The Madhouse Nudes

a novel

Robert Schultz

simon & schuster

SIMON & SCHUSTER
Rockefeller Center
1230 Avenue of the Americas
New York, NY 10020

SIMON & SCHUSTER and colophon are registered trademarks of Simon & Schuster Inc.

Designed by Elina D. Nudelman

Manufactured in the United States of America

10 9 8 7 6 5 4 3 2 1

Library of Congress Cataloging-in-Publication Data
Schultz, Robert.
 The madhouse nudes : a novel/Robert Schultz.
   p.   cm.
 I. Title.
PS3569.C5535M33   1997
813'.54—dc20

96-38619
CIP

ISBN 13: 978-1-416-59355-3

ISBN 10:   1-416-59355-1

 The first two chapters of this work were published as "The Madhouse Nudes" in *The Hudson Review*, XLVI, 1 (Spring 1993). The poem "Winter in Eden" is reprinted from *The Hudson Review*, XLV, 1 (Spring 1992). Copyright © 1995 by Robert Schultz.
 Psalm 51:7–9 and portions of two hymn texts—"Alas, and Did My Savior Bleed" by Isaac Watts and "Deep Were His Wounds" by William Johnson—are reprinted by permission from the *Lutheran Book of Worship* ©1958 by Augsburg Fortress.

After Sally, *this book is for*
Frederick Morgan, *in memorium, and* Paula Deitz
and for
David Wyatt *and* Ann Porotti

Winter in Eden

There are no fences, no gates in the snowy
Fields and wrecked orchards; only the sword-blade

Winter light swings north to south, east to west
Where the straight horizon locks itself with ice

To a sky too bright to look at. We are free
Among the trees of knowledge, gleaning

Shriveled apples and berries, sweet
As they melt in our hot mouths. Memory

Flares as we walk beneath the torn limbs.
At home each night the dream arrives, insistent

As a chanted word: the slim trunk rises,
Branches dense with scalloped leaves protecting

Their fruit--globes the colors of perfect bodies,
Naked, shameless in the tree of life.

— R. S.

Preface

      I'm sitting in a storage room above my gallery on Spring Street in New York City, surrounded by drawings and paintings made by John Ordway between November 1990 and June 1991. The group consists of 237 drawings and 12 oil paintings, nearly all of them female nudes produced in the second year of the artist's two-year stay in Delphi, Iowa, a small town in the northeast corner of the state. The paintings are large, some measuring over 48" x 72". Most of the drawings are charcoal studies for the paintings, but a small group of pencil drawings made at a local slaughterhouse depict the carcasses of animals. My gallery has handled Mr. Ordway's work since 1982 and I have come to consider him one of my closest friends. At John's request, I have not shown or sold any of the paintings or drawings.

      John has granted me permission to collect and publish the letters he sent to me during the period when this work was produced, along with two letters he received from his companion, Jamie Stephens (she also generously granted permission to publish her letters). I suspect John felt that if there was to be a hiatus in his exhibiting career the book might explain the reasons for that interval. Some of the New York art papers had run brief stories about the circumstances that had befallen John in Iowa and about the confiscation of the paintings in the course of the legal proceedings. Also, the critic Delia Sommers had published her extended magazine piece, "The Strange Case of John Ordway and His Midwestern Nudes." (She had sought, through me, permission to see the paintings, and I hope my inability to grant her request did not contribute to the unfortunate tone of her story.) It would be natural if John were to wish the record of the letters to stand in counterpoint to speculations he has read in the press, though I hasten to add that he has never said this to me. He has only joked that letting me publish the letters is the least he can do, since I can't show or sell his paintings.

      John's letters to me were intimate, sent from one friend to another, and I found the intimacy flattering. He confided in me during a time of terrible difficulties, and I did what I could to help. Many letters passed between us, but I have omitted my own from this collection because I feel they would distract from the main story, which is John's. As the letters arrived—sometimes three in a single week—I felt that I was receiving something extraordinary. They often provided accounts of an artist's workings, and this interested me, of course. But even more striking was the human story they told—the story of a man looking at women.

Wyatt Arends
New York City
December 1991

1

John Ordway
503 Lime Bluffs Road
Delphi, Iowa

Wyatt Arends
261 West 10th Street
New York, NY

June 16, 1990

Dear Wyatt,

Well, I'm back, though it wasn't easy. My flight out was canceled because the plane was broken, and it looked like I was going to be all day zigzagging home on other flights. But I ran with a bag in each hand from one end of the terminal to the other and caught a plane with another airline. Stepped on just before they rolled back the jetway and was still breathing hard when the stewardesses handed out the little foil packs of peanuts. On the connecting flight out of Milwaukee in a small twin-engine plane we bobbed on the drafts between thunderheads. Jamie was at La Crosse with the van to pick me up and we drove through rain and lightning across the steel bridge at Lansing and all the way to Delphi. Who says there's no adventure left in travel? Of course, if I'd been going to L.A. or Paris it would have been simple, but to penetrate to the remote heart of North America is another matter.

Though I was only away two weeks, the apartment feels strange and the studio seems bigger. I'm at the studio now, sitting at the table under the north window, watching the crows sway in the top of a pine across the road. Behind me, the place seems empty, now that you have the canvases that had been leaning against the walls. The hardwood floor down to the big windows feels like a dance hall. The humidity is almost tropical today and the red bricks of the walls are sweating.

I have a model coming over in a few minutes. I want to do some studies for a series of big nudes. The small ones I left with you are half measures. I've just decided.

Since getting home I've been stuck on what that woman said at the party the last night (what was her name? she writes for one of the papers). When she leaned toward me her condescension was masterful, or was that pity for the visiting provincial? "But the nude is simply unavailable," she said. "Especially the female nude. Even the women should leave it alone for thirty or forty years." Well, that sounds like an opportunity to me. Whenever something is declared dead, I circle in.

I said the apartment feels strange. While I was gone, Jamie painted the front room a kind of adobe orange (she said we need warm colors for the long winters), but that isn't it. I think it's just that sense of the uncanny you feel when you return to the familiar, a ripple of displacement at seeing your home as a new place to come to. It reminds me how much work it is to stay awake in your life. Does it happen to you when you've been away? After New York's vertical grays strung with lights, we drove home from the airport through horizontal greens undulating between the farmsteads all the way to this little town of wood frame houses and three-storied brick storefronts. Suddenly I understand Thomas Hart Benton—the land in his paintings like the pelt of something alive.

After a year, it's still odd to call this place home. Coming back, even Jamie seems different to me. That first night back in my own bed, lying behind her with my arms around her, she felt both like herself and someone new. In the dark our bed was a pool with no bottom.

I think I hear my model coming up the stairs. It was fine to spend a few days with you and Alice, to make the rounds of the museums and galleries, and to visit some of the old spots. You are dear friends. Thanks.

John

July 3, 1990
Dear Wyatt,

Good to hear about the sale. You worked quickly. Thanks. Yes, I had thought of the nude by the yellow table as companion to the one with dark blue trees through the window—morning and evening pictures. Maybe your client will eventually want the yellow, now that he has the blue, but don't worry about splitting them up. Again, thanks. Jamie will be glad to hear the news when she gets back. She's selling some of her things at a fair in St. Paul and will drive home in two days.

It's late and I've been reading in the front room. The lamplight on the adobe-colored walls is restful, even in summer. I worked all day and am tired. I'm working with two new models, sometimes in the same day: today Ellen in the morning and

Jean early evening. Really, it was a waste of Jamie's time to model for me, especially with the way her own work is selling. Finally, in the middle of a session she said, "John, I don't think I can do this anymore." So I put an ad in *The Weekly Oracle*: "Professional painter seeks female models for life studies. Pay by the hour with flexible scheduling. No previous experience required. Telephone for interview appointment." I was a little surprised when I actually got calls. Of course, most ended quickly once it became clear that I was talking about nude modeling. Finally, though, I was able to hire two models.

In our first session Ellen seemed to me the archetypal young woman of these parts: very fair-skinned but with high color in her cheeks, hair so blond it's almost white. She undressed behind the curtain to the right of the platform, then stepped out from behind it, tall and lean, but strong in the shoulders and thighs in a way that goes with her square jaw. But for all her appearance of physical vigor and strength, she was ill at ease with her body. She moved stiffly and didn't know what to do with her arms. The frankness of the morning light, combined with her self-consciousness, was very poignant. She appeared bright to the point of overexposure.

Jean, on the other hand, comes in, drops her clothes, and lounges on the platform as if she's leaning back into a warm bath. I never pose her; her instinctive physical comfort, even grace, is feline. She's about thirty and has long straight brown hair and tanned skin. She's a cashier at a store downtown and is married to a man who works in a small local factory. The two of them go to the bars most evenings. She usually takes her hours here after work and seems to relax, as if slipping into her natural element.

Sometimes all my years of painting—the hours in figure studio at art school with the tired, bored models; the last years in New York when the sense of the "business" of art was so wearying—sometimes they all fall away and I'm struck by the strangeness of waiting in an upstairs room for a woman I know slightly, if at all, who arrives, undresses, poses before me for two or three hours, then dresses and leaves. Here, in a small Midwestern town, with models who are doing this work for the first time, a sense of the nonconformist—even the illicit—hangs in the air. We are wrenched into a strange intimacy, though we take pains not to acknowledge it. And so the subject of the pictures, as when I began, is the fact of nakedness. I feel like I'm starting over, having recovered the first things.

John

July 4, 1990
Dear Wyatt,

I know I just wrote yesterday, but there's nothing to do today. Jamie's still in St. Paul and I can't get a model on a holiday. It's too hot to do anything, anyway. It's 90 degrees and humid. I'm sitting in the bright kitchen, idling over a bottle of beer. The corn in the fields just outside town is knee high and higher. On days like these I really do think you can hear it grow, the leaves reaching out and bending over with a little snap. We had a cool spring and early summer, so I'm not used to the heat. My head feels thick and my arms and legs heavy. I think the best I can do is sit here in front of the fan and write this letter.

Today is an anniversary, of sorts. Last year we moved to town, arriving in our rented truck a little after dawn. We finished moving our things into the apartment that afternoon and, because it was hot inside, wandered up to the city park on a bluff overlooking the river. We spread out a blanket and fell asleep under the big oaks. We woke as townspeople gathered for an Independence Day celebration, carrying their own blankets and lawn chairs and arranging themselves around the elevated, gazebo-style bandstand. Soon popcorn and ice cream cones were being sold to the children, the mayor recounted the town's ethnic history and welcomed visitors from out of town, a congressman talked about the U.S. Constitution, and the municipal band played marches and patriotic songs. We felt as though we had moved not only 1,000 miles west but also forty years into the past. We sat up on the blanket, still exhausted, but stunned into tranquility by the clarinets and flutes and by the calm civility of the ritual. By now we recognize the element of willed innocence and self-conscious nostalgia in these ceremonial occasions, but I'm not tempted to irony when I describe them. There's enough truth to sustain the moment, however fragile.

I'm still pleased by the coincidence that we arrived on the day Thoreau went to the woods. A sense of economy something like his brought us here. The rents on the apartment and studio are low; we've been lucky with our health so far, so have gotten by all right without insurance; we don't eat in restaurants and our "entertainments" are cheap. We can almost live on Jamie's pots and weavings, and when I sell a dozen paintings in a year we feel flush. We have tried to live simply and directly, to be able to survive by the work we most want to do, rather than do something else to buy time for our best hours.

Last year in St. Paul Jamie sold all the weavings she took, several pots (including two of the tall ones), and she picked up two commissions. We lived for two and a half months off that show. She's good. In the summer, with the regional fairs and festivals, she's on the road quite a bit. I go along sometimes, but my paintings don't sell at those places so I'm better off staying home and working. She says she doesn't mind.

But I'm worthless in this heat. I find myself sitting and staring for minutes at a time. The sun is pouring through the window onto the blue and white checked tablecloth. In the middle of the table, in a steel bowl, are red and green grapes, spotted bananas, ripe peaches. The scent of the peaches is strong in the humid air. My life seems to spread out in rings from the steel bowl of fruit. I think of my sketches in the studio five blocks away, my neighbors gathering across town in the park, Jamie tending her booth in St. Paul, you and Alice in New York. A line moves out from the center through the rings, and all I want to do is to show you all how the light in July on a ripened peach is more solid than my own body around me.

We're not supposed to paint bowls of fruit these days. But if I could do *this* bowl, *this* peach . . . The aim is that we see for a moment with the same gaze. All art that I care for is about intimacy. I have looked at one of Jamie's undecorated jars and seen the poise we both long for but seldom feel. We bump through our lives to-gether, anxious, hopeful, sad—it changes by the hour—and suddenly there it is. The slender form is waist high, rising from the floor, widening as it goes—a stretched amphora. There is a coolness in it, and a delicate certainty. In that mo-ment I know her better than I have for weeks.

Well, even without a model, perhaps I can work this evening when the heat lets up.

John

July 9, 1990

Dear Wyatt,

Hot and bright today, less humid. Very clear. I can look out the studio's north window, over the rooftops and past the big pines, to the ridge at the far side of town. Jamie did very well in the Twin Cities, was back just long enough to glaze and fire some pots, and now is at a show in Milwaukee. So I've had a lot of time to myself. Now it's early evening after a full day working with Ellen this morning and Jean late afternoon. I'm doing sketches one after another as quickly as I can, shak-ing out ideas for the next paintings. If there were more light, I'd go for a walk and sketch in one of the parks. I'm interested by the possibility of setting my figures in natural places—without pastoral absurdities. It feels very different to be drawing nudes here, different from working with the body in New York. Jamie quipped the other day that I'm either going to be on the cutting edge, discovering the true feminist-ecological nude, or earn the world's scorn by yet again equating men with culture and women with nature. We joke sometimes—a little nervously, I think—about trends, movements, orthodoxies. I guess it's our way of holding them at arm's length.

I like working on two tracks with two different models. In the studio's hard midmorning light Ellen's skin and hair are brilliant. The subject that comes to mind when I work with her is repression and the effort to work free from it. Her presence on the platform seems an extraordinary act of will, a difficult performance.

Today I gave her a simple pose. I placed a wooden chair in front of the platform and said: "Why don't you just sit as naturally as possible. Maybe you could put your hands together in your lap." She sat rigidly in the chair and held the pose with difficulty, tiring quickly. After just fifteen minutes her wonderful square shoulders began to sag. So we took an early break. She wrapped herself in the robe I gave her and sat on the platform's edge, almost as uneasily as before. When we began again, I tried to relax her with conversation. I asked her if she'd always lived in Delphi.

She pulled in a deep breath before she spoke. "I grew up here," she said. "I came back from college four years ago. I'm living back home now—with my mother—but that's only temporary."

I asked her what she did. Again, she tried to compose herself with a deep breath. I sketched the fluid line that ran down the inside of her arm, alongside the breast, across the stomach, to her hands upturned in her lap. "I work at the public library afternoons and some evenings," she said. "I'm just trying to save some money right now."

I asked her what she was saving for and she said she wasn't sure yet. She said she answered my ad because it seemed like a way to earn money with hours that would fit around her library job. She sat rigidly in the chair as we spoke. I worked quickly, trying to capture the almost physical sense of vibration she communicated.

After half an hour she was flexing her hands unconsciously and gulping for breath, so I cut the session short. When she'd dressed and left, I didn't think she'd come back. Really, the session had been a little brutal, but I assume she answered my ad for her own reasons and it's my task to find the truth in the figure she presents, if I can.

On the other hand, it's hard for me to concentrate on Jean as an individual. My imagination keeps slipping away from her to archetypes or myths. She's utterly unself-conscious. Since I'm doing a lot of sketches, I tell her to move around as she wants to, and so she holds a position for about ten minutes and then rolls over or crosses her legs or moves to a chair. She luxuriates in the studio as if it's a lazy Saturday at home with a magazine, and yet she is instinctively graceful and attractive. Her nonchalance gives her sensuality an air of command. A couple of times I've asked her to bring an object along that she'd like me to include in my sketches of her. The first time she brought a shallow dish filled with the small blossoms of a local rose. Another time she brought something she'd gotten on a vacation—a big white conch, fluted at its lip, and pink inside. Well, you get the idea. When she's in the room, everything's a symbol. It's been a long time since a model has made me feel self-conscious about the pencil in my hand.

Downstairs the landlady, Mrs. Tolman, must be frying onions. They smell wonderful and are making me very hungry. I'd better go home and fix some supper. When Jamie's not here I lose track of time. The sun's gone down and a couple of thin high clouds over the western ridge are lighting up like neon tubes. Sometimes it's a good life.

John

July 13, 1990
Dear Wyatt,

Something's happened. I was at the studio yesterday when Jamie got home from Milwaukee. I walked into the house and she was sitting on the little couch in the front room. When she looked up I knew there was something wrong. She said, "I've got to go away for a while. Things just aren't working out here the way we had hoped." She said, "There's a current in New York that carries you along, or that you navigate in or against, but it's all still water here. There's nothing to keep you moving or to push off from." She was talking about her work, but I felt she meant everything else, too.

I was just standing there across the room, completely stopped. After a minute I asked, "Are you moving away from this place or from me?"

She looked away, out the window. After a minute she said, "It's been a lot of work lately. I don't know. I can't sort it all out. I think I want to go back to New York, but I've got a place to stay in Minneapolis while I think things through."

She collected her things, going up and down the stairs and out to the van while I sat like a stick in the front room. I couldn't move. Finally, she was standing in the entry and saying good-bye. I stood up. "I don't understand," I said. "You've got to talk to me. Why can't we talk about this? Why do you have to leave to think things through? Can't we do it together? I don't know what's happening."

She looked at me, shook her head, and went out. When the door shut its latch made a little click.

That was two days ago. I'm still numb with surprise, and in the quiet house I find myself rereading the past weeks and months. I hadn't understood anything correctly. Jamie had been quiet for stretches this spring and summer, and I had taken it for preoccupation with her work. And, of course, she's been gone a lot. But she's been remarkably productive and that made me glad. I had been busy, too. I thought we were settling into the kind of routine we had hoped for when we left New York. Now I think her silence was the distance building as she gradually pulled away.

I'm unhappy—I'm miserable—but I'm not angry. I don't blame Jamie. I can see things her way, now that she's pointed it out to me. There's a heave to get started every morning. It's all up to us. There's not a sense that the kind of work we're doing is in the air. There aren't other artists, galleries, critics, and buyers around to assure us that our work is important. In fact, when I step outside the apartment or the studio, my painting seems the oddest thing around. I see now that Jamie and I were thrown back upon each other in a way we hadn't been before. She had to be my prop and mirror, and I had to be hers. It *was* a lot of work.

But for me—and I thought for her—there were compensations. Most days I'm glad to be out of the clamor of the "profession." We've both felt lonely, have missed our friends, but I haven't missed the desperation and ambition, everyone calculating their prospects and plotting their next move. I got sick of trying to be the boutonniere on the world's lapel.

But I've known all along there's a kind of ambition which is a good, clean thing—the attempt to see a thing and feel it as fully as you can, and to get it down. It's like telling the truth, and I thought we could do it here. Maybe we still can. Maybe I can. I don't know what's going to happen.

John

July 18, 1990

Dear Wyatt,

I've been trying to work this week, doing studies with Ellen for a big canvas. As always, technical matters are most immediate, breaking the pose down to bone and muscle, the charcoal stub rebuilding the body in line and value. Then, since it's a study, a detached part of mind is considering the possibilities for the composition in paint, imagining colors, textures, surface tension. And all this is lightly overseen by the attempt to bring into focus a vaguely yearned-for picture—something I need but can't see clearly yet. And so the emotions and imagination brood over tone and meaning, tugged by old obsessions, new objections, sharpened this week by the ache in my side that seems to be the physical sensation of loss. Ellen's whiteness starts to my eyes, her tension exaggerated by my own so that while I sketch I'm guided by the memory of a Dutch still life, a scaled and scrubbed fish on a silver plate, shocking among the plump fruit and gorgeous flowers. The silver of the tray suggests the hook no longer in the fish's mouth.

Now it's late back at the apartment. Jamie hasn't called all week, and I haven't called her. My instinct is to let a little time pass. Maybe I'm hoping time by itself will change something. But I do need the time, myself, to reflect. There's so much I hadn't seen before.

I had imagined it was the same here for the two of us, but it wasn't. Things were changed here for Jamie more than they were for me. I was happily detached, working in privacy away from distractions, but I was still selling, through you, to the same people in New York. Jamie, though, had been taken away from the shops where she had been selling her things. To ship them east would have cost almost her whole profit. So she was on the road, out of the studio, selling at fairs which, good as they are, don't compare to her old markets in either return or prestige. How could I have failed to recognize this? What kept her from saying anything until she had decided to leave?

I'm going to drive up and see her. I'll write again in a few days.

John

July 21, 1990
Dear Wyatt,

I went up to see Jamie. She's living in a small, tidy apartment in a complex. It belongs to another artist she'd gotten to know at the fairs. They both travel a lot so aren't often there together. The woman, Andrea, is a photographer. I didn't meet her. Jamie says Andrea was glad to find someone to help with the rent for a while.

Seeing Jamie there reminded me of visiting her in the hospital in New York two years ago when she had that kidney infection. I felt the same strangeness and anxiety—the tense air of convalescence. But this time I was the sick one. I caught myself watching her face for clues the way you watch a doctor's.

We sat across from each other in the apartment's small living room, me on the tan couch, Jamie in a matching chair. Around us on the light blue walls were hundreds of Andrea's photographs hung in neat rows. She's a portraitist and every photo was a black-and-white headshot of a woman looking straight into the camera. Jamie's gaze at me was multiplied by the photos behind her.

I told her I had done some thinking, and I talked about the kinds of things I described to you in my last letter—my realizations about the way the move has worked out for her. When I finished there was a long, unbearable pause. Then I remember her exact words. She said: "There used to be space. We used to have fun. But since the move it's like we've been on some kind of mission. My work is important to me, but you think *everything* is about work. Maybe if it gave you more pleasure . . . but it's always there, I don't know, like some kind of big black bird perched on your shoulder."

I asked why we couldn't have talked about this before, why she had to leave first, and she said it seemed like heresy to question what we were doing. Finally she just had to break away to think things through. We said we'd talk again in a few days. I don't know what happens next, and I don't think she does, either.

I started home that night, but it was late. I stopped at a picnic area out in the country at the side of the road and got my sleeping bag out of the trunk. It was a clear, quiet night and I fell asleep quickly. At dawn, when I woke up, my face and hair were wet with dew, but I wasn't chilled. I was at the edge of a broad, sloping cornfield extending down to a line of willows where a creek ran. Beyond the creek, farms stretched to the horizon, each house with its barn and silo, windbreak and sheds, surrounded by the big fields—hay, soybeans, more corn. I stood and listened to the birds calling from the tops of poplars like muezzins in their minarets. I didn't understand anything I saw. Where do I belong?

John

July 23, 1990
Dear Wyatt,

A bad night tonight. Even if she left a situation, a place, she also left me. She *could* leave me. She conceived of it and she did it. I had been avoiding taking that in. I've been out walking. I needed to stretch out my arms and legs, to take deep breaths. It's hot and close and everything is pressing in.

She had the idea to leave and it grew in her mind. When she looked at me then, she was thinking about it. She thought about it, and she looked at me, and after a while the reasons for leaving became more important than the reasons for staying.

When I'm in the apartment things flash at me. It was another hot night and we were cooking. Mrs. Tolman had given me some fresh sweet corn from her garden. We were boiling it and the steam in the small, hot kitchen was unbearable. Even with the window open, the room got hotter and hotter. We peeled off our clothes and stood there naked, making a salad, slicing some cold cuts. When everything was done we moved the table out to the sitting room and ate there. We were so hungry and so hot, we didn't bother to get dressed. We sat across from each other, our faces smeared with butter from the sweet, yellow corn.

I remember another night in the kitchen. I was cutting up a head of cauliflower for a soup and the knife slipped. I cut the fleshy base of my thumb on the left hand. Jamie tried to bandage it closed for me, but it kept gaping. She said it needed to be stitched but I didn't want to go to the emergency room. I didn't think we could afford it. So she boiled a needle and some nylon thread from her weaving box. I sat in the kitchen with my arm on the table and clenched my good hand while she stitched the cut. She was always a good seamstress. She finished making the soup, we ate, and then she came around and sat on my lap and kissed me. Then we went upstairs and made love sweetly. The stitches were so close and fine, today there's almost no scar.

I don't know where it all went. Lately, we just struggled ahead, living our own inward dramas—for weeks at a time they barely overlapped.

I hope you don't mind me writing to you like this, Wyatt. Tonight I just can't stand it alone.

John

July 27, 1990
Dear Wyatt,

Very hot and humid again this week. A big fan in the studio makes it just bearable, and I've been taking walks evenings when it cools a little. I go out to one of the little parks and walk the ridge trails or sit by one of the cool springs. There's a point after sunset when the trees flatten into silhouettes and the sky shows through their branches in bright copper ingots. For me, the impulse to paint comes from seeing such things alone. They are uncontainable.

I think Jamie feels stuck. She's not ready to break things off entirely and go back to New York, but says she can't come back here. We talked on the phone this week, and I feel she may stay where she is for a while as we both try to figure things out. I feel stuck, too. I know I can't go back to New York—if that's what Jamie wants me to do. (I haven't asked.) But I have thought about the possibility of moving up near the

Twin Cities. I've wondered if that would work as a kind of compromise. At the same time, I know it's too soon for that sort of thing, mainly because I still don't know how much of our problem really has to do with geography. Maybe it's all about me. We still have a hard time talking.

In the meantime, I try to work. Today more studies with Ellen, and I may be getting somewhere. I'm working out the details of a composition in which she is seated, facing forward, in a kind of crouch with her knees together and pointing left. At the same time, she's looking to the right, her face in profile. There's a difficulty in the posture which communicates unease, and I've added to the stiffness by flattening the rendering, giving the whole a hint of the primitive. She's situated on a grassy bank beside a stylized version of our local Redding's Spring, which spates out of a limestone bluff and down a rocky creekbed. The stream riffles down beside her arm on the left, mirrored by her white-blond hair which flows behind her arm on the right. Her left side, from breast to hip, will be painted against small plants lush with red berries, and the outer border will be dense with foliage and a few wildflowers. But she looks to the right, away from the berries and the running spring.

I think I can start painting soon. All best until next time.

John

July 30, 1990

Dear Wyatt,

It seems clear that I'm going to have to get some kind of job. The checking account is Jamie's. It was always the money she made with her pots and weavings, supplemented by withdrawals from the small (sometimes very small!) savings account where we put the checks from my sales. She'll keep the checking account and I'll live out of the savings. To split up our finances seems a harsh symbol, but we can't very well go on living out of the same accounts as things stand now. Jamie will be fine—better off than when we were together. And I guess I'll find out to what extent she was subsidizing me. I figure I'm all right for two or three months, depending on new sales. Beyond that I'll have to supplement my painting income.

The picture is progressing. I find myself thinking of it as Milton's Eve troubled after her dream, but that's not exactly right. It's slightly vertical: 42 x 38 inches. The green in it is the dark, heavy shade of late July in Iowa, a green just crossing from vigor to weariness. But the figure, apart from the torsion of the pose, is all ravishment. Above the tense legs and below the averted face, the high white breasts look you straight in the eyes. Health, beauty, pleasure—it could break your heart. I don't know how much of this I'm getting from Ellen and how much is projection, but that hardly matters as far as the painting is concerned. There's far to go, but I'm very hopeful about it.

John

August 9, 1990

Dear Wyatt,

Your idea about a show is interesting. I have mixed feelings about it. Certainly a few sales would help right now. On the other hand, I feel the new work I've just begun will be a real advance over the things I brought out to you this summer, so it's hard for me to think about representing myself with the old work just now. You can see how I'm torn between the feelings I have about the pictures and the economics of the situation. What do you advise?

I'm tightening my belt. I've sublet the apartment and moved into the studio. The bed fits into the foot of the studio's L, along with a small refrigerator and a hotplate, and I've separated off that space with a curtain. Two chairs and lamps fit at the north end of the long room, so I still work under the big south windows.

Of course, Ellen wondered what was going on the next time she came to work. I saw her looking around, noting the furniture I'd moved into the studio and the curtain that defined my "bedroom." When she stepped behind the curtain to undress I started to explain. "Jamie's left me," I began. Saying the words out loud for the first time shook me. "She's left Delphi," I said. "I don't know if it's permanent." As I talked I realized how little we had actually spoken. After that first meeting when we had agreed on the terms of her job, I'd done little more each time than say hello, make a little polite conversation, then give her directions for the poses. I generally don't talk while I work, and it must have been strange for her. She's not a professional model, after all.

She listened carefully but didn't comment on what I had told her. As I painted I thought I could see it working behind her eyes. Maybe she felt a little funny about the bed behind the curtain. So I made conversation, asking how she felt by now about being painted. The charcoal studies were taped to the walls all around. She glanced at them and said, "At first I felt uncomfortable, but now most of the time I think the pictures have very little to do with me. I'm just here—like a vase of flowers or a bowl of fruit—and you're over there doing your work. That's when it's easy. But once in a while a sketch will surprise me and I'll feel like I've really been seen in a way people usually aren't. But that doesn't happen so often."

I asked if any of the studies really "saw" her. She nodded at a small one taped high on the wall across from us. "The eyes and the hands," she said. In the study her head points to the right, but the eyes glance out at the viewer with a startled look, as if she's just discovering that someone is looking at her. The hands are apart from her sides, pressing the bank as she leans back on her arms. But the fingers are spread as if her hands have just flexed out, ready to push her up, and the muscles are tightened into the arms and shoulders.

Tonight I'm scraping down the eyes and hands on the big canvas to repaint them as they are in the small study. But I may have to start all over. I don't know yet.

John

August 17, 1990
Dear Wyatt,

I have to tell you a story. I almost burned down the studio last night.

Jamie came down with the van yesterday to pick up her kiln bricks, iron, and batting. She's found space for her wheel at Andrea's photography studio and the apartment complex is letting her build a kiln off in a corner of its yard. Andrea came with her and when Jamie introduced us we shook hands. Andrea's tall and lanky with slightly stooped shoulders. Her long black hair was tied back, but loose strands of it swung around her face. "Hello, John," she said, and fixed me in dark steady eyes above a strong, rather Roman nose. She's very tall—maybe over six feet tall. At any rate, I had the impression she was looking down at me from a height as the three of us carried the bricks from behind the sublet apartment and stacked them in the van. When we finished, Andrea offered to drive downtown and pick up something cold to drink, so Jamie and I sat on the front steps and had a few minutes to talk.

It was a lovely afternoon, hot, but with breezes under the maples. Jamie had on a white T-shirt and a pair of old jeans. Her bronze-colored hair was bright in the sun, and it reminded me of other times we had sat there, sometimes with our morning coffee or for a few minutes after lunch before we went back to work. But the recollection of those times only made me feel odd and desperate. There was a strange feeling in my chest, like a ball in there was pumped up too tight. My heart was pounding and I had the wild notion that I wanted to hold out my arms and shout "Stop!" to freeze everything. But I clamped down hard and tried to listen.

She was talking about the pots she had sold in Minneapolis, getting to know the town, and plans for new work. "I'm doing very little weaving, now, because the pots are doing so well," she said. "They're getting even bigger—and wilder." She held her voice low, as if restraining her enthusiasm out of deference to my feelings, but clearly she was happy and excited. There was the light in her eyes of a person for whom all the windows and doors have been thrown wide open.

"And how's your work going?" she asked. I described the new painting, but I was wrestling to keep down a rising panic so the words sounded hollow as I spoke. Just the same, Jamie nodded encouragingly. Then Andrea came back with a carton of juice and some paper cups. She poured out our drinks and we sat on the steps and talked about the town.

"It doesn't look like Iowa," Andrea said. "Too many hills and trees. It reminds me of villages I saw in Yugoslavia."

When we had finished the carton of juice, we all stood up. My heart pounded as if I'd been running. Andrea said good-bye and walked to the van. Jamie gave me a hug and smiled, walked to the van, and they left.

It was worse than when she left the first time. She seemed so brightened by the move away. I stood there in the sunlight, feeling like some kind of shadow, all chilled and darkened. Was life with me really such a jail? I turned and started up the steps, and my hand was on the doorknob before I remembered the place wasn't mine anymore. As I walked across town toward the studio, I was still picturing the apartment's front room: its walls the color of fired, unglazed clay; the furniture we had collected together, some of which I sold when I moved into the studio; the small couch, Jamie looking up from it and shaking her head and saying, "I have to go"; Jamie looking up from it another time and saying in a low voice, "Come here." I couldn't stop the chain of associations.

When I reached the studio the car wasn't there, and I remembered that I had driven to the apartment. So I turned around to go back for the car, but after a couple blocks I stopped and sat down on a bench at the edge of a small park. I sat there like a dry stick blown out of a tree and couldn't imagine getting up, couldn't think where I had to go. After a long time I heard the six o'clock whistle, stood up, and started walking toward downtown. When I got there I went into a dim place called Sammy's, sat down at the bar, and ordered a beer. When it came I sipped at it, but swallowing was hard because the tight ball in my chest had risen to the base of my throat. Then I heard a woman's voice call my name out of the dark somewhere behind me and I turned around.

I couldn't see very well into the row of booths with high, darkly stained wooden backs, but then an arm rose from one of them and a face leaned forward into a little light. It was Jean. She waved me over and introduced me to her husband, Jerry, and to another guy, Ron. I recognized Ron as the electrician who had been to the studio to wire in the line for my refrigerator and hotplate. His name was stitched onto the breast of his blue shirt. Jerry grinned from under a broad reddish mustache as Jean motioned for me to sit down.

Ron topped off my beer from their pitcher and said, "You here for supper? It's not much fun cooking on a hotplate, is it?" He smiled and I shook my head. Then Ron told Jean how we had met at the studio and Jean asked me what I was doing living there. When I explained, she looked stricken. She looked so sorry I expected to see tears in her eyes, and I was so taken aback that for a minute I thought I was going to cry myself.

Jerry said, "Listen, Jean and I just got back from a trip up north, and tonight we're driving out to check on the cabin we have over by the river. Why don't you come, too?" I had the impression that both Jerry and Ron had heard a lot about me from Jean. They were trying to be very friendly. Suddenly I felt exhausted, and I let myself relax toward all three of them.

They were just ordering food, so I ordered with them, but I didn't have much appetite. We finished the beer and ordered another pitcher. They talked and I listened, adding a word once in a while. We drank some more beer together and it was dark when we went outside. Ron said good night and I went with Jean and Jerry and got into their old white Chrysler.

Out in the country on the secondary roads it was almost completely dark. I sat cradled in the spacious backseat as the car plunged on its lush shocks. Over his shoulder, Jerry asked me smart, practical questions about how I support myself. Up front the dashboard gauges softly glowed between the two of them as they listened. I let myself sink into their care. It was like traveling with my parents and sister on our long trips to the Rockies when I was a child. Whenever we drove late, Vivien slept in the backseat and I used to lie in the back window ledge. It was soothing to remember. She had a funny way of lying on her side, clutching handfuls of her long red hair under her chin, as if to keep her throat warm. The brightness of the stars in the dark countryside reminded me of how I used to lie with the cool glass a few inches from my face, and look out at the constellations as if I were an astronaut in my capsule.

The big car rolled languidly as we pulled off the blacktop onto gravel. I was drunk with comfort, not just the beer. In a few minutes we turned again, this time into a narrow dirt driveway arched over with trees and low brush so that the headlights lit a curving tunnel. It was like driving down a throat.

Finally we rolled onto grass and stopped. At the far edge of a small clearing, in the lights, I could see a small log cabin with a covered porch built out from the door and a stone chimney rising at one end. Jerry stayed in the car, waiting to turn out the lights until Jean and I had made our way to the cabin. Jean unlocked the place, went in, and lit a gas lantern. It was one simple room, but comfortable, with a brass bed across one end, a round table and three chairs in the middle, and a large open fireplace at the other end. Jean hung the lantern on a hooked wire over the table and Jerry came in and started to build a fire in the fireplace. "This may feel good after a little swim," he said. Then Jean tapped me on the arm and said, "Come on, I'll show you the river."

We made our way through the dark about fifty yards, moving away from the cabin and the car into an open space where the stars showed brightly. When we reached the riverbank there was just enough light to see that the stream was about thirty feet wide. The water riffled through shallows on our left, quieted when it flowed into the pool in front of us, then turned and ran smoothly into the dark woods to our right. Across the stream a hillside blotted out the low stars.

We stood and listened to the sound of water until Jerry came up behind us. Jean said to me, "You'll like this place," and the two of them began to take off their clothes. I did the same and followed them onto the sand at the inside of the river's crook. The night air was chilly against my skin and as we waded into the pool the water felt warm. The pool deepened quickly and the sand gave way to velvety ooze that rose to the tops of my ankles. Jerry hung in the still point at the pool's center, treading water. Jean swam to the base of the cutbank where the water moved quickly around the bend, rolled onto her back, and let the current carry her to the tail of the pool, then she kicked over to the sand and sat in the shallows. I followed, and as I edged into the current I felt the warm water gliding by like a big muscle. I pushed myself in and rolled onto my back. The current, surprisingly swift, pulled me into the broad curve, turning me like a dial. I was moving feet first, then head first, then feet first as the little swirls and eddies at the edge of the main current caught me. My ears were covered by the dark water and everything was hushed as I turned. I looked up as I went and the stars wheeled.

When I reached the pool's tail I rolled over and swam to the shallows. I could see Jean sitting on the sandbar and smiling at me, resting with the warm water up to her breasts. "I told you you'd like this place," she said. I smiled back and waded to the beginning for another float. Jerry was backing into the current at the pool's inlet, making the water hump over his shoulders as it flowed. I launched myself into the head of the pool and rolled onto my back. As I swung again with the strong current the night sky turned around and around.

At the end, a little dizzy, I climbed back onto the sandbar and sat down next to

Jean. Then Jerry waded over to join us. He said, "That fire will feel good now," and Jean added, "Let's go see if it's still burning." So we stepped out onto the grass, picked up our clothes, and walked back to the cabin through the cool night air.

The fire was low, so Jerry added a log. Jean got some towels out of a wooden trunk at the foot of the bed and handed one to each of us. Then we all stood by the big fireplace, drying and warming. Jerry helped Jean with her back and Jean reached over with her towel and dried mine. In the firelight our bodies looked ruddy and perfect.

Jerry went to the bed and pulled off its quilt. He spread the quilt on the floor in front of the fireplace, sat down cross-legged, and set his clothes in a heap in front of him to warm. So we all sat in a row by the fire with our clothes in front of us, Jean to my left and Jerry on her other side. Jerry produced a bottle of blackberry brandy from somewhere, took a drink, and passed it down the line. The brandy was hot and sweet in my mouth. Then Jean turned to me and said, "I'm so sorry to hear that Jamie's moved out. You must be awfully lonely."

The low vibration of sympathy in her voice called to my self-pity, which quickly rose in my throat. Suddenly I was exhausted again. The fire and the brandy made me want to lie down. I imagined resting my head in Jean's lap and going to sleep. I must have been drunk. I've never felt so maudlin. I looked at Jean and tried to an-swer, tried to say "yes," but my voice cracked and I sobbed hard once before I caught myself. But that was enough. She quickly slid behind me and put her arms around my shoulders. She stroked my chest and murmured, "That's all right. That's all right."

I had drawn her many times, but now her body was soft behind me. I let myself relax against her. Jerry said, "That's okay, man. I know it's tough," and he leaned over and put his hand on my leg.

I came back to myself with a start and shot a glance at Jerry. His gray eyes were blank and unreadable. I sat up straight, then said with forced casualness, "You're both very kind. You know, I'm really tired."

Jerry said, "Sure. It's late. We should take you home," and we all stood and dressed.

We were quiet on the drive to town. I slumped in the big backseat, woozy with fatigue. I just wanted to sleep, but my mind wouldn't stop. I wasn't sure what had happened. I looked at the two of them in the front seat and wondered who they were. I closed my eyes, but I started to spin and a wave of nausea swept over me. So I opened my eyes and focused on the highway's center line until we reached town and my studio.

I got out of the car, said good-bye, and went upstairs. By the single overhead light the studio seemed harsh and desolate, with shadows extending from my reading chair, my work stool, and the easel. The big painting of Ellen, almost finished, stood on the easel at the far end of the long room. I've been working on it steadily for three weeks, but suddenly it looked strange to me. I walked over to it and my eyes jumped first to the very white torso. It was the only part of the figure facing straight out of the canvas, recommending itself—despite itself—to my sight. Upon the white breasts the pink of the aureoles intensified into the beads of the nipples, red like the berries along the left flank. I thought: this isn't Eve, it's Susannah in the eyes of the peering elders. Then I thought: no, it's Ellen. And then my eyes snapped to her startled eyes, the flexed hands, and the knees brought up awkwardly, as if caught halfway in a gesture of concealment.

Nausea rose again so quickly that I just had time to drop to my knees over the wastebasket before I was sick. After a few minutes, when I was able to steady myself, I went and got a mat knife and cut the canvas out of its stretchers. I took it down the stairs, went outside, and found Mrs. Tolman's wire incinerator stowed in the garage. I carried the incinerator to the backyard, rolled the canvas into a long tube, dropped it into the blackened wire container, and struck a match.

The flames rose along the sides of the big rolled canvas. Quickly, the oil in the fresh paint flared up hard. The canvas was tilted in the wire cage like the barrel of a cannon and I heard a low moaning sound as the fire sucked air into the bottom of the tube and flames began to shoot from the hole in the top. The rolled canvas spouted like a Roman candle and chugged like a chimney fire. It burned wildly, flames shooting four feet out of its top. It lit up the whole backyard and then I saw that, in the darkness, I had set the incinerator under a tree and the high flames were licking the lowest branches.

I kicked the incinerator over, but the tindery leaves on a dead branch had already ignited. The fire swept up through the tree, branch by branch, until its whole top was engulfed. I stood and watched as the big yellow sheets of flame rose and folded on themselves, leaping as high as the rooftop. The entire tree shook and roared. It was the only tree in the yard, but it was near the house, so when the flames jumped they touched the eaves.

I shook myself and ran for the garden hose, turned on the outdoor spigot, and sprayed down the back of the house. The screen door slammed and I saw Mrs. Tolman standing at the edge of the yard in her bathrobe, struck dumb and still, staring up into the fire. As quickly as the nausea had come in the studio, a wave of laughter swept up and shook me. Then I looked and saw the adjacent yards lighted by the flaming tree and the neighbors lumbering forward heavily in their pajamas and robes. The firelight colored them all yellow and orange, with long black shadows shifting behind them on the lawns. I expected to see a fire truck wheel up next with its spotlights and clamor, but, strangely, no one had called the fire department. Everyone stood dumbstruck as the fire peaked and began to subside.

I kept the hose on the siding and eaves of the house until the flames had dropped. Then I turned the hose on the tree and soaked down the branches. Gradually everyone—even Mrs. Tolman—just turned away and went back inside. When there were no more coals glowing in the tree I shut off the hose, went inside, and fell into bed.

I woke up to a knock on the door at eight o'clock. It was Mrs. Tolman and she asked me to move out right away. I nodded, closed the door, and went back to bed. This afternoon I've been packing.

Wyatt, I feel like a sleepwalker. I'm staggering in slow motion and everything else is racing in a blur around me. Just a few weeks ago I thought I knew who I was and what I was doing. Now that's all gone and I don't know what's going to happen next.

I just want to sleep. Writing this whole thing out to you has made me very tired.

John

2

John Ordway
423 River Street
Delphi, Iowa

October 1, 1990

Dear Wyatt,

I'm sorry that I haven't written before now. I've wanted to but didn't know how. I can only tell you the truth, and I haven't known how to do that. I can't say that I know yet how to tell you about the things that have happened in the last seven weeks. I've thought about it quite a lot. And just now I've been sitting at this table writing and not writing for about thirty minutes. Can you hear the long silences?

Here are the bare facts, as inadequate as they seem.

After the long night of August 16th, after the trip into the country and the fire in the yard at the studio, and after I wrote you the last letter, I went to sleep and couldn't wake up. Eventually someone came and took me to the hospital. I was there for three or four days, and then was taken to the state hospital at Liberty for psychiatric evaluation. After a week I was released. I came back to Delphi and took a room in a small residential hotel. Two weeks later Jamie came down and insisted that I move. She helped me find the small upstairs apartment where I am now. I've taken a job bookkeeping for a recycling organization in town. It pays the rent, but I'm drawing down my savings for food and gas. If you still think you can arrange a show, go ahead. Whatever sales you can make would be very helpful.

I know you must have a lot of questions. But I think I'll break off, now. I've been at this quite a while and I'm getting tired. I'll finish tomorrow.

10/2

This is a struggle. I feel embarrassed and confused about my time in the hospital. I don't know what happened—something just gave way.

After I fell asleep in the studio, I would stir every once in a while and remember that I had to pack my things and find another place, but then I would go back to sleep. I was sluggish, I never woke up completely, things were a blur. When I did wake up a little I felt like I was at the bottom of a well and the effort of climbing out was more than I could muster. When I think back my sense of time is pretty hazy. I remember people coming in a couple of times. Then somebody got me up and helped me to a car or an ambulance—the fact that I can't remember which it was scares me now. Then I was at the hospital.

Mostly, they let me sleep there. I was tired like I'd never been tired before, and every time I tried to think about what was happening something in me fell, plummeting deeper and deeper away. I remember a couple of exams, some blood tests. A nurse roused me once to talk to a dark-haired woman who asked me how I felt. I felt like lead. Like a smooth lead pellet sinking toward some dead center of sleep. For the short periods when I was awake I felt very tense, very anxious, exhausted. But I slept most of the time, a heavy, wrenched sleep, the kind where you wake up more tired than before.

I'll finish this tomorrow. It's late. It feels late, anyway.

10/3

In the hospital here, the woman who had spoken to me earlier came back and told me that all the medical tests were negative. She said my symptoms suggested depression, and recommended that I be evaluated at the state hospital in Liberty. I was beginning to be awake more of the time, but the feeling of tension stayed with me. A quiet older man in a brown sweater drove me down to Liberty in a state car. I sat next to him in the front seat and tried to stretch and relax my arms and legs, but in a couple of minutes they were all flexed again. I'd been feeling something like that for quite a while this summer, but it was much worse now. The only relief I had was when I slept.

That's what I told the doctor who talked with me when I arrived at Liberty. I sat in a soft chair in the corner of his beige office while a small, sparse tree in the far corner dropped yellow leaves into its pot of dirt. The doctor sat with his elbows on his desk, turning a pencil in his fingers and gazing at his blotter and a sheet of paper there with typing on it. The window in front of him looked out into a parking lot. Then he began to ask me questions and seemed to be satisfied with the broad outlines of things. He didn't probe. I think I was being categorized—sorted into the proper bin to be matched with a treatment. And maybe that was all right.

He'd heard about the fire and did want to know about that. "How did it start?" he asked. I told him it was an accident, that I was burning a painting I didn't like.

"Would you mind telling me about the painting?" he asked, gently, as if I were a child.

"It was a nude of one of my models," I answered. It seemed a great labor to speak. I noticed that I was sighing deeply, almost between each sentence. But I didn't want to withhold anything. I hoped he could help me. I felt tired and dizzy and my heart was pounding with the effort of sitting upright in the chair.

Then he asked me to tell him about my work as a painter, and as one thing led to another I told him how Jamie and I came to live in Delphi and that we had split up. Several times as we spoke I noticed that my feet were flexed back under the seat of the chair and my torso was hunched over in a tight curl. Each time I noticed I sat up straight and tried to relax. The interview must have lasted about an hour, but it seemed much longer. At the end I was exhausted again.

Most of our friends in New York have been in therapy at one time or another—and you've told me about your own experience—but this was my first brush with all that, so I didn't know how to judge this man, Dr. Turnstile. I remember feeling a little let down. I don't know what I expected. A shaman in a beard and bow tie, perhaps. Dr. Turnstile was tired and kind. The elbows of his sport coat were shiny. At the end of my interview I tried to rally myself. "Do you ever get any jokes about your name?" I asked.

"No," he said.

After my interview, a nurse showed me to a small, tidy room with a bed, chair, small dresser, and one window. She gave me a pill and a little plastic cup filled with water. "Dr. Turnstile prescribed this," she said. "It will make you feel less anxious." When she left I fell into the bed and slept until a different nurse roused me for dinner. I felt her touch on my shoulder and heard her voice and dragged myself back to the surface. At dinner in the cafeteria the young man across the table from me suddenly put his hands in his lap, leaned over his tray, and began to sob.

10/4

Reading what I've written so far, all the facts are right but it doesn't sound true. This is what kept me from sending a letter earlier. (I did try to write to you from the hospital, but those letters—if you can call them letters—were even worse. I destroyed them.) But I don't want to be out of touch anymore.

My few days at Liberty passed in a sparse routine punctuated by meals, group therapy sessions, and free time, most of which I spent in my room sitting up in bed and staring out the window. I remember becoming aware one time that I had been sitting and staring outside at the bright side of a corrugated steel garden shed—for how long, I don't know—it could have been an hour. There were times when I felt very emotional—I cried sometimes about nothing, just all of a sudden—but over-all my strongest feeling was relief that the drug Dr. Turnstile had prescribed had stripped away the tension and I could just sit and be still.

I wasn't that way all the time. There were exercise periods in the morning and afternoon when we could go out into the big fenced yard if we wanted to. I'd walk the fence line, stretching out my legs, while other patients leaned against the high Cyclone mesh and watched me pass. On basketball courts in the middle of the yard awkward bodies lunged at each other and shouted. Sometimes I walked around in-side. There was a lounge with card tables, couches, and chairs. At one end a clus-ter of patients watched TV while a nurse or intern sat quietly in a corner, reading or crocheting.

There was a small reading room that I liked. It had a couch and large glass doors opening to a small patio. I had to have special permission to go there—probably because of the glass doors. The view through the tall double doors was of the slop-ing yard, a line of big oaks going bronze in front of the fence, and beyond that a broad cornfield starting to brown and dry toward harvest.

Group sessions took place in the afternoon, in a windowless upstairs room that was meant to look like a living room but failed with chrome and leatherette and travel posters vibrating in fluorescent light over the cheap carpet. At my first ses-sion a staff psychologist I hadn't seen before asked me to introduce myself to the group. There were eight of us, plus the psychologist and a nurse, arranged in a cir-cle of chairs. I said my first name and the others said theirs back to me, one by one around the circle. Most of the names flew out of my head as soon as I heard them, but the faces and bodies stuck. The young man from the cafeteria was there, look-ing down into his lap where his hands were folded. I saw the top of his head with its close-cropped black hair and the smooth, boyish features of his lowered face, a face which would have been almost pretty if it hadn't been drawn into the expres-sion of abject sadness. He mumbled his name into his lap and the group leader did not press him for an audible performance. An old man with a big head of white hair that stood out in every direction wore a red and white striped cardigan sweater over his caved-in chest. He pronounced his name loudly and clearly, then dropped his chin to drowse or brood—I couldn't tell which. Not everyone was so passive. Two men whom I guessed to be in their mid-thirties sat on opposite sides of the cir-cle, one obese and the other skeletally thin. The thin man was the last to introduce himself, then he shouted immediately: "I'm not starting this time! I went first yes-terday! Make Roger. He never says anything."

"Shut up, you skinny hell-dog," said the obese man, narrowing small eyes that were nearly lost already behind the curve of his full cheeks.

"Fat pig!" shouted the thin man, standing up and clenching his fists at his sides. "Look at those dead little pig eyes!"

"Please," said the leader, calmly. "This is not the way we want to begin, especially with a new member joining us." The antagonists both glared at me. "John, would you mind telling us something about yourself?" the psychologist said.

"I'm a painter," I said. "I lived in Delphi before I came here, and before that I lived in New York City."

"Hoo, hoo!" said the thin man, mocking me. "A painter from New York City. I guess you had enough houses there to keep you busy. Why'd you have to come out here? Get in trouble?"

I didn't want to answer. I didn't want to be a part of this group at all. I felt as though I'd slid down a long chute and landed in the vestibule of hell. I tried to sit up straight and draw a deep breath. I untucked my feet from under the chair where they'd locked themselves and stretched my legs out in front of me. Maybe if I could appear relaxed I would feel that way.

Then the young man from the cafeteria began to sob again. His shoulders shook and tears fell straight down out of his eyes into his lap.

"Charles, what's bothering you?" the leader said in a flat, neutral tone. "Is all this shouting upsetting you?" The leader made deliberate glances at the thin and fat men. Charles shook his head. "Then can you tell us what it is?"

"Annie, Annie," Charles wept. "My little Annie."

"What about Annie?" asked the leader.

"Oh, she's gone, she's gone, she's gone, she's gone." Charles was swaying back and forth in his chair, now. "She's gone, she's gone, she's gone . . ."

"The same thing every day," groaned the thin man, interrupting the chant. "Be a goddamn man!" he said, and struck his rib cage with a fist. Charles stopped swaying and sobbed quietly, the tears still dropping straight down onto his folded hands.

"Ha, ha, ha, ha, ha, ha, ha!" Laughter boomed out of the huge chest of the fat man, who was peering through eye slits at his antagonist. "Be a man! Look at you—more like a scurvy dog than a man."

The old, white-haired gentleman continued to drowse or brood. To his left, a man only slightly younger, bald except for a fringe at ear level, cowered sideways in his chair, making himself as small as possible. I glanced at the middle-aged man next to me, who was decked out in pastels like a golfer. His eyes were bright with glee, taking in the whole scene.

The leader spoke again. "I want you to notice something," he said, then paused. "Anger, grief, and fear. Look around the circle. You have more in common than you think." The fat man snorted. "Anger, grief, and fear," the psychologist said again.

"They're all connected, deep down, like springs that rise up from the same underground river." The comparison struck me. I hadn't expected poetry from this earnest young man in a plaid shirt and name tag. "We need all these emotions, but sometimes we get stuck on one and we make it do all the work." He'd left his metaphor, but the image stayed with me. A river running in the dark, under the ground, issuing at the surface in three springs. Two get blocked, and the other spurts up, too hard and wild. So what was it for me? I knew instantly. I'd called it anxiety. That was easier than to say I was afraid all the time. So afraid that my body tightened and twisted and wore me out. But afraid of what? I didn't even know anymore. Lately I'd just held myself rigid against it, afraid of the fear, afraid of feeling that way. I'd held myself rigid, as if I could clamp down and stop what was rising, wildly, in my chest, as if I could clamp down and not feel anything.

I held myself and rode out the session. A glass wall slid down around me and I sat, looking but not seeing, listening but not hearing. And when it was time I went back to my room and sat and stared out the window at the sunlight beating hard on the bright steel shed.

10/5

On the third day of my evaluation at Liberty I was called in for my "staffing." A nurse I recognized from group sessions came to my room and led me down hallways, around corners, up a stairway, and finally to the end of another hall and a door which she opened. She smiled and nodded me into a room where I found eight doctors and nurses sitting around a large conference table. When I entered, the silent group of white-coated figures turned in unison to look at me. My guide steered me to an empty chair at the head of the table and I sat down. Then she took her own place at the table.

I recognized Dr. Turnstile, who smiled at me in what appeared to be a gesture of reassurance. Also there was the young psychologist who had led the two nearly chaotic group sessions I'd attended. Aside from my introduction, I'd spoken at neither. And I'd seen all three of the nurses who were there. The others around the table were strangers.

Dr. Turnstile made introductions. The men I didn't know—and one woman— were other staff psychiatrists or psychologists. "We'd like to talk with you for a few minutes," Dr. Turnstile said, "to get to know you better. It's nothing to worry about; it's part of our routine."

The group continued to regard me, their folders and notepads in front of them on the table. Clearly, they had been discussing me. I felt my heart beating in my chest, a little too quickly, a little too hard. I recognized the adrenal trill that ran through my body, and everything I looked at—the faces around the table, the appraising eyes, the yellow walls, the empty blue sky through the one high window—started to my eyes with unusual clarity. Suddenly I felt all alert, like a fox in the woods.

"How have you been feeling, generally, in the past few days?" The voice came from a man down the table to my left. His long dark hair was combed straight back and he wore thick glasses which blurred his eyes.

"Better," I said. "I've been able to relax a little. And I sleep less." What were the right answers, I wondered. What would get me away from here?

The doctor behind the thick lenses followed up: "What differences have you felt, if any, since starting the medication prescribed for you?" I told him I felt less anxious, that I was able to just sit still for periods of time, and that that was a relief.

Now an older man with a tanned, deeply creased face spoke. "Do you sometimes feel really down, really blue?" He smiled sadly, sympathetically.

"Of course," I said.

"How long do these times last?" he asked.

"They come and go. A couple of days, usually." I thought of the wild, wordless, animal fear and the despair that followed, clamping down like metal on bone.

"And do you ever feel so badly that you just want to throw yourself in front of a truck or something?" He said this recklessly, almost lightly, with a little gesture of his arm, as if he were tossing something away.

My guard went up at the question, but I thought about those patches of despair as clearly as I could. They didn't make me want to end my life. They made me want to escape the way I felt—fear and dread so intense I'd chew off one leg to escape. I looked at the kind, tanned face and said, "No."

"Are there particular thoughts that come back to you again and again? Or any dreams that are especially vivid or that you have often?" This came from the young doctor to my right. His brilliant blue eyes fixed me in a steady gaze.

The dream. I had to give them something. I said, "Sometimes I dream that I wake up in my own bed, that it's morning, but I can't move."

"How do you feel in the dream?" he asked.

"It's very distressing," I said. "A panic builds until I finally wake up, sometimes with a jerk or a jolt." Several pens around the table moved across their yellow pads. The blue-eyed doctor sat back, satisfied, as if he'd scored a point over the others.

Next the woman who had been introduced to me as a psychiatrist spoke up. She was attractive, probably in her late forties, with long dark hair tied back loosely.

She wore half-framed reading glasses which she took off now and placed on the table. "Is there a time or a place that makes you feel best, or safest?"

I answered without thinking. "When I'm working," I said. "I feel best, most at ease, when I'm painting." She nodded.

"Tell me about the painting you burned, if you don't mind," she said.

A wave of adrenaline swept through me. The question seemed dangerous, but I had to answer. "It was a life study of one of my models, Ellen Swensen," I said.

"It was a nude, then?" she asked.

"Yes," I said. "That's my subject. It's what I'm known for among the people who buy my work. My agent, Wyatt Arends, of the Arends Gallery in New York City, handles the paintings."

She ignored my little speech. "What were you feeling when you burned the painting? Why did you do it?" She looked at me directly, but with a skillfully produced air of pleasant curiosity.

I searched for a safe answer, but invention failed me, and I went blank. I took a deep breath and stretched my legs out under the table. Then I searched myself for a true answer. It occurred to me that all I could do was to tell the story of the whole, long evening. At the thought, a wave of exhaustion swept over me. I groped for a short version, the shortest way through. I sighed and said: "I came home late one night and the painting looked different to me. Maybe it was the electric lights, a bare bulb. I felt sick. I threw up in the wastebasket. But that could have been the beer on an empty stomach. I'd been with friends." That sentence—I'd been with friends—didn't sound right. "For some reason I couldn't see it as a painting," I said. "It was just Ellen and she looked scared. It felt wrong."

There was a silence around the table, but nobody wrote anything down. They were all looking at me.

"Dr. Turnstile tells me you had seen your companion, Jamie, earlier in the day," the woman continued. "How long had the two of you been together before you separated?"

"Three years," I said.

"And how do you feel toward her now?"

"I miss her," I said. "Very much." I was truly exhausted now, just hanging on.

"Do you ever feel angry with her? Angry that she left you?"

I took a deep breath that probably sounded like a sigh. "I don't feel that. No," I said. The woman looked at me for a long moment, then glanced at Dr. Turnstile to signal that she was finished.

It was his turn now, and I hoped that meant we were near the end. He asked,

"Do you feel particularly angry at anyone right now? Do you hold anyone responsible for the way you've been feeling lately? Or for the fact that you're here?"

"No," I answered.

Dr. Turnstile continued: "Tell me again, please, what differences, if any, you have noticed in the way you've felt since starting medication a few days ago?"

"Less anxious. Easier to relax sometimes," I said. I heard myself and tried to muster the energy for complete sentences.

"Just one more question," he said. "Here at the hospital, do you feel like you want to stay or leave?"

The image of the fat man and the thin man shouting at each other rose in my mind, and behind them, the old man turning sideways, cowering, and the young man with his head down, sobbing. Anger, fear, and grief. I wanted to leave the place of anger, fear, and grief. "I want to be released," I said.

Dr. Turnstile turned and nodded to the nurse who had brought me in. She got up and ushered me back to my room. I lay down on my bed, on top of the covers. Grief welled up from somewhere deep. Tears filled my eyes briefly, then ebbed away. And then I went to sleep. I shut my eyes and let myself sink into the deep, easeful, bottomless dark.

10/6

The next day I was called into Dr. Turnstile's office. I sat in the chair in the corner and he leaned back in his desk chair as he told me the staff agreed that my depression and anxiety were, as he put it, "short-term responses to recent trauma." He smiled sadly as he said this, and reassured me that he didn't feel I was "ill" in any long-term way. He gave me the name of a counselor in Delphi to see once in a while, someone at the county human services agency who turned out to be the woman who had spoken to me in the hospital. He also recommended that I seek out some contacts in town, spend less time alone. He wanted me to stay on the pills for a while. He explained that they were for anxiety and he said that if they didn't seem to be working we could try an antidepressant.

"I feel funny about taking drugs for emotions," I told him.

He said, "If you had some sort of chemical imbalance that affected your kidneys, you wouldn't feel funny about taking something for that, would you? So, if you have too much or too little of a particular enzyme at your synapses, why should there be anything wrong with taking something to help with that problem?" The physician's view of the body and the self had never struck me quite so forcefully. He saw me as a bundle of chemical reactions jilted out of balance.

He stood up and I did, too. He shook my hand and wished me luck. I took a bus back north and checked into the cheap residential hotel adjacent to Delphi's small business district.

10/7

My little hotel, absurdly named The Broadway, was a dim place that smelled like wilted lilacs. Its lobby was actually a wide hallway with a narrow reception desk built into one side, and it always seemed like the middle of the night there, even at noon. Behind the desk and a single lamp, a sixty-year-old woman with silver hair and a lot of heavy rings watched me—warily, I thought—as I came and went.

My room was small and rectangular. A single bed just fit across the far end, under a window with faded yellow curtains that smelled like dust. The bathroom— toilet, sink, and shower—was down the hall. The hotel was a grim little place, but that didn't concern me at the time. I felt different than I ever had before. I don't know whether it was depression or the effects of the drug I was on, but I still felt heavy and listless. I roused myself to go out for meals or buy groceries, and I looked in the paper for a job.

Within a week, I'd been hired by Earth Day Industries. I keep records of how many pounds of newsprint, cardboard, plastic, glass bottles, and crushed cans are shipped out in semitrailers to reconstitution plants. The recycling company is housed in a new corrugated metal building about a half a block long—not much to look at, but well lit and ventilated. Inside are a couple of simple offices, a big sorting room, another big room where the machinery for crushing cans, cardboard, and plastic jugs operates, and an adjoining holding area that opens into the loading dock.

I was hired to work six hours a day. If I finish figuring and recording the previous day's totals in less time than that, I help with the sorting. A lot of that work is done by employees who, when I was in school, we called mentally retarded. There's a house where they live together with some kind of supervision, and they walk to work together across town every morning with their lunch buckets. In the sorting room, one guy, Rich, showed me the ropes. He has a wandering eye and a thin mustache that twitches sometimes when he speaks. He walked me around the sorting room, pointing and explaining. "Metal caps and rings have to come off the glass bottles," he said. "Then the bottles go here." He pointed to a bin. "Plastic jugs and bottles go in this bin." He pointed with his other hand. "We sort the cans and put them in these long plastic bags. Except we crush some kinds into bales." I had seen the oversized bales glittering in the sun—gaudy, crunched hunks of silver and primary colors next to the loading dock. I looked around the big room. It smelled like

stale beer, but the work seemed peaceful, everyone milling carefully past one another from bin to bin, sorting.

At the end of my first week Rich told me they went bowling every Friday night
and I was invited.

10/8

One morning, before work, when I was sitting at the little table in my room, there
was a knock on the door. I said "Come in," the door swung open, and there was
Jamie.

She exhaled a long breath and let her shoulders sag. And then we just looked at
each other. I didn't know what to say and I guess she didn't either. And then she
opened up like a mother scolding a child who's been lost: "My God, what's going
on?" she said. "Don't you know how we've been worrying? I got a call from Wyatt
last night and he said he hadn't heard from you in weeks. He said he'd tried to call
and your phone had been disconnected. Letters came back 'addressee unknown.'
He reached me by calling nearly every J. Stevens in Minneapolis." Her distress
drummed down on me like a hard rain. Finally, she paused.

"How did you find me?" I managed.

"First I tried to phone Jean or Ellen, but they weren't home. When I did reach
Ellen's mother, she said she thought you'd been in the hospital. Ellen had spoken
to your landlady, she said. So I called the hospital, scared out of my wits, but they
wouldn't tell me anything except that you weren't there. I drove down in a panic
and got here around midnight. I went up and down streets until I spotted your car
in front of the hotel, then took a room at the motel out on the highway." When she
finished I looked down at the tabletop.

"I'm sorry," I said. Then I realized that she was still standing out in the hall. I
stood up, asked her in, and pointed toward a green chair. I shut the door and we
both sat down. Then there was a long, awkward silence and the room closed in. I
felt like we were crouching together inside a shoe box.

"What happened?" she said, finally. Her voice had softened now. Mixed with her
tone of complaint were concern and relief. "Why didn't you call anybody?"

"I guess I didn't know what to say," I told her. And then I recounted, in bare-
bones fashion, what had happened since the last time I'd seen her—the day of the
fire.

She listened with what looked like great concentration. Her eyebrows were
pulled together and a little vertical crease formed between them. Her eyes looked
out at me, then glassed over with reflection, then looked out at me again.

"I'm not really *sure* what happened," I finished. "Something just gave way." And then we sat quietly for what felt like several minutes, in an aura of wilted lilacs and dust. She looked down, somewhere into the space between us.

I broke the silence. "I have to go to work," I said. Her eyes came up to mine and brightened. "I'm keeping books and helping out at Earth Day," I explained, and her eyes went dim again. Then she asked when I got off and I agreed to meet her for lunch at Lu's Café downtown.

When I arrived at Lu's, Jamie was already at a table covered by a newspaper marked with circles and notations. I sat down and she said, without looking up, "We've got to get you out of that terrible hotel. I've found some places for you to look at." And so, after lunch, Jamie took me in the van and I went along, docile and grateful as she drove me from place to place, questioned the landlords for me, and scrutinized the rooms. In the late afternoon we settled on a place upstairs in a house on the south side of town.

A flight of exposed wooden stairs attached to the side of the house went up to a landing and a private entrance on the second floor. There was a full kitchen with a table in it, a sitting room, a little bath, and one bedroom. "There's no studio space," Jamie pointed out. I hadn't thought about studio space all day. It was the farthest thing from my mind. "But it's clean and freshly painted." I nodded.

I took the day's events as a simple extension of the past weeks, when the forces that moved me had shifted from inside to outside. Before, I'd thought of myself as having made a bold move away from New York. I was a man moving toward the heart of his work. Now—I just don't know. I let Jamie arrange everything and I was grateful.

10/9

Before Jamie left, she made me promise to get back in touch with you right away. But then I had to move, had to get my things from Mrs. Tolman's garage. After work each day I still felt very tired, and I decided that I couldn't afford to install a telephone—I make calls from the pay phone at the drugstore downtown. So more time passed.

I know Jamie's told you what's been going on, generally. But I'm sorry. She said you were worried, and I've been inconsiderate. Finally I guess what's kept me from writing, most of all, is embarrassment.

But now I've written all these pages. I hope you don't mind. It seems to help to go over these things in this way. It calms me, somehow.

Your friend,
John

October 12, 1990

Dear Wyatt,

Yes, it's good to be back in touch. You said on the phone that I sound different. I feel different. There's a heaviness that I don't remember from before. Sometimes I just drag down to a full stop. I find myself sitting, staring out the window at a tree-top waving. There's a vague melancholy, but more than that simply a physical sensation of weight, of fatigue. I can't tell whether it's sadness over the whole messed-up situation here—whether it's missing Jamie and feeling that my life is all tangled up—or the drug I'm on. I've seen the woman at the county health services a couple of times—Caroline Evans. I don't know what her training is, but she's interesting, someone I can talk to. She's putting me in touch with another doctor nearby to have my medication checked. She doesn't think it should hit me so hard.

Ellen stopped by the apartment to talk for a while yesterday. It was late afternoon and at that time of day the sun pours into my little kitchen. We sat at the table and drank tea. She said she was sorry, but she couldn't work with me anymore. Her mother had pleaded with her, told her people were talking, especially after the fire. Ellen said: "I know they're wrong, but it's a very small town and there are a lot of people who assume that a woman with her clothes off in the presence of a man can mean only one thing. Some people had started to look at me differently. Then, after the fire, I guess there were a lot of people who said to each other, 'See, I told you.' At the library, I only catalog and reshelve now," she said. "Mrs. Steegers took me off the circulation desk. She says some people have told her they don't feel comfortable around me. Can you believe it?"

I shook my head. I told her, as far as I was concerned, she shouldn't worry. I understood. She looked pretty down about it, so I tried to lighten things up. I smiled and said, "Well, Ellen, I suppose they're right. A woman with her clothes off in the presence of a man is always about sex in some way or another."

As soon as I said that, I felt nervous about it, but she smiled back and said, "You know, you really blew it with that fire. My mother says Mrs. Tolman's neighbors can't stop telling the story. They say: 'The whole tree was on fire, shaking like a big torch in the dark!'"

I said, "You should have seen them standing there in their pajamas, gaping up at it! I almost turned the hose on them." Then we both cracked up. We laughed hard and couldn't stop. We bent over the table holding our sides, laughing, and then we tipped back in our chairs with our mouths wide open and laughed some more. We howled. I can't remember the last time I laughed like that.

Afterward, we just sat there and grinned. Ellen was still smiling when she asked, "How did you manage that, anyway? What in the world were you doing?"

So I told her about burning the painting.

She asked why, her face serious now.

I tried to tell her how it struck me that night, how I had seen it differently. "Suddenly it felt as though I had done you wrong, that I'd taken something from you and used it."

"You make it sound very personal," she said. "I didn't think it was supposed to be like that. You can do what you want in your paintings, can't you?"

I nodded. Then she said, "It was a pretty interesting painting. You probably shouldn't have burned it." She stood up, put her hand on my shoulder, leaned over, and gave me a friendly kiss on the cheek. We smiled at each other and I let her out.

It pains me—it torments me—that Ellen is being talked about because of her work with me. But she must have known she was taking a risk modeling for me, that some people would talk. She knows her town better than I do. So why did she do it? And, after all that's gone on, she certainly wasn't timid in coming up to my apartment. That was considerate and brave. And for a moment, laughing hard in my kitchen, we were together under that burning tree. There's a fire in her, too. I shouldn't have destroyed the painting.

John

October 19, 1990

Dear Wyatt,

We're well into fall here, and mornings are cold when I walk to work. This morning a couple of women were sweeping their porches. A man was trimming a hedge. One maple still held a few yellow leaves.

I finished my bookkeeping by noon and ate my sandwich with Rich and Kevin and Linda out back at the picnic table pulled up next to the side of the building. The warmth off the corrugated steel felt good. It's Friday, and Kevin says the whole crew is going bowling tonight. He wants me to come. He looked at me hopefully from under the brim of his green baseball cap, his straw-colored hair winging out from under it on both sides. Last time I rolled an 86, despite Rich's earnest coaching. He stood with me at the end of the lane, looking up at me almost plaintively, explaining how if I would hold my hand a little to the side of the ball as I released it, I could start it at the right side of the lane and it would curve into the sweet spot for a strike. He focused me hard in his good eye while the other seemed to gaze off in serene contemplation of something in the distance. I tried, but threw the ball down the right gutter. The girls tittered, but then immediately shouted encouragements. Rich showed me how to lock my wrist, his crooked mustache twitching. My second ball caught three pins. Mocking applause from the girls, then laughter. I smiled at them as I walked back to my seat, and they patted my shoulder with sympathy. Then it was Rich's turn. He knocked down nine pins with his first ball, but missed the spare. His delivery is furious. He almost runs toward the end line and hurls the ball with all his might. The pins jump and thrash in the air. He's the crew champ, but Linda comes close. She's more accurate than Rich, which is remarkable given her form. She stands at the end of the lane—tall, gangly—with her long, thin arms hanging at her sides. She can't find sweatshirts or flannel shirts with sleeves long enough, so her white, thin wrists stick out. She stands perfectly still at the end of the lane, holding her ball at her side with one hand. Then she starts it swinging like a pendulum until finally she's whipping it quickly back and forth, back and forth. I don't know how her arm stands it—she must use a very light ball. When she releases, it always goes right down the middle.

Spending time with the crew members is oddly settling. I don't have to ask myself how much they know about me. They don't care—I'm just somebody new at work. It's hard to guess their ages. Rich could be in his mid-thirties. Kevin and Linda are probably in their early twenties. The others might be a little younger. No matter their ages, at work the staff always refers to them—even Rich—as "the kids."

As we finished lunch, Rich reminded me how much better I had done when I started locking my wrist. Linda and Kevin were holding hands under the picnic table; I think they're going steady. We made plans to meet at the bowling alley and then went back to work. I helped Kevin crush and stack cardboard.

I look forward to my chances to do some repetitive physical work. I can lose myself in it. This afternoon I broke down cardboard boxes and shoved them into the hopper of the big, yellow hydraulic crusher. Kevin secured the machine's door with the heavy sliding bolts, pushed the buttons to operate the crusher, then opened the lower door so we could pull out the compacted bale. For an hour and a half my mind was a restful blank. When we finished, I stood in the doorway between the machine room and the holding area and watched a semi back up to the loading dock. The driver eased the rig in expertly until the back of the trailer kissed the timber that forms the edge of the dock. There's a whole world of practical work—of clean-smelling oil and gears—that I've had no part in until now.

When I got off at 2:00 I walked home by way of the library. As I'd hoped, Ellen was working in the stacks. She helped me look for the books on Goya I needed, but we didn't find much. As we searched she told me for the first time that she had been an art major in college. We sat cross-legged on the floor up on the second level, whispering next to the art shelf. She'd had a lot of art history, she said, and some coursework in painting, including figure classes. That was partly why she had answered my ad. "I wanted to watch you paint," she said, "without making you self-conscious."

"Why?" I said. I was taken aback.

"I still sketch quite a bit, but don't paint very much," she said, "and sometimes I think about doing some things, putting together some slides, and trying to get into an art school."

I asked to see some of her work and she said she'd think about it. But I told her to be careful. Then we heard footsteps on the iron stairs leading up to the second-floor stacks. So I moved off to another section and Ellen continued her shelving.

Wyatt, if you have some Goya books—or better yet, some slides—could I borrow them for a while? I particularly want to take a fresh look at his madhouse paintings and drawings. Give my love to Alice.

John

P.S.: *The doctor that Caroline referred me to reduced my dosage and I don't feel quite as listless as before.*

J.

October 24, 1990
Dear Wyatt,

Yes, a show in November would be fine. It won't be a big one, and those paintings seem like ancient history to me now, but I'll be happy for the chance to sell some things. Yes, November is sudden, and all the stress and strain of preparations will be on you, I'm afraid. I hope you haven't juggled the gallery schedule and made a lot of headaches for yourself. As always, thanks. I'm very grateful. God knows I need the money as soon as possible, if anything sells.

No, I haven't spoken to Jamie for about three weeks. The last time I saw her was when I went up to help with a raku firing. I drove up on a Friday afternoon and we did the work that night. (In Delphi we got into a pattern of nighttime firings, partly because it was cooler, partly because we liked the long unbroken stretches of time and the way the flames and sparks looked in the dark.) In the big triangular yard of her apartment complex, she had built a kiln and connected it to tanks. It was a small kiln and her pieces were big, so we could only do one thing at a time. We put in a large covered jar and started to bring the heat up. While Jamie kept an eye on the temperature, she sent me into the apartment to eat some supper. I sat at the kitchen table with the soup and sandwich she had saved for me, browsing the magazines stacked there. In the pile was a folder of photographs Andrea had taken of Jamie.

There were pictures of Jamie among her pots and weavings at an outdoor setup at a fair. I've always been taken by photos of artists among the things they have made. There's a poignance and triumph in them. The individual who has labored through difficulty and confusion stands at last among the realized conceptions. Jamie sat in a director's chair, at ease between two slender jars. The one on the left, rising to her elbow, was decorated with fanciful uneven stripes in different shades. The taller one, to her right, was lightly mottled with an organic pattern something like clusters of narrow leaves. Its elegant, stretched shape makes you think of a palm tree or a woman. Jamie's leg, crossed over her other knee, swung out in front of the tall piece so the curve of her calf and the side of the jar cut the same shape. Behind her, a woolly horizontal weaving with vertical strips in coarse textures set off the smooth line of her hair and cheek. Her personal beauty was reflected and magnified in the beauty of the things she had made.

There were more pictures, some of Jamie at her wheel and close studies of her hands raising the sides of a bowl; there were photos of her shot through the harnesses of her loom and from above as she pulled the reed down the warp strings. At the back of the folder there were nudes. When I came to them my throat tightened and panic surged up. What did this mean? In each picture Jamie's figure was lit in the foreground against a dark backdrop. In one, she was seated in a simple wooden chair, sitting up straight but relaxed, her knees and ankles together and her hands in her lap. Above the familiar curves of her shoulders, breasts, waist, and hips, she looked directly into the camera. Her smile was changed by the tilt of her chin, which was raised a little, proudly. In another picture, her back formed a white shape, and her hair, wound in a single thick braid, fell between her shoulder blades. I recognized the three birthmarks that make a small triangle near her waist.

As I looked at the photos I saw Jamie as I had in those early weeks in New York, when we were first living together, but she was also changed. There was a new dignity and stature and accomplishment. I saw her freshly, but it was through Andrea's eyes. I felt admiration and confusion, love and jealousy and fear. In a single gesture, the pictures had given Jamie back to me and taken her away.

~·~

I went back out into the yard. It was dark, and Jamie's silhouette interrupted the kiln's dim light when she moved back and forth. The air had grown cold after the sun went down. I went to my car and put on an extra sweater. I got a blanket out of the trunk, walked back to the kiln, spread my blanket on the ground nearby, and sat down. Jamie was sitting on another blanket. There was no moon, and though we were only seven or eight feet apart, I couldn't see her. Her voice came out of the dark when she said, "The kiln's working fine, but it'll be a good while before the first piece comes out." Then it was quiet except for the low hiss of the gas jet.

I was lying on my back with my hands behind my head. The stars were dim because of the city's lights in the distance. Once in a while a car went past on a nearby road. There were bits of conversation at wide intervals. Sometimes Jamie switched on a flashlight and looked at her watch. We may have slept a little.

I was awake later when she got up to check the kiln's temperature gauge. "How's it going?" I asked.

"Fine," she said. "We're about half an hour away." I heard her shift on her blanket. Then she asked, "How's it going for you, John? What are your days like?"

I shifted onto my side and faced her voice in the dark. The sudden question surprised me. "Well," I said, "I work until early afternoon at easy tasks with people as different from me as I've ever known. I go home and make tea. Then I read or take a walk along the river. I go to bed early."

"God, John," she said. "It doesn't sound like you."

I barked out a little laugh that startled us both. "No, it doesn't sound like me, does it? Everything is such a surprise."

It was quiet for a minute.

"How are you feeling?" she asked.

Having her so near but invisible, hearing her familiar voice coming out of the pitch black as we sat on our two blankets as if on separate rafts, struck me as eerie and true. "I hardly know how to answer that," I said. I wondered if this was what it was like to sit in a confession box and talk back to the disembodied voice coming through the screen. I kept talking. I don't think I was trying for pity. I was just answering her question as accurately as I could. Finally I said, "I can't imagine the future and that scares me."

We sat quietly in the dark. The gas jet hissed.

"I can't imagine the future right now, either," she said. "I try to sort things out, but I just draw a blank. I feel like there must be a key, but I can't find it."

I peered hard toward her, but it was like sitting in a cave—no light at all. After a while Jamie said, "I think we can get that pot out," and she got up and went to the van to put on her protective clothes. I rolled the empty oil drum near the kiln, filled it with some of the shredded newspaper from the big plastic bags, and leaned the lid against the drum. Jamie came back and turned off the gas. "Okay," she said. I pulled on the padded gloves and stepped up to the detachable kiln door. I carefully lifted the door out of its stays and used it to shield my face from the heat as I took a couple of steps back.

Orange light poured out across the yard in a wide V. In it, Jamie stepped forward with her leather apron tied on and her hair tucked up into the old leather pilot's helmet. Thick asbestos mitts reached above her elbows, and the clear plastic welder's visor that protected her face shone with the reflection of the glowing pot. I peered around my shield and felt the heat blast my forehead. In the kiln's yellow mouth, the big jar glowed red and shimmered, almost translucent, shining from the inside out like a Chinese lantern. Jamie reached in and grasped its curved sides and slowly drew it out. It glowed in her hands as she carried it at arm's length, carefully but quickly, like a newborn or a lit bomb, and nested it in the drum with the shredded newsprint. The paper ignited and flamed up, and Jamie covered the drum with its lid.

I stepped back and put down the metal door. We stood in the light of the glowing kiln bricks. "Well, that looked good," I said.

She tipped up her visor. "We'll see. Do you still have your eyebrows?"

"I think so," I said. "And you're not on fire, as far as I can tell." She smiled and we went inside to make tea while the kiln cooled for the next piece.

That was the pattern of the whole night. We did three more pots—big shallow bowls about six inches deep and over two feet across, decorative pieces for a low table or to hang on a wall. While they were in the kiln we rested on our blankets and talked a little. I couldn't help but remember other nights, in Delphi, next to another kiln, when we were wrapped in the same blanket, watching together for the occasional sparks to rise and swirl against the fixed stars. We used to play a game: we would each pick a star and locate it, murmuring close in the other's ear, and then we would see whose star was nearest when the spark went out. The sparks were different from the stars in three ways: they were yellow, they swerved and veered as they rose, and they didn't last.

After midnight when it became very cold we waited inside, napping with an alarm set for when the next piece would be ready to come out. I slept on the little couch in the main room. By the time the last piece came out it was dawn and bunched gray clouds were lit a soft peach color at their edges. While the last bowl was cooling we lined up the other pieces that were still covered with carbon char, pulled out the hose, and started to scrub them. First we worked on the shallow bowls. Both of them are handsome pieces, but I especially like the big covered jar.

It stands about two and a half feet high, becoming wider as it rises until it curves gently into an almost round top. The shape is something like a hot-air balloon and the jar has the same appearance of buoyancy, as if it might lift and float. We cleaned the pot together, one on each side, both gripping its rim and scrubbing with the stiff brushes. It's remarkable that a piece so lyrical can be so tough. The walls that seemed almost transparent coming out of the kiln—all red and shimmering—were thick and heavy as we muscled the pot hard, scrubbing at the char. We knew this was a really good one, and we were excited as the colors began to show. The flat round cover and the wide band around the opening were done with a smooth cream glaze, so they came clean quickly. The smooth areas were crackled with little gray veins. The body of the jar had a coarse, pebbly finish the color of a lustered penny. As she had hoped, the raku process had introduced a lot of variety, with coppery greens and deep violets showing through in a muted iridescence. Her familiar willow pattern rose from the bottom of the jar, but with a variation. There were rectangles tumbled among the leaves, like floating windows that the leaf shapes twined into and out of as they curved toward the jar's top.

When it was clean we sat back on our haunches, wet and chilly with the hose spatterings, and grinned at each other. We both knew it was a breakthrough piece for her. Then we went inside and ate a big breakfast of pancakes and eggs.

When we had finished, I needed to sleep before driving back to Delphi. Jamie told me to take her room where I could pull the shades. She went back outside to scrub the last bowl.

Jamie's room was small and unadorned. The walls were the same pale blue as the rest of the apartment, with nothing on them except for the woolly tapestry hung over the head of the bed. It was the tapestry I had seen in the photo, and the same tall jar stood in one corner of the room. I pulled the shades, slipped off my shoes, and sat down on the edge of the bed. Jamie's hairbrushes were on the small dresser across from me. Next to them was the small coral necklace that she usually wore, the one we found in Key West in the little shop near the fishing wharves. I stretched out on top of the covers and shut my eyes. The pillow held the light scent of her perfume.

I couldn't sleep, felt vaguely restless. I sat up on the edge of the bed, facing Jamie's dresser. I could hear the water spattering on the concrete of the parking lot below the window as Jamie cleaned the last bowl. I reached over and pulled open the dresser's top drawer. Jamie's T-shirts and underwear were folded and stacked

neatly. I lifted each shirt, searching between them. I sifted through the light un-
derthings, the delicate sculpted lingerie in colors—the things I had bought for
her—and the more practical, comfortable items she had bought herself. I felt behind and beside the clothes with both hands, looking for—I don't know what. I
told myself that if I were to find something that could help me understand what
was happening—a letter, more photos, anything—it would help us both. That's
what I told myself as my heart beat in my ears so hard I felt dizzy.

I slid the drawer shut quietly and opened the next. Shorts, jeans, corduroys. I
shut that drawer and opened the bottom one. Socks, stockings, the long knit
nightgown she liked to wear, the short white gauzy one I liked her to wear. Underneath the clothes I found the familiar leather case. Inside, the antique jewelry in-
herited from her grandmother shone dully in the gloom. The tiger's-eye earrings
were there, the serpent bracelet, the pomegranate ring. I returned everything to its
place and shut the drawer. When I straightened up I went light-headed and
thought for a moment that I would pass out.

When I recovered I got up and stepped to the closet near the head of the bed.
Inside, in the cool darkness, Jamie's scent hung in the blouses and dresses. I remember feeling ashamed, but I was helpless to stop myself. I put my arms around
the clothes and pulled them to me. It was like embracing ghosts. I dropped my face
into the light, cool fabric and sobbed. —Wyatt, my friend, my confessor, I think I
am still not very well.— After a while I lay down on the bed again and instantly fell
asleep.

Sometime later I heard footsteps and a light click. The bedroom door opened a little and Jamie stuck her head in. "Are you awake?" she said. "You told me you
wanted to get home tonight, and it's late afternoon. I thought I'd check on you."
The room was dim. A little sunlight leaked in around the edges of the drawn
shades. I rolled onto my side. The hairbrushes and coral necklace sat on the dresser
next to their images in the mirror.

"If you're hungry, there's some soup left from last night," she said. "Or we could
order something."

"Thanks," I said. "I'll be out in a minute." Jamie pulled her head back and shut
the door. I sat up on the edge of the bed. Across from me in the mirror I saw a man
sitting in a darkened room. On either side of the mirror rectangles of light glowed
in the narrow space between the shades and the window frames. I rubbed my face
and looked again at my reflection, flat and indistinct in the half-light. It looked like
a man cut out of paper and glued to a stick.

Jamie waved as I pulled out of the parking lot. In the rearview mirror I saw her wrap her sweater more tightly around her against the chill and turn away to go back inside. I followed the branching roads out of the city, recognizing the landmarks and turns, finding my way south toward the highway. It had rained and the roads were slick with reflections. Sunlight angled through the empty trees, and it was late enough that a few clouds were a deep delft blue. Somehow it reminded me of the day over a year ago when you and Alice helped us fit the last of the boxes into the van and waved as we started threading our way toward our new life out here. This time I couldn't tell if I was driving toward something or away from something.

John

3

John Ordway
423 River Street
Delphi, Iowa

October 31, 1990

Dear Wyatt,

Went for a long walk earlier this evening. I like to follow the little roads that crest the ridges and overlook the town and the river and the fields. There's a park along one of them. I stopped there when it was nearly dusk and looked out. The people in town had been raking their yards and piling the leaves at the curb and burning them. I could see dozens of little orange fires through the smoke that hung in the trees. Beyond them stood the church steeples and the municipal building's small dome. The distance and the smoke and the fires made the town look ancient.

Tonight's Halloween. It's dark now, and out my kitchen window I can look down and see the small draped figures quietly moving up and down the street, going door to door in their sheets or tall black hats or plastic skeleton suits. They won't come up to my second-floor entrance, so I can stand here on my landing and watch them pass. They move under the trees' bare branches like so many fears or wishes that only come out at night.

This angle is interesting, with the streetlights projecting the limbs' crooked shadows across the yards and the street. I think I'll break off now and do some sketches.

John

November 3, 1990

Dear Wyatt,

I'm astonished by the news that you've managed to sell three more of the paintings in advance of the show this month. The check is a godsend. Many, many thanks.

And thanks for sending the Goya slides. I checked out a projector from the library and looked at them last night, shining them on my bedroom wall. The room is long and narrow, with an unbroken white wall at one end above my bed. I placed the projector on my small writing desk at the other end, sat on the floor next to it, and ran through the marvelous pictures.

Well, "marvelous" isn't exactly right. This time they frightened me—the aquatint *Giant* under the crescent moon, looking up over his massive shoulder like an immense, wild version of Rodin's *Thinker*; *The Witches' Sabbath*, with the great black goat in the circle of women, its horns wreathed with vine leaves and its yellow eyes turned in, self-absorbed, dead, mechanical; *Prison Interior*, its chained figures under that massive black arch which fills the top half of the painting; the frontispiece to a set of dreams, with the artist burying his head in his hands while bats and owls swing around him in the dark; the chalk drawing of the *loco furioso* with head and one arm thrust through the bars, his face and eyes deceptively serene.

I can tell you, when that wonderful self-portrait, *Goya Attended by Dr. Arrieta*, came up, it was a relief. I gazed and gazed. Do you remember? Goya, in his seventies and desperately ill, sits up in bed and slumps back into his physician. The doctor is almost cheek-to-cheek with his patient, supporting him from behind. His left hand is on Goya's shoulder as he reaches around with his right arm to offer an elixir. Arrieta's back is to the black background, as if shielding Goya from the dim figures looming there. It is a tender, affecting painting.

Thanks again for sending the slides. Thanks again for everything, my dear Dr. Arrieta.

John

November 9, 1990

Dear Wyatt,

I've decided it's time for me to get back to work, one way or another. So for the past three days I've been drawing in a slaughterhouse. There's a locker plant in town run by a man named August Stortz. I asked for him there. The young girl tending the counter where they sell packaged meats, candy bars, and soft drinks went back to get him, and he stepped out of the meat-cutting room wearing a white apron, wiping his hands in a towel. He's a short, solid man—about sixty years old I'd guess—with thinning gray hair combed straight back. I was the only one in the shop just then. I introduced myself, told him that I was a painter and that I'd been living in town for sixteen months. He nodded, as if he knew that. I asked him if I could do some drawings while he was working.

He didn't say anything and he didn't move. The young girl behind the counter looked at him expectantly, her mouth hanging open a little.

I explained that I didn't intend to draw *him*. I said I wanted to draw the cattle and pigs he was butchering. I opened the book I had brought, leaned over the frozen food case, and showed him a Flemish painting with a ham in it. I told him I needed to practice.

His eyes rose from the book to take me in again. The girl looked at me now as if I had just materialized from a distant galaxy.

There are two kinds of people. Those who need a reason to say *yes*, and those who need a reason to say *no*. August Stortz fixed me in his blue eyes, considered all the perfectly good reasons why he should not grant my strange request, and rejected them as unworthy. After a minute he said, "Well, I don't see why not. I'll be butchering tomorrow at two o'clock."

Do you think this is bizarre? For the past three months I've been having dark thoughts about all those men and women being flown to Saudi Arabia. And recently, of course, I've been looking at Goya's *Disasters of War*—etchings like *Heroic feat! Against the dead!* with the terribly mutilated bodies and the body parts tied up in trees. So it occurs to me that if my subject is bodies, there are realities I've got to register which aren't in my nudes. (And even if I wanted to continue with the nudes, it's a little awkward to find a model here at the moment.)

I arrived at the slaughterhouse at exactly two the next day. It's not a big processing plant, just a local operation in a small T-shaped frame building with a high peaked roof. The structure is painted dark red like the boards of the holding pen next to it. A black steer was in the pen and, in a separate area, two pigs. Alongside, a little creek ran under an iron bridge and a stand of poplars shook in the breezes. A pickup with a tall wooden box built up from its bed was already parked in the yard. The sign painted on its door said "Stortz Locker Service." I knocked on the slaughterhouse door and August's voice said, "Come in."

I stepped in and shut the door behind me. August stood about fifteen feet away, at the other end of the building's single room, holding a small rifle which he pointed down at the concrete floor. In front of him a steer lay on its side, its neck through the bottom of an iron stanchion. Another man holding a large sledgehammer stood over the steer's head, straddling its neck with his back against the stanchion. August gestured toward a stool against the wall behind him. I went and sat down with my sketch pad and pencils.

The men put away the rifle and sledge. August's assistant fastened a chain around the dead steer's back legs and connected the chain to an electric hoist suspended from a rail that ran along the roof's peak. August hoisted the animal into the air, slit its throat, and waited while the carcass bled into a drain. After several minutes he let it back down as his assistant positioned a metal rack under it. Now the animal lay on one side and the two men went to work skinning it. They worked quickly and without speaking. There was some sawing, to remove the head and hooves. When one side was fully skinned, they hoisted the carcass again in stages, skinning the other side. With the carcass fully hoisted, they opened it along the chest and spilled the innards into a steel drum for the rendering truck. Finally, August's assistant, a very big man, sawed the carcass from neck to tail until it swung apart into two sides of beef, each hanging by a chain from the overhead rail. The whole process took less than an hour. I looked down at my paper and realized that I hadn't made a mark.

But I sketched while they repeated the process with the second steer. This time I saw how the animal was led into its stall and fastened in the stanchion. And I saw how August spoke to it in a quiet voice so that it raised its head and he could shoot it cleanly through the forehead. The steer collapsed and then the assistant struck it hard three times on the forehead with the sledge to make sure it was finished. Part of me was stunned by the violence. But what surprised me was the calm, deliberate competence with which the task was done. Stortz was almost gentle in his motions, and the two men knew their jobs so well neither spoke. It finally seemed to me that they performed an ancient task with reserve and dignity. Maybe they didn't speak because I was there, and maybe it was the silence which gave the whole an aura of ritual.

I sketched the folds of hide drawn back from the fat. I drew the ribs packed in their muscle. I quickly sketched an impression of the offal plunging out of its cavity into the steel barrel. I sketched the two halves of beef as they swung in opposite directions at the moment the saw cut through. I studied the animal mechanism and thought how much more we are than what I had seen, what I had drawn. That night when I got home something strange happened. I sat down at my kitchen table, put my face in my hands, and cried hard. Not for the cattle, certainly. I don't understand. I suppose it could be the drug.

I went back the next two days: three more steers, four squealing hogs. There were no gilded horns or muttered prayers, but each day the same aura of solemn ritual surrounded the acts. And each day I went away shaken, feeling as though I'd run hard into something true about the world. At night sometimes I dreamed of skin and blood, muscle and bone. And I dreamed once that I peeled the skin off my left hand, peeled it off like a rubber glove and watched my fingers flex, the tendons working like piano wire.

John

November 16, 1990
Dear Wyatt,

No, I don't plan to come out for the show opening the 27th. I don't see the point, unless you particularly want me there. Actually, even thinking about the exhibition lately makes me angry. It seems so much the result of my troubles—the breakup, the breakdown, being broke. I shouldn't say these things, I know, because you're doing me a great kindness, and I sound ungrateful. I am *very* grateful. But that's part of the trouble. The show feels like a charity event to me. If I were more sure about the paintings . . .

Anyway, I'm inclined not to come out—the expense is part of it—unless you think my being there can serve some practical purpose.

John

November 18, 1990
Dear Wyatt,

I'm sorry about the tone of my last letter. I get agitated whenever I think of the show. But the bottom line is that I need to sell some paintings. Thanks, truly, Wyatt.

It's been a full weekend. I went to the Mississippi with Ron, the electrician, and his girlfriend, Iris. I remet him when I saw a "for sale" sign taped to the frame of a bike in the front yard of a small beige house. I went to the door and knocked. Ron came to the door. It was his bike—a ten-speed—and I think he gave me a good price. I told myself I'd pay for it with the gas I save going to work. And I imagined riding it up through the parks on top of the ridges at the edge of town. But then the weather turned cold. Anyway, I'm glad to have it.

After that I saw him at Sammy's. There's a good, cheap fish fry there on Fridays. This weekend when I went, he saw me walk in and waved me over to his table. We ate together—battered and fried northern pike out of red plastic baskets lined with waxed paper—and it turned out we had Chicago in common. He'd grown up in Delphi, then went to the University of Chicago. He started in biology and graduated in religion! I asked him how he'd decided to come back home. He looked down at the table and then back up. "I didn't get along very well with the city," he said, with a sheepish smile. "Nerves," he said.

His dad was the town's electrical contractor and Ron came home after college to join the family business. A few years later, when his father died suddenly, Ron didn't want to run things, so he sold the business and stayed on as an employee.

We went to the river yesterday. Ron and Iris came and got me at about 6:00 A.M. in Ron's pickup and we headed for MacGregor, the little river town about 35 miles away where Ron keeps his boat. Iris sipped coffee between us as we drove through the dried cornfields, most of them harvested, and then descended through a wooded valley to the river. They had packed lunch and the idea was that we'd do some fishing and then picnic somewhere on the river.

Ron's boat turned out to be a small aluminum outboard with thin plastic pads on the metal seats. It was tied to a wooden dock in a little marina with a few other boats like it. I don't know what I was expecting—big river, big boats, I guess. Ron and Iris made preparations expertly, arranging the gear and tending the motor. Soon we pushed away from the pier and were scudding across the wide water, me in the front, Iris in the middle, and Ron at the back with one hand on the throttle. The cold was astounding. I sat in the prow in my denim jacket, cutting the frigid air. I could feel the river's chill make its way through the hull, the soles of my sneakers, and up into my legs. I noticed that Ron and Iris were wearing insulated boots and down coats.

Iris spoke over the noise of the engine, explaining that at this point the river has two channels. We were crossing one of them, she said, heading for the long, wooded islands between, where the backwaters hold panfish, bass, and northerns. Behind her as I looked back, a series of high bluffs rose above the river, limestone outcroppings and scrub brush climbing to hardwoods and pines thick on the tops. My head was numb with the cold so that my nose ran and my eyes teared. Ron noticed, slowed the boat, pulled a stocking cap out of a coat pocket, and tossed it up to me. I said thanks and put it on.

The channel we were crossing must have been half a mile wide. The water was green—dark green and opaque—with small waves and a few whitecaps. I thought to myself, Here you are on one of the world's great rivers—pay attention, but really I was hunkered down inside myself, braced against the cold.

At last we pulled between two narrow strips of land, turned north, and slowly cruised into a chain of backwaters. We were close enough to one large island to see deer and raccoon prints on the mud bank. Across the way, beside another island, a great blue heron stood in the shallows. Ron steered us between the gray woods on each side. Iris poured me a big cup of hot coffee and I gulped at it as we moved slowly ahead. "It's been a warm fall, but this late in the year, with the water temperature going down, the fish will be deeper," Ron said. "We'll try some deep holes we know just ahead."

We rounded a bend and Ron cut the engine, letting us drift into an arm of water curved along a sandy shore. A large pile of drift timber had accumulated at the near end of the beach. "It's deep here, from the drift pile to the far tip of the island," Ron said. "Maybe this would be a good place to start." I told them I'd watch for a while to see what I could learn. I'd fished quite a bit out west on small creeks and rivers during family vacations as a kid, but I'd never fished on a large river or lake.

Iris baited her hook with a nightcrawler and pinched some lead onto her line. Ron snapped a large silver spoon onto the swivel at the end of his line. Iris cast near the driftwood and watched the bait sink. Ron cast far up parallel to the beach and let the spoon sink for a few seconds before starting to reel it in. The coffee going down made my chest feel warm, so I poured myself another big cup. There was no feeling in my feet.

Ron's spoon came up out of the dark green water and flashed next to the boat. He lifted it and cast again. Iris kept one finger on her line, letting her bait lie still. "It's late for this kind of fishing," she said. "But we don't mind if we don't catch anything." Her black hair is cut straight across her forehead and she has a pretty smile. She works as a legal secretary in Decorah, a lovely little town with a college about 20 miles from Delphi.

I was looking at Iris when Ron jumped to his feet in the back of the boat and jerked his rod up. I turned and saw a rolling splash about 30 yards from the boat. Then Ron's line started to cut through the water, first one way, then the other, and his rod tip bowed hard. Iris reeled in her line and picked up the landing net. When Ron tried to reel in, his drag clicked fast. A strong fish was taking out line.

Still a long ways from the boat, the fish rolled again, its tail breaking the surface. "What is it?" Iris asked.

"I don't know yet," Ron said. He was starting to get back some line. "When it gets near the boat, I've got to keep it from getting into the brush."

"I'll pull us away from it," Iris said. She stepped to the back of the boat and started the motor. Ron kneeled on the middle seat and kept his rod straight up. Its tip jerked hard. Slowly, Iris steered us away from shore.

The fish was about fifteen feet away now, but deep. "It's tiring," Ron said, as he worked it up.

I was leaning over the boat's prow, peering into the dark green water while Ron pumped his rod and cranked the reel. Suddenly out of the dark almost directly below me a silver flash and then a very big fish appeared, rising quickly. I straightened up so fast that the boat rocked and Ron sat down hard. "Here he comes," he said.

The mouth gaped, trailing the flashing spoon from one corner of the jaw. Then the fish turned and its flank, nearly as long as my arm but thicker, glided by. I could see its dark back, silvery side, and the paler belly. It shook its head, but the hook stuck fast.

Ron guided it to the back of the boat and Iris netted it and lifted with both arms. The fish came over the side, thrusting and twisting, throwing water over the three of us. In the nylon mesh, it pounded the bottom of the boat with its head and tail.

"It's a brown trout!" Iris shouted, as she carefully grasped its back behind the gills. Then, with her other hand, she struck it sharply on the head with a rounded wooden stick. The fish shivered once and went still. She disentangled it from the net and held it up. "It's heavy!" she said. "It must go over 20 inches!"

Blue spots the size of nickels shone on the fish's sides. Its lower jaw hooked up over the top impressively. "I've never heard of a trout being caught in this part of the river," Ron said. His eyes were wide with excitement.

"It must have been washed out of a stream during a storm," Iris said. "But, at this size, it's been in the river for a while."

"Well, John, I guess this means you're invited for supper," Ron said, grinning.

Iris took a knife from a holder on her belt and inserted it in the fish's vent, then slid the blade up the belly to the tip of the lower jaw. When the knife went in, a little milky fluid dribbled out. "Male," Ron said. Iris made cuts below the lower jaw, from one end to the other, then cut the bright red gills and the gullet free. When she pulled, the innards came out in a single tangle—tongue, gills, and guts—and she dropped them over the side. Then, holding the emptied body upside down over the water, she ran her thumbnail along the inside of the spine, scraping membrane and blood away. When she dunked it in the river to rinse it clean, the body waved languorously, like a rag. Then she held it up, dripping, for us to admire. I noticed that I was shivering hard, or trembling.

Iris put the fish in the cooler under her seat, started the engine, and pulled us back near the shore. Ron checked his spoon and made a long cast. Iris rebaited her hook and tossed it next to the brush pile. I poured myself more hot coffee and watched. But I couldn't stop shaking and I couldn't relax my arms or legs. My heart was pounding. I wondered how long it would take to get to the truck and then drive back to Delphi if we had to get home as quickly as possible. Then my heart skipped a beat and a bright wave of adrenaline swept through me.

I fought panic and embarrassment. I wanted to flee. I didn't know why. Could I say something measured and plausible to Ron and Iris that would prompt them to take me home? I put down my cup and gripped the seat with both hands. Could I ride this out? My heart skipped a beat. I sucked in a sharp breath. My heart skipped another beat.

I looked at Ron and Iris, as if through the wrong end of a telescope. They were absorbed in their fishing. I said, "I don't feel well." Maybe I didn't say it out loud. Neither of them heard me. Ron was standing near me. I reached out and touched his leg. He looked down and I repeated, "I don't feel well."

He sat down and looked at me. "You're really cold, aren't you?" he said. And then, "Iris, let's go ashore here. John doesn't feel good." They reeled in their lines and Ron picked up an oar and paddled us to the beach.

Ron helped me out of the boat—it was strange to walk on the sand without feeling my feet. He led the three of us into the trees and cleared a small area of its twigs and leaves, sweeping them into a pile. Iris told me to sit down and she put a blanket over my shoulders. Ron gathered more sticks and downed branches, lit the heaped twigs with a match, and fed in the larger pieces. Yellow flames and acrid white smoke rose quickly in front of me. Iris tucked the blanket tighter around my shoulders. "He's shivering hard," she said.

"Hypothermia, maybe," Ron answered, and then said to me, "Why don't you drink some more hot coffee?"

"I don't know," I said. "I've had a lot, and I'm not used to it." My teeth were chattering. My heart skipped another beat.

"We've got to get you warmed up," he said, but he didn't pour more coffee. Iris fed some branches into the fire and sat down next to me, close. Ron sat next to me on the other side. They met eyes across me and I saw worry in their faces.

"I've got an idea," Iris said. "We'll make a sandwich out of you. Come on, Ron." She turned and straddled me, one leg behind my back under the blanket, the other crossing in front of my stomach. She unzipped her down coat and reached it around me the best she could, pressing the warmth of her sweater-front against my side. Ron did the same from his side, meeting arms with her. My legs stretched forward toward the fire.

"This ought to do you some good," Ron said.

"Thanks," I said. "I'm sorry. This is embarrassing." I could feel myself shivering against them.

"Nonsense," Ron said. "Hypothermia's something you've got to watch for on the river this time of year. We should have paid closer attention. You don't have enough clothes on."

"I guess that must be it," I said, unconvinced.

We sat that way for a few minutes, their bodies warm on each side of me. The memory of my strange night by the fire with Jean and Jerry flitted through my mind, but this felt different. When the fire burned down Ron got up and put on some more wood and then resumed his position next to me. There was less smoke, now, and red coals at the base of the fire gave off an even heat.

"Are you warming up at all?" Iris asked.

"I think so," I said.

"We'll stay here as long as it takes," Ron said. "Just let me know if you want me to blow in your ear."

"Oh, stop it!" Iris said, reaching across me to slap him on the shoulder. Then she tipped back her head and started to laugh—a lovely, deep laugh. Her throat was very white against her black hair. Ron grinned and laughed, too. They shook on both sides of me and I took a few deep, slow breaths. The feeling was slowly returning to my feet.

I remembered that I hadn't taken a pill yet that morning. I took the bottle out of my breast pocket, tipped out one tablet, and swallowed it dry. Ron noticed the label and said, "I've taken those before. Anxiety attack?"

"Feels like it," I said. "Plus the cold. But I'm warming up."

"When I was a student in Chicago I went to the emergency room three times," Ron said. "I thought I was going to die." He shook his head.

I was surprised and it must have shown. I met eyes with him and he glanced down and then back up. "When I was in school I almost always felt like there was too much juice in my wires," he said. "My lips and fingertips tingled. My heart pounded. I really only felt good when I was in a pickup basketball game, or right after, when I was tired. I still get that way sometimes, but I manage better now." He's slim and tall, and moves with an athletic ease. I wouldn't have guessed.

The fire had fallen down to its coals and Ron got up to gather more wood. Iris, still straddling me, rested her head on my shoulder and said, "How are you doing?"

"Better," I said. "Thanks."

After Ron built up the fire, he went to the boat and brought back a small cooler. He sat down next to me, opened it, and passed out sandwiches. Iris swiveled around and we all sat in a row with the blanket over our shoulders. The sandwiches were thick slices of pork roast on dark bread with fresh onion and hot mustard. "Good sandwiches, Ron," said Iris. I ate mine hungrily. It was delicious.

When we had finished we all bent over the fire for a last warming, then Ron scattered and buried the coals. We got back into the boat and slowly moved between the islands and back across the channel to the marina. In the truck, we all sat quietly on the ride home. The heat blowing out of the dash made me drowsy, comfortable at last. By the time they dropped me off, I felt fine.

That evening Ron came back to get me for dinner. He and Iris had stuffed and baked the fish with diced carrots, onions, and herbs. It was a good night with new friends.

John

November 20, 1990
Dear Wyatt,

A real cold snap here—colder than the weekend. Arctic air swept down and a heavy frost stayed on the lawns and the rooftops until past noon. It was chilly at work all day. When Rich, Kevin, Linda, and I ate lunch in a corner of the sorting room, Linda put on her down parka to stay warm. Kevin sat close to Linda and we all chewed our sandwiches tranquilly. When we finished, Rich stood, grasped my arm and said: "Come on, John. I want to show you the new pickup we got. It's green." So I went outside with him to admire the new Earth Day truck, our breaths making little clouds in the brilliant air.

As soon as I got home this afternoon I boiled water for tea. That's when Ellen came by. A surprise—I hadn't seen her for a month. For an instant, I didn't recognize her at the door. She had cut her long blond hair short, and she wore a scarf up around her mouth—it didn't get above freezing all day.

I let her in and offered her some hot tea. She said she could feel the steam from the kettle and it felt good. I took her coat and scarf and we sat down at the kitchen table. She wrapped her hands around her tea mug and started talking.

"I've got something to tell you, John," she said. "I've let my apartment go and I've rented space in what used to be the hotel downtown. It's half the old ballroom on the second floor—lots of room, a high ceiling, and big windows. They built a wall down the middle of it and put in plumbing years ago, thinking shops would move in, but nothing ever happened. It's been standing empty, so I got it cheap. I'm living at one end and I want to paint there. I'll share the studio space with you and do some modeling in exchange for instruction. I want to work with you. What do you say?"

Her cheeks were still flushed from the cold and her light blue eyes were fixed on me, wide with expectation. I had always sensed a deep reserve in her, and a tension, but not now. Leaning over the table with her sleek new haircut, she was all forward motion. Somehow it made me uneasy.

"This is big news," I said. "Congratulations. But what about Mrs. Steegers at the library, your mother, and all that?"

She straightened in her chair and ice came up in her eyes. It was breathtaking. "I've made up my mind," she said.

"Well, I'd like to see your new place," I managed.

"Let's go," she said.

Ellen drove us downtown and we went up a dark stairway between Lu's Café and the Hair Affair in the old Delphi Hotel building. At the top of the stairs she unlocked a big oak door and we went in. I must have stood with my mouth hanging open because Ellen was looking at me with an amused smile. It is a remarkable space. The wooden dance floor stretches from the front of the building to the back—about 80 feet—with three big windows at each end. The windows must be twelve feet tall with semicircular tops and broad bench-style sills. The walls are covered in old paper that has weathered to a dark olive green so that the pattern barely shows. Above it and all around the edge of the high ceiling there is what appears to be a white plaster cornice cast in a motif of grape bunches and cornstalks, with a fiddle in one corner and crossed flutes in another. The ceiling itself is tin, painted white. There's one wooden pillar of varnished wood in the center of the space fitted at the top with a white Corinthian capital. From the floor to a height of eight feet it carries initials and pierced hearts and mottoes, roughly carved or burned in who knows when. The wall with the door in it is recent drywall, painted white, cutting the room in half so that it's about 40 feet wide. Ellen's living area is at the back of the big open space. In one corner there's a closet-sized enclosure with sink and toilet. In the corner along the far wall, she's set up a long table with a hotplate, dishpan, and cupboard sitting on it. Underneath there's a small refrigerator. Between the bathroom and "kitchen," a round table with four chairs and a double bed stand under the tall windows.

"This is great," I said. "How do you heat it?"

She said that could be expensive but would be partly offset by the break she got on the rent. And some heat came up through the floor from the café below. "What do you say?" she asked.

"It'll be a wonderful place to work if you can heat it," I said. Sunlight from the back windows stretched across the floorboards. It was late afternoon and the air glowed. It made me want to work. "Now, what's the arrangement?" I asked.

"I want you to paint here," she said. "I'll be working, too. In return for studio space and ten hours of modeling a week, we talk about painting, yours and mine."

I'd never seen this side of her before, direct and resolute. I grinned and said okay. She fished a key out of her coat pocket and held it out to me, smiling back.

"I'll still have hours at the library. You can work here whenever you want. I'm sure we can sort out a schedule as we go along." She was crisp, pleased, excited. She stretched up on the toes of her boots, hugged herself, and grinned. Then she drove me home. I told her I'd bring my easels and things over the next day.

Best,
John

November 21, 1990
Dear Wyatt,

I've been mulling over our phone conversation after the opening and I'm afraid I'll have to ask you not to sell the small nude of Jamie looking out the window of the mauve room. I realize that it may be awkward, especially if, as you say, the buyer is a longtime client of yours. I won't pull anything else, I promise. I just didn't realize how I felt about that one until you told me you might have it sold. I'm sorry. I know I've been difficult about this show, but I'm very grateful for all that you've done. Everything else in the show is definitely for sale. I won't do this to you again.

John

November 23, 1990
Dear Wyatt,

Ellen had a group of people over for Thanksgiving dinner yesterday, a kind of housewarming for the new loft. I arrived a little early because Ellen said she wanted to show me some of her college work. It was a surprisingly interesting portfolio—predominantly still life and architecture studies, some of them promising. She draws with a strong, fluid line.

I only got a brief look before Ron and Iris arrived, and then Caroline, my "counselor." A woman I didn't know, someone named Sarah from the library, also came. And there was another couple I hadn't met, friends of Ellen's named Ed and Sue. Then Jean and Jerry walked in. It was the first time I'd seen them since our trip to their cabin three months earlier. I should have guessed they'd be there, but it caught me by surprise. I didn't know how to behave, so busied myself at the back of the loft setting out the plates and glasses.

Ellen has no real kitchen, so everyone brought something from home, salads and potatoes and casseroles. Ellen had gotten turkey from the supermarket, baked and sliced and laid out in an aluminum foil pan. I'd brought beer and a jug of wine and some soft drinks. After our various offerings had been deposited on Ellen's makeshift counter, everyone stood in a knot in the center of the studio, looking around with what I took to be a mixture of wonder and bewilderment. They were virtually hushed, at first, standing in the big space as the sunlight slanted in through the tall windows. Ron and Caroline and Jean looked intrigued. Faint smiles showed on their faces as they turned around and took everything in. Jerry was inscrutable, but he looked around, checking the scene out carefully. And I saw a little vertical worry crease gather itself between Iris's eyebrows.

I didn't know the others, but Sarah from the library spoke up: "Just look at all this empty space!" she said. "And you're camping like a Girl Scout over in one little corner!" Her word "empty" struck me. She couldn't fathom, apparently, what might occur in the space and light that Ellen was buying with her monthly rent. Ellen seemed amused as she watched her friends take in the signs of her new life. I gazed at the sunlight angling among them and thought of empty canvases—the space to be filled with what you need and can't find anywhere else.

We set out the food, filled our plates, and scattered around the big room in small groups, talking and eating. At the back of the room Iris and Ellen sat in one of the deep window benches, leaning over their plates and talking seriously. Iris was doing most of the speaking, and she seemed to be trying to convince Ellen of something.

Jerry and I had the same idea, pulling chairs up next to the model's platform I'd banged together the previous day. We put our plates on the platform and faced each other across the small square of smooth wood. I hadn't meant to wind up alone with Jerry over dinner. We ate in silence for what seemed like a long time, each of us glancing around the room and out the windows as we forked up the turkey and trimmings. I tried to think of something to say to him, but my mind came up blank. When his plate was empty, Jerry propped his boots against the platform and tipped back in his chair. I was still trying to conceive of a possible topic of conversation. Then Jerry took a pull from his beer bottle, smoothed his red mustache with the back of one hand, and said: "Well, how's it going?"

"Could be worse," I said, grasping for the vernacular.

There was a pause.

"Looks like a good place for your kind of work," Jerry said, tipping his head up in a way that acknowledged the space around him.

"Yes, I think it will be," I said.

"If you can heat it," he said.

"Right." I nodded.

We fell silent again. Jerry sipped his beer contentedly.

Then Jean sauntered over and crawled slowly on her hands and knees to the middle of the platform and stretched herself out between the two of us, centering herself in a bar of light from the near window. She rolled onto her back, put her hands behind her head, crossed her ankles, and sighed, "Now I'm nice and full." Jerry gazed at her appraisingly, then looked up at me. I avoided his eyes.

The others gradually finished eating and brought their chairs to our end of the room, where we made a group around the platform. Light conversation went around the circle. Jean still luxuriated in the platform's center, but gradually the sky grew dark and then, suddenly, big snowflakes were swirling at the windows. Everyone went to the front of the loft and looked out over the main street. It was empty of people, with just a few cars parked in front of the closed storefronts. Flakes blew in circles on the stained concrete.

"Here we go," said Ron. "Into the long tunnel."

"Oh, don't be so gloomy," said Caroline, with a teasing smile. "Don't you like the first snow, the change of seasons, the sense of something new coming?"

"I know what's coming," Ron said. "Wind chill." Everyone laughed, ruefully.

The sun went down and the snow outside began to accumulate. Sarah, Ed, and Sue went home first, and Jean and Jerry started to gather their things. Caroline and Iris and Ron were helping Ellen straighten up, so I walked to the door with Jean and Jerry. As they stepped out, Jean turned back and said, "If you're going to start working again, I'm ready, too." I glanced at Jerry. He gazed at me, his face unreadable. I glanced back at Jean and nodded. Then they turned and descended the stairs, Jerry guiding Jean down with his hand on the back of her neck. I watched them until they went out into the street.

Back inside, the cleanup was finished, and Caroline, Ron, Iris, and Ellen were sitting at the table having a last cup of coffee. I joined them.

Ron looked at me and said, "What's on your mind?" He must have seen something in my expression.

"How well do you know Jean and Jerry?" I asked.

"I thought that was it," he said, and smiled. "We have a few beers together sometimes. And I've taken Jerry fishing. And they've had me out to their cabin. How about you?"

I said I didn't know them well but that I was curious why Jean had answered my ad and had modeled for me.

"Oh, they're always looking for something different," he said. "They have a sense of adventure, I guess."

"What kind of adventure?" I asked.

Ron grinned. "Oh, I don't know," he said. "They like to travel a lot. They'll go up to Lake Superior for a weekend, driving all Friday night to get there, and come back just before work Monday morning." He paused before he went on. "And I guess I was thinking that, in school and just after, Jerry got into trouble a few times before he settled down. And Jean always had a reputation growing up as being kind of wild." Iris nodded as Ron spoke.

"I'm not telling you anything everybody doesn't already know," he added. "I like them. It takes guts to be different in a town like this."

Iris and Ellen met eyes. Ellen turned her coffee cup in her hands.

"Well, if they're looking for something different," Caroline said, "the baby will shake things up." Ron and I looked at Caroline.

"You mean you didn't notice?" she said. "John, I'm especially surprised at you. I thought you were a professional when it comes to looking at women's bodies." She flashed a mischievous smile. "I'd guess she must be at the end of the first trimester," she said.

I hadn't noticed, though I'd been absorbed by Jean's presence as she'd reclined on the platform.

The four of us sat around the oak table, quiet in the cold, gray light of the snowy evening. Finally, Ron stood up. "Good party, Ellen," he said. "Thanks." We all stood and Ellen helped us gather our things.

As she walked us to the door she turned to me and asked, "Do you want to get to work in the next few days?" I said yes, and we made our arrangements. Tomorrow we'll begin.

John

4

John Ordway
423 River Street
Delphi, Iowa

November 30, 1990

Dear Wyatt,

Thanksgiving's inch of snow lasted a day, then melted. We've had a stretch of gray days with temperatures in the mid-30s. I've worked with Ellen a few afternoons since my last letter. Starting up with her again, there's a sense of familiarity and repetition, but also difference. This time I'm as much in her employ as she's in mine. That shouldn't make any difference, but it seems to. Or maybe it's that she initiated this whole arrangement, and now we're working in her space. I'm the "guest." Or maybe it's something else.

The other day she was sitting on a chair on the platform while I stood at an easel with a big pad of paper clipped to it. She was wearing jeans and a blue cotton shirt and I held the brittle charcoal stick, sketching tentatively. I softened the shading at the base of her neck with the side of my thumb and realized how much I'd missed the pleasure of drawing and painting.

We spoke as I worked, and I tried to explain what she'd be getting as I "instructed" her in painting. I wanted her to know how old-fashioned I am. I was working on the way her collar fell open, the shadows on her shirt and neck.

"I'm out of step with most contemporary painting," I said. "My paintings have subjects, I work with forms in pictorial space, I sometimes still aim for 'beauty,' and I work by hand, applying paint with brushes."

She nodded. She'd had a good education. I said, "Anyway, people can do just about what they want these days, because we've come to the end of something and have to find a way to start again. The game's wide open. Only, in New York, you've got to have a theory." She smiled.

As I tried to work there was a new tension in the air—at least for me. Ellen

71

shifted her pose, crossing and recrossing her legs, but not out of nervousness. I read it as impatience and thought again of how our new arrangement differed from the old one. Before, I'd bought her time, paying her an hourly wage. Now she was buying mine, paying in modeling. Or perhaps my uneasiness came out of the difficulty of beginning again after all that strange, lost time. Whatever the reason, I felt more hesitant now about giving her poses, more tentative, generally.

I drew for about forty minutes and stopped. It wasn't going very well. Then Ellen showed me some of her recent sketches, very different from the college things I'd seen before. These were of places in town—Redding's Spring, a limestone church, a neighborhood street. And there were interiors with people. She said she did a lot of these from memory, inventing things as she liked. One in particular interested me. An older woman sat at a big desk, her wide jaw fixed in an unsettling smile. Books were stacked in front of her like a rampart. Next to her sat a dented globe. "Mrs. Steegers," Ellen said. She smiled at me, mischievously. I hadn't taken her for a satirist.

"That's good," I said. "Paint that." And then we talked about the colors she had in mind.

I've never taught. And so I'm uneasy about this. But I can look at what she shows me, and comment, and talk with her about the things that interest her, and I think that's what she wants.

She surprises me. Her decisiveness about the studio arrangement and the wit I see in some of the drawings don't square with the nervous woman on the platform I remember from before. I thought I knew her, but I don't.

John

December 5, 1990

Dear Wyatt,

Had dinner with Ron at Sammy's again last Friday. It was raining outside and then the rain turned to big, wet snowflakes. The news was on the TV above the bar. Pictures from the desert—men filling sandbags, then sitting on cots in a tent, then driving a truck and looking through binoculars.

Ron hates winter. When he saw the snow outside he pulled a face and shook his head. Iris was driving down from Decorah for the weekend, and he worried that the roads would be slick. He had seemed to be tense anyway, eating quietly and fussing with his beer glass. He didn't say much.

Afterward, when we stepped outside, he asked if I wanted to come over to his place and wait for Iris with him. I apologized. I told him it was bowling night for the Earth Day crew and that I had promised to meet them. We said good-bye and I walked toward the bowling alley, about five blocks away.

It had gotten dark, and the big flakes had become lighter and fell more slowly, drifting straight down through the calm air. I cut through an alley to get behind Main Street. As I came out, I saw Rich and Kevin and the rest of the group across the street. Rich was in the lead. Kevin and Linda were at the back, holding hands. I stopped and watched them go. Rich tipped back his head and stuck out his tongue to catch snowflakes, holding his arms out straight from his sides to steady himself as he went. Two girls behind him shuffled their feet, watching intently the grooves they made in the accumulated snow. One of them stooped down and quickly drew something in the snow with her finger, then stood and ran to catch up with the others. They all moved with a kind of chunky deliberation, except for tall, skinny Linda. She strode with an almost swooping motion, and a little waver of her left arm with every other step. I wondered at their bodies, the given facts which have so much to do with who they are.

Rich stopped to steady himself, his head still tipped back and his mouth open to catch the snow. The two girls watching their feet—I could see now that they were Dot and Patty—walked into him and bumped him forward. Rich shouted, "Hey!" and then they all laughed. Nobody fell.

I let them go ahead and then met them in the bowling alley. The snow had cheered them, unlike Ron, and they clowned and joked together. When we started bowling, Linda was in good form, with her pendulum delivery. She scored highest. I broke 100 and received rousing congratulations.

So the wheel turns and the days slide by. I keep the accounts at Earth Day, sitting in a beige chair in a small beige room. I spend some time sorting cans and bottles with the others. I take my medicine and see my counselor. I sketch some. And at home I sit at my kitchen table and go over it all again in these letters to you. It's just that I can't quite believe it. This life that I've fallen into is so strange to me. What Jamie said seems true to me now: "It's all still water here." Maybe if I tell it out to you I can find the thread that leads forward.

Your friend,
John

December 10, 1990
Dear Wyatt,

Bright and cold today. Only patches of last week's snow are left on the roofs and lawns. I'm at home in my kitchen after work at Earth Day. Over the weekend I put in a lot of hours with Ellen at the loft, trying to get started again.

It's been hard. In the two weeks since Thanksgiving, I've done about fifteen hours of sketching with her, all very preliminary. Saturday I worked for a while sitting on the floor with my back against the central supporting column, while she sat on her haunches above me on the platform, her forearms resting across her thighs, looking athletic in bare feet, jeans, and a red T-shirt. With my angle from below, she was framed by one of the high, bright windows. Every once in a while she ran a hand through her hair and tossed her head. It occurred to me that she was impatient, that she thought I was dithering.

Maybe she was just bored or tired, but I knew I was dithering, casting around for an idea, but tentatively. Finally I stood up and said, "Let's change the pose. Do you mind undressing?" We hadn't done any nude work since before.

She stood and shook her head, then hopped off the platform and trotted to the bathroom. In a minute she came out wearing a white terry cloth robe, crossed the big room, and stepped back onto the platform. Then she untied the belt, slipped the collar off her shoulders, and let the robe fall. She stood, facing me, waiting for my instructions.

I was not prepared for my reaction. The frankness of her body in the strong light struck me hard. She stood, waiting, in the pose before any pose. And I looked, not through an idea for paper or canvas, but directly. It was almost unbearably personal. I could remember what it had been like before, what it was supposed to be like, but this was something else. I felt an unaccountable shame.

"That's fine. Just like that," I said. My voice came out low, almost inaudible.

I drew almost without looking down, quick drawings like gesture drawings, though she stood still. I did ten or twelve, tearing off the sheets and dropping them to the floor. Then I said, "Move as you want to," and she let her hips ease into a lovely *déhanchement*. And her arms relaxed, falling more naturally from her shoulders. She shook her head once and her short, bright hair fell neatly around her ears and neck.

Her beauty, surging at me, made me want to look away. I felt as if I had been blinded, though I could still see. I made a show of continuing to draw. The pencil moved over the sheet, but my hand was slack. I couldn't register, couldn't muster myself to make a response. I felt overwhelmed—"unmanned" I was going to say.

The sound of a dog barking down in the street brought me back to myself. And then another dog started up somewhere behind the building. I closed my sketch-book. "That's all, I think," I said to Ellen. She looked surprised for a moment, then picked up her bathrobe, put it on, and tied the belt around her waist. "It's getting late," I said. "I should go." It was 4:00 P.M.

I left my sketchbook on the chair and went across the room to get my coat, which was lying across her bed. I tried to go slowly, casually, to counteract the impression that I was fleeing. I put on my coat. Ellen had stepped off the platform and was looking at me from across the room. I said good-bye and went out.

I hurried down the stairs, stepped out onto the sidewalk, turned my collar up against the cold wind, and stuffed my hands into my pockets. I took two strides and then flashing teeth and a vicious din exploded beside me. I literally jumped away from the street and my hands flew up out of my pockets. From the backseat of a parked car a Doberman barked convulsively, cocking its head, trying to force its muzzle through the four-inch gap where the window was partially rolled down. Its black lips curled back from the white teeth and spit rolled down the inside of the window. The dog barked at me frantically, straining against the glass.

Badly shaken, I hurried to my car and drove home. That was Saturday.

We had agreed that I would look at some of Ellen's new drawings Sunday. I delayed as long as I could, out of embarrassment, I think. But finally I went over in midafternoon. She greeted me as if nothing had happened, made us a pot of tea, then took me over to her work area in one corner at the front of the loft. Her drawings were laid out on two tables and we walked around them, looking together. I made little comments about the compositions. There were more neighborhoods—winter trees arching over wide streets and prim houses. The drawings seemed ambivalent. "I don't know how to feel about the houses," I said. "I don't know whether, under the bare trees, you think they're havens or jails." I told her I couldn't gauge their temperature, how cool or warm, and suggested she begin to paint and see what emerged.

She agreed that she should start painting. She knew she was hanging back. "It's been a long time," she said.

I told her I understood. I said it was hard for me to start up again, too.

"I know," she said. "I'm not surprised. After all, you burned the last painting you did of me." She gave me a level look. "Do you know why?"

The sudden question startled me. "No, I guess I don't," I said. "Not entirely." She nodded.

The memory of that night—almost four months ago now—sickened me a little.

Recollections of my confusion and rout the day before mingled with the older memory and I felt all at sea. My stomach rolled over.

"Well, I'll help you the best I can," she said. Then we went across the room and sat down at her table. She brought out some cookies and warmed our tea. I had no appetite, so only sipped at my tea. When we had finished she asked if I wanted to do some work. I told her I didn't think so. Then we arranged a schedule for the coming week and I went home.

John

December 11, 1990

Dear Wyatt,

I went to work at Ellen's this afternoon with the strange sensation of steeling myself for battle. A battle with her or with myself? I didn't know. In retrospect, I think I just felt afraid that I would never be able to work again.

It was chilly and overcast, the sky a uniform gunmetal gray. Inside Ellen's loft it felt surprisingly warm. She had been waiting, sitting on the bed in her robe, folding laundry. We started right away. I said I wanted to warm up with some charcoal gesture drawings. I went to my chair and pulled up the easel with the big sheets of cheap paper clipped to it. She slipped off her robe, bent to lay it across a folding chair, then stepped onto the platform. She knew this routine well, from before. Standing up, she held a gesture for twenty or thirty seconds, then another, then another, while I quickly stroked out a shoulder, an arm, a flexed leg. As we began, I held myself tightly, willing a concentration on line and space that fell over my eyes like a protective visor. Ellen moved more fluently than I could remember, pose upon pose like a stop-action dance. It was as though I weren't there. Or I was there as a kind of secretary, taking down the notations of a private reverie expressed by her gestures.

The light was not very good. The room was warm—too warm, really—but the December light was chill and blue. I began to feel irritable. The poses she was taking now didn't please me. Some of them were striking, but they felt remote from me—it was all happening over there, on her side of things.

I was about to tell her to lie down when she turned her back to me and raised one arm above her head. One knee was slightly bent, so her hips took a lovely angle. I couldn't remember that she had ever turned her back to me without an instruction. It surprised me, and I had two simultaneous reactions. As I had Saturday, I felt stunned by her flashing beauty. And I got angry. The first is easy enough to understand. The soft, muscular line from her raised arm, through the back, waist, hips, and legs, was perfect. She radiated beauty and erotic power. I didn't have to look to see. It was coming at me. It overcame me, and I felt ravished by it.

My anger is harder for me to understand. It was sudden and hot. When she turned her back, the pose seemed almost coquettish, or daring. Like the matador turning his back to the bull. Irrationally, I felt the sense of an affront, a dangerous challenge. Was it going to be like Saturday? The anger was my only power.

"Fine. Now lie down, please," I said. "On your back with your head toward me." She did so. "Raise your knees, and rest your arms above your head. Cross the wrists." I drew this pose in a heavy, thick line, omitting the face and fine details. I was sweating with the effort, like a wrestler, but I was working. I labored over the page, struggling for coherence. My heart was pounding and my face was hot. It sounds crazy, I know, but every line felt like a lifeline into my future, a stay against obliteration. She lay there at her ease, soft and white, while my shoulder knotted and cramped. My anger built.

"Now let your knees drop to the sides," I said. She hesitated, then slowly complied. I sketched this pose in the same heavy line, bearing down hard. The charcoal stick broke from the pressure. I picked up another and continued, working from the crossed wrists nearest me, down the torso, to the line of the inner thighs and the tufted pubis.

I snapped the big sketch pad out of its clips and turned to a fresh sheet. I had to grasp the charcoal hard because my hand was trembling. But the line seemed strong, and the drawing powerful. I permitted myself a flush of exhilaration.

I stood, stepped closer, and did a quick sketch from above. Then I walked to the other side of the platform to begin again. From this angle she was completely exposed, as to a lover or midwife. I drew quickly, avidly. My anger was gone now, or had changed. I was towering, now, totally absorbed, in full command of my abilities. I felt extraordinary relief.

Then her thighs began to tremble and I looked up to her face. Suddenly, she rolled onto her side, curled up, and sobbed, "I'm sorry. I'm sorry. I'm sorry."

It was like being shaken out of a dream. Ellen lay there crying hard, her ribs heaving up and down. "Oh!" I heard my voice. I lunged to the chair by the platform, picked up Ellen's robe, and placed it over her. She flinched at my approach, and I stepped back.

"Ellen, I'm sorry," I said. "It was a mistake."

She was still crying. "No, I'm sorry. I'm sorry," she said.

My face was hot with shame. I wanted to comfort her, but knew I couldn't. There was nothing I could do. Helpless, I walked to the door and looked back. She still lay on the platform, curled under her robe, sobbing. I went out and shut the door.

Tonight, I write this in desperation. There's no one else to turn to. I feel awful. This can never be undone.

John

—*I realize now why I burned that painting. I was right to do it.*

December 12, 1990

Dear Wyatt,

It's been a long day. This morning I called Caroline at home before she left for work and asked if she could find a reason to drop by and see Ellen. I was vague and she didn't press. She said she would go. Since then, I've been to Minneapolis and back.

I felt sad and restless—about yesterday—so I just got into the car and started to drive. I drove aimlessly around town at first, and then out into the country, trying to get away from myself. When I came to the highway I turned north and the idea of going up to see Jamie presented itself. I couldn't decide whether to go or not, which meant I just kept driving. And if I did go, what was my purpose? After an hour on the road I knew I wanted to see Jamie, but I still didn't know what I expected, what I might say or do. After another two hours, when I found myself standing at Jamie's apartment door, ringing the bell, I had no better idea of what I was doing. I'd last seen her almost three months ago. Since then, I'd phoned twice, but not for over a month. I had no reason to expect she'd be happy to see me.

The door swung open and it was Andrea. She took a step back, surprised to see me. "Oh, hello," she said. "Jamie's not here. Was she expecting you?"

I think there was just a little relief mixed with my disappointment. I told Andrea I was in town and had stopped by on impulse. She gathered herself and invited me in for a cup of tea. It was midafternoon.

She led me to the tan couch and went behind me to the open kitchen and started the tea. I sat facing a coffee table, a tan chair, and, behind it, the rows of portrait photos hung on the blue wall. The women in the photos stared out of their frames at me.

From the kitchen Andrea said, "I'm not expecting Jamie home tonight. How long will you be in town?"

I fought the impulse to ask where Jamie was. I briefly considered getting a room and staying over to try to see her the next day, but remembered I only had enough money in my pocket for gas and a sandwich on the way back. I told Andrea I was on my way home.

It was quiet while she fixed the tea. One of her cats slept on a nearby rug. The other sauntered over, jumped into the tan chair, and stared across at me. I stared back absently, listening to the sound of cups and saucers clicking onto a tray behind me. I wondered what Andrea's relationship with Jamie was, then tried hard to put the thought out of my mind.

"How's your work going?" Andrea asked, as she brought over the tea and a plate of breads. The cat jumped down and Andrea took her place.

"Fine," I said. "How about yours?"

"It's paying the rent these days," she said. A 35mm camera sat on the coffee table next to a dozen film canisters. "Great about Jamie's pot, isn't it?"

I must have looked blank.

"She didn't tell you she has a pot in a group show at the Walker next month?" Andrea said. "The big pot, with the leaves and windows."

"Yes, I remember," I said. "I helped her fire that." We both nodded. The cat jumped onto Andrea's lap, situated herself, and resumed her stare.

I couldn't think of a thing to say. And what could Andrea have to say to me, a drop-in she hardly knew? The silence grew longer and deeper. I began to get angry. I was acting like a fool, embarrassing myself. What was I doing here? Andrea picked up the camera and fiddled with its settings. I sipped at my tea, though it was still too hot.

I was looking down into my tea when I heard a click. I looked up into the lens of Andrea's camera. It clicked again.

"Do you mind if I take your picture?" she asked. A belated request, I thought, as my anger flared a little.

"Why?" I said.

"It's what I do," she answered. "Unless you mind."

This seemed strange, and I had every right to say no. But my own behavior didn't seem any less strange to me.

"Why pictures of me?" I said.

"You interest me," she said, speaking from behind the camera. It clicked and wound.

"I didn't think you photographed men," I answered, glancing at the rows of women's faces behind her.

"Sometimes," she said. "If they interest me." The camera kept firing.

"And what makes a subject interesting?" I looked from the camera down to the cat, which lounged in Andrea's lap and continued to stare.

"I'm interested in what you do," she said. And then: "Why the female nude?"

I looked up. Her face was still behind the camera. My neck and face began to feel warm. "Why not?" I said. "It's always been a subject for painters."

"Yes, but why did *you* choose it?"

"Is this going to be an interview, too?" I said.

"I like to talk to people while I shoot," she said. "And I usually talk to them about what they do for a living. How do you choose your models?"

"Different ways. Sometimes I put an ad in the paper." I was getting annoyed.

"And you take everybody who answers?" she asked. The camera fired and wound.

"Of course not," I said.

"So how do you choose the ones you want to work with?" She lowered the camera and changed film without looking down. Her eyes fixed on mine and she smiled, disingenuously.

"I suppose I find them interesting," I said. She tipped back her head and laughed. I tried to decide whether she found it amusing that I had echoed her or was laughing for another reason.

She finished reloading and raised the camera. From behind it she said, "I'll just tell you. As far as I'm concerned, most nudes are for men to get off on. A king showing off his mistress, making the dukes and barons envious." She took a shot. "Or it's like a guy who wants to remember what he had for lunch, or drool over what he's going to have for dinner. Woman as steak platter." There was steel in her voice. She squeezed off a couple more shots. "Now, I can't believe you're doing that sort of thing in this day and age. So, I'm curious. What are *you* up to?"

Fair enough, I thought. That deserves an answer. So I said, "I'm interested in the relation of the body and self, appearance and identity, that sort of thing." I'll have to admit, it sounded a little bloodless.

She made an aperture adjustment without lowering the camera. "And these are always nudes?" she asked.

"Yes, for the most part," I answered.

"Do you do any men?" she asked.

"No," I said.

"And these naked women," she continued. "What are they doing? Are they running, jumping, dancing—I mean, are they ever *doing* anything? Or are they always *lounging*?"

She drew out the word "lounging" so that I had to laugh. "Mostly lounging," I said.

"Hm," she said. "Sounds like woman-as-lunch, to me. I've got to tell you, John, I don't approve."

"With your photography, have you ever done any nudes?" I asked.

"No," she said, without missing a beat. I gave her a level look, but she just kept firing.

She finished another roll and started to reload. "Would you mind trading places? I'd like to shoot the other way." I hesitated—how long was this going to go on?—then finally stood up. She stood and the cat jumped down. I took her place in the tan chair. She pushed the coffee table and the small couch out of the way and began to shoot again from various angles, standing and kneeling.

"Let me ask you something else," I said. I had answered her questions and she was getting her pictures, so I thought I was entitled. "Is Jamie happy?"

Andrea kneeled and took a few shots from a low angle. "You mean, does she miss you?" she said from behind the camera.

"No, I didn't ask that," I said. "Is she happy?"

"Her work is going very well," she said. "But I wouldn't speak for her. You should ask her yourself."

"Is she seeing anyone?" I blurted out. I didn't like the pleading I heard in my voice, but there it was.

Andrea lowered her camera. I don't know if the look on her face was pity or something else. Her voice was a little softer when she said, "John, you really should talk to Jamie. She's in New York trying to line up a gallery. I think she'll be talking to your friend Wyatt. She'll be back in three days."

I stood and thanked her, got my coat, and said good-bye.

I made it home by about 10:00. Now it's around 2:00 A.M. Wyatt, if you have seen Jamie, can you tell me anything about her plans? Does she talk about moving back to New York? I'm sorry—ignore those questions. I shouldn't put you between us. Andrea was right. I'll speak to Jamie myself when she gets back.

John

December 16, 1990

Dear Wyatt,

Sunday afternoon at the kitchen table. A band of sunlight cuts across the salt shaker, sugar bowl, and my stationery. On the radio there's piano music, then news from Washington and Baghdad, then more music.

Thanks for your good letter, which came yesterday. I'm glad Alice's tests came back negative. That kind of worry is a terrible strain—for both of you. I wish you'd told me about all this earlier, when I might have been of some support. Now I feel simultaneously jangled by the scare you had and relieved at the outcome. Please give Alice a long squeeze for me.

You must have mailed your letter the day before Jamie arrived in New York, and before my last couple of letters reached you. I'm very happy about the two sales, and the check is going to help a lot. As always, thanks.

Friday evening I called Jamie and asked if I could drive up to talk to her. I've decided to ask if she'll have me back. I'm willing to move to Minneapolis or return to New York. Whatever she wants. I've made a botch of things here. She said she had another trip to make—this one to L.A. Apparently there's a gallery there that's interested in her things and she's going out to talk to them. She'll be back in about a week. She agreed to see me then. After all this time, maybe we can finally discover what's really going on between us.

On Saturday I worked up my courage to go to Ellen's. When she answered the door I gave her key back to her and apologized for what had happened. She took the key and said, "Look, we've got to talk." She got her coat and went ahead of me down the stairs and out into the street. I had to hurry to stay at her elbow as she strode down the block and turned right. She was headed for the small municipal park at the edge of the business district. It was a cold, clear day, and our breaths puffed out ahead of us. As we walked, Ellen spoke without looking to the side.

"I don't know what you expect of me," she said, hotly. "You've got to remember, I'm not a professional model. I'm sure I'm not as sophisticated as others you've worked with." She drew out the word "sophisticated" with contempt.

She strode ahead. I tried to keep up, eyeing the sidewalk's patches of ice. In the park, the big burr oaks were empty except for snow along the horizontal branches. There were small footprints in the snow around the swings and slide, but we were the only ones there. A statue of the town's first settler held a ring of snow on its hat brim. Ellen stopped and wheeled to face me. She drew herself up and fixed me in a hard glare. "I don't know what was going on Tuesday, but I didn't like it one bit," she said.

"I'm sorry," I said. "I pushed you across a line. I didn't know I could be so brutal. I don't know why I did it."

"Well, you'd better get it figured out, dammit!" She was shouting now, and she swung at me hard. We both heard the loud, hollow thump when her fist struck my chest.

We stood still, facing each other. I didn't know what I could say. I opened my mouth—I really don't know what I was going to say—but she cut me off.

"Listen," she said. "We've got to straighten things out and go on. We don't have any choice." She pulled her scarf up against the cold. "I'm going to leave Delphi as soon as I can get into an art school. I need your help with my portfolio. And you need my help, too. Without me, you don't have a studio or a model." She bit off her words. "And from now on, I'll refuse any pose I don't like!" She turned and strode off, back the way we'd come.

I stood for a minute. An older woman in a black coat across the street was sweeping snow off her front steps. When I noticed her she looked down at her broom whisking back and forth at her feet. I walked back downtown, got my car and went home.

So, after everything, Ellen wants to try again. I'm astonished. I wonder if I can be as brave as she is. I didn't say anything about the possibility that I'll leave Delphi before she does. I don't know what's going to happen when I see Jamie.

John

December 18, 1990
Dear Wyatt,

Tuesday afternoon and I've just come from talking with Caroline. The session seemed too short today, and I suppose that's why I went straight for my stationery when I got back to the apartment. There's something about my ritual of boiling water, brewing tea, and sitting down at the kitchen table to write. These letters and my conversations with Caroline are my only ways to sort through what's going on. And, more than ever, I feel that events are flying at me. Things *befall* me—that's the word that comes to mind. I'm not in control. Talking to Caroline, at least, I can reflect.

I sit in the brown, overstuffed chair and talk. Caroline's calm presence is very soothing. Ron has told me a little about her. She went to school at the University of Minnesota, lived in Minneapolis after that, and has been in Delphi for about ten years. She married late, Ron said—a man who moved down from the Twin Cities after the wedding and opened a law practice. But her husband got sick two years later, suffered a long decline, and died about three years ago. I think she must be in her forties, five or ten years older than me, but it's hard to tell. She seems to know everybody in town and is well liked.

Today I told her what happened with Ellen. She'd probably already heard the story from Ellen's point of view, but I didn't feel judged. She asked some questions and seemed only to want to understand. She asked about my previous experiences with models and how I establish limits or ground rules. "Among painters, is there a sense of conventions?" she asked at one point.

I had to smile. "The conventions," I said, "if you can call them that, are not particularly reassuring." Her face clouded with worry. "I'm just thinking of some infamous historical examples," I explained. "And the word 'conventions' sounds funny when I think about the studio situation. It's exactly the right word in some ways, but things aren't that cut and dried." I gazed past the African violets on the windowsill to a patch of blue sky. "Of course, there has to be respect and a mutual understanding," I said. Her question had started me musing. "But rules and art don't get along very well. There has to be a sense of possibility, even danger." I wasn't really thinking anymore about what happened with Ellen; I was thinking about art, in general. But Caroline didn't know that, and when my gaze shifted back to her face I saw that her look of worry had only deepened. I fumbled to explain myself. "When I said 'danger' I was talking about taking risks in a painting," I said. "I didn't mean the model should feel that." But what *did* I mean? I was in a tangle.

I went on with my explanations, but soon Caroline glanced at the clock on the low table between us. "Well, our time is up for today," she said. As I stood to go, I groped for a last remark—something that would reassure Caroline about me—but I couldn't find it. She recognized my discomfort and offered up a smile. "We'll continue this next time," she said, reassuringly.

But I don't feel terribly reassured. Maybe I couldn't explain myself to Caroline because there's no satisfactory explanation. It startles me now to recognize how easily I slipped away from Ellen and her feelings into abstracted ideas about painting. Maybe that's what happened in the studio, too.

I'm eager for the next session with Caroline. I don't want her to feel uneasy about me. And, despite all my awkwardness, her small high-ceilinged office with its violets on the wide sill has come to feel like a safe haven.

John

December 20, 1990
Dear Wyatt,

This was my first day back to work with Ellen modeling. Earlier in the week we painted a still life setup together, with talk about colors, ways to handle a palette, possibilities for composition. She's warming up to begin on some of the work that I've seen as drawings.

Today it was so cold that she turned the heat way up and boiled pans of water on the hotplate to put humidity into the air. She managed to get the loft reasonably comfortable. The insides of the big windows froze up, though. Frost patterns shaped like barbed wire and feathers covered every window. It was beautiful, in a way, but disturbing. The windows themselves were shining brilliantly, all white and glittering—it was sunny and 5 degrees outside—but the light in the big room was dimmed and eerie.

It gave Ellen's skin a blue pallor. She sat on a straight-backed chair up on the platform, her chin up, knees together, hands in her lap. The chill blue light was so remarkable, especially in the shadows of her neck and breasts, that I worked directly with oil on canvas, without preliminary sketches. To my great relief, the session went well.

Afterward, Ellen got dressed and heated a pan of apple cider. We sat together with our warm drinks and talked about the painting she was about to begin. At one point I walked over to the window by the table and scraped a hole in the frost with my thumbnail. When I bent and peered out, I felt like I was looking into one of those fancy eggs with a scene inside. Houses stood in blocks like crystals between snow-packed roads. Snow covered the roofs, and lines of white smoke rose straight out of the chimneys. Beyond the houses, ice clung to the limestone bluffs, and the pines and cedars on top made a dark border between the white town and the pale sky. I tried to imagine the people in the quiet houses, the lives below the white smoke that rose and disappeared, but I drew a blank.

When I straightened up and turned around, I was snow-dazzled for a minute. Ellen's voice swam at me out of a cavelike darkness. And, because I couldn't see her, I couldn't make out what she was saying. Gradually, the dim, bluish light in the loft came back to me and she was there again.

When I got back to my place, there was a big envelope from Minneapolis in the mailbox. I opened it at the kitchen table and pulled out an 8 x 10 black-and-white photo. There wasn't anything else inside. I saw my face and, in the photo's background, the portraits on the wall behind me. I'm looking at the picture again right now. Both my face and the ones looking over my shoulders are in sharp focus. The composition is horizontal, and behind me you can only see two of the portraits entirely. One hangs over my left shoulder, one over my right. On the left, an attractive young woman with short, light hair stares straight ahead, hard and serious, either angry or afraid. On the right, a somewhat older woman with dark, curly hair appears to be laughing. Her mouth is open and her eyes are shut, but this image is ambiguous, too. She could be crying. Between them, my own face almost fills the picture from top to bottom. It looms forward, too big and too close, and my eyes are round with a startled look. My mouth is pursed and my cheeks are belled out a little—I'm probably chewing a piece of food. I look and see a man self-conscious and discomposed, completely unaware of the faces that float above his shoulders. Looking at the picture, I winced, just as Andrea intended, I suppose.

John

December 23, 1990

Dear Wyatt,

We're still in the deep freeze here. I think the high today was 10 degrees, with bright sun and a wind full of knives. The windows at Ellen's are still frozen over: one looks like it's overgrown with big white ferns that shine and glitter.

I painted again yesterday, taking a pose directly into oil. Ellen sat in a chair again, facing me with her arms folded under her breasts. Her hair took a bluish cast from the room's icy light. An electric space heater glowed orange next to the platform. We talked while I worked. At one point I told her about getting the photo in the mail, and about how Andrea had just picked up her camera and started taking pictures during my visit. I told her how peculiar it had made me feel to have Andrea's lens trained on me while trying to carry on a conversation.

Ellen laughed. She found it very amusing. "That was something new for you?" she asked, still smiling. "You've never modeled before?"

I said I'd taken my turn modeling a few times in art school when a group of us did extra work some evenings.

"Nude?" she asked.

"Nearly," I said.

"Then you should model for me," she said. "Don't you think I should have some figure work in my portfolio?" She was still grinning at me. I forced a smile and kept painting.

We worked in silence for a while. Ellen gazed over my head, deep in thought. I worked to get that serious expression into my picture. After a few minutes she said,

"I do think you should pose for me, John. I think it's a good idea." There was an edge in her voice. I kept working. I was trying to decide whether to use the light from the space heater in the painting. Its orange cast shone on the outside of her left leg and arm and just touched the nipple of her left breast.

"I think you should model for me *now*." Ellen stood up.

She wasn't kidding. She looked very determined, maybe even angry. She had caught me by surprise. I sat with my brush in my lap, looking up at her. She stepped off the platform, crossed the room, and carried over the drawing easel. She set it down next to my easel, picked up a stick of charcoal, and looked at me. She stood there, still completely naked, and stared me down.

I made a quick calculation. I knew I had two choices: go along or get out, this time for good. I sighed, put down my brush, and stood up. I walked over next to the space heater, undressed down to my briefs, and stepped onto the platform.

"You can take the same pose I was in," Ellen said. "But first . . ." She gave me a meaningful look. I took off my briefs. I sat down on the chair and crossed my arms.

She stepped over to the edge of the platform, picked up my shirt, and put it on. It was a white, long-sleeved shirt with long shirttails. Then she walked back to the easel and began to draw.

The skin on my arms and legs stood up. I shivered some, but that may have been partly tension. I'll admit, I was uneasy. But I knew that Ellen's sense of justice had come into play, and I submitted. It felt like a ritual atonement.

She drew intently, scrutinizing me for long moments between rushes of activity. In the room's chill, I was—well, I was very crumpled and small, almost childlike. Of course, Ellen had never seen me naked before. I felt painfully self-conscious.

Ellen tore off a sheet and said, "Would you mind standing now?" I stood up.

"Can you stand any straighter?" she said. "Your shoulders are hunched. Are you cold?"

"No, I'm okay," I said. I straightened my shoulders.

"That's good," she said. "Fine." She sounded chirpy now. She began drawing again. She drew freely, in long vertical strokes. When she looked up, I found myself trying to guess where her gaze was focused. She did not meet my eyes. She continued for several minutes, finished another drawing, and tore off the sheet.

"Who knows, maybe you'll learn something from this," she said. "Maybe it will get into your paintings." I nodded and took a step nearer the space heater, holding my pose.

"You *are* chilly, aren't you?" she said. "We can stop." She came out from behind the easel and stepped toward the platform. "I'll give you your shirt back," she said.

She unbuttoned the shirt. She unbuttoned it slowly, holding my eyes with hers.

I shifted my weight, uneasily. I was still on the platform and she was at its edge, two or three feet in front of me. She slipped the shirt off her shoulders in a lingering, expert gesture which kept her breasts covered suggestively. Despite the chill room, I began to respond. I had to sit down quickly on the chair. It was very embarrassing. Ellen stepped onto the platform, slipped off the shirt, and laid it across my lap.

"Let's call it even," she said. "Tomorrow I'll be nice." Then she turned and walked across the big room, went into her small bathroom, and shut the door.

I got dressed and waited for a couple of minutes. I heard water running behind the door. I waited for a few more minutes and then guessed that I had been dismissed. So I went home.

The next day both of us pretended nothing had happened. We talked about some of her sketches. She modeled for me and I continued working on the painting I had started the day before. I guess she felt that she had made her point. I guess she had. I'll be modeling for her from time to time now. And I'll make a monthly contribution to the heating bill.

John

5

Jamie Stevens
2663 Lilleskare Road #110
Minneapolis, MN

December 20, 1990

Dear John,

I know we've spoken of you coming up for a visit. I know you want to talk about things. You've asked me before what I imagine for the future and I haven't been able to tell you. I just haven't known. But I can tell you how I've tried to think things through, and I can tell you some of the things that have occurred to me. And maybe it will be easier in a letter. We've had a hard time talking about this face-to-face.

I try to think about the future, what I want to happen, but it's hard to focus. I keep thinking about the past, trying to figure out what has happened. It's like weaving. I tell myself that if I know the pattern, then I'll see what comes next.

I tell myself stories, but there are too many. One starts in Watkins Glen, New York, growing up in a small town and saying to myself when I left for college, "Never again." At the end of that one I'm standing at my kitchen sink in Delphi peeling potatoes and asking myself, "How did this happen?" I'll never live in a small town again. I just can't.

Another starts at a pottery wheel in a studio at Cornell next to the Fall Creek gorge. It was probably the spring of my sophomore year, and I'd just finished throwing a copy of a big Chinese jar. I stepped outside into the sunlight and heard the sound of the falls, then looked back through the door to the shape of the jar on the wheel and felt a deep, calm satisfaction with what I'd done. From then on I knew that, whatever else I was doing, I wanted to make things. All those stupid jobs in the city after I graduated just earned the money to keep my days free. Bartender, radio dispatcher, message service operator. Then the good job at the gallery uptown kept me from working, and so when you came up with the idea of the move, so we could try to live on the art, I agreed. The funny thing is, after the move, when it was all art, it wasn't enough. I'd get up from the wheel or my loom, step outside, and wonder, "Where's the rest of it?" I'd gotten used to the back-and-forth in New York. I used to do pots or weaving as long as I could, then go off through the crowded streets to a job or a show or to see some friends. And when I'd get back to my work I'd have seen something, I'd be someplace else, with a new idea or a new angle on things. But in Delphi it was all me. And you. I felt, in a funny way, like I was living off my capital. No new income.

I haven't forgotten those early days at the Loft Co-op when you kept finding reasons to drop by during my studio hours. I remember how casual those little visits seemed. You always acted surprised to run into me, but I could see how deliberate those drop-ins were. You were very attentive and cheerful and funny, then. God, I was being courted! I was usually covered with clay and you were rummaging around looking for stretchers or rags, but it felt like we were on a porch swing somewhere sipping lemonade. You were very sweet and careful, and I was flattered. It was a good time, with your show that spring and my first run of good sales and commissions. We'd both been in New York for quite a while, but we met just as things were beginning to break for each of us, so we felt like good luck to each other. We had a lot of fun with the Loft crowd, with Mary and Tina and Judd and all the rest. We were almost never alone, except when we were working.

And then in Delphi we were always alone. When we'd decided to move, the whole idea of a retreat seemed okay. We were starting to get worn out. So when Judd came back from Iowa City and talked about the writers he'd met out there who'd been to the workshop and decided to stay, it started us thinking. And he was so enthusiastic about this little pocket up in the northeast corner of the state where somebody had taken him fishing and canoeing. It did sound nice. The rents would be cheap, we'd be out of the city hassles, and you said you felt comfortable with the Midwest since you'd grown up in Chicago. I thought of it as a kind of experiment.

I thought I wanted peace and space and time, like you did, and for a while things were pretty good. But I hadn't expected the loneliness. When I started to have doubts, I thought of the story that Tina had written. The one about the woman who goes to visit an old friend and her husband who live in a big dream house up in the country somewhere. Do you remember? The couple latch onto her and don't want her to go. They seem desperate to keep her and talk to her and show her things and take her places. She's having a good time and everything, but it feels a little strange. Every time she mentions leaving, her friend gets very anxious and the husband suggests two or three things they still want to do. Finally, up in a corner of the big house, in a little sewing closet or something, the woman confides in her friend. She says being married is so hard that it's too much for just two people. They're lonely, and they can't do it by themselves. They need help.

John, we were just so alone. I was so lonely! Even you got more and more distant. I can't come back to Delphi. I'm not sure what to do. It's not like weaving. I can't find the pattern, or there are too many.

But I think I want to go back to New York. I miss the city and my friends there terribly. And I don't want to drag you back. That wouldn't work. It would always be between us.

Jamie

John Ordway
423 1/2 River Street
Delphi, Iowa

December 24, 1990
Dear Wyatt,

I got a long letter from Jamie. She finally opened up and talked about her reasons for leaving—loneliness, mainly. She said she thinks she wants to go back to New York, but she didn't sound too sure about it. I felt mainly encouraged. I read the letter, left the apartment, walked straight to the drugstore, and called her. I told her: "I just got your letter. That's the most you've been able to say to me since you left. It's a start. We have something we can talk about now. When can I drive up to see you?"

The line was quiet for a moment. Then she said: "I don't know, John. What do you think can happen?"

I said: "Look. You wouldn't be dragging me back to New York. I've botched things out here. I'm willing to go back. There's really nothing left for me here. I want to be with you."

There was a long silence on the line. A woman came down the aisle of the drugstore looking for something among the elbow braces, trusses, and elastic bandages. The fluorescent lights cast a blue-white pallor over her. I turned toward the wall. There were toothbrushes hanging there: red, blue, yellow, green. Some, for kids, had little silver flakes embedded in the plastic.

Finally, Jamie said: "Please, John. Don't make this harder." Her voice came to me as if from a great distance.

Then I realized what was happening. "I just don't understand," I said, my voice rising. "When I came up for the firing—things seemed better, didn't they?"

"I'm sorry," she said. "I'm very, very sorry."

I lost heart for a moment, then came back to myself with a rush. "You haven't told me anything!" I shouted into the phone. "You owe me some kind of explanation, dammit!" I looked over my shoulder and saw the woman in the aisle, frozen, staring at me. I listened for an answer. Jamie hadn't hung up but she didn't speak. I listened to the silence on the line. Then I slammed down the phone, left the store, and walked hard through the streets until I was tired. The cold didn't touch me. I was too angry to be cold.

12/25

The town is very quiet today, everyone settled in for Christmas. Ellen is with her family. Ron's with his, too. Caroline has gone to St. Louis to be with her mother. When I went out to call my parents this afternoon, the drugstore was closed like everything else. So I walked the five blocks down Main to the other end of the business district. There was nobody on the street at all. At the crosswalks the wind barreled between the buildings so hard it took my breath away. When I stepped into the phone booth in the corner of the Shell station parking area, the booth shook with the gusts. The wind in the vents made a howl. I dialed and wondered if I would be able to hear over the noise.

My father answered. His voice sounded old. I could picture him standing at the phone table in the dark of the downstairs hallway, his full head of white hair lit by the one lamp hung on the polished walnut paneling. "It's John," I said. "Merry Christmas." He called for my mother to get on the bedroom extension. "Betty, it's John," I heard him say. I heard the click of the other phone being picked up and then my mother's voice: "Hello, John, where are you calling from? What's that noise?" I told her it was the wind. "It's windy here, too," she said. "We haven't been outside all day." She asked if I had any special Christmas plans. The pauses as we spoke were a little too long, the talk too polite. She didn't mention Jamie or my work. There seemed to be a tacit understanding that these matters were strictly my own.

I suppose they assumed everything was more or less as it had been the last time we had spoken—almost a year before. I pictured my mother sitting on the edge of their bed. She would be facing her dresser, with the framed pictures in a row beneath the mirror: her parents in a formal portrait; me at twelve, my hair cropped short, my chin leaning on balled fists; Vivien, eighteen, in the school photo taken the same year as mine. On the dresser it's as though time has stopped: my mother's parents are there, her daughter is alive, and I'm a boy gazing dreamily over the photographer's shoulder.

Time did stop in our house that year. My sister's death loomed up in front of us and my parents couldn't find their way around it. At school that year we learned a song: "So high, can't get over it; so low, can't get under it; so wide, can't get around it . . ." I forget the rest of the words.

I listened to my mother—"The neighborhood isn't the same since Mr. Orson died and Doris moved to Arizona where her son lives"—and I could almost smell the lavender she kept to scent the drawers and closet. My father stayed on the line and listened. I knew this when I said "Good-bye, Mom" and he added his "Good-bye, John" at the end. When I hung up the sound of his voice saying my name rang in my ears.

After the walk home, climbing the stairs to the apartment, I touched the handrail with my gloves off, and its cold iron made my hand ache. I can't think of anything colder. That's what I think of when I think of being dead: the touch of that iron handrail in midwinter.

The apartment was quiet so I switched on the radio. I sat down and reread your Christmas card and the enclosed letter. It was snowing a little. I was watching it out the window, sitting on the old red velvet couch in my small living room. I'd stood and sweated in the August heat to buy it for $40 the previous summer when I'd moved into the studio on Raven Street. But today it was impossible to imagine summer—going outside in a T-shirt, the sound of leaves when the wind blows. When I tried to remember lying down in the grass under the big tree in the front yard, it seemed like something I had dreamed once, something that could never really happen. And the same thing happened last summer—I couldn't imagine winter, this bare-bones life, the same hard sky through the empty trees for days and then weeks and then months.

Last night I went to a little Christmas Eve party at the Earth Day house. Rich and the others had invited me. "You have to see our Christmas tree. It's cool," Rich said. I was glad to have someplace to go. I took along a jar of popcorn and a bag of tangerines as gifts.

The house is only a few blocks from my apartment, so I walked over. The sun had just gone down and the sky in the west flared a violent magenta. In a few minutes I reached the big, turreted Victorian, went up the five stairs onto the wraparound porch, and knocked on the door. Kevin let me in and, with studied formality, asked if he could take my coat. Off the foyer to the left a staircase went up. Straight ahead a hallway led to the back of the house. And to my right, in the brightly lit front room, everyone sat on the floor or on the long brown couch, chattering excitedly. In one corner a tall, garishly decorated Christmas tree throbbed with color.

Kevin disappeared with my coat and I stepped into the front room. Linda, sitting cross-legged on the floor next to the tree, raised a gangly arm, waved, and smiled broadly. "Look, everybody," she said, "John's here." Everyone turned and shouted "Hi" and Rich jumped up, took me by the arm, and led me to the tree.

"Look, we made these," he said, pointing to the cardboard stars wrapped in tinfoil that reflected the colors of the blinking lights. His wandering eye darted back and forth with excitement. And then he showed me the blue ball with his name written on it in silver sequins stuck on with white glue.

"Sit here with us, John," Dot said, so I went and sat with her and Patty on the couch. Everyone had on new sweaters, white or red or green.

"You're just in time," Patty said. "Barbara is making popcorn." It reminded me of the gifts I'd left in the foyer, so I got them and brought them back into the front room.

"Here's some more popcorn, in case we run out," I said. "And here's a bag of tangerines. Does anybody want a tangerine?" Their hands flew up, so I opened the bag and passed it around and we all ate tangerines.

Linda went to the back of the house and returned with a paper bag. "Here's for the peelings," she said, and everyone brought their peelings and tangerine seeds and dropped them into the bag.

Then Barbara appeared with a huge bowl of popcorn. A round, easygoing woman in her early fifties, Barbara lives in an apartment on the ground floor and supervises the house. She put the bowl on a low table in the middle of the room. Kevin, wearing his green baseball cap, as always, handed out cereal bowls to everyone. They filled their bowls, sat cross-legged on the floor, and ate contentedly. Barbara and I sat on the couch, eating like the rest.

"Watch this, John." Rich tossed a kernel into the air, tipped back his head, and opened his mouth. The kernel bounced off his forehead and fell to the floor.

"No, like this," Dot said. Her kernel fell straight down into her lap.

"You've got to keep your eyes open, dummy," Kevin said. "Watch me." His throw went wide and he rocked over sideways in pursuit and tipped over.

"You try," Patty said to me, her eyes swimming behind her thick glasses. She turned to the others. "I bet John can do it." I glanced at Barbara, who was leaning back into the cushions and smiling broadly.

I took a kernel, gave it a careful toss, tipped back my head, and opened my mouth. The kernel bounced off my chin and everybody laughed hard.

"Here, this way," Rich said to Kevin. "Open your mouth." Kevin complied and Rich fired a kernel that bounced off Kevin's forehead. Everyone laughed and Kevin grinned. Then everyone's mouth was opened and everyone was throwing popcorn, either straight up or at someone else's open mouth. I sat and watched the puffs flying and bouncing around the room. A white accumulation spread across the brown carpet.

"Okay," Barbara said, "now let's pick up before everything gets ground into the carpet." And for the next few minutes everyone gathered the kernels and dropped them into the paper bag with the tangerine peels.

"Can we turn out the lights now?" Rich asked Barbara.

"In just a minute," she said. "First get me my Bible story book." Linda ran to Barbara's room and brought back the red-bound book. Everyone seemed to know the ritual. Still sitting on the floor, they turned to face Barbara as she read the story of the child in a barn among the quiet animals, of the kings and the guiding star and the gifts they brought to the child, and of the shepherds who heard angels singing among the stars above their hill.

Barbara finished and Rich stood up and turned out the lights. Only the Christmas tree glowed and blinked in the dark room. And then, all together, they sang "Silent Night." I sat in the dark and listened to the off-key voices, sounding in heartfelt unison. They knew all the verses and sang them to the tree as if to a glowing totem. And at the end there was a long hush of satisfaction.

Later, walking home through the snowy streets, I looked up at the stars, which showed bright and sharp in the cold air. Between the pinpricks of light, the dark shone in its own way—vast, vivid, and bottomless.

John

Jamie Stevens
2663 Lilleskare Road #110
Minneapolis, MN

December 25, 1990

Dear John,

You're right. I do owe you more explanation.

I've realized some things, John. This July at the big fair in Milwaukee, Andrea and I had our setups together. We'd been at a lot of the same shows in the past year, but we'd never really talked. It was awfully hot and Andrea had an awning, so we sat together in her shade and took turns going to fill the water jug. We talked a lot and she took some photos of me at my booth. When I saw the pictures later they surprised and pleased me. I was sitting between two of the tall jars with a big, woolly tapestry behind me. The photos really struck me. What shall I say? I hadn't felt seen like that for a long time.

We sat under the awning, and as the day went along and we got to know each other better I started thinking out loud about the year since you and I had left New York. It was a relief finally to say some things that had been on my mind, and some of what I heard come out of my mouth surprised me. Before, when you and I had talked, we'd always done a careful balancing act. Every complaint had to be followed by something good. We were making less money, but our costs were down. We were isolated, but we were free. We were lonely, but we had more time for each other. But talking with Andrea, I blurted out, "God! I miss my friends, I miss seeing what they're doing, I miss the streets, I miss the smell of the Italian bakery down on our old corner. I even miss the smell of the bus exhaust!"

Andrea asked about you, and what I said then surprised me, too. I didn't even think. I just said straight out, "We never fight. We're good to each other. But, if I had to, I could live without him."

It stunned me when I said it. But, John, you're not the man I was with in New York. You've tunneled deep inside, away from me. And the last few times I've seen you—since the fire and the hospitals and all that—you've seemed so listless. Of course, I can't help but feel partly responsible. If I thought that getting our little house back and trying to make everything the way it was before would do us any good, I might try it. But, God, it was just so joyless! We were making pots and weavings and paintings as if our lives depended on it. It wasn't just the money thing. It was like there wasn't anything else. We worked like demons. Or maybe we weren't the demons. The demon was at the door with his big mouth wide open, and if we didn't keep throwing pots and paintings down his throat, he'd come in after us.

Maybe I felt that more than you did. The desperation. You still talked about the progress you were making, about the next project or series that would be "an advance." I loved that in you, like I always have. But after the move it was all so grim.

Yes, it's been better when we've seen each other lately. The night when you came up and helped me with the firing was nice. It felt like being with an old friend. But it was only better because of the split. In Delphi there was a "party line," and it was your line. A lot of what I was feeling just didn't fit. And you didn't even know it. I was starting to become invisible to you. Even when you looked you didn't see me. I remember lunches or dinners after we'd both been working. You stared at the walls, chewing and brooding. I'd pull you back for a minute with a comment of some kind, but then you were off again, thinking about your work, probably. It reminded me of something my mother said about you in New York that Christmas, the first time she met you. "He's like one of those talking bank machines," she said. "He's courteous and complete, but there's no one there." I yelled at her then, but in Delphi it was true.

And I remember something else she said. "Either he's from another planet, or someday he's going to explode." She'd been watching the way you took things in without anything coming back out. I remember what I said, too. I told her that I loved the calm steadiness of your body while your nervous eyes took in everything around you. I told her that things came back out when you painted, and that's why you didn't have to explode. So when I heard that you'd burned the big, new painting, I wondered, "Is this it? Is this the explosion?" It scared me—even more than the loneliness when we were together.

I'm going back to New York. Tina is helping me look for a place to live. I'll always remember what we had for a while. Believe me, I wish things had turned out differently. We tried to put our lives together and it just didn't work.

Jamie

John Ordway
423 River Street
Delphi, Iowa

December 28, 1990

Dear Wyatt,

Another letter from Jamie yesterday. And an hour after the mail arrived I had a regularly scheduled appointment with Caroline. I dropped myself into the brown chair and held out the letter. I wanted her to know. Caroline looked at me with concern, reached forward and took the letter out of my hand, then leaned back and read it. She read with a look of intense concentration. The letter spoke of loneliness—mostly the loneliness. Jamie's moving back to New York, Wyatt, and she doesn't want me to come.

Caroline looked up when she had finished. The sympathy in her eyes made my throat tighten. "I'm sorry," she said. "What are you going to do?"

I looked down and shook my head. "I don't know," I said. "The finality of the letter shocks me. I wasn't expecting this. It's hard to take in." I paused. A hot feeling rose suddenly in my chest. "I know what I *feel* like doing," I said.

"What is that?" she said.

I looked up. "I feel like shouting," I said. My voice rose a little. "I feel like shouting out, 'You can't do this! You just can't do this to me!'"

Caroline nodded. "Maybe you should do what you feel like doing," she said.

That night I called Jamie. In a calm, even voice I told her I would not allow her to end our relationship with a couple of letters. I said she owed it to me to see me one last time. I said I was willing to drive up the next day or any day she would name. She agreed—reluctantly, I thought. We'll meet tomorrow at a café in Dennis, Minnesota, about halfway between Delphi and the Twin Cities. I'll write again after I've seen her.

John

December 31, 1990

Dear Wyatt,

I had a dream last night. In it, I woke up in my bed with the sense of someone standing at my feet. I couldn't see in the dark but knew it was Jamie. She stood there silently, then turned to the side and stepped to the window. The pale light from the streetlight lit her, and I saw that she was naked. Her skin took a mauve cast from the walls. Then the light from outside became brighter. It intensified into a strange glow, and she looked out into it, intently. I wanted to get up and look out the window, too—to see where the light was coming from, to see what she was looking at—but when I tried, I couldn't move my arms or legs. I strained, but my limbs were heavy, unresponsive. I began to struggle and pant, and panic started to rise in my chest. I broke into a sweat, but I still couldn't move. Then the light through the window snapped off with a metallic click. I opened my eyes.

The bedroom door had opened a little and a woman spoke from behind it.

"John?" she said. "Are you there?"

"Yes," I said.

She stood behind the half-opened door and said, "I'm sorry I let myself in. There was no answer when I knocked, and the front door was open. Are you all right?"

I said yes. I was half awake.

"You missed your last two sessions with Ellen. She phoned me. She sounded worried," the familiar voice said.

It was Caroline. I asked what time it was and she said 10:00 A.M. She asked if I wanted her to go to the kitchen and start some hot water. I said, "Yes, thanks," and told her I'd be out in a minute.

The room was dim. I guess I'd slept all day Sunday and then all night. When I sat up on the edge of the bed, my arms and legs felt like lead and my heart pounded. A rectangle of bluish light glowed around the drawn shade. I sat there for a minute. I saw myself in the dresser mirror and looked away. Finally I got up, pulled on some clothes, and went out to the kitchen. Caroline had put a kettle of water on the stove and had found the tea and teapot in the cupboard.

"I'm sorry I intruded," she said. "I would have called if you had a phone. I'll leave now." We were both embarrassed—she because she was checking up on me, I because I needed it. Aside from the people at Earth Day, I hadn't seen anyone for a while. I had increased my dose of pills back to where I started in August.

I asked Caroline to stay and have a cup of tea before she left. I had been keeping to myself, but now that she was here I couldn't stand the thought of her leaving right away. When the water boiled I made the tea and we sat down across from one another at the kitchen table. I'd only talked with her at her office before. When she asked how I was, I tried to think how to answer, tried to think how professional or personal this conversation was going to be. But that was too much effort. Her dark eyes were serious and receptive, so I just started in and told her about my meeting with Jamie. She listened quietly, and before she left she put her hand on my shoulder and told me to call her at home if I needed anything. It was a relief to talk to her, but I couldn't tell her everything.

The meeting with Jamie was a disaster. I drove through light snow and arrived at the Dennis Café on the highway at the edge of town around 4:30, half an hour early. There wasn't much to do while I waited. In the café, I looked at the postcards and gifts near the cash register. There was a sweatshirt with a picture of heavy snow boots printed on the front; underneath them were the words "Minnesota Aerobic Workout Shoes." I went outside and walked to the edge of the parking lot. It was getting dark. Next door was a small field covered by snow. Weed stalks the color of rusty barbed wire stuck through the snow and shook in the gusts of wind. Beyond the field, behind an aquamarine one-story house, a dog was chained to a tree. It sat on its haunches in the snow, facing the house, and didn't move. I went back inside.

Forty minutes had passed and Jamie was a little late. I sat in a booth at the front of the café and watched the road for her van. The snow was getting heavier. I could see it falling sideways through the orange glow of the mercury vapor streetlights. I had told the waitress I was expecting someone, and she left me alone. People came and went. A couple in the next booth ate in silence.

As more time passed I started to worry. I looked out the window and watched the snow sizzling across the road in the wind. It could have been sand in the desert. I felt like I was in another country, in a far corner of the world. The café's fluorescent lights glared hard off the gray Formica tabletop, and everything began to look grotesque to me—the toothy grin of a stuffed pike hanging on the wall; the beefy figures at the other tables, quietly chewing; the snow wheeling out of the dark and hitting the big plate of glass next to me.

She was almost an hour late now, and I sat there imagining the worst. I clung to the image of Jamie's van pulling up, of her stepping through the door. I followed each pair of headlights that approached. As they glided past, one after another, my chest tightened as if a balloon in there were being slowly inflated. At 6:30 I didn't think I could stand it any longer.

At 7:00 I was completely overcome by dread and anxiety. She was two hours late and I was sure something had happened, otherwise she would have called. I didn't know what to do.

At 7:30 I sat in the booth with my face in my hands. Then I heard a little bell and looked up to see Jamie step through the front door and shake the snowflakes out of her hair. She spotted me and strode over, swinging off her coat. She sat down and said, "Oh, John, you won't believe it. I sat on the highway in a line of cars behind a jackknifed truck for two and a half hours. It's getting awful out there. I'm so sorry. Were you worried?"

I exploded. "Of course, I've been *desperately* worried," I said. "Couldn't you have called when you got through the traffic? Do you realize the thoughts that ran through my head? Can you imagine how I felt? Do you care at all about the way I feel?" My voice shook. All my relief that she'd finally arrived poured out as bitter anger against the way I'd been made to suffer.

She defended herself. The accident had been just 30 miles to the north. Once she'd gotten past it, she'd considered calling, but thought it would take her as long to find a phone as to reach the café. "My nerves are jangled, too," she said. "I sat in the van wondering if I'd get through, knowing you were waiting for me."

We fell into a chilly silence.

The waitress came over and asked if we were ready to order. We said no, and she went away.

I apologized. I said, "I'm sorry. I was just so miserable. I wasn't in control of myself."

"I understand," she said. "I was upset, too." And then we fell silent again.

Finally, we ordered some food. At first I could barely swallow, but gradually I settled down. As we ate we began to talk, and by the time we'd finished the tension had eased.

I told her a story about worry and anger—about the time my mother had taken me shopping at Marshall Field's department store when I was twelve. I guess it must have been a few months after Vivien had died. I walked off while my mother was talking to a clerk. I sat in a chair next to a rack of spring coats, ate peanuts out of my jacket pocket, and watched a woman dress some mannequins for a display. The arms came off and were interchangeable. They lay around the saleswoman like an assortment of pipes at a muffler shop. And there was a head with red hair, but not like Vivien's hair. This head rested upright on its neck, with its big startled eyes wide open, as if she had just popped up from under the floor and the rest of her body still swam under the reddish carpet.

About twenty minutes later my mother found me, still watching the saleswoman assembling and disassembling the mannequins. She grabbed me by both arms and shook me. Her face was so red and contorted as she scolded me that I can still see it. She shouted at me, "What are you doing? What are you doing to me? Do you know what you just did to me?"

"So," I said, "I guess in my family we express relief with anger." I tried to make a joke out of it, but it didn't come out that way.

There was a long silence then. And finally we talked seriously about the future. Without drawing things out, all I really need to say is that we could not agree. We must have talked for about two hours. My word, spoken hopefully, was "maybe." Her word, spoken sadly, was "no." At the end, in desperation, I did what I knew I would do. I reached across the table, took her hand, and asked her to marry me. I said I'd willingly go back to New York with her, that the move had been a mistake. "If you want," I said, "we can live together for a year first, to make sure. Things would be different for us in New York. They could be like they were before."

Jamie's eyes filled with tears and she shook her head. "Oh, John, I knew it would be like this," she said. "Please, please, please, please stop." Then she kept her eyes down, looking at the gray Formica tabletop.

We were silent for a few minutes, then we walked together out to the parking lot. Jamie gave me a nervous kiss on the cheek and got into the van. I went to my car and we drove in opposite directions.

In ten minutes we were both back at the café. The state patrol had closed the highway because of drifting snow. And so we had an awkward reunion. Jamie said there was a motel at the other end of town, and we went in the van to see if there were vacancies. There was one room. "I'll go back to the café," I said.

"You don't have to," Jamie said. "I'll go."

"No, don't be silly," I said. We stood there for a minute in awkward silence.

"This is silly," Jamie said, finally. "There are two beds. We ought to be able to handle this." And so we checked in.

In the room Jamie said, "I think I'll just take a shower and go to bed."

"I feel the same way," I said. "You go first." Of course, neither of us had packed a bag.

I sat on my bed while Jamie was in the shower. I listened to the shower water and stared at the stains on the dark red carpet. When she came out, wrapped in a towel, I went in and took my shower. When I came out she was sitting on the edge of her bed, drying her hair with another towel and then brushing it out. I sat down in my T-shirt and shorts on the other bed, facing her.

Then we both just stopped. Jamie was looking at me with a mournful expression, and I must have looked the same. Then tears were going down her cheeks and down mine, too. She opened her arms and I went into them. We cried as we made love. It was a way of saying good-bye.

Tonight is New Year's Eve—the loneliest night of the year, you used to say. But when you get this letter, you mustn't worry. I feel strangely calm. Like something's been settled. It's an odd feeling, and vaguely familiar. It's not resignation, exactly, but a kind of hush. I had a funny thought: that this is the way Jonah must have felt sitting in the belly of the whale. There he sat in the dark, and though something terrible had happened, it was also something big, something real. The night feels very big tonight, and we're all inside it.

John

6

John Ordway
423 River Street
Delphi, Iowa

January 9, 1991

Dear Wyatt,

I need to get off this drug. I can't tell what's me and what's the medicine. The other night, late, I was filled with such anxiety and dread that I knelt down in my dark bedroom and pressed my face against the cold windowpane, first one cheek and then the other, over and over. The sting of the cold was something to focus on, to hold to. When that didn't work anymore I got up, put on my coat, and walked over to Ron's. It was around midnight and I woke him up. He looked startled when he let me in. I told him I couldn't sleep and that I felt desperate—panicky nerves, skipping heart, couldn't catch my breath. He nodded. He told me to take my coat off and lie down on the couch. Then he went out to the kitchen to get me something warm to drink. In a minute he came back with a cup of hot cider and a blanket. "Drink this," he said. And he spread the blanket over me. Then he pulled a wooden chair over close to the couch and started talking.

"I know how you feel," he said. "This has happened to me. It will go away. Sometimes it helped me if I could just listen to somebody talk. Just listen—you don't have to say anything." He kept talking as he got up and walked over to one of the bookcases. "Maybe I'll read to you," he said. "Here's something." He pulled down a book and came back to the chair and started to read. I recognized a chapter out of *Walden*. He read softly, evenly—the part about clay thawing and running out of a railway embankment in spring, taking the shapes of things. I clung to the sound of his voice, like the cold window against my cheek. He was in a blue bathrobe and old moccasins. His hair stuck out on one side from sleeping on it funny.

After a while he stopped and went back to the bookshelf. I stretched out my arms and legs, tried to relax. "Well, what's next?" he said, as if to himself. "Here, maybe a little of this." He came back with two books, sat down, and began to read again. First he read for a long time from a slim paperback, *The Way of Life* by Lao Tzu. I could see the cover. I shut my eyes and listened, tried to take deep breaths. After a while he put that down and picked up a thick book in black binding. "Parts of the King James Bible are soothing," he said. He read out of it for a long time. I remember a passage that said, "Our bed is green. The beams of our house are cedar, and our rafters are fir." I could feel my neck muscles knotted against the arm of the couch.

It must have been very late when he stopped reading. He set his book down on the floor beside him and said, "Something just came to mind, I don't know why. Maybe it would interest you." He got up, went to the kitchen, came back with a glass of water, took a drink, and sat back down.

He said: "This happened last summer, in early August during that really hot stretch. Do you remember the heavy all-afternoon rain we had that broke the heat for a couple of days? I finished work at about four o'clock and went for a bike ride in it. I put on my poncho, baseball cap, and a pair of old shoes. I got some funny looks from people in their cars as I headed for the edge of town, but it was a beau-tiful, drenching rain, and I just wanted to be out in it. Big drops drummed down on the bill of my cap, and the gutters were full of runoff. I rode out to Sand Pit Road and started out of town between the river and the bluffs. The air smelled good, and out by the woods the sound of the rain beating through the leaves sounded like the ocean, except it didn't come in waves, it just kept on in a steady roll.

"I decided to turn in and go back to Redding's Spring. I like the way the trees arch over the little road there, and I wanted to loop by the waterfall and see how hard it was running with this rain. When I came up to the turnaround near the falls, I saw a red pickup. While I was coming up behind it, a guy slid out of the cab and started walking forward toward one of the trailheads. His legs were bare under a green poncho like mine and he was wearing a pair of flip-flops. The funny thing was, he wasn't wearing anything else—nothing at all—just a poncho and a god-damn pair of flip-flops. I knew because of the way the poncho had shifted up when he got out of the truck. I was coming up behind him and he didn't know I was there because my bike was quiet and the rain was loud. He palmed a jar of petroleum jelly in one hand.

"I went ahead to the turnaround, glanced at the waterfall running hard, and started back out. This time I passed the guy face-to-face. He gave me a shy smile—an embarrassed we're-both-a-little-crazy-to-be-out-in-this-rain sort of smile. It wasn't anybody I recognized.

"I rolled back out to the main road and continued on toward the sand pit, but I was thinking about that guy. I wondered if he was just going off by himself or whether he was meeting somebody. Whatever it was, I imagined him at work somewhere that afternoon, looking out at the rain pouring down, and feeling drawn out into it. The rain came down and this fantasy developed and he thought of this thing he wanted to do. After all that heat, day after day, the rain was cool and heavy and sexual, and he just had to do this thing. And the possibility of getting caught, of losing everything in this little town if anybody found out, only made it sweeter and more irresistible. And so he formed this plan, thought just how he'd do it, and he crossed the line. He acted out this secret desire of his.

"I don't remember feeling any sort of judgment. Well, I guess it did seem pathetic to me. But mainly I had a feeling of awe. It's not every day you stumble across somebody else's obsession. I'd glimpsed this guy's private imagination, the most secret part of his life. I rolled on through the rain, hearing some thunder off in the distance once in a while, and that naked guy under the poncho seemed like the name for something true about that afternoon and the rain in the trees.

"When I got back home Iris was there. She had come over and fixed some supper, so I took a quick shower and put on dry clothes. We sat down and started to eat. She'd made a nice salad of mixed greens and had fried a couple of chicken breasts. I told her about the bike ride and my strange encounter. She stopped eating and put down her fork. She had this worried look on her face and she said, 'How long ago was this? Do you think he's still there? You've got to call the police.'

"This surprised me. It hadn't occurred to me that he could be dangerous. That hadn't been my sense of the situation, and I told her so. But she pressed me. She said, 'That's not normal behavior, Ron. You don't know what he'd do if somebody ran into him out there. Kids play on those trails around the spring.'

"'He just didn't seem dangerous to me, Iris,' I said. 'He seemed like a harmless, pathetic guy acting out a little fantasy.'

"'You can't know that,' she said. 'You don't have any idea who he is or where he comes from or what he might do, today in the park or someplace else some other time. He could be a rapist or a child molester. You've got to call the police.'

"I still didn't want to, but she'd gotten to me now. I wasn't so sure of my own judgment. I could understand how it seemed to her when I told her about it. And, most of all, it was very clear that if I refused to report this, it would be a big deal to her. I could sense that it was a very serious matter in her eyes, and if I failed her in this she would never be able to think about me in quite the same way as before.

"I got up and phoned the police. She listened to me make the report and answer the officer's questions about the guy and his pickup, describing them the best I could. It was a hard call to make. At one point, I thought I heard the officer snort.

As I spoke, I felt torn between the roles of good citizen and informer. It was confusing. And the stakes seemed very high. It seemed possible, I guess, that I was reporting somebody dangerous. But it seemed more likely that I was ruining some poor lonely guy's life. Afterward, I felt a little shaken.

"We finished our dinner in silence. Iris left the table and started reading the paper. I cleaned up the kitchen and went out to the garage to wipe off my bike. The police didn't call back and we never heard anything else about the matter.

"For a while I kind of noticed red pickups, but I never saw that one again. And I haven't really thought about it much since then. But tonight, with everything frozen solid in the middle of winter, it's kind of nice to remember that heavy rain and the streets all full of water."

Ron stopped talking and fell into thought. His hair winging out from the side of his head was bright in the reading lamp. After a while he came back to himself and asked me how I was feeling. I said I was feeling quite a bit better.

"Why don't you just go to sleep here on the couch, if you can," he said. He went and got me a pillow and an extra blanket. Then he went upstairs to bed.

I lay in the dark for a while. I could still hear Ron's voice in my head. At last I could manage a few deep breaths. I felt very grateful.

When I woke up the next morning I felt silly and ashamed. It was about nine o'clock and apparently Ron had gone to work. I used his phone to make an appointment with Caroline, then went home and got cleaned up. That afternoon in Caroline's office I told her what was going on.

Wyatt, I have these very bad patches. I can't tell why they come on when they do. When I'm inside them it's like falling down a well—twisting in free fall down a dark shaft. I can't tell whether it's my mind doing this to my body or the other way around. And I can't sort out from hour to hour whether my feelings are my own or are caused by the drug. Caroline said it's possible that I'm having a reaction to my medicine. Or else, if I'm not taking just the right amount on the right schedule, I could be having something called "rebound anxiety." As she spoke to me her face moved in that smile of hers that starts in sad acknowledgment and makes its way gradually toward hopefulness. She spoke gravely and warmly and that complicated smile moved over her face like shadow and light on a lake in summer. I told her I feel like I'm caught in a labyrinth, and I said I wanted to get off the drug. I want to know, at least, that my feelings are my own. So she sent me to a doctor who's put me on a schedule to taper off. We'll see how that goes.

Earlier this evening Ron came by. It's been a few days since my bad night. I thanked him again for helping me out. I gave him a beer and we sat at my kitchen table and talked. After a while, I asked why he had thought to tell me the story about the guy in the park. He said he really didn't know, that it just came into his head. Then he paused.

"Now that I think about it, there's something I hadn't remembered," he said. "I recall now that when I turned my bike around and was about to see that guy's face, I half expected it to be you. This was about a week after that fire in Mrs. Tolman's backyard, and I guess I'd heard some of the talk around town. Of course, I didn't know you then. I'd wired your studio and we'd met at Sammy's that night with Jean and Jerry, but I didn't really know you. I guess maybe that's the link that made the story come to mind the other night. I hadn't thought of that." He looked down the neck of his beer bottle. He seemed embarrassed by the admission.

"So, are the town fathers keeping me under surveillance?" I said in what I hoped was a good-natured voice. "Can't have sexual deviants running around unwatched." He grinned at me, then shook his head.

"Go ahead and joke," he said. "Just remember this is a very small town. You can't assume you're invisible just because you mind your own business."

I got him another beer and we talked some more, about other things. He left about 10:00. I've been wondering since then whether he was sending me some sort of signal, flashing me a warning either knowingly or unknowingly, both with the story and with his answer to my question tonight. This is something to think about.

John

January 11, 1991

Dear Wyatt,

Thanks for your kind letter. Give my love to Alice and tell her how glad I am that she's fully back into her old routines. It must be a great relief to both of you. And thanks, Wyatt, for passing along the information and cautions from your doctor concerning the medicine I'm taking. I do feel that my care is good here. Caroline Evans, especially, is very sharp and knowledgeable.

Yes, I've been working a little lately. Ellen and I seem to have reestablished our equilibrium. Things have gone smoothly enough lately, anyway. We model for each other and we've gotten Jean back involved, too. She's an untiring model, seems actually to enjoy the work. This way, Ellen and I can paint at the same time, and I can make suggestions when she asks my opinion about something. I have several canvases going right now, myself, but I'm not ready to talk about them just yet.

Ellen has finished her painting of her old boss, the librarian Mrs. Steegers. She used a lot of olive and yellow and dark blue in a dour, effective way. It really is a very devastating portrait. And she surprised me the other day by pulling out a completed painting of *me*. She was very dramatic about it, in a mocking, ironic way. "I've got a present for you," she said, and she walked me over to an easel facing one of the big windows. The painting was covered by a sheet, which she swept away with a grin and a flourish. "Here it is," she said, "I call it *What the Model Sees*."

In the immediate foreground, along the left side of the painting, the line of an inner thigh curves up. Beyond it, I'm a smallish figure standing in the middle distance. Seen from below, I'm looking down, palette in one hand, brush in the other. My white shirt starts out against the dark background. Around my head, the hair is a furious corona. My face swims up in impressionistic swirls of pink and red strokes. She's given me eyeglasses. My gaze is intent, but at the same time it seems to be clouded with a kind of bemused preoccupation. I stood looking at the picture, very surprised, while Ellen grinned at me with her hands on her hips. It's a striking picture. Lately, she seems to conceive of painting as revenge.

I still see Caroline regularly. This week, during our session, she suggested that I start to keep a journal to discuss with her. I told her: "I almost feel as though I do keep a journal, but one that I write and mail away." She looked at me, questioningly. "I write a lot of letters to my friend Wyatt in New York," I explained.

"Do you keep copies?" she asked, and I told her I didn't.

"Does writing seem in any way therapeutic?" she said.

I nodded. "It's calming," I said. "It's another way of going over things."

"You're lucky to have such a good friend," she said, gazing out the window. The way she said it made me wonder if she was lonely. I had assumed she was more or less happy. She's a woman with a secure, respected position in town, and when I notice her in public—in the grocery store, for instance—she greets everyone with a warm smile. But now I thought of her dead husband, and I thought of what it must be like to be a widow in a small town like this.

When my hour ended I turned on my way out the door and saw her sitting still and gazing out the window past her African violets.

Before closing, I need to ask you something that's been on my mind. Were there any notices or reviews of my show? I kept waiting for you to tell me. There must have been *something*. And the fact that you haven't mentioned any makes me suspect the worst. I'd rather see what was actually written than continue to imagine what you might be shielding me from. Please send them out.

John

January 16, 1991
Dear Wyatt,

The UPS driver delivered your overnight parcel today. Thanks for the paints. I do appreciate the significance of the gesture. Don't worry, I'm not going to stop painting because of the reviews you enclosed. If I thought that much about critics I wouldn't be doing the kind of work I do in the first place, would I? But some of the remarks stung: "*Does Mr. Ordway believe that figurative, realistic painting—and indeed the threadbare tradition of the female nude—is at the moment so out of fashion that the attempt to revive it is a revolutionary gesture? If so, why are these paintings so quiet and earnest? One can only conclude that the artist's motives are private, and so detached from wider cultural deliberations on matters of both art and sex, that this work will be, for most of its viewers, almost entirely beside the point.*" How does *The New Yorker* find so many twitchy little reviewers who write like they've got cobs up their butts? (I heard that expression at the gas station the other day. Two mechanics were talking about the banker who'd just dropped off his Cadillac for an oil change. It comes in handy.)

It's easier for me to read the women. At least you feel like they've got convictions. The feminist paper from downtown was comfortingly predictable: "*At least since the early Renaissance, Western oil painting has been obsessed with woman as erotic spectacle. Women bathing, women sleeping, women preening, women swooning. Women in the woods playing 'nature' to man's 'culture.' Women with their heads shadowed or cropped, and their torsos arched for the male gaze sweeping over them. So much surveillance and plunder. We've had quite enough. And so John Ordway's nudes currently at the Arends Gallery on Spring Street, however 'tasteful,' however 'well painted,' just won't do.*" Tell me, Wyatt, is that really what I'm doing? They'd say that about any female nude painted by a man. The woman who wrote for the Voice said about the same thing, only she was angrier. "*John Ordway needs a good shaking. His languorous women in those enigmatic interiors are the warmed-over dreams of a snoozing patriarchy. Hey, wake up!*" I suppose most nudes are what they say. It just makes you feel steamrolled—flattened into a dough with all the old pornographers.

The positive notices were almost as bad: "*No one has attempted to render flesh in oil with such delicacy since Renoir.*" Renoir—Christ!

Well, thanks. I asked for it.

John

January 17, 1991

Dear Wyatt,

So, after the terrible countdown, it's really started. I was in a booth at Sammy's with Ron, having a cheeseburger platter for supper. He was telling me about a problem at the office where Iris works that was going to keep her in Decorah through the weekend. Next to us, outside the plate glass window, big snowflakes were blowing sideways under the streetlights. At the bar, Sammy was showing his newest bowling trophy to two big men in flannel shirts and baseball caps. It had blue metal-flake strips inlaid into the walnut pedestal with the inevitable gold man in mid-delivery fastened to the top. Sammy turned and made a space for it with the others on a shelf under the Hamm's Beer clock with the lighted river that seems to flow from background to foreground. I was listening to Ron as I watched the scene at the bar over his shoulder. Then somebody behind me shouted, "Look! Sammy! Turn up the TV!"

At first I didn't know what I was seeing. The screen above the bar seemed to have turned into an aquarium. A city shone phosphorescent green while fountains of light arced over it. Sparks sprayed up and out of view while slower glowing balls rose in lines that tipped like fronds of seaweed. Flashes at the horizon lit banks of green clouds. Then I heard the name, "Baghdad."

Everyone had turned to look. Customers had turned away from their pinball machines and stared at the screen. Ron had turned around and was looking over the high back of our booth. There was no sound except for the television. John Holliman was holding his microphone out a window of the El Rashid Hotel and we heard the bombs exploding and the anti-aircraft fire. Bernie Shaw was saying something about the pit of hell.

There was no cheering. Nobody said anything at all. The room was very tense. Baghdad under aerial bombardment, live at the corner bar. But it was eerily inhuman—just buildings and lights and a little smoke. And the green light of the night-vision camera lens made the whole thing strange and unreal. It could have been happening on Venus, except for those American newsmen, somehow in the middle of things, their voices tightened by fear. But even their presence, peering out their hotel windows, boosted the weird sense of spectatorship. This was manifestly something to be *watched*, and I was riveted. We all were. Everyone not sitting at the bar moved to tables closer to the television. Sammy brewed some coffee.

I stayed three more hours while the news anchors tried to piece together what was happening. There was low murmuring at the other tables. Ron and I said very little, and when we left we parted quietly in the snowy street, both of us pensive.

Downtown was quiet, muffled by the new snowfall. A front had come through and the temperature had gone way down. It was the kind of cold that makes your skin hurt the minute you step outside. I walked to my car, which was still parked in front of Ellen's place three blocks away. When I got there I looked up to see if there were any lights on. Suddenly, I didn't feel ready to be alone. But the windows were dark, so I got into the car and drove home.

It was very dark away from the downtown streetlights, despite the new snow on the ground. There was no moon. I hadn't left my outdoor light on, so the side yard where my steps go up to the apartment was in total darkness. As I walked, I felt ahead of myself for the iron handrail. I found it and my hand ached. At the top of the stairs I paused and looked up. The sky had cleared, and the stars were as thick and bright as ever.

John

January 22, 1991

Dear Wyatt,

The bitter cold continues. It has been very bright—blinding at midday—but you can't *feel* the sun. It's so cold that the packed snow squeaks on the roads and sidewalks underfoot. People hurry from one warm place to another, outside only long enough to make the transit. Their heads are covered with hats, scarves, and hoods, and their breaths puff out in front of them in little clouds. I bought a second space heater for Ellen's place and we boil pans of water on the hotplate continuously. Of course, the windows are covered by deep frost. With the sun on them it looks like we're working in an ice cathedral.

I worked on a composition involving both Ellen and Jean the other day. Earlier, Ellen had asked me to pose with Jean. Jean is about six months pregnant, now, which presents a new subject. I had never thought of doing a Madonna.

When we finish working, it's my habit now to stop at Sammy's to watch the news. Often, Ron meets me there. Sometimes I end up staying a couple of hours, watching the reports and briefings and the film released by the military. I'm appalled and fascinated. Certain images stick in the mind—a camera gazes steadily at a square building marked by crosshairs, and then two streaks, one right after another, sweep into the frame and enter the building by the door. Smoke puffs out and the structure sags. There's no sound.

And did you see the tape shot from the nose of a bomb? Again, that monomaniacal gaze at a squat, gray building. The structure grows larger and larger until, in a rush at the end, it fills the whole screen and then the picture is replaced by empty-channel static. In that one, you're left to imagine the smoke. Again, no sound.

There was an audiotape that made a big impression on me—of a pilot during a bombing mission, dodging antiaircraft defenses. The military had released the tape to show that these missions "aren't video games." The pilot spoke in brief, tense bursts. Through the jargon I understood something about a target, a radar lock, and an anti-aircraft missile. It sounded like someone had found a key and tightened the pilot's vocal cords the way you tune a banjo. I imagined that he was very cold. Behind it all, there was a high mechanical whine, exactly like the sound my car's defroster fan makes in the extreme cold. And so a funny thing happens now when I drive. I'm hunched in my coat, looking out at the packed white streets, with that high whine in my ears, and I think of the pilot in his cockpit at altitude in the war. It happens every time. It's half empathic imagination trying to know what that experience is like, and (this is the embarrassing part) half Walter Mitty fantasy. There's a secret, guilty part of me that thrills to all this. It's boyhood stuff: ships, planes, bombs, heroism. And, most seductive, the omnipotent feeling of action-at-a-distance, doubled when you're peering at an aerial strike through the keyhole of a television.

Of course, I know we're being shown a war shaped by a massive public relations effort, and I make my mental objections continuously. "Necessary" or not, every war is a disaster. And, of course, I know the whole sordid history of our involvements leading up to this. But I'm fascinated nonetheless. The eye has a mind of its own.

John

January 25, 1991
Dear Wyatt,

Bowling night tonight. Something was bothering Kevin. He didn't want to bowl—sat behind us at a table and hid under the brim of his green baseball cap. At first Linda went and sat with him between her turns and held his hand, but later

112

she just left him alone. The whole group was subdued. Only Rich seemed to ignore the distraction. He rolled a strike in the eighth frame and punched the air in celebration. When he sat down next to me I finally asked him what was going on.

"You mean about Kevin?" he asked. I nodded. "He's sad," Rich said.

I asked him what Kevin was sad about.

"He can't be in the army," Rich said.

Dot rolled a ball that went into the gutter almost the moment it left her hand. Rich jumped up and offered instruction, pumping his arm back and forth and pointing to his wrist. Dot turned stiffly away and reached for her second ball. Rich shrugged and returned to his seat. Dot's second ball went halfway down the alley and fell into the gutter. She walked back, impassive, and sat down. Patty stepped up for her turn.

I was puzzled. "Kevin wants to join the army? Who talked to him?" I said.

"The man in the office said no," Rich answered.

"What office?" I said.

"The army office downtown. Kevin went down there and they told him he can't join because he can't get a driver's license." Rich looked down.

I didn't understand the remark about the license, but knew that Kevin wouldn't pass a service physical. I glanced back to where he was sitting. He was slumped in his chair with his arms crossed and his legs out straight. His chin was on his chest and the bill of his cap hid his face.

Patty had quickly dispensed with her turn, knocking down three pins with her two balls. Linda stepped up for her turn.

I asked, "Should I talk to him?" and Rich shrugged.

"He yelled at supper," Rich said. "He said we aren't normal. We know that, but we have jobs. Now everybody's sad. Nobody wanted to go bowling, but Barbara made us."

I wanted to be able to do something, but didn't know what. Linda stood at the end line and swung her ball back and forth, faster and faster, then let it go and knocked down eight pins. With her second ball she picked up the spare. On her way back to her seat she looked to see if Kevin had seen, but his head was still down.

I took my turn and we went around quickly until the game was finished. Everyone seemed relieved when it was over. I bought popcorn and we sat in the orange plastic chairs at the round table with Kevin. He accepted his bag of popcorn and we all sat in a circle and chewed as if we were fulfilling a duty.

Patty, who was across from me, stared over my shoulder, her eyes enlarged by the thick lenses of her glasses. Next to her, Dot was spelling her name on the table with kernels of corn. Rich, on my right, had swiveled around to watch the other bowlers. On my left, next to Kevin, Linda reached her long, thin arms across the table and helped Dot cross her "t."

Kevin watched and chewed idly. He's thin and slight, but as he brought another handful of popcorn to his mouth, I saw how thick and stiff his wrists are. He's serious—something of a brooder—and he can be prone to moods. I wondered where this business about enlisting was coming from. I would have expected it from Rich, maybe, but not Kevin. Where Rich is excitable, Kevin is always very deliberate and gentle: I've noticed him carefully straighten the collar of Linda's coat before they walk home together after work.

When we finished our popcorn everybody was ready to go. We walked in a group the few blocks downtown to my car and I drove everyone back to the house. It was a tight squeeze. Patty had to sit on Rich's lap in the seat next to me. But we rode in near silence. Only Rich spoke. He said, "John, you should get a Dodge Caravan. They're nice."

I can't get them out of my mind. There's no denying that their lives and choices are limited by the bodies they were born with. Kevin is running up against that hard right now. But, more than that, their very selves are tied to their physical makeup. When I think of Patty I see an abnormally square face, a stiff, shuffling walk, and eyes like grapes swimming behind thick glasses. Sure, there's more than that—she's patient and tender, her feelings are easily hurt, and she tunes in quickly to the way others are feeling—but every trait comes through her bodily carriage and features. In the same way, with Rich there's no separating that wandering eye and twitching mustache from his energy and volatility. His eye is like a gauge—the more excited he gets, the wilder it moves. Am I any different when I have to go over to Ron's house in the middle of the night because I can't draw a deep breath? I was born with a particular nerve net, one that trembles like a spider's web in the slightest breeze. It has everything to do with my abilities and my miseries. And now I'm taking a chemical to change the traffic at my synapses.

Where does the soul live? Do we even have a meaning for the word? And let alone *soul*—what about "self"? When I say the word, you know what I picture? An empty sky. It gets light, it gets dark. Weather blows through. There are curious formations, sudden gusts, and an infinite variability in the qualities of light. But it's all meteorology. The sky is an empty dome, a receptacle or medium, in itself almost nothing. I get a chill at the thought.

I think I'll stop now. It's getting late. It was windy earlier, but is still now. The temperature must be dropping because I can hear the house siding pop as it contracts.

John

February 1, 1991
Dear Wyatt,

Working these days in our ice palace we are a cozy threesome. I arrive from Earth Day after lunch. Jean comes almost every day. Ellen paints diligently, making real technical strides. Working in oil from sketches and memory, she's doing places around town. I think it's part of her psychic leave-taking, putting distance between herself and home, putting a frame around it so she can be outside it. I'm surprised she has so few attachments here, aside from her family. When I mentioned it, she said most of the friends she grew up with have moved away. But it also seems to me she's withheld herself by a kind of discipline. I saw the same thing growing up in Chicago—girls being very deliberate, knowing that if they married someone from the neighborhood it was a decision to stay for life. This air of unavailability made them, of course, all the more desirable. I remember conversations in high school with guys obsessed over the distant, beautiful Anita Capelli. She walked through the halls with that clear, brown-eyed gaze and all that dark hair falling down her straight back. Whoever won her would be distinguished for life, we thought. But she escaped. She's a physician in San Francisco now, I believe.

Ellen may be like that for some local men—the fascination of what is withheld. And her very act of standing apart—the discipline of it—gives her stature. There's the sense of a power narrowly channeled. A filament shines when current meets resistance, and she has that kind of incandescence. It's more than her blond hair and fair complexion. Sometimes she looks like she's lit from within. The last few times I've painted her, I've found myself thinking of a candle—the way the top glows near the flame.

Most of the time lately I've worked with Jean, while Ellen does her own projects. I've painted one nude with Jean, in which she lies on one side, curled around her wonderful belly. I guess I've never had the occasion before to really see a pregnant woman. I find myself pausing here over the page with a mass of impressions that I don't know how to get down. I'd like to be able to describe the way in which Jean is beautiful now, a way different from before. As she appears to me now, she may be the most completely sexual woman I've ever looked at. She's all softness, weight, and plenitude—a rich center. She's heavy with sex, drenched in it, perfected in it.

But it's sex completed, brought to a momentary still point, a rondure. I hope some of this got into the painting.

I love women. I love to be around them. I think if I were a woman I wouldn't have to paint. Somebody else would have to paint *me*. He'd never get it right. I'd drive him crazy.

John

February 9, 1991
Dear Wyatt,

Something awful happened at work yesterday. I was finishing the bookkeeping just before lunchtime in the office out front when Don, a foreman, burst in, his face white, and shouted, "Call an ambulance! There's been an accident!"

I jumped up so fast my chair flipped over backward, and as I dialed I heard a cry from the loading area. A male voice gave out a long, low moan that rose into an hysterical scream. Then it was joined by other cries and moans. I finished the call and ran out. Linda was sitting on the concrete floor near one of the loading bays. Her right arm was bent at an angle that made my stomach turn over and her shirt-sleeve was bloody. She sat silently, her face white and vacant. Kevin crouched be-hind her with his arms around her, wailing in distress. His green cap was lying upside-down on the floor beside him, and his yellow hair stuck out in all directions. The other cries came from the workers who had streamed in from the sorting room. They stood in a huddle, some covering their eyes with their hands, some hugging each other and rocking back and forth. Rich was among them, staring at Linda, his fists clenched at his sides, shouting "No. No. No."

Barbara grabbed my arm and pulled me toward them. She leaned into me as we went and said, "Help me get them out back and settle them down." The two of us put out our arms and gently urged them toward the sorting-room door, making soothing sounds as we went. I heard myself repeat: "It's all right, the doctors are coming, they'll take care of Linda." I glanced over my shoulder. Linda's eyes were closed. Kevin was still holding her up. Don was tying a handkerchief around her arm above the wound.

When we got them back to the sorting room, Rich and the others still hung to-gether in an anxious knot, groaning and crying. Rich said, "Barbara, what's going to happen?" and his wandering eye darted right and left. Then the ambulance came.

"Why do they have to run that awful siren?" Barbara said, hunching her shoulders. "We've got enough to contend with." Over her head, out the back window, I saw red lights sweep back and forth over the white siding of the house next door. The siren stopped but the lights continued to dart and sweep. Then the screen door of the white house flew open and a roundish woman came running over, holding both arms above her head as she ran. In one hand was a wooden spoon and in the other a red-checked kitchen towel. As she approached our back door she opened her hands and let the spoon and towel fly, then reached down with both arms to fling open the door. She burst in and cried, "Oh Barbara, what's happened?"

"An accident," Barbara said. "Help me settle the children," and they waded into the group, hugging and caressing.

I returned to the loading dock just as the ambulance sped away, its siren starting again. Don said to me, "I'm going with Drake and Mr. Johnson to the hospital. You stay with Kevin." Drake is the other foreman, Johnson is the director.

Kevin stood in the loading bay, watching the ambulance disappear and then the station wagon with the three men. The front of Kevin's plaid flannel shirt was blood-soaked. I led him to the bookkeeping room and sat him down. He moved stiffly and didn't say anything, seemed stunned and docile. I wondered if he could be in shock. I helped him out of the bloody shirt and stuffed it into my lunch bag. I could see all the ribs of his narrow, concave chest. I was wearing a sweater over a T-shirt, so pulled my sweater off and helped him get it on. Then I went out to look into the sorting room. It was empty and I guessed that Barbara and the neighbor were walking the others back to the house. That left just me and Kevin. I didn't know what to do.

I called Caroline at her County Services office and she came right over. She suggested we take Kevin away from where the accident had happened, so we went in her car to my place. No one said anything in the car or as I led them up the stairs and into my kitchen. Kevin and Caroline sat down across from each other at the table and I filled the sink with water and put Kevin's shirt in to soak. It was startling how quickly the water turned dark red. I drained the sink, rinsed the shirt, and started again. The water turned pink and I turned away to fill a pan with milk and put it on the stove. Kevin followed me with his eyes as I took three mugs and a tin of chocolate powder from the cupboard. Caroline reached across the table, took his hands, and asked him if he had any questions about what was happening. "Where's Linda now?" he asked.

"She's at the hospital," Caroline said.

"Did she die?" Kevin looked straight at Caroline and she looked over to me.

"I think she fainted," I explained.

Caroline turned back to Kevin: "After a while we can call the hospital and find out how Linda is doing. And tomorrow or the next day, when she's feeling better, I'm sure you'll be able to go see her." I was grateful for the way she was taking charge. Her warm, level voice was soothing. It was doing as much for me as it was for Kevin. She had spoken the same way often during my weekly visits—warmly, sensibly, honestly. What had surprised me in some of those later meetings, though, was the humor, when she sensed it was safe. And I liked her curiosity—not offensively personal, but intellectual. Once she asked, "What do you learn about a woman when you paint her body?" I remember thinking that she had a way of seeking the little statue buried inside a person, the shape of one's individuality. She works to find it, then fights to keep it from getting broken.

Kevin had put his head down on his arms and was sighing heavily—in relief, it seemed to me. Caroline patted one of his arms. I felt another flush of gratitude, and thought: what kind of person puts herself in the way of other people's troubles? I looked at her. She's small, compact. Her short, black hair has a little gray in it. With the angle of her dark eyebrows and the strength in the lines of her nose and mouth, she could almost appear fierce, if it weren't for her eyes. It's a clear and definite face, but open, receptive.

I mixed the cups of hot chocolate and put two of them on the table. Caroline looked up and I said, "I'll walk to the drugstore and call the hospital. You and Kevin can move into the next room to be more comfortable."

Then it was a relief to be outside and walking. The day was bright and cold. Suddenly the accident seemed like something that had happened a long time ago. When I reached the phone and dialed the hospital I expected to hear a kind, cheerful voice tell me that Linda was fine, that she was on her way home with a cast on her arm. In fact, a nurse told me that she was in surgery. Then Johnson came on and said Linda's elbow had been crushed. He had been out back talking to Don and saw the whole thing. Linda had started to climb up into the bay from outside after watching a semitrailer back into position. As the driver reached to set his brakes the truck had lurched back against the deck of the bay, catching Linda by the arm. Kevin was the first to run up. He had been operating the cardboard compactor at the far side of the big room. When the driver managed to pull forward, Kevin, slight as he is, lifted her up to the loading area floor, then held her and wailed. Johnson seemed surprised when I told him they were a "couple."

I asked Johnson about Linda's condition and he said they were trying to save her arm. I pictured her gangly form at the end of the bowling alley, the ball swinging back and forth like a pendulum before she let it go.

When I got back to the apartment Kevin and Caroline were sitting in the middle room. Caroline had turned on the radio and there was piano music. Kevin had his eyes closed and Caroline got up to greet me, signaling for me to be quiet. We walked into the kitchen and I told her what I had learned. She said she'd drive Kevin back to the house when he woke up and that she'd stop by to see him tomorrow.

"He's exhausted," she said.

"So am I. Thanks for coming over." We both leaned on the counter next to the sink and looked out the window into the snowy yard. A few dry leaves shuddered on the big oak tree. Otherwise, the yard was empty.

There was a long silence. I still wasn't sure how to talk to her outside her office. I looked at her and she smiled in that way I had come to recognize, a smile that started in sad acknowledgment and grew into something warmer. Then we heard movement back in the living room and Kevin appeared in the kitchen door.

He was pulling the green cap back on over his tousled blond hair. "Would you take me home now?" he said to Caroline. So she collected her coat and they left.

The piano music from the radio sounded hollow in the empty apartment and I decided to go for a walk. I went down to the frozen river and along a path to the edge of town and through the bare trees and the open fields beside the flat, snowy place where the river used to run. There were a few small weed stalks sticking up through the snow next to the path, and dried, brittle vines clung to the brown trunks of the trees. I looped back through the edge of town, stopped at the drugstore, and called the hospital again. Johnson was still there. Linda had lost a lot of blood, but she was stable now, he said. "She's going to be okay," he said. "They removed her arm just below the shoulder."

I walked home, rung out Kevin's shirt, and hung it in the bathroom to dry. I went back into the kitchen and poured the pink water out of the dishpan into the white sink and watched it swirl down the drain.

2/10

Let me finish telling you about the other day.

I hadn't felt like eating supper. I was tired, really tired, but didn't want to go to bed. It felt as though there were something important going on that I had to pay attention to. It was something like sitting up at the bedside of a sick friend—Linda, also Kevin, Rich, and the rest. But there was something else I couldn't bring into focus. I was in the middle room, sitting at the end of the old red couch in the floor lamp's circle of light, staring at a book. After a while I just let myself lean over on the couch.

A knocking at the door woke me and I jumped up as if I had been caught at something. On my way through the dark kitchen I saw the clock: 1:00 A.M. It was Caroline.

"I saw your light," she said. I was groggy, and my heart was pounding from jumping up so quickly.

"Come in," I managed. She looked tired.

We went inside and sat down on the couch. She had been at the hospital waiting to see Linda all this time. She told me what I already knew about the operation. She said that, finally, they had decided to keep Linda asleep through the night in intensive care, so she hadn't been able to see her after all.

I asked if she wanted a cup of tea, or maybe a glass of wine, something to relax. She seemed very tired, but restless. She hadn't taken off her jacket and as she sat, with her back very straight, she tugged at one of the buttons on her right sleeve. Every once in a while she ran her hand up her arm, as though she were rubbing off a chill.

"No thanks, I just saw your light, and I thought you'd want to know about things," she said.

"Still tending your flock?" I said. I was going to say something else but at that moment she leaned into me hard, actually drove into me with her face and shoulder against my ribs so that I went back against the arm of the couch. Her arms tightened around me and she pressed her face against my ribs and held still.

I lay there, half reclining against the end of the couch, with my arms up in the air, stunned. Slowly I let my arms settle down on Caroline's back and lay there blinking up into the floor lamp's glare. She pulled her feet up onto the couch, sighed once, and went heavy against me. In a minute her breathing was deep and regular. She was asleep.

I lay there blinking. When I shut my eyes against the lamp, its light glowed red through my eyelids. My back was torqued at an awkward angle and my neck was pressing against the wooden strip on the couch's arm, but I didn't want to move. Caroline was breathing hard in her sleep, almost panting like a runner, and the wool of her gray jacket moved up and down against my hands. I straightened myself a little, managing to get more comfortable, and she didn't wake up. I took a deep breath and tried to relax. I smelled the wool of her jacket and the clean, womanly scent of her hair.

We stayed like that for a long time, and I felt like I was going to have to make some sort of decision. My shoulder was starting to cramp. And then she heaved a great sigh, like someone who's just completed something, and lifted her head.

"How long did I sleep?" she said.

"About half an hour," I answered. She put her hands against my rib cage and pushed herself up.

"I'd better get home," she said, and stood. I got up and walked with her back through the kitchen. She opened the door herself and turned. "Thanks, John," she said. And then I watched her walk down the stairs and get into her car.

I slept late the next morning, then walked to the drugstore to call the hospital. The sky was low and a light snow was falling. A nurse told me that Linda was still in intensive care, but that she was going to be "okay." On the way home the snow gradually became heavy and started to blow.

I wish it weren't Sunday so I could go to work at Earth Day and see how everyone there is doing. I wish there were somewhere to go.

John

February 13, 1991
Dear Wyatt,

Linda is stable and out of intensive care. We were able to visit her for the first time today. Caroline and I went with Kevin and Rich. Dot, Patty, and the others didn't want to go—they don't like hospitals. Neither do I, to tell the truth.

It's a relatively new hospital. The beige walls and floor tiles are clean and smooth, with light green trim the color of scrubbing powder. In the rooms, the curtains drawn around the beds or pushed back on overhead tracks are a deeper green, like the disposable clothing surgeons wear. The smell of laundry soap and alcohol brought back hazy memories of my own hospitalization there in August. The place seemed only vaguely familiar, but details would start out at me: the tone that preceded an announcement over the speaker system, or the square-faced clocks and their heavy, inelegant numbers.

Some of the rooms were dark. Passing by, I would catch a glimpse: someone dim in the bed, quiet, head back, mouth open. Is it pain or sleep? It struck me like something in a dream. For some reason I think of a small boat at night on moving water.

Linda's room was bright, with the curtains open and the sun glaring in off the snow. As the four of us stepped tentatively into the room, a nurse sitting in the far corner nodded and smiled. Linda's eyes were closed. The light in the room was snow-colored, and Linda looked pale, grayish. Something was dripping from a clear plastic bag through a pale green tube and into her left arm. Bedding was pulled up over her other shoulder, up to her chin. Beyond the bed, two red plastic helium balloons stood on their strings, tied to the arm of a chair. There were flowers on the nightstand—forced daffodils.

The nurse stood and came over. "She's been waiting for you. She naps on and off. I'll just wake her." She bent over and put a hand lightly on Linda's chest. "Linda, your friends are here," she said.

Linda's tongue came out and went around her lips. Then her eyes flickered open and she squinted against the harsh light. The nurse stepped back. When Linda saw us she reached across with her left arm to tug the covers up on the other side. The nurse leaned forward, anxious about the IV drip, then moved back again.

Caroline stepped to the side of the bed and took Linda's hand. "It's so good to see you," she said. "Kevin and Rich are here, and John." She turned and held out her arm, inviting Kevin forward. He stepped up, shyly, and Caroline took his hand and put Linda's in it. She held their two hands in hers and said, "We've been looking forward to this visit. And everybody else at work sends their best wishes, too." Rich and I arranged ourselves at the foot of the bed.

Caroline looked at Kevin and smiled encouragingly. He looked at Linda and said, "How are you?"

"Fine," Linda said. "How are you?" Her voice was hoarse.

"Fine," he said. "Does your arm hurt?"

"Not now," she said.

There was a pause. Linda was shy about looking at Kevin. She glanced toward the windows and at the nurse and up to Caroline. I moved down to the other side of the bed, easing past the balloons. "Some of your friends sent cards with us," I said, fishing the bundle out of my coat pocket. I held them up one by one, showing her first the front and then the insides, reading aloud. On the cards there were flowers and spring landscapes and cats. Dot and Patty had sent valentines.

The nurse said, "I can stand those on the windowsill where she can see them."

Then Rich said, "I bet you can learn to bowl left-handed." We all looked at him.

"Everybody hopes you get better and come home as soon as possible," Caroline said, smoothing over. "Do you want to rest some more now?" Linda nodded. She did look tired.

Caroline stepped back and Rich and I walked to the door. Kevin kept his hold on Linda's hand and she looked up at him. "See you later," he said.

"See you later," she replied.

Then he put her hand down on the bed, palm up, carefully, as if it were a delicate china cup. We left the hospital, and I drove everyone across town. Rich and Kevin sat together in the backseat, while Caroline sat in front, gazing straight ahead through the windshield. It was almost noon. Rich and Kevin were quiet, brooding. When I stopped in the Earth Day parking lot, Rich asked me to go to church with them that evening. He said it was Ash Wednesday. I nodded, said I'd pick them up at the house, and they got out.

When I pulled away from the curb, Caroline turned sideways to face me. "I should say something about the other night," she began. "That was unprofessional of me. I'm sorry."

I glanced at her. She was leaning forward slightly, and her face was composed, purposeful. "Don't worry about it," I said. "Even the counselor needs to lean on someone sometimes. Believe me, I understand."

"Thank you, John," she said. "But it won't happen again." Then she turned in her seat and straightened her coat.

When I stopped at the County Services building she opened her door and said, "Well, I'll see you next week, as usual. Take care." I nodded and she got out.

Back at work, I skipped lunch and finished with the records by 1:00, then drove to Ellen's. Jean was already there, modeling for Ellen, sitting in a chair on the plat-form with her shirt off and a white sheet wrapped around her legs and hips. Ellen was standing at an easel, working in pastels. They both said, "Hello, John," and continued. I took off my coat, found a sketch pad, and joined them. After a few minutes I stopped drawing and just looked. In contrast to Linda's ashen face and long, white arm this morning, Jean's flesh had a rich, olive cast, despite the studio's winter light. It was restful simply to gaze at her: she's swollen with life, extravagant with it. She seemed vital and languid at the same time, like an engine idling. It was very restful. It set a kind of purring going in my head—very pleasant—and sud-denly I felt extremely tired. I realized then how tense I had been all day, how tight I'd been during the visit to the hospital. I put down my sketch pad, walked to the back of the studio, and lay down on Ellen's bed. At that end of the big room, away from the space heaters, the air was chilly. The bed was covered by a down quilt. I pulled the sides up and folded them over me. The two women across the room kept working, ignoring me. Their presence was like coals radiating. Once in a while they murmured back and forth, but I couldn't hear what they said. I relaxed. I shut my eyes and went to sleep.

When I woke up it was dark, except for a single lamp somewhere nearby. Jean was gone. I could see Ellen to my right, at the big round table between the bed and makeshift kitchen area. She sat with her elbows on the table, holding a cup of cof-fee in both hands, sipping at it. She was looking at me. "Tired?" she said, quietly.

"I guess so," I said. "What time is it?" She told me it was 6:15. It seemed like I'd just shut my eyes a moment ago. I asked her how long she'd been watching me.

"Just a few minutes," she said. "I've cooked, eaten, and cleaned up. You were really knocked out."

"I hope you don't mind," I said. I'd never done this before. I don't think I'd even been at her place past sunset.

"It's all right," she said. The studio was quiet—hushed, in fact—and I realized that during the day there was a steady run of muffled sounds coming up from the businesses below, a background noise that I'd stopped hearing. But now, with it gone, the silence was like a third presence, and we both were speaking in low voices, almost whispers, not to disturb it.

I should have gotten up, but I didn't want to change anything. There was a stillness I wanted to linger in. Lying there in the near darkness, with Ellen sitting nearby, I'd awakened into one of those moments—rare for me—when two people arrive together at a still point, calmed but alert. It's a kind of intimacy, necessary like food and sunlight, but how do we get there? Maybe that's what sex is for, but even sex doesn't work that way most of the time.

"Are you hungry?" Ellen said. "I left some supper on the hotplate for you."

Immediately, I felt starved. I hadn't eaten since early morning. "Yes, thanks," I said, and got up. Ellen stood, went over to the hotplate, and spooned some beef stew out of the pot into a bowl.

"Sit down," she said. "I'll get you a slice of bread and a glass of cider to go with that." I sat down and she put everything on the table in front of me. Then she poured herself a fresh cup of coffee and sat down, too. She watched me eat. It was good stew.

Then I remembered. "My God! I'm supposed to take Rich and Kevin to church!" It was 6:30. I still had time. But now the stillness was broken. Even Ellen's posture changed. Now she sat back, straight in her chair, arms crossed. I asked if she wanted to come with us.

"Sorry. I'm not a churchgoer," she said.

"Neither am I," I said. "This will be my first time, actually, except for some weddings and funerals." Ellen shrugged. It made me sad. Something had been lost. I finished my stew and thanked her, then found my coat.

It was time for me to go, but I stopped by the door, trying to think of something to say. I said thanks, again, and good-bye. Ellen half turned from the plate she was wiping and said good-bye without looking. I went out, descended the stairs, and stepped into the chilly night.

As I drove to the Earth Day house to pick up Kevin and Rich, the defroster fan whined in the cold. I remembered the war, turned on the radio, and scanned the dial until I found the news. They were talking about the bunker or shelter that had been hit in Baghdad, whether it was somehow a military target or whether a mistake had been made. Now they thought 400 civilians had been killed, a lot of them kids. A BBC reporter in Baghdad described rescue workers carrying out charred bodies. And he reported seeing one man that he described as "incoherent with grief" who "fell to the ground and buried his face in the earth." Then there was tape of men and women screaming in a language I didn't understand, but didn't have to.

When I pulled into the driveway at the house, Kevin and Rich came right out. Patty was with them, too. They got in and we drove back across town toward the church they go to—St. Paul's Lutheran—a big limestone building with a spire you can see from all over town. I asked Rich to tell me about Ash Wednesday. I didn't learn that kind of thing growing up. According to my mother, my father was raised Catholic—intensely so—and rebelled. She'd been a Protestant of some kind, but bowed to his hatred of religion. If the pope came on the evening news, he'd get up and leave the room. But I didn't inherit those feelings. Religion is simply unknown to me, exotic.

Rich said Ash Wednesday was the night when we got ashes on our faces. This struck me as strange. I wondered if he could be mistaken, but I drove on with my interest piqued.

We parked as near as we could and walked a half block to the church—toward the lit spire and glowing colored windows. At the entrance, we climbed the wide steps and went in. Just inside, a middle-aged couple greeted us and shook our hands. Rich led us through the vestibule and into the sanctuary. Ushers handed us bulletins at the back of the church and Rich said we should sit where they usually did, in a back pew. We sat down in a row, Rich, Kevin, Patty, and me. I sat on the aisle next to the red strip of carpet leading down to the altar area. The church was about three-quarters filled. There was organ music, a prelude. I looked down the row at the others. Rich was staring into space, his wandering eye drifting serenely. Kevin and Patty were looking at their hands folded in their laps.

I scanned the church, feeling anthropological. The tall colored windows extended up the high walls. From inside, the windows were dim, because of the dark outside, but I could see the images at the top of each one: a lamb lying inside a crown, an open book, an anchor, a chalice. The high walls and high peaked ceiling were plastered and painted a light yellow. Large wooden beams embedded in the walls between the windows followed the ceiling's curve and met at its peak. Big stained-glass light fixtures the size and shape of vacuum-cleaner canisters hung from the ceiling by chains. They were a swirled yellow with metal crosses on them.

All the wood at the front of the church was painted white with gold trim. There was a lectern on one side. On the other, a pulpit stood on a wooden pedestal, with a small curving stairway leading up to it. There were two carpeted steps up to the railing and the altar behind it. On the wall above the altar there was a simple wooden cross about five feet tall, lit by spotlights so it cast multiple shadows.

The prelude ended and the congregation stood and chanted a psalm. It was written out in the bulletin and part of it said:

> For behold, you look for truth
> deep within me,
> > and will make me
> > understand wisdom secretly.
>
> Purge me from my sin,
> and I shall be pure;
> > wash me, and I shall be clean indeed.
>
> Make me hear of joy and gladness,
> > that the body you have broken
> > may rejoice.

Then there was a prayer, followed by a confession that everyone read aloud. It was a pretty tough confession, I thought. And then the imposition of ashes.

Rich was right. Beginning with the front pews, the congregation filed up and kneeled at the railing around the altar. The pastor, inside the rail, moved from one to the next, grinding his thumb into a small container in his left hand and touching their foreheads, saying each time: "Remember that you are dust, and to dust you shall return." When the people stood and walked back to their seats, I could see the dark, cross-shaped smudges in the middle of their foreheads.

Row after row filed up, old men in brown suits leaning on canes, their white-haired wives, young couples trailing small children, lovely young girls in crisp dresses, athletic young men. They kneeled and received their marks, even the children. The church was quiet except for the repeated phrase, "Remember that you are dust, and to dust you shall return."

Another row stood and filed to the rail. I saw August Stortz, the butcher, and his wife. Maybe the pretty blond woman and her tall husband were part of his family, and the little girl his grandchild. Then there was a woman in a blue dress, and an older woman with short brown hair, and a schoolboy, probably her son. And then,

126

with a start, I recognized Caroline among them. They moved to the rail, kneeled, and received their ashes: "Remember that you are dust, and to dust you shall return."

I thought of Linda and looked over at Kevin. He was staring forward. His unruly straw-colored hair had been combed down wet, but was drying now and curling away from his head. I thought of Ellen and Jean and Ron and Iris. For each individual the phrase was repeated.

An usher nodded at us and I stood to let the others into the aisle. Patty and Kevin stepped by me. Then Rich came out of the pew, grasped my hand, and started toward the front of the church. I almost cried out. As I trailed him helplessly, I wanted to whisper something in his ear and disengage myself, but he strode ahead. Now it was too late. We were in front of the congregation. I couldn't turn back and make a scene, but could I go forward? Wouldn't that be some sort of trespass? We stood in a short line, waiting for a space at the rail. Rich still held my hand, as if I were a child. My face felt hot and my heart was pounding.

It was our turn. I should pull free and walk calmly back to my seat. That would be best. I wasn't a member. I didn't belong here. It might be some kind of sacrilege to go forward. Kevin and Patty walked up the two carpeted steps to the rail. Rich clamped down on my hand and followed. I couldn't escape.

We were all standing at the rail around the altar. Then Kevin and Patty and Rich kneeled. I went down with them. Rich released my hand and folded his in front of him, bowing his head. I imitated him, gasping for air as quietly as I could.

The pastor came down the line, thumbing the ashes onto each forehead. He came to Patty. "Remember that you are dust, and to dust you shall return." He marked Kevin. "Remember that you are dust, and to dust you shall return." Out of the corner of my eye I saw him smudge a small cross onto Rich's forehead. "Remember that you are dust, and to dust you shall return." Then he was standing in front of me. The greasy black ashes were in a scallop shell cradled in his left hand. His right thumb was black. He pressed it into the shell and reached forward. I felt a gritty cross pressed onto my forehead. "Remember that you are dust, and to dust you shall return," he said to me.

I was the last. Everyone at the rail stood and turned. I pressed myself up. When I turned I saw the whole congregation sitting in their rows looking forward, the whole body marked with ashes—every man, woman, and child. Each forehead carried its dark smudge. Tears started to my eyes, but I squelched them and walked back to my seat.

Then there was a prayer, but I didn't hear it. My face was hot and my ears were ringing with the blood rushing through them. The congregation stood and there was some singing. And then there was a communion service, with the congregation filing to the altar again for little wafers and sips of wine. This time when the usher came to our row I stayed seated, even clamped my hands to the pew and looked down when Rich slid by me. They came back with the scent of wine on their breaths,

Then there was a last prayer and it was over. The pastor strode to the back of the church and people spilled into the central aisle. I went out with the others, self-conscious about the mark on my face in that sea of marked faces. We filed by the pastor and he shook my hand, smiled, and greeted me like all the others. This seemed remarkable to me.

And then we were out in the night. I took a deep breath of cold air. It felt good in my lungs. We walked to the car and I drove everyone home. Kevin was silent. Patty said, "Thanks for going with us, John."

Rich said, "Yeah, thanks." He was sitting next to me in the front seat. "It's not sad," he said.

"What's not sad?" I asked.

"Ashes to ashes, dust to dust—that's just the way it is," he said. I looked at him by the green dashboard lights. He wiped the back of his hand across his forehead and smeared his ashes. "In heaven we get new bodies," he said.

We drove on in silence, under the streetlights. When I stopped in front of the Earth Day house, they slid out. "Good-bye," they said, in unison.

"Good-bye," I said.

Back home, in front of the bathroom mirror, I looked for a long time and then washed off the ashes. And then I wanted to write all this out to you while it was fresh in mind. It's been a full day. I can hardly hold it all in mind at once—Linda pale in her bed, the terrible war news, the ashes on our faces. And pushing back against it all, Jean and Ellen, those glowing bodies, so lovely. "Remember that you are dust, and to dust you shall return." Yes! But what does that mean we should do? It only makes them—all of them—more beautiful to me.

John

7

John Ordway
423 River Street
Delphi, Iowa

February 15, 1991

Dear Wyatt,

Bright today after a string of gray days. Cold but not windy. Thanks for your letter of the 11th. I'm glad to hear that Jamie seems well settled in her new place out there and that she's living not too far from you and Alice. I hope you'll see a lot of her, and, no, I don't feel awkward about that, at all. I like the idea that she's living in your part of town.

Here, I've started on something new. I made a trip to the fabric store downtown, picked out some black material—a kind of satin with a matte finish—and hired the woman who works there to sew two big rectangles of it together into a kind of sack. I had her leave openings on one side and at the two adjacent corners. The opposite end is left completely open. When she'd finished and I went in to pick it up, she couldn't bring herself to ask me what it was for, and I didn't feel like explaining. But I saw the way she watched me as I went out the door.

My idea is to paint Jean—and Ellen, too, if she has time to model—wrapped in the black material. She'll slip into the open end and put her head and hands through the holes at the other side. Only her head, hands, and feet will show. The rest of her body will be draped. The image came to me last Wednesday night, after that long day I wrote about last time.

By the way, I'm completely off medication. I feel about the same, maybe less tired. I quit very gradually, so didn't really notice anything. At least I can know, now, that what I feel is my own.

John

129

February 17, 1991

Dear Wyatt,

I've started on the new pictures I mentioned. We covered the platform with an extra sheet of the black fabric, and Jean wrapped herself up and lay down. I can't really do any studies, because what I have in mind will only work in oil, so I started right in. And I have to lay out the picture in a single sitting, because there's no way to get the drapery just the same a second time. This will be tricky. But the effect, so far, is about what I had in mind—with a few surprises.

These will be somber paintings. In the back of my mind is the Ash Wednesday service and a news photograph of an Iraqi woman wrapped in her *ábayeh*, mourning. And when I think of Linda's injury and all the smaller pains and indignities of the body, I want to curse or cry out: "Why should this be so?"

Working today, I was struck by the eerie, unsettling quality of the image when Jean is in the black sack, reclining on a dark sheet, her eyes shut, and her head resting on the platform's floor. The hands lie on her shrouded torso, and, farther down, the feet reach out of blackness. Her face, hands, and feet seem to float, disembodied. They could be remnants of a broken statue lit by the moon in a dark field.

The ruling emotion is grief, yes. But working with Jean yesterday and today, I've also seen something else. Her form under the drapery is irrepressible. There are moments when the black draping, meant to cover and subdue, only intensifies her body's presence. It's as though her legs, belly, and breasts are rising out of mud. Especially her belly, with that drooping roundness which means fecundity. The dark fabric swirls around it, its sheen slick and primordial, and the body looms forward, powerful as ever. Ellen is working beside me, making drawings. I wonder what she sees.

This afternoon, when we'd finished painting and Jean had gone, Ellen told me some things. "Jean has left Jerry," she said. "She moved out a few days ago after a big fight. Apparently, when they first learned that Jean was pregnant, Jerry pressured her to get an abortion. She refused, and there's been trouble ever since. Finally, he hit her, and that was it. Jean's living with a friend in town, now, while she looks for her own place."

I saw real pain in Ellen's face as she told me this. I hadn't realized how involved she and Jean have become as they've spent time together in the studio. Ellen said she's been talking with Jean about these troubles since Thanksgiving. Jean must be a little older, but Ellen has assumed the role of elder sister, fierce and protective. We spoke for about an hour, while a gusty wind rattled the big windows, then I went home.

The wind had calmed by the time the sun went down. I stood on my landing and watched while half the sky turned a vivid magenta then gradually darkened through shades of rose and purple to black.

John

February 20, 1991

Dear Wyatt,

Linda continues to recover. She'll probably be in the hospital for about two more weeks. I went with Caroline to visit her again this morning. She was sitting up in bed wearing a bulky red sweatshirt with a picture of a cat printed on the front. It was hard not to look at the empty sleeve. Caroline and I sat in chairs and talked with her.

The way Caroline was able to draw her out amazed me. I'd never heard Linda "chat" before. Caroline had asked what she's looking forward to doing when she's able to go home. Linda looked up at the ceiling and said: "I miss walking home after work. There's a small house we go past. I look at it and think of living there someday with Kevin." Then she turned to Caroline and asked, "Do you think we could ever do that?"

What she'd said stopped me, and I didn't hear how Caroline answered. I thought: of course that's what they want—to live like everybody else. And that's why Kevin wanted to enlist. To go to war with all the others would be to live the life of a normal man, as he understands it. If he could be a soldier, surely everything else would be possible afterward—a marriage, a home, an adult life.

When we left the hospital I asked Caroline whether she thought Kevin and Linda could ever live together on their own. We were walking across the icy parking lot toward her car, and there was a steady wind. I could see in her face that she was tensed against the cold. She shook her head and answered, "I wish it were possible. It would be very difficult."

We got into the car and Caroline started the engine. Our breath froze on the inside of the windshield, so we waited for the defroster air to warm up. We sat hunched in our coats in the cold car in the hospital parking lot, staring ahead at the fogged glass. Caroline said, "She's very brave." There was a long pause. Then she said, "I've seen middle-aged men, secure professionals, go through less than she has and fall apart. I counseled a man in Minneapolis who lost two fingers and spent a year in severe depression. He was vice president of an insurance company. Buttoning his shirt in the morning, he'd break down crying and stay home from

131

work. There were other things going on, of course, but aren't there always? I think of everything that Linda had to deal with even before the accident. And she's still able to dream about the future." She shook her head in wonderment.

It was the farthest thing from her intentions, I know, but I felt shamed by what she'd said. I looked out the window to my right at the row of bare trees that lined the parking lot. Against the background of the gray sky, their tops shook in the wind. Beyond them, a snowy hill rose and stopped. I looked at the bleak landscape and wondered what I had inside to put up against that cold, empty space.

The defroster had cleared the windshield halfway up—enough to drive. Caroline put the car in gear and pulled out of the lot, heading toward my apartment. We rode in silence, each of us thinking our own thoughts. Halfway across town, I looked over and saw tears going down her cheeks. It startled me. I asked her if she was all right. She nodded, wiped her face with the end of her scarf, and said: "I was thinking about Linda. I remember how I felt eight years ago, when I lost my son and then my husband got sick. I didn't think I could go on. Ordinary, daily courage like hers . . ." She broke off.

Ron had told me about Caroline losing her husband. I didn't know she'd had a son. "Your husband and son died in the same year?" I said.

"No, my husband was sick for a long time," she answered. "He died three years ago. Our son died at birth."

"I'm sorry," I said. "You don't think of that happening very much anymore." I meant children dying at birth.

"He had a heart defect that we didn't know about," she said. "He couldn't stand the stress of labor. They tried an emergency cesarean when the trouble showed up, but it was too late. We had chosen the name John." She looked straight ahead, out the windshield.

I nodded. We were crossing the river. I looked over the bridge railing to the flat white space between the snowy banks. "How *did* you keep going?" I asked.

"Of course, we were both desolate," she said. "Then, once Terry got sick—that was my husband's name—we just dealt with the emergencies as they arrived. There wasn't any choice. I was the healthy one. That became my role, no matter how I felt." We came to my apartment and she pulled to the curb and stopped. "On the days when I didn't think I could get out of bed, I would roll over and see him, the one who was truly sick. Toward the end he needed quite a bit of care. And then he was in the hospital. Fortunately, we had a long time to prepare for what was going to happen, a long time to talk about it. When it was all finished, it almost felt like we—like both of us—had accomplished something. We lived through his death, and then it was over. I think I did most of my mourning before he died."

"And you've been the healthy one ever since," I said.

"Well, you find out what's possible." She smiled, sadly.

I asked if she wanted to come in for something hot to drink, but she had appointments. I got out of the car and went up the wooden stairs to the apartment.

Tonight I'm writing at the kitchen table. I didn't work at all today. After Caroline dropped me off, I ate lunch and then just moved through the apartment, sorting through piles of books, papers, sketches. I felt agitated, thinking about her and the things she'd said.

In midafternoon, the sky blew clear and the temperature plunged. I decided to go for a drive and found myself on a secondary highway with icy fields stretching to the horizon on both sides. The sun poured down blindingly over the snow and the temperature kept falling. At sunset the whole sky turned copper-colored. Wind blew snow across the road in low sheets. Then the sky blackened and filled with stars.

Driving home through the polished fields, the world seemed hard, sharp, factual. Tonight, starting from this white disc, it feels as though you could add one thought at a time, feeling your way, building sturdily block by block. Maybe that's what winter is for.

John

February 22, 1991

Dear Wyatt,

Took today off from Earth Day and worked nearly the whole time at Ellen's. In the morning I finished my latest draped figure of Jean, while Ellen sat at her table across the room filling out art school applications. At noon I went out and brought back sandwiches and a Des Moines *Register*. Sitting at the big, round table, we ate and read, passing around the sections of the paper. As we were finishing lunch, Ellen asked me to go through her applications with her and look over the choices she'd made of drawings and paintings to photograph as samples of her work.

She and I went through the paperwork quickly, then Ellen leaned her canvases in a row against one wall and taped several drawings to the wallpaper above them. Jean and I walked with her, back and forth, looking and commenting. Much of the work I'd seen before, of course, but there were some new paintings and drawings. And until then, I hadn't looked at the whole body of her recent work. Seen together, it's a full and complicated reaction to the town she's planning to leave, with portraits, buildings, neighborhoods, landscapes. In the various pictures there are affection, pique, satire, and cool appraisal—it's a real accomplishment.

But what struck me hardest were the figure studies. She and I had worked side by side, drawing and painting Jean. We had worked on the same poses, and now I was intrigued by the differences between my pictures and hers. I looked at Ellen's paintings, saw Jean in a different aspect, and felt the ground of my perception shift. It was fascinating and disconcerting. In several of Ellen's paintings Jean's eyes appeared deep-set, with dark circles under them. In two more, the arrangement of the limbs suggested tension, heaviness, fatigue. And a recent drawing of Jean draped in the black fabric was frightening: viewed from near her feet, she was dramatically foreshortened, her head mostly obscured by her belly, and she looked inert—dead and shrouded.

I looked at Jean standing thoughtfully before Ellen's pictures, and I could see now the fatigue in her eyes and posture. I looked at Ellen and saw the dark circles under her own eyes. They had both been under a terrific strain in the last few months. I had been idealizing them, underestimating the difficulties Ellen had chosen when she defied her mother, rented the studio, and took her own way. And, of course, Jean's marriage has been coming apart. I had chosen, without realizing it, to ignore all this when I painted them. I had looked at both of them through the lens of my own need.

Some of my pictures of Jean were leaning against the wall across from Ellen's. I could see in my paintings the drive for poise, harmony, composure. All the things I felt I lacked I had invested in Jean's form. And running through the series was my preoccupation with her remarkable sexuality. Even in the new picture, in which I had thought I was protesting the body's fate, the drapery led the eye to linger over Jean's lovely shape. I think what I had seen in her—and painted—was true, but partial. Finally, my paintings had more to do with my own obsessions than with Jean.

But maybe Ellen's pictures were projections, too. Those dark circles under the eyes were Ellen's as much as Jean's. If I had painted my desire, Ellen had painted herself.

But there was still something else. One small drawing taped to the wall—it must have been very recent—caught my eye. It shows Jean standing on a chair in front of one of the big windows, reaching with a watering can toward a hanging plant. It is a delightful drawing, light and airy. Jean is on tiptoes on the seat of the wooden chair, balancing her full belly and maternal breasts delicately as she reaches high to the plant. Her light dress swings with her reach, and the can's spout curves like one of the plant's arching stems. Looking, I realized how little a part of Jean I had been concerned with in my paintings. In my work, she was always "lounging," to use Andrea's word. I had painted her sex and not much else.

In my paintings, Jean is an idea. But in Ellen's drawing she's an individual who lives and suffers and tends to daily things, like the watering of plants. Ellen has taught me more than I've taught her.

John

February 23, 1991
Dear Wyatt,

The letter I wrote yesterday is still lying on the table, unmailed, but I'm so filled with thoughts tonight that I want to write again. I'll send these two together.

Earlier tonight I went to Sammy's, hoping to run into Ron. He was there, sitting at a table with Jerry, and he waved me over. It was about 8:00 and the two of them were drinking beer. Jerry, it seemed, had had quite a bit. He was talking too loudly, going on about Saddam Hussein. "After dealing with that cocksucker all these years, you'd think we'd have somebody close to him," he said. "Some agent willing to strap on his balls and do a job." Ron and I exchanged looks. "I'd volunteer in a minute," Jerry continued. "I'd sit in a rathole Baghdad apartment for weeks if I had to, staking out one of his goddamn hideouts." He shook his head boozily and slumped back in his chair.

Ron turned to me and said, "Did you hear that the ground war's started?" The news sent a bolt of adrenaline through me. "About an hour ago," he said.

I looked up at the TV behind the bar, fully expecting to see flames and black smoke on the screen. I had been reading in the papers about the gauntlet of defenses along the Kuwait border—the sand berms and wire and mines, the ditches filled with oil ready to be lit, the gun configurations and the "killing zones," the poison gas. I felt an awful foreboding. On the television a man was pointing with a stick at a map covered with arrows.

"What are they saying?" I asked.

"Not much, yet," Ron said.

Jerry roused himself. "We're going to kick their butts," he said. Then he stood, walked heavily to another table across the room, and sat down with two other men.

Ron and I watched him go, and I asked, "Is he like this much?"

"Not really," Ron said. "He's hurting pretty bad right now. Did you know that Jean moved out?" I nodded. "He's pretty torn up about it," Ron said.

"Ellen told me there was trouble over the pregnancy," I reported.

"He liked things the way they were, and he didn't want them to change," Ron said. "Before you got here he told me: 'If I'd wanted a threesome, I'd have moved to Utah and got me a goddamn harem.'" I rolled my eyes. "A baby *will* shake things up," Ron continued. "They used to take off in their car at the drop of a hat, go off who knows where for a few days. I can't picture Jerry as a father. And he says he doesn't like to see Jean changing."

We looked at each other and shrugged. Ron shook his head. Then we both turned back toward the TV.

There were more maps and arrows—a lot of speculation, but not much real news. I didn't think I could sit up half the night in a war vigil. I just wasn't ready. My imagination conjured the image of a billowing black cloud, petals of it opening, drawing me down a tunnel of smoke that darkened as it went.

Jerry walked back over and sat down across from Ron without acknowledging my presence. He reached for the pitcher and filled his glass. I told Ron I thought I'd go. He nodded and said good-bye.

Outside, I didn't feel ready to go home. There were places I didn't want to be— Sammy's, where the war loomed over the bar, my apartment, where the walls were closing in further with each winter's day—but where could I go? I walked down the block under the yellow streetlights, opened the familiar door, and climbed the stairs to Ellen's. At the top of the stairs, I stood by her closed apartment door and listened. I didn't hear anything. I knocked on the door softly. There was no answer. I thought I'd seen some light in the studio from down in the street, so I knocked a little more loudly. Still no response. It was only about 9:00 P.M. Where could she be? I realized how little I knew about her life outside the studio. And, suddenly, the only thing I wanted in the world was for Ellen to come to the door and open it.

But what did I want, exactly? I didn't know. I wasn't even thinking that way. I simply felt drawn. Behind the door there was another world, a place where I lost myself in the contours of somebody else. And, sure, I was remembering the evening I'd fallen asleep on her bed and had awakened into that wonderful calm.

I leaned against the door and listened again. There was still no sound. Then, upset, I drew back and kicked the door. A loud boom sounded in the stairway. It startled me, and afraid of being found there, I hurried down the stairs and back out into the empty street.

Back home now, I wonder at my behavior. I'm a mystery to myself. Acts and feelings rise up, unforeseen. It's as though my body is a big house, and I'm living in a small room up in one corner. The other rooms are dark, but there are drafts, noises.

John

February 27, 1991
Dear Wyatt,

Yes, there are quite a few new paintings of different kinds now, but I just want to work ahead for the time being without trying to think of them as a group. I do wonder how they'll look to me this summer, since they've all been done by winter light. And, after the comments on my show in November, it's hard not to think occasionally of how these new paintings might be received. But I really don't brood on that. What you wrote is true: I'll get lost if I try to follow anything other than the logic of my own feelings.

I worked today. Ellen modeled. Jean had stayed home after a doctor's appointment, feeling tired. It had been a while since I'd painted Ellen. For the past several weeks she had been very busy getting her art school applications together. Today was the first time I'd painted her wrapped in the material we've been using. She undressed, slipped into the black fabric, and lay down on the platform. She found a comfortable pose and I knelt over her and arranged the drapery. Then I went to the easel and began to work. In ten minutes she was asleep.

It was a peaceful afternoon. We had a bit of a thaw today, and the windows were clear. A murmur of sounds came through the floor from the café below. I painted Ellen as she slept. I felt marvelously relaxed and free as I worked. I painted without forethought or afterthought, without pursuing any preconceived idea or theme. I just painted what I saw. I suppose it was easier in some ways, painting a sleeping model. There was no freight of interaction. In sleep, Ellen's face was entirely relaxed, with none of that look of scrutiny or interrogation I've come to recognize in it. She must have let down, feeling relieved that her applications were finally in the mail. I felt flattered that she was comfortable enough with me to sleep while I worked. And the painting went well. Her hands lay loose near one another on her chest, white against the black satin. I painted her draped torso, her hands, and her head. She slept soundly, without moving. So lovely, so lovely. I didn't want the afternoon to end.

I worked a long time. Finally Ellen stirred a little and opened her eyes. "I must have slept," she said. It was late afternoon and the light had changed. She stretched herself and sat up.

"I've just finished," I said. "You slept all afternoon."

"Was that okay for you?" she asked.

"Fine," I said. I asked her if she wanted to go get something to eat, but she said she wasn't awake yet, that she thought she'd just have a quiet night at home. So I cleaned my brushes and left.

I went to Sammy's, ate a sandwich, and watched the news. Thank God the war is over.

John

March 2, 1991
Dear Wyatt,

I was awakened in the dark this morning by someone knocking. I rolled over in bed and looked at the clock: 5:00 A.M. I pulled on some clothes, went to the door, and found two policemen on the landing. I turned on the kitchen light and let them in. When they took off their caps I noticed the red stripes across their foreheads. They stood in my kitchen and the taller one asked me if my name was John Ordway. He asked when I'd gotten home and who I'd been with. I said I'd been alone since eating supper downtown and that I'd spent the evening at home. He asked if anyone could vouch for my whereabouts—if I'd gotten any phone calls. I told him I didn't have a phone.

He took a leather glove out of a bag and asked me if I recognized it. It was my glove. He asked if I had the other one. They followed me as I looked through the apartment, but I didn't find it. I told them I hadn't used my gloves for a few days, I hadn't seen them for a while, I sometimes misplaced them. I didn't know how long it had been since I'd last had them. "What is this about?" I asked.

The shorter policeman said: "Someone broke into Ellen Swensen's apartment last night and attacked her. This glove was left behind." They both looked at my hands.

We were in my bedroom, next to the closet. I had to sit down on the bed. I managed to ask: "How is Ellen? Was she hurt?"

"Mr. Ordway," the taller policeman said, "we have a search warrant here. We'll need to search your apartment."

I sat on the bed and watched them go through my closet and drawers. They asked me to get off the bed. They looked under the bedding and mattress. Then they moved to the sitting room and the kitchen. They were very thorough. I assumed they were looking for my second glove, which they didn't find. But they gathered all my sketchbooks and the three paintings that I had in the apartment. They stood by the door with my work under their arms, much of it of Ellen. They told me not to leave town. They said they would need to talk to me again. The taller policeman, the older one, was sweating from his exertions.

I said: "Can you tell me where Ellen is now? I want to see her. I'm very worried about her."

The shorter policeman said: "Under the circumstances, I don't think it would be appropriate for you to see Miss Swensen, Mr. Ordway." I saw judgment in his eyes.

I said: "If you think I did this thing, let me tell you that I work with Ellen. I'm at her apartment nearly every day. I've probably left my gloves there many times."

The shorter policeman held up the glove in his free hand. "This glove was left in Ellen Swensen's mouth, Mr. Ordway. Is that where you left it?" They turned and went out.

I needed to find out what had happened to Ellen. I put on my coat and walked to Ron's house. A third policeman in a car slowly followed me. Ron came to the door in his bathrobe and let me in. I followed him to the kitchen, where he put some water on the stove and got a pitcher of orange juice out of the refrigerator. It was Saturday morning and I'd gotten him up. "What's going on?" he said.

I told him that something had happened to Ellen and that the police had been to my apartment. As I spoke, Iris came in, wrapping her robe around her. She picked up the phone and dialed Ellen's apartment. There was no answer. She called the hospital, but Ellen wasn't there. "I'll get dressed and go over to her mother's house," Iris said, and she went back to the bedroom.

I called Caroline. She had just gotten up and hadn't heard anything. She asked me what I wanted her to do. I told her that I just wanted to find out what had happened to Ellen. She told me to stay at Ron's and she hung up. I heard Iris go out the front door.

For the next three hours I sat with Ron at his kitchen table. He fed me and we talked and I sat quietly while he read the paper. We passed the time the best that we could. When I went to the front window and looked out I saw the policeman sitting in his car across the street.

We moved to Ron's living room and passed another two hours. It was excruciating.

At last, at about noon, Iris and Caroline arrived together. They had met at Ellen's mother's house. Ellen was there and they had spoken to her. Ron and I sat in chairs in the living room. Iris and Caroline sat on the couch. Iris sat up straight with her arms crossed and looked at me steadily while Caroline spoke.

"Ellen is shaken," she said, "but she wasn't badly hurt." I exhaled heavily. "She was in bed, asleep, in the middle of the night. Her door came open and woke her up. There was someone crossing the room in the dark. She froze. She could see a black silhouette standing over her bed. She stayed still and quiet, hoping it was a burglar who would take something and leave. Instead, he stood over her for a long time, then bent toward her. She was going to cry out but a gloved hand came over her mouth. He rolled her facedown on the bed, keeping his left hand over her mouth. With the other hand he ripped her nightgown and got down on top of her. He was pretty rough. She's got some bruises. She's sure he would have raped her, but she struggled and got her mouth open and bit down hard on his hand. The man cried out, jumped up, and ran. He'd pulled his hand out of the glove to get away when she bit him and the glove was left between her teeth." Caroline stopped and sighed.

"John," Iris said, "it was your glove."

"I know," I said. "The policemen showed it to me this morning. They searched my apartment for the other one, but didn't find it. I must have left them somewhere. I may have left them at the studio. The attacker could have picked them up there last night when he got in." I tried not to sound defensive. These are my friends, I told myself. "Thank God Ellen's all right," I said, belatedly.

"Does Ellen have any idea who it was?" Ron asked.

"She couldn't see him," Iris said. "There's only the glove and the mustache."

"Mustache?" Ron said. He shot a worried look at me.

"She felt a mustache against her back when he was on top of her," Iris said.

I began to feel sick in the pit of my stomach. Iris looked at me, then glanced away, out the front window to where the police car was parked.

"That doesn't mean anything," Ron said. "I've got a mustache, too. Hell, half the men in the county wear mustaches—mustaches and feed caps."

Then we all fell silent. No one could think of anything to say.

After a couple of minutes I got up and found my coat. "I should go," I said.

Caroline got up and crossed the room. She stood in front of me and looked me straight in the eyes. "May I stop and see you later?" she asked. I looked at her dark eyes taking me in. She looked at me steadily, almost fiercely. I felt a rush of gratitude. I nodded and went out.

The first thing I noticed when I stepped outside was that there were now two cars—the Delphi police officer had been joined by two county deputies sitting in a marked sheriff's car. All three men got out of their cars as I walked down Ron's sidewalk toward the street. They came straight for me and I stopped. They stood in a line in front of me and one of the sheriff's deputies said, "Mr. John Ordway, we have a warrant for your arrest." He told me my rights, led me to their car, searched me for weapons, and handcuffed me. Then they put me in their backseat and drove me to jail.

I sat, stupefied, behind the wire mesh that separated the front and back seats of the sheriff's car. I looked out the side window at the corn stubble jutting from the wet, black soil. In the ditches brown weeds were matted between piles of dirty snow. I wondered if Ron and the others had been looking out the window and had seen my arrest, or whether they had turned to each other to discuss me as soon as I'd left, so that only the police and the deputies knew where I was. I wondered where Ellen was, how she was, what she thought, what she thought about me. And I simply wondered. I sat there in a state of wonder and disbelief and stared out at the corn stubble, the dead weeds, and the snow.

When we'd been on the road for several minutes the officer who was driving picked up his radio mike and reported in. Then he said to me over his shoulder, "Do you have a lawyer?"

"No," I answered.

"Arrange for assigned counsel, Margaret," the officer said into the mike. And then we were silent for the rest of the drive.

When we reached Decorah the officer steered toward the Winneshiek County courthouse, a tall limestone building topped by a columned tower and a small green dome. The sheriff's office squatted next to it, a square, one-story brick building in the adjacent parking lot. A few steps away, an old, two-storied jail building was stuccoed and painted yellow with white stone caps above the barred windows. When we stopped, the officers let me out of the backseat and directed me to the jail. We entered, walked through a tiny visiting room with a paneled booth, and into a small room with a table and chairs. I was told to sit down and one of the deputies sat across from me. The other stood by the door.

The officer at the door was young, clean-shaven, and strong-jawed. He hadn't spoken at all. The one across from me—the one who had driven—was older, a little heavy, and tired-looking. He rubbed his eyes with the thumb and forefinger of one hand, looked at me, and said: "You're being charged with sexual assault. We're going to ask you some questions. You can have a lawyer here. I suppose you know that already. A public defender has been assigned to your case but you can hire anybody you want to."

"I don't know any lawyers," I said. "I want to talk to the person who's been assigned to me before I answer any questions."

"All right, then," the man said. "We'll book you and you can wait upstairs." He put both hands on the table, pushed himself up, and left the room. The young officer stood silently by the door. He didn't say a word as he stared at the wall somewhere over my right shoulder. Then a woman in a deputy's uniform like the others' came in carrying a book and a Polaroid camera. She took down my name and address and then had me stand against the wall. She took my picture as I held a small plaque with numbers on it in front of my chest. After that, another woman came into the room, identified herself as a nurse, and showed me a piece of paper which she said was a search warrant. "It authorizes me to draw a sample of your blood," she said. "Please roll up your sleeve." She drew some blood and then examined my hands and photographed them.

Then the young officer led me upstairs. The top floor of the building was a single large room with a kind of cage in the middle of it. This cage, in the high-ceilinged room, looked like a picnic basket turned upside down, but woven out of broad strips of steel instead of wicker. There were others in the room in the single narrow corridor that ran around the cage. One of them lay in a bunk hung on the outside of the cage. Everyone turned and looked at me. The deputy put me into the cage and locked the door. The ceiling was low, so I sat on the bunk in the dim space. Light from the windows of the outer corridor came through the small holes between the thick, flat iron strips. The late winter light fell into a stretched checkerboard pattern on the floor.

That was early this afternoon, before my bond hearing. It's evening now, and I'm writing in my cell. I fully intend to call you in just a few minutes. They said I could make a phone call. So writing this all out on paper is unnecessary, I know. It's just that when I'm looking down at the page, writing to you like always, I can almost forget where I am.

John

8

John Ordway
423 River Street
Delphi, Iowa

March 3, 1991

Dear Wyatt,

Thanks for talking with me on the phone yesterday. Your voice was something to hold to. Everything is out of control. These things that are happening—where do they all come from? The lawyer assigned to me—his name's Storley—says I'll probably be out of here later today, as soon as the money arrives and the papers are filled out. I didn't expect you to post bond for me. It's too much. The idea of you becoming involved in all this. And the amount required . . . It's all too much. I'm very sorry. All I can say is thank you.

I'm not sure I could stand another night in here. Last night in this cell . . . The thing's low and dark. If I stand up straight the top of my head is just a few inches from the ceiling. When Storley came to see me for the first time yesterday he asked the deputy: "Why is my client in the tank?" and the deputy said: "Charged with a violent offense. No prior knowledge of the defendant. Standard precaution."

Last night in here I sat on the edge of my bunk and stared down at the front of my shirt. A streetlight shone through a window in the outer wall and came through the woven iron strips of my cell. I stared at the big black and white checks it made on the front of my white T-shirt. I was restless, agitated, and when I moved the squares stretched and distorted, wrapped around my arms and chest. I got up and paced. I looked down at my shirt, arms, and legs as I strode back and forth in the little space. The patches of light and dark rippled over me like a pelt. Thoughts came from a long way off, strange thoughts that flew in and skipped away. I couldn't concentrate and I couldn't rest. I was panting and sweating. My heart skipped a beat and then another beat. I felt light-headed and sat down, but I couldn't sit still. I stood up and paced. "This is only a panic attack," I told myself, but the words had no force. I remembered that I didn't have my medicine with me. Adrenaline crackled in my arms and chest. My lips and fingertips tingled. Then my chest began to ache. "I'm going to have a heart attack," I thought. "I'm having a heart attack right now." I sat down on the bunk and the black and white squares stopped moving, fastened to me. I covered my eyes with my hands. I pressed the heels of my hands into my eyes until I saw sparks. There wasn't enough air. I fell back onto the bunk. The mattress smelled of stale sweat and urine.

"Hey, are you all right?" The voice came from just above my head. "You all right in there?" It was a man in one of the bunks fastened to the outside of my cell. "Are you sick?" the man asked.

"I don't know," I managed.

"Take it easy," he said. "Just take it easy."

I fastened to the sound of his voice and tried to slow my breathing. Deep, slow breaths, I told myself. Just take it easy. I heard the man's voice in my head, replayed it deliberately, over and over. Just take it easy. A low, groaning sound came from outside, like a truck straining up a hill.

I lay in my bunk with my eyes open for a long time, concentrating on breathing slowly and deliberately. When I thought I might be able to sleep I shut my eyes. When I did, the room slipped, like a car swerving on ice, then righted itself. Eventually I must have slept a little.

3/4

I'm back at the apartment now, thank God. The money you wired came through yesterday and Storley had me out of there by early afternoon. He drove me home himself.

You asked on the phone whether I feel well represented. I think Storley's all right. He's very young. I was a little surprised about that when I first met him. His short blond hair was parted neatly on one side. He wore roundish tortoiseshell glasses and a green double-breasted suit. A deputy let me out of my cell and led us down to the room where I'd been examined and photographed. When it was just the two of us, Storley said: "I understand that you've been charged with attempting to rape Ellen Swensen last night in her apartment. How do you intend to plead?"

"I didn't do it," I said.

"All right," Storley said. "I'll need to ask you a few questions. I don't suppose anyone can testify as to your whereabouts at midnight that night?"

"No. I was at home asleep," I said.

"Tell me about the evening."

"I ate supper at Sammy's Bar and Grill in Delphi and watched the news there," I told him. "I went straight home, read, and listened to music. At about 10:30 I went for a short walk in the neighborhood and then went to bed—it must have been about 11:30. The Delphi policemen woke me up when they arrived."

"When had you last seen Ms. Swensen?"

"Ellen models for me. I'm a painter." Storley nodded. He'd been told about me. "I'd last seen her that afternoon in her apartment and we'd worked. She fell asleep while I painted, actually. I left at about 5:00 and went to Sammy's."

"Okay," Storley said. "Now I guess the police talked to you about this matter of the glove. What can you tell me about that?"

"I hadn't had my gloves for a couple of days," I said. "I could have left them anywhere. They could have been at Ellen's apartment. Someone could have picked them up. I misplace them sometimes. It's happened before." My skin felt hot. I knew that wasn't a good answer.   Storley paused. "May I see your left hand?" he said. I put my hand on the table. The middle finger was badly bruised on each side and the skin was torn around the middle and top knuckles. "How did you hurt your finger?" he asked.

"Oh, that," I said. "My hands are always a little dinged up—from stretching canvases, handling the wood I use, and I do some framing."

"But how about this wound," Storley said.

"I was at Ellen's preparing stretcher frames one afternoon last week . . ."

"What day?" Storley interrupted me.

I had to stop and think. "It was Wednesday," I said. "I was hammering together stretcher frames—the rough frames you stretch the canvas over. I was working on the floor and some finished stretchers were leaning against the wall. They're big— four feet by five feet or bigger. I must have bumped them because they tipped and fell. I saw them out of the corner of my eye just before they landed. I jumped back but didn't get my left hand completely out of the way. The pile slammed down and caught my finger."

"These wooden stretchers fell and only injured the middle finger of the left hand, making a crushing wound on both sides? How could that happen?" Storley asked.

"I don't know," I said. "That's just how it happened." I heard the irritation in my voice.

"Was Ellen there?" Storley asked. "Did anyone witness the accident?"

"Ellen was at the library," I said. "I was alone."

Storley gave me a long, doubtful look. He paused, then said, "Blood found in the middle finger of your left glove after the attack on Ellen matches your type. Did you have your gloves Wednesday? Did you wear them after this accident?"

I shook my head. "I'm not sure," I said. "I might have."

Storley leaned forward and put his elbows on the table. "You'll have to think hard about those gloves—when you last wore them, when you lost them, where you may have lost them. It's important. You can see how it looks. There's a wound on your left middle finger, the same finger of your left glove has blood in it that matches your type, and that glove was left between Ellen Swensen's teeth when her attacker fled. You can plead not guilty, but you've got to give me something to work with."

We looked at each other across the table. I tried to read his eyes. Behind the roundish lenses of his glasses, they were a pale blue. His face was almost completely unlined. I guessed he must be twenty-seven or twenty-eight years old. I couldn't tell whether or not he believed me.

Storley went to the door and called in the two officers who had arrested me. With Storley present, they asked me most of the same questions that he had and I gave the same answers. When that was finished, Storley stood up and reached out his hand. I stood and we shook hands. "I'll see you tomorrow afternoon," he said. "There'll be an initial appearance. You'll enter your plea and the judge will set bail. We'll have more to talk about after I've done some work." Then the young officer took me back to my cell.

It was a terrible night, but I've already told you. Now I'm back on the medicine, and that's helped some. Storley says my trial will probably be in late April. I'll keep you informed.

John

March 11, 1991

Dear Wyatt,

I've just gotten back from Earth Day. It was my first day back at work, and Johnson called me into his office. He said he was in the habit of giving his employees the benefit of the doubt and, as far as he was concerned, nothing would change for me before the trial.

Ron has been great, too, but I'm afraid my case has become an obsession for him. He's begun to cruise the county roads and the other little towns in the area two or three evenings a week, looking for that red pickup. The last time I saw him he said:

"I'm racking my brains, John. I'm trying to remember if that guy I saw in the park had a mustache."

The only other person I see outside of work is Caroline. I go to her office twice, sometimes three times a week now. The first time after the attack on Ellen she explained why she hadn't visited me in jail. Sun streamed through the one big window with the wide sill and the flowers. "After the police questioned me," she said, "I realized that I'd be called as a witness in your trial. My testimony could help you, but only if I maintain my professional credibility. Even as a defense witness, I've got to appear neutral—not an advocate for you." I nodded. "And of course that means I can only see you in my office. A prosecutor might try to make something out of visits to your apartment."

"Right," I said. She was leaning forward and there was a note of apology in her voice. She was upset. "What did the police want to know about me?" I said.

"They asked about your medical record, of course. They wanted me to tell them about my evaluation of you here at the hospital last August and they wanted me to talk about your committal to the hospital in Liberty. I reminded them of the client privacy protections but told them I would cooperate in every legal way. I made a point of telling them that, in my view, you were not dangerous."

I looked down at the floor. That she'd had to form a judgment of me—dangerous or not dangerous—made me sag. The weight of suspicion, of judgment, bore down on me. In little shocks, the whole impossible situation was becoming real.

"I can see the way it all adds up for the police," I said. "I'm a relative stranger—from New York City. I've been the subject of talk around town: The woman I'd lived with left me. I lost my first apartment when I burned down a tree in the yard late one night. Then I was hospitalized with a mental disturbance. I've drawn carcasses at the slaughterhouse. And the police have seized my drawings and paintings, most of them nudes of the woman I'm supposed to have assaulted. And—God—my glove was in her mouth!"

I saw Caroline glance at the wound on my hand. A sad, stricken look came into her eyes. And then she flared: "Keep hold of yourself and fight this," she said. "If you know you're innocent you've got to fight this."

That night—in the middle of the night—I woke up in a sweat. The bedding was on the floor except for the sheets tangled around my feet. I'd had a dream. My heart was pounding and I was breathing hard, but I wanted to jump up and run away. The dream hung all around me, still vivid in the room. What did this mean? Did it mean anything? In the dream I'd stood in a big dark room for a long time, leaning with my back against a door. Gradually, as my eyes adjusted, I had seen the bed at the far side and the shape in it. I stood still and looked as the shape moved and a woman sighed in her sleep. I stood still for a long time and it was very quiet. As my eyes continued to adjust I could see the soft glow of dim light that came through the room's big windows. The blond head above the bedding picked up the light and shone a little in the gloom. I reached into my jacket pocket and took out my gloves.

Sitting in the bright kitchen writing to you, now, I'm sure it was just a dream. I'd been told the particulars of the attack. It's easy to imagine—all too easy. It must have been terrible for her. I can't stand the fact that I'm not allowed to see her, to talk to her.

John

March 13, 1991

Dear Wyatt,

Sometimes the prospect of standing trial on a charge of sexual assault overwhelms me. It's a nightmare. It draws me outside myself into the way that others must see me. Yesterday, as I was sitting in Caroline's office talking with her, it struck me so forcibly that I couldn't draw a deep breath. She said I looked gray. I had been telling her how I can imagine what they think—my former landlady Mrs. Tolman, the librarian Mrs. Steegers, the sullen clerk at the gas station, and the others who believe they know something about me. It must all look so clear to them. Seen from the outside, especially after my arrest, it all becomes something other than it is. But now I can see it that way, too, through their eyes, and it makes me unsure of things. At the grocery store yesterday the cashier rang up my purchases silently, then gave me my change, carefully, without touching my hand.

I sat across from Caroline, telling her these things. She said: "You must not let others caricature you." I nodded.

Of course she's right. But sometimes lately I've had to wonder. I'm haunted now more than ever by that awful day in December when I made Ellen cry. If the prosecutor were to ask her if I was always completely professional in my sessions with her, what could she say?

Ron and I go out a couple of evenings a week, cruising the back roads, looking for that red pickup. And I've been back to Decorah for another meeting with Storley. As we drove one night, Ron told me a little more about him. He's a local kid who went to the University of Iowa. He's been back home practicing law for a year, mostly court-assigned cases. Not much experience, certainly, but he seems smart enough. His office is a room in a renovated brick house across from the courthouse, and as I sat across from him he leaned back and rested his head against the bookshelves behind him.

"I've been doing some work," he said. "The people who live downstairs in your house heard you go out for your walk and come back at 11:30. They didn't hear anything the rest of the night. That's good, but it's still not an alibi. We can't establish an alibi—you live alone and you've got no telephone, so you certainly weren't with anybody or talking to anybody at midnight Friday night." I nodded. "Do you know of anyone who might have done this thing—a jealous boyfriend, any creep hanging around, anybody who's made any sort of comment to you about Ellen Swensen?"

I thought for a minute, then shook my head. "I can ask around," I said.

Storley continued: "The stuff the prosecutors will offer about your 'character' is meaningless, all that circumstantial stuff about your hospitalization and the fact that you paint Ellen nude. All they've really got—the only thing that gives the rest of it any weight—is your glove in Ellen's mouth the night of the attack." He leaned forward over the desk, propped his head in his hands, and said: "Tell me again about the gloves. You've got to remember something."

I sighed. "I'm sorry. I just can't think of the last time I had them. It's not the kind of thing I pay attention to. I tend to leave them places for days at a time—at Ron's, at the studio. One time in January I lost them for about a week. Then, paying for some gas at the Standard station, I saw them stacked neatly on the glass countertop by the cash register, and claimed them. The guy down there—Sarge—was real nice about it."

Storley closed his eyes and shook his head. Then he tipped back in his chair, took a deep breath, and looked at me again. "We *could* have the blood in the glove DNA-tested. If it turns out to be somebody else's blood, you'd be acquitted. But you've told me there's a chance you wore the gloves again after the accident that injured your finger. It could be your blood, even if you didn't assault Ellen. And the prosecutor has the right to the results, even if we run the tests. You see what I'm getting at?"

I nodded. "The test could come back looking like solid evidence against me." I gazed to my left, out the front window, toward the courthouse across the street.

"Yeah," Storley said. "It's a risk—a double-edged sword. And expensive." I looked at him. "With the testing and the expert witness, it could come to something like $4,000. And the state's not going to do it. They feel like they've already got their case and they won't want to gamble on a test that could mess it up."

"Well, that settles it." I shook my head. "I don't have the money. And, if there's a chance the test could hurt me, anyway . . ."

Storley stood up behind his desk and held out his hand. "Look, I'll do the best I can for you," he said, but his voice sagged and there was no light in his eyes. Before I left he told me that the trial date had been set: May 1.

John

March 16, 1991

Dear Wyatt,

It's not a dream, really—more of a reverie. I'm on the witness stand. My paintings are hung on the courtroom walls, all the way around. The prosecutor is gesturing at them with an outstretched arm, a kind of leer on his face. He's asking me what these paintings are about, what they're for, though it's clear that he thinks he already knows. Ellen is sitting somewhere behind him, among the other townspeople, her face hidden in her hands. Andrea is in the back row, observing.

This is my chance. If I can just find the words, they will understand. Surely they have some knowledge—some memory—of beauty, desire, pleasure. I have to make them see.

I make a speech. It goes on for a few minutes. When I finish I look out at the people in the courtroom. They are sitting still, perfectly quiet, looking back at me. I can't tell what they're thinking.

Then I start again at the beginning, replaying the reverie like a tape. I come again to my speech, which seems, somehow, the key to my defense. I speak again, revising as I go, keeping some phrases, trying new ones. Over and over I repeat the scene, fiddling and polishing, perfecting my defense of the paintings. If I can make the people in the courtroom see . . .

It's a foolish dream. But late at night or in the middle of an empty afternoon, the mind goes where it wants to go.

John

March 18, 1991

Dear Wyatt,

I worked at Earth Day until 2:00 today, then went to Caroline's office. At work, it's been hard to tell how much Rich and Kevin and the rest know about what's going on with me. Most of the talk last week was about Linda coming home from the hospital. She's back at the house and doing well, but hasn't returned to work yet. She needs to rest some more and get stronger.

There's been no talk of my arrest. And I never have known how much they know about my painting. Today, though, after lunch, I was helping Rich bundle newspapers and magazines. He came to a box of old Penthouse magazines, opened one, and held it up to show me. He got a crooked smile on his face and his mustache twitched. "Hey, John," he said. "What do you think of this?"

I shook my head. I must have looked grim.

"What's the matter?" he said. "I thought you liked it." He sat down on the floor and began to page through the magazines. I turned back to my bundling and stacking.

In a few minutes he finished, stacked the magazines neatly, tied them with twine, and heaved them onto the recycling pile. I added a bundle of my own to the same pile, and he reached over and slapped me on the back. When I turned he flashed me that same crooked smile, and gave me a wink of comradeship with his good eye. The other glided eerily to the left.

I looked at the floor and stood still. I didn't know how to respond. Finally, overcome with sadness, I put my arms around him and patted him on the back with both hands. Then I stepped back and said, "It's time for me to go. I'll see you tomorrow."

At Caroline's office this afternoon I wanted to discuss my encounter with Rich, but she cut me off. She was uncharacteristically directive. There was something on her mind. "Do you think about your trial, John?" she asked. I told her that I did, of course, all the time. "And what do you think about it?" she said.

I started to tell her about my reverie, but she cut me off again. "No, I mean your real trial, not some imagined version of it. Have you thought about what could happen?"

I said: "Yes, sometimes I picture myself sitting in jail, guilty. But I try not to dwell on that." She took a deep breath and gave me a level look.

"But John, your trial," she said, "are you prepared for it?"

"It all seems so unreal," I said. "Part of me still doesn't believe this is happening.

But I'm trying to prepare myself." She shifted in her chair. I had made her impatient. She leaned forward and spoke quietly, but urgently.

"John, I'm not talking about your trial as something to be coped with. I'm talking about it as something that is going to happen to you, something that could go one way or another, depending on how you and your lawyer prepare for it. I've talked to Storley," she said. "You're not giving him much to work with."

"What have I *got* to work with?" I said. I felt stung and my voice was rising. "I don't remember where I left the goddamn gloves!"

She sat back in her chair and took another deep breath. She turned her head and looked out the window. The icicles outside were dripping and shrinking. Then she looked back at me. "If I can help you in any way . . ." Her voice trailed off.

When I left I felt empty. I had disappointed her. I was like the insurance man, staring down at his buttons and his newly awkward, unrecognizable hands. The shame burned in. I've got to do something.

John

March 21, 1991
Dear Wyatt,

It's late, past midnight. I'm writing at the kitchen table. When Ron got off work this evening I rode with him as he cruised the county again, looking for the red pickup.

We drove the back roads south of Delphi, slowing near farmhouses to scan the vehicles. The sky was gray over the narrow asphalt and gravel roads. The weather has turned mild, with highs in the 40s and 50s, so most of the snow has melted. Brown weeds, uncovered by the thaw, lay matted in the ditches. The fields were muddy around the rows of corn stubble. The landscape made me think of a patient with the bandages just removed after a terrible surgery.

We're doing a systematic search, taking the county section by section. Ron's pretty sure the pickup carried Winneshiek County plates, but he had no reason to take down the number when he saw it last summer.

Near sundown, we were on a gravel road that humped up and down over rolling hills. Thawing fields contoured the tops and sides of the hills, while gray trees filled the small creek valleys between. The farmhouses here were close to the road. Yard dogs chased us past the properties, barking frantically. When we approached a yellow farmhouse, Ron slowed. No red pickup. We drove on. "The sheriff says they're looking for this guy, too, but I don't know," Ron said. "I feel like I'm being humored."

"Well, they've made an arrest and they're building a case," I said. "They think I'm their man." Ron nodded.

"Is Storley doing any investigating?" Ron asked.

I told him he was. Ron looked at me, then back out the windshield. He was quiet for a minute, then said: "Without other suspects, their case against you looks pretty strong."

I nodded. "What about boyfriends?" I asked. "Does Ellen have any old boyfriends around who might have gotten upset about her posing for me?"

Ron gazed out the windshield. "I don't know," he said. "I can give you a couple of names, but I don't think they . . ." His voice trailed off. Then he gave me two names and I wrote them down.

We rode for a while without speaking. Then I said: "I appreciate all the time you're spending on this, Ron."

"It's important," Ron said.

"Well," I said, "I hope Iris doesn't mind that you're away like this so much."

"Things are tense, anyway," he said. "Iris is very loyal to Ellen, you know." I nodded. What he'd said grieved me. But at the same time, I wasn't sorry he had a personal stake in trying to help me. He was also trying to help himself. Somehow, it put me less in his debt.

The rest of the evening we saw three red pickups. One of them made Ron stop and look hard, but it wasn't the one he'd seen at Redding's Spring. We rounded back to Delphi after dark. When we pulled up to my apartment I recognized the unmarked police car parked across the street and the officer sitting inside. I said good-bye to Ron and went upstairs.

I made myself a late supper, ate it, and washed the dishes. I turned the radio on and sat at the kitchen table. In a few minutes I got up, tuned in a new station, and looked out the window to the street. The car was still there. I got a beer out of the refrigerator and drank it, standing by the sink. I changed stations on the radio. I drank another beer. It was about 10:30.

I turned off the kitchen light and went to the bedroom, changed into my black jeans, and pulled a black sweatshirt on over my T-shirt. In the middle room I turned on the reading lamp next to the red couch. Back in the kitchen, I went to the door, opened it, and stepped onto the landing without turning on the outside light. I went down the steps slowly, staying close to the side of the house. When I stopped at the bottom of the stairs and looked across the street, I thought I could see the policeman's head tipped forward, his chin on his chest. I turned under the stairs and moved along the side of the house to the backyard. I cut through the yard of the house behind mine, reached the next street, and started across town, staying in the shadows.

I had no plan, but I knew where I was going. After twenty minutes of walking, I found the block where Ellen's mother lives. In the middle, behind the houses, an alley cut through, running past detached garages and untilled garden plots. It was about 11:00 and there weren't many lights on in the houses. I went up the alley in the dark.

It was hard to pick out the right house from the back, but I found it—the third one in, on the left. A stepping-stone path ran from a garage that faced the alley to the back of the house. A large pine in the backyard provided cover. A back porch was in shadows. The room off the porch was brightly lit and someone was in it.

I stayed close to the garage, moved under the pine, and made my way to the steps of the porch. I could see into the room now, through the glass of the door and two adjacent windows. It was the kitchen. The person inside was Ellen. She was standing at the stove, her back to me, stirring something in a saucepan. Very quietly, I took the three steps onto the porch and moved across it to the door. Ellen kept stirring, staring down into the pan.

Now what? Here I was. She was just across the room. The rest of the house was dark and Ellen's mother, no doubt, was upstairs, asleep. I'd had tremendous luck. But how could I get her attention without startling her? If I knocked lightly on the door and she saw it was me, would she be frightened? At that moment, looking at her, I couldn't believe that Ellen really thought I'd been the one. I thought there must be a part of her that wanted to see me as badly as I wanted to see her—to clear up this mess. There had to be a way. I stood on the dark porch, looking through the pane of glass at Ellen standing in her mother's kitchen.

She was wearing white tights and a gray sweatshirt. She stood on one leg, with the right one lifted and bent, the raised foot resting against the left knee. She looked down and stirred. After a minute, she turned off the burner, stood down on both feet, reached a cup to her right, and poured hot chocolate out of the pan and into the cup. As she raised the cup to blow it cool, she turned around and leaned against the counter. Quickly, I stepped back away from the door.

She seemed to be looking right at me, but blankly. I stood still in the shadows of the porch. I didn't know if I was visible. I was afraid to move, to draw her attention. But, at the same time, I wanted her to see me, wanted her gaze gradually to focus and calmly take me in.

She held the cup in both hands, blowing across it. Then she raised her right foot and braced it against her left knee. She took a few sips. I thought hard. What did I have to lose? Everyone already thought I was guilty.

Her hands on the cup were small and delicate. Something like yearning moved through me. I gradually raised my right hand in a sign of greeting. She sipped at the cup and looked blankly into the dark porch. I took a slow step forward.

Ellen screamed and both of her arms flew up. The cup fell to the floor and burst. I turned and ran.

I ran all the way across town, through my backyard, and crept up the stairs to my apartment. I stood panting in my dark kitchen and looked out the window to the car across the street. It hadn't moved.

I was streaming with sweat. I pulled off the sweatshirt and tried to get my breathing under control. Then I heard a car door slam and looked out the window. The officer was crossing the street, walking toward my stairs. I ran to the bathroom and toweled the sweat off my face. I took deep breaths to slow my breathing. I kicked off my shoes, which were muddy from the run across town. I heard a knock at the door.

On my way through the sitting room, where the lamp was on, I picked up a book and opened it. I went into the kitchen and turned on the light, then answered the door.

The officer stood on the landing. He looked like he'd been sleeping, but he was edgy now, shifting his weight from foot to foot. "Mr. Ordway," he said. There was a pause. He didn't seem to know what to say. Finally he said: "I got a radio call asking me to speak to you." I forced myself to breathe slowly and evenly. "Have you been at home all evening?" he asked.

"Yes," I said. "I've been here since about 9:00, and you've been parked across the street the whole time." We faced each other. He looked me up and down. Holding the book open in one hand, I rubbed my eyes with the other. Finally he nodded, turned, and started down the stairs. "Good night, then," he said, over his shoulder.

3/22

When I got home from Earth Day at about 2:00 today Storley was sitting in his car out front, waiting for me. I invited him in and we sat down across the kitchen table from one another. He was excited.

"Somebody was creeping around Ellen Swensen's house last night," he said. "She called the police. They went over and talked to her. She couldn't give much of a description—it had been too dark—but they know it wasn't you because they had your apartment staked out."

"I know," I said. "The policeman came up and talked to me."

"That's great," said Storley. He was very animated. "They must have radioed him when they got Ellen's call. I've already filed a motion for dismissal, which Judge Haugen will deny, but this is a tremendous break."

I stood and went to the stove. "Do you want a cup of tea?" I asked.

"No thanks," he said. He didn't want to be distracted. "We can get reasonable doubt now. Here's our case: You can testify that you don't remember about your gloves, that you often lose them. I can call Sarge Elton to tell the court about the time you left them at his Standard station for a week. We can say that anybody could have picked them up, someplace around town or right in Ellen's apartment the night of the break-in." He stared across the room as he spoke, concentrating, gesturing with both hands.

"To suggest that almost anybody could have attacked Ellen, I'll call a few witnesses to show that your paintings were widely discussed in town, that it was common knowledge that she was modeling nude for you in her apartment." A smile was forming on his face. "There are people who will say that Ellen was getting a certain kind of reputation, the kind of reputation that might attract attention." He looked at me to see if I was following him. I stared back from across the room.

"After the break-in and attack, the police charge you and put you under surveillance. But the perpetrator can't stay away. He comes back and peeks through a window, scares her half to death. And the *police* have to testify that it wasn't *you*. *They* give you your alibi on the Peeping Tom incident." He was tipped back in his chair, now, grinning at me.

"What's the matter?" he said. I wasn't smiling back.

"You're going to attack Ellen's reputation?" I said.

"*I'm* not going to attack it," he said. "I'm just going to establish that, in some people's minds, she *had* one." I looked down. "We've got to give the jury a reason why it could have been anybody," he said.

"I understand," I said. "I just don't like the idea."

"Well, I'm sorry you don't like it," he said. "It happens to be the way you're going to be acquitted. And it happens to be the truth." He stood, crossed the room, and patted me on the shoulder. "I'll talk to you again in a few days," he said, then turned and left.

Before today I could think of myself as "innocent." My lawyer wants to bring Ellen's "reputation" into the courtroom. Her modeling gave people ideas about her. If I didn't attack her myself, my paintings made her a target. They gave her a reputation that made somebody else go after her. And Storley will make the other man real for the jury by using that unidentified figure—me—looking in at her from the dark porch.

John

9

John Ordway
423 River Street
Delphi, Iowa

March 24, 1991

Dear Wyatt,

When I close my eyes I see Ellen's face taut with fear and the small explosion of glass and liquid at her feet. I know I'm guilty. I just don't know what I'm guilty of. This weekend I've given a lot of thought to my trial. And finally, this afternoon, I felt I had to talk to Caroline. I wanted her counsel before I spoke to Storley again. I was frustrated that it was Sunday. I was worked up and didn't think I could wait until Monday to see her at her office. So, late this afternoon I took my bicycle out for a ride.

During the day, the police make only a halfhearted effort to keep an eye on me. They don't post the car across from my apartment until evening. But, to be safe, I went on a long, circuitous ride, then hid my bike in some bushes at the foot of Quarry Hill and took a small hiking path to the top where Caroline's house sits alone, overlooking the town.

Caroline and her husband had cleared the lot and built the house soon after they were married. Ron had told me about it, but I'd never been there. The trail through low brush and pines was muddy, but passable. It opened into a sloping yard that ran up to Caroline's house—a small, modern house with a deck and lots of glass overlooking the town. Stepping-stones led around to the left where a gravel driveway circled next to the front door. I stepped up and rang the bell, hoping Caroline wouldn't be angry with me.

She opened the door, her eyes widened, and she said: "John! Is it safe?" I told her I'd been careful, and she hustled me into the house, saying, "Come in! Come in! Quickly."

Inside, I looked to my right into a large, open room that was all windows on one side. A small couch and two chairs were arranged around a low table. Caroline led me to the chair facing the view over the river and town. She sat across from me in the other chair and leaned forward, anxious. "Do you think this is wise?" she said. "If someone saw you . . . I'm thinking of the trial."

"That's what I want to talk to you about," I said. "I've been thinking. Perhaps I should plead guilty."

She sat up straight, something like fear coming up in her eyes. "What are you telling me?" she said.

I realized she thought I was saying I had done it—that I had attacked Ellen— and alarm jolted through me. "No, no!" I said. "I mean, if I plead guilty there won't be a messy trial. I'm thinking of Ellen. My lawyer is going to say she brought on the attack by posing for me."

Caroline relaxed and eyed me, appraisingly. Behind her, through the windows, the town was spread out under a gray sky. "Well, that's very noble," she said. I heard skepticism in her voice. She paused, then said, "Is this really about sparing Ellen?"

"I just don't want to cause any more trouble," I said. "In a way, maybe I *am* guilty. I don't know how to think about the paintings anymore."

She had a ready answer for this. It was as though I'd stepped through a trip wire. "The trial isn't about your paintings, John. It's about somebody breaking into Ellen's apartment and trying to rape her. You may want to speculate back through endless chains of cause and effect to find out where you fit in. And you may want to look at your paintings in the light of all this. But I don't think you attacked Ellen, and I want to know who did.

"I'm sorry," she continued. "This trial isn't only about you. It's about trying to find out what really happened—for all of us. If you're thinking about Ellen, think how safe she'll be if you plead guilty and the man who attacked her is still out there."

She spoke evenly, but I glimpsed how frightened and angry she was. "I'm talking to you as a friend now," she said. "You haven't thought through the consequences—for yourself or anyone else. You've got to wake up a little. Sometimes I want to shake you."

I stood and walked to the windows. The river, curving near the base of Quarry Hill, ran high with snowmelt. Beyond it, the houses stretched away in lines toward the small cluster of businesses. On a far hill, the limestone spire of St. Paul's rose out of bare trees. Caroline came and stood beside me. She nodded toward the town. "These days, when I'm walking or driving, I'll see a man with a mustache and think, 'Is he the one?'" She paused. "These are people I know. That's not what life here is supposed to be like."

We looked at each other and I nodded. We stood quietly for a minute, staring out over the town.

Finally I said: "I had an awful thought the other day." She looked up at me but I didn't turn. "I was bundling magazines with Rich. He showed me a centerfold, slapped me on the back, that kind of thing. When he grinned at me, all I could see was his mustache. Since then, I've wondered what he knows about my work, what it makes him think, and what kinds of ideas he might have formed about Ellen." I shook my head and took a breath. "I really don't think he'd do anything like that, but the nagging doubt feels terrible."

I looked at Caroline. Her face was lined with worry. "Yes, that's troubling," she said. "I don't know. There's really no reason to suspect him." Her voice trailed off.

I tried to change the subject. "Ron and I are still driving the county, looking for that red pickup."

Caroline looked up. "Well," she sighed, "talk to Storley. Make sure he's asked Ellen if she can think of anyone else." We stood for a minute. Then she went to the small couch and sat down facing the windows.

I told myself that I should get back to my apartment before the police showed up. Off to the right, the sun was about to sink behind the limestone palisades that border the town on one side. The river below them was already in deep shadow. Inside, the light in the lovely, high-ceilinged room was starting to dim. But I didn't want to leave. I went to my chair and sat down.

We both sat quietly for a while. Caroline was lost in worried contemplation. I gazed around the room, admiring the high bookshelves on the walls adjacent to the big windows. After a few minutes, Caroline came back to herself and said, "I think I'll make myself a drink. Would you like something?" I told her I'd have whatever she was having, and she went up the four wide steps behind me to another level of the house. In a minute she called out, "Is a whiskey sour all right?" I said it was.

I heard the sound of ice cracking and cupboards opening and closing, then Caroline returned, handed me my drink, and sat down again on the couch to my right. We sipped and gazed out the windows. "This is very nice," I said. "Does it help you think?"

"What do you mean?" she said.

"Sitting here in this room on a hill, with your view over the town," I said. "There's such a feeling of calm and detachment—a sense of 'overview.' Does it lift you out of the welter?"

"I hadn't thought of it that way," she said. "It is relaxing to look out at evening."

"You like it here, don't you?" I said.

"In this house?" she asked.

"The house is wonderful," I said. "But I meant in Delphi."

"Yes." There was no ambiguity in her tone, but she paused. "It was supposed to be different, though. Downstairs, off my bedroom, there's a study where Terry was going to work. And there's a child's room. I planned a life here that didn't happen."

I nodded. "My plans haven't exactly worked out here, either," I said. As soon as I spoke the comparison seemed foolish. I shot a worried glance in her direction. At first I thought she was starting to cry. Then I saw, to my surprise, that she was trying to stifle a laugh. In a moment she *was* laughing—quietly, and she was still trying to resist it—but clearly she was laughing.

"What is it?" I said.

"I'm sorry," she said. "It just struck me as funny." She couldn't stop. "Here we are, two tragic figures, sipping whiskey sours and gazing out over the cruel world."

I adopted a mock-serious tone: "How can you laugh at a time like this? I could go to jail!" Perversely, this made her laugh harder. I'm sure she wasn't drunk. She laughed at me and I grinned back.

"I'm going to take offense in a minute," I said. This made her double over, and I laughed out loud with her, though I don't know why.

"I'm really sorry," she managed, composing herself. She shook her head, smiling at me.

"It feels good to laugh," I said.

Then neither of us could think of anything to say. We lapsed into a silence that was uncomfortable at first. Then the discomfort eased. And then the silence deepened—into a kind of brooding. We looked out the window and finished our drinks, alone with our own thoughts.

Finally I stood up. "I'd better go," I said.

She stood and walked with me to the door.

"You probably shouldn't come here again," she said. "I have to remember my professional ethics."

I looked at her. "Now *I'm* going to laugh," I said, then realized it was a mistake. She didn't smile. "We can break off the appointments," I said. "I'd rather see you here, as a friend."

"Not before the trial," she said.

I paused. I knew she was right. I nodded and turned to the door.

"Normally, I'd turn on the outside lights for you," she said. "But maybe I should leave them off this time."

"Yes, I'd better sneak out like a scoundrel," I said. We both smiled.

She reached up and put her hand on my shoulder. "Be careful," she said.

She let me out, and I found my way through her yard and back down the slippery trail. I pulled my bike from the bushes and rode home through the dark. On the way, I decided there was no need to hide my arrival from the policeman across the street. What did it matter as long as he had no way of knowing where I'd been?

John

March 27, 1991

Dear Wyatt,

I had a surprise visitor today. I was sitting at the picnic table behind Earth Day, eating my lunch with the others, enjoying the mild weather. I was eating my sandwich and listening to Rich and Kevin argue the merits of plastic milk jugs versus paper cartons when a big blue station wagon came to a stop across the street. August Stortz, the butcher, stepped out and walked straight over. I stood to greet him and he announced that he'd come to see me. He said he wanted to ask me something.

I took him inside to the room where I keep the records and we sat down on folding chairs. I couldn't imagine what was on his mind. "I understand you're a pretty good painter," he said. "You sell paintings in New York City, somebody told me." I shrugged at the compliment.

"Well," he continued, "I wondered if you might be interested in painting a picture of my family. There's me and Ruth and our daughter, Emmie. Then there's her husband, Tom, and their little girl, Tracy. Five in the whole group. Now, I don't know what you'd charge. Maybe I can't afford you. But, on the other hand, I thought maybe these days you could use the work."

I looked into his clear, blue eyes. He regarded me steadily, patiently, awaiting my reply. He knew, of course, about my upcoming trial. Everyone did. He would know, too, that I'm not able to paint now in the downtown studio with my usual models. But there was nothing of opportunism in his proposal. This was an offer of work at a time when I badly needed it. And we barely knew one another. I had sketched at his slaughterhouse maybe half a dozen times over the winter. It sounds quaint to put it this way, but I was touched. "I would be proud to paint your family," I said.

He asked about the length and number of sittings that would be required and we discussed the money involved. He was straightforward, businesslike, sensible. We quickly and easily came to terms that suited both of us, then stood and shook hands. I walked out with him, he said good-bye, and he left. And as the station wagon pulled away I found myself gazing after him with a feeling something close to wonderment. What an inexplicable kindness! For the rest of the day the air around me has been sweetened by the unexpected gesture.

John

P.S. *I've begun to taper off my medication again. I'm determined to get off and stay off. It's too complicated to explain. I suppose it's a symbol of health for me.*

J.

March 31, 1991
Dear Wyatt,

Easter Sunday night. Rich insisted on taking me to church this weekend—Friday night and this morning—and I feel like I've been through a pageant. After Ash Wednesday, I'd gone with the group to some other Wednesday night services. They had seemed routine and dull. Mostly I remember the smell of homemade soup drifting up from the church basement. There were meals for the congregation after the service, and Rich, Kevin, Patty, and I would go downstairs together, pass through the line for our soup, bread, and pie, and sit and eat at the corner table off at the edge of things where they felt most comfortable. Compared to what I usually eat, the food was wonderful: I remember the meatball-vegetable soup with the fragrant broth I'd been sniffing upstairs while the pastor took strange, mysterious Bible passages and methodically boiled them down to platitude and cliché. I ate hungrily, relishing in particular the cut pieces of flat green beans that probably had been canned out of somebody's garden. When I got to the bottom of the bowl I imitated Rich, mopping up the last drops with thick slices of white bread smeared with butter. Then there was homemade pie with fillings made out of the fruit put up in somebody's freezer—blueberry or raspberry, it was hard to choose. I read somewhere that Lent was a season of fasting and self-examination, but I looked forward to those Wednesday nights for the aromas rising through the floor of the sanctuary, then the good, simple food afterward. I was glad, one night a week, not to eat alone.

The Good Friday service was later in the evening, there was no meal, and the church was different. We walked into a dimmed sanctuary and took our customary places at the back. Most of the light was from eight candles in the front, a large one at one side and seven smaller ones at the other. The big cross on the wall behind the altar was draped with a black cloth. Linda was with us for the first time, wearing a simple dress with the right sleeve pinned up. She sat on my left, then Kevin and Rich and Patty.

When a somber organ prelude ended, we stood for the opening hymn. There were only a few others scattered in small groups through the darkened church. I guess it wasn't a very popular service. With so few voices, the hymn echoed weakly off the walls and empty pews:

> Well might the sun in darkness hide
> And shut its glories in,
> When God, the mighty maker, died
> For his own creatures' sin.

When we finished and sat down I squinted in the dim light at the crucifixion scene on the cover of the bulletin. It was the reproduction of an oil painting—probably from the seventeenth century—but I didn't recognize it. It looked Spanish. The ghastly body on the cross hung almost inert. It made me think of one of those carcasses hoisted in chains down at Stortz's slaughterhouse.

There were prayers, some readings, and then another hymn. The small congregation sang:

> Deep were his wounds, and red
> On cruel Calvary,
> As on the Cross he bled
> In bitter agony.

As the others sang, I sat still, suddenly conscious of Linda's empty sleeve hanging next to me, just touching my shoulder. It must have been hot in the church. I was starting to sweat. And I felt restless, agitated. I could see why the church was mostly empty. The gloom and the ghastly Good Friday imagery were genuinely troubling. The sensational crucifix on the bulletin cover and the words of the hymn called up some of the most difficult things I'd seen in the past months—war pictures from television, slaughterhouse scenes, Linda bloody on the floor of the Earth Day loading dock. My God! What a thing to be a body in this world!

The hymn had ended and the pastor was speaking now, his face illuminated by the large candle in front of the lectern. I tried to listen. He was reading the seven things Jesus said from the cross, one by one, and commenting on them. After each brief meditation, an acolyte extinguished one of the small candles that burned next to the altar. The church grew slowly darker. It was powerfully distressing. I felt a tightness in my throat and was conscious of my heart—that fist-sized muscle—flexing and flexing in my chest.

Ending one of his meditations, the pastor quoted another hymn: "May we in our guilt and shame, still thy love and mercy claim, calling humbly on thy name: Hear us, holy Jesus." There was a shuffling sound to my left and a deep, audible sigh. Startled, I peered over and saw Rich leaning forward, his face in his hands. I looked at Kevin and Patty, who sat on each side of him, but neither was reacting. Strangely, they just sat quietly and looked straight ahead.

At last the pastor said, "Father, into Your hands I commend my spirit," and the last of the seven candles was put out. Then the acolyte walked over, picked up the large candle in front of the lectern, and carried it down the middle aisle and out of the sanctuary. We sat in the quiet church in near-total darkness. I could just make out the form of the pastor as he moved to the altar, turned his back to us, and bowed his head beneath the black-draped cross. All around, the tall, colored windows glowed faintly.

Then a loud bang made me jump. It had come from the front of the church and sounded like someone dropping a big book or slamming it shut. I looked around, but no one else was reacting. Then I heard Rich sob out loud, over and over. Everyone heard him, I'm sure. I looked over in the darkness and saw his hands gripping the back of the pew in front of him. He leaned forward, his forehead on his hands, and his back heaving up and down. My heart beat wildly. A voice in my head sounded like it was coming from a great distance, repeating "Oh no. Oh no." I sat rigid in my place.

Kevin and Patty each had an arm around Rich, now, patting him on the back. The other groups made their way slowly out of the dark church, leaving us alone. In the quiet, Rich's sobbing was the only sound. I looked over at him, feeling stricken and helpless. One terrible thought gripped me hard, but I didn't know what I should do. Somehow, for me to acknowledge Rich's outburst seemed dangerous. I didn't know where it might lead.

In a few minutes, Rich managed to compose himself and we stood to go. I stepped, shaken, into the aisle and turned to let the others file out ahead of me. Linda took Kevin's hand and they walked out together. Rich, his shoulders hunched and his head down, stepped by me without looking up and walked heavily away. To my surprise, Patty stepped up and took my arm, so we walked side by side out of the sanctuary, through the vestibule, and down the wide stairs into the night air. The others had turned toward my car, which was parked about half a block away, but Patty stopped. I looked down at her. In the corner streetlight I saw her round eyes swimming up through the thick lenses.

"Don't worry," she said. "He's just like that. He cried last year, too." I stood for a moment, looking down into her broad, square face. I felt as though I had just heard the pronouncement of a sibyl, but surely she didn't know what I'd been thinking about Rich. Then her mouth stretched at its edges into a kind of smile. She was trying to comfort me. She didn't want Rich's emotion to upset me. I tried to smile back, then we turned and went to the car.

No one spoke on the ride home. When we reached their house, I promised to pick them up Sunday morning, as we had planned. They got out and trudged silently up the driveway. The porch light came on and I saw Barbara swing the door open to let them in.

I drove to the phone booth next to the Shell station and tried to call Caroline. When there was no answer I remembered that she'd told me she was going to be out of town until Sunday. I didn't want to talk to Storley yet about my growing suspicions of Rich or how I should or shouldn't act on them, so I went home and kept to myself that night and all day Saturday.

When Linda, Kevin, Patty, and Rich filed back down the driveway Sunday morning and got into my car, they were wrapped in pastels and a cloud of colognes and perfumes. Patty's dress was pink with a white flower pattern on it. Linda wore a light green skirt and a white blouse with flowers stitched into the front. Kevin and Rich both had on white shirts, and their shoes were polished. Rich even wore a tie—a wide, blue one with big, gold Greek-looking jugs. The jugs were tipped and gold water poured from one to the next down the length of the tie. When everyone was settled I rolled down my window and started across town. The morning was bright and mild, and the four of them chattered serenely about flowers and chocolate. Friday night's gloom had completely vanished.

We had to park two blocks away from the church. People were streaming into it from all directions. When we stepped inside, we could barely squeeze into our usual places in the back pew. In front of us, there were little girls in their puffed sleeves and white straw bonnets. The whole congregation looked scrubbed and polished. Even some of the old men had exchanged their brown suits for sports coats in country club colors like light blue or aqua. In front, the black cloth was gone from the cross, and in its place dozens of real lilies were somehow fastened all over its trunk and cross beam. More white lilies crowded the altar and the stairs leading up to it. I blinked at the brightness of everything. I'd never been in the church in daylight before.

Trumpets sounded from the balcony and everyone stood up and sang a jubilant hymn. The music pumped up the packed church like an overinflated tire—the air was taut with it. As everyone sang, the pastor came down the middle aisle, led by acolytes carrying banners with sewn pictures on them: a lamb in a crown, an open book, a rock split in two by a plant sprouting. When the singing stopped, the pastor stood in front and proclaimed, "He is risen!" and the congregation shouted back, "He is risen, indeed!"

I had not realized Christianity is so pagan. The blood sacrifice had been accomplished. And now the morning unfolded as a festival for a dead and miraculously risen god—a kind of Osiris or Adonis. The pastor talked in his sermon about "the death of death" and "the new body." And, inevitably, after nearly six months of hard winter in this little farming community, he spoke about the ground thawing and a buried seed cracking open in spring.

I looked down the row at Linda, Kevin, Rich, and Patty. Their faces almost glowed. Even Linda, who still looked pale much of the time, was bright and vivid this morning. The flowers on the front of her blouse were red tulips.

The service was celebratory all the way through, with lots of music. And when it was over, the trumpets played a recessional filled with fanfares as we spilled out onto the greening grass of the church grounds and milled about in the sun. In the crowd, August Stortz came up to me, pumped my hand, said "Good morning," and introduced me to his family. He reminded me that our first sitting was coming soon, and I promised not to forget. Then I saw Caroline and made my way over to her.

When she saw me approaching she smiled broadly and waved. She looked so bright, so cheered by the holiday, that when I got to her I couldn't bring myself to mention what was on my mind. And, besides, Jean was with her. I was glad to see them both. I hadn't seen Jean for something like five weeks and I was taken aback at how big she'd gotten. Jean's belly was astonishingly full and round under a light blue dress and her dark hair was brushed straight back, shining in the sun. The due date is about three weeks off and Jean has taken a new apartment, where she lives alone. She talked about preparing a nursery. "John," she said, "if you see an old changing table at Earth Day—something that could be fixed and repainted—set it aside for me. And I'm looking for a high chair. And Doris at the doctor's office said I can have her old playpen." She continued excitedly down her list as Caroline and I smiled and nodded.

Then I felt a tugging at my sleeve and turned. It was Patty, straining up on her tiptoes. I bent down and she said, "Everybody wants to go. Is that all right?" So I excused myself, and Patty led me to where the others were waiting at the corner.

On the drive home Rich sat in the backseat, and I found myself cutting glances at him in the rearview mirror. As we drove, he gazed serenely out the window with his good eye, watching the town slide past. The iris of his other, wandering eye bounced lightly up and down like a bobber on the surface of a pond when a fish down below is nibbling at the end of the line.

John

April 2, 1991

Dear Wyatt,

Yesterday morning, before going to Earth Day, I went to Caroline's office for a serious talk. I told her about Rich's outburst in church Friday night. I said I was tortured now with the thought that he had attacked Ellen. I asked her what could happen to him if it was true.

As I spoke I saw alarm rising in her face. When I had finished she spoke without hesitation: "He's subject to the same legal processes as you or me. If it's true and he's convicted, he'd probably be sent to Liberty or someplace like it. He'd be institutionalized under very strict controls. His life would be completely changed and I doubt that he'd ever get out."

I remembered some of the other patients I'd seen at Liberty last August. A number of them had looked like they were drugged pretty hard.

"We've got to be sure," I said. "Before we talk to anyone else about this, we need to have some kind of proof. If Rich were picked up for questioning . . ." I paused. "He's so emotional, I don't know how he'd react. He shouldn't have to go through something like that if he didn't do anything."

Caroline nodded. "Yes," she said. "You're around him a lot. There must be some way." She turned up her palms and shrugged her shoulders. "And at the same time we need to check out every other possible suspect. That's the other way to find out about Rich. Will Storley be of any help?"

"I'll see him this week," I said. "He's checking a couple of names Ron gave me." We were both leaning forward in our chairs, our heads near one another, almost whispering. We were thinking hard, and despite the dire circumstances, something in me thrilled to the situation. I think it was the intimacy of the two of us conspiring together—the sense of something to do, and a partner to do it with.

It was time for me to go. We both stood up and took deep breaths, as if we'd been under water. Caroline's forehead was lined with thought and worry, but there was a strange lightness in me. I felt the impulse to smile broadly, but checked it. I felt almost giddy. I said good-bye and almost bounded out the door.

The day at work passed without incident. Linda came down to eat with us. We all sat in the sun at the picnic tables behind the building. Everyone was cheered to see her back, even if it was only for a visit. She said the doctor would let her start to work half days in another week or so. She had a red bow tied in her short black hair and Rich told her it looked pretty. Kevin stiffened and looked at him with a pained expression, but Rich didn't notice.

That night after supper I walked to Ron's. He greeted me at the door but didn't invite me in. I could see that Iris was there, sitting in the front room with her back to me, listening to music. I wanted to ask Ron whether he'd come up with any other names for me to give Storley. But this didn't seem like a good time. I told him I'd catch him later.

"Sure," he said, and nodded. He gave me an apologetic look. I said good-bye and left.

On the walk home, the air was cool but not cold. The sky was clear and the stars shone brightly. I could see the faint trace of the Milky Way, and that strange buoyancy I'd felt in Caroline's office returned to me. The shapes of things started forward—the jutting branches between houses, the angles of the roofs, the bright yellow squares of lit windows. I walked home and stayed up late looking at pictures, reading, and looking at more pictures.

John

April 4, 1991
Dear Wyatt,

Thanks for your kind last letter and the welcome news that you've sold another painting. The news comes as if from another world or another lifetime. After the reviews of my show, where are you finding these buyers? The check, of course, is very welcome. Storley tells me there's only a limited amount of money allocated to him by the county for his investigations, so if I have some of my own resources it may make some things possible. I met with him again today over in Decorah.

It was a cold, dark day. In Storley's office, the two of us sat among his books with a bare tree pitching outside his one window. He's still feeling happy about what he called "our good luck," referring to the man in black who had peered in at Ellen from her mother's back porch. He seemed complacent to me, and I asked him if we weren't relying too heavily on things that couldn't be nailed down—vague rumors about Ellen's "reputation" and what they might have prompted some unidentified person to do.

"Of course, it would be better if we could put another suspect in front of the jury," he said. "A courtroom confession would be best." He paused to see if I had appreciated his tone. "But all we have to do is knock enough holes in the prosecution's case to establish a reasonable doubt. And I think we can do that." I tried to ignore his condescension.

I asked if he'd investigated the two men Ron had told me about.

Storley nodded. "I asked Ellen about them when I deposed her," he said.

A wild impatience rose in me suddenly. It seemed incredible that I had to trust this stranger to say and do the right thing for me, that I couldn't sit down with Ellen myself and try to get to the bottom of this mess. I made myself hold still and waited for him to continue.

"The first one—Dean Tyler—was just a high school boyfriend," he said. "But the other—Charlie Anderson—seemed interesting for a while. She'd known him in high school, they went to different colleges, then remet back here. She says they dated for about a year and then she broke it off in November."

"So she was seeing him when she modeled for me in my old studio last summer," I said. "What did he think of her modeling work?"

"I asked her that," Storley said, pleased with himself. "They quarreled about it, but that's not why they broke up." It always astonishes me when I learn something new about Ellen. Her life keeps unfolding before my eyes. Storley continued: "She broke things off when he complained about her plans to go off to art school."

"He sounds like a suspect," I said.

"I thought so, too," he said. "But he took a job in Des Moines in mid-December—before the attack—and his parents say he's only been back once when he visited at Christmas. And I checked with his employer. No absences, good work record, promotions. And, besides, it's a good family. Mr. Anderson has run the Super Value in Delphi for twenty years. I've checked it all out."

I must have looked upset. "Don't worry, John," he said, leaning back and crossing his arms and tucking his hands under his suspenders. "Our case is shaping up just fine."

"One thing, though," he said. "Would Jamie Stevens do you any good if she were asked to come back and testify?" He paused for a moment. "What would she say, for instance, if I asked her whether you were ever unfaithful to her or whether you'd ever, to her knowledge, had an affair with one of your models?" He gave me a level look.

I looked back at him. "I hope she doesn't have to testify," I said. "But I was not unfaithful to her, and, contrary to presumed custom, I do not have affairs with my models."

I got up to leave. I was at the door when Storley said, "How well do you feel you know Ron Tappet, the electrician?"

I stopped and turned. "I consider him a good friend," I said.

"Has he told you that he and Ellen spent a lot of time together for a while?" he said. "There were rumors."

I stood at the door and tried to take in what Storley had just told me. Ron and Iris had been together for a long time. Ellen had only been home from college for a couple of years. Iris and Ellen were close friends. I looked at Storley. He was behind his desk, tipped back in his chair with his arms folded across his chest. "You and your rumors," I said. "I'm not interested in them." And I left.

Driving home, the weather was bad—an overcast sky and intermittent rain thrown down by gusty winds. Storley's insinuation about Ron turned in my head like a puzzle piece that wouldn't fit. I tried to dismiss it. The sky darkened as I drove. Below solid overcast, the wind pushed fast-moving, lower clouds until they stretched and twisted into tatters. Something twisted in me, too. When I finally recognized what it was it surprised me. It was jealousy.

John

April 6, 1991
Dear Wyatt,

I spent this evening—Saturday night—with Rich at the house. He had asked me several times in the past months to come over, and I feel guilty that I only agreed this time because I wanted to look for evidence that might implicate him in the attack on Ellen. Of course, I hoped I wouldn't find anything. But, at the same time, I knew that if I did I would be cleared of the charge, myself.

It was a mild evening, so I walked over. The sun had just gone down and a soft, peach-colored light was in the air. Next to the foundations of some of the houses I could see crocuses blossoming and the first tulip leaves pressing up. As I walked, the light gradually failed, and when I rounded the final corner and approached the Earth Day house, its sharply peaked roof and turret stood in silhouette against the sky. Rich and Kevin and Dot were sitting on the big front porch and when they saw me they waved in unison. When I came up the stairs they all stood and we went inside.

I'd only been in the house once before. Off the foyer to the left, the big wooden staircase ascended. Straight ahead, the hallway leading to the back of the house was dim. To the right, in the sitting room where the Christmas tree had been, Barbara sat on the brown couch with Patty, staring across the brown shag carpeting at a television. They looked up, said, "Hi, John," and turned back to the TV. Dot went over and joined them.

Rich and Kevin led me down the hallway to the kitchen at the back of the first floor. Linda was there, sitting at a yellow Formica-topped table, eating a bowl of ice cream. When we entered she looked up, smiled broadly, and said hi. I said hi and leaned against the doorframe, trying to look casual despite the nervousness I felt. The strong fluorescent light from the circular tubes of the ceiling fixture made us all look a little ghoulish. Rich leaned over the sink and peered out the back window. "Are those guys still playing croquet?" he said. I heard voices coming in from the backyard.

"Yeah," said Linda. "They can't even see. All they do is argue." Kevin sat down next to Linda and watched her eat.

"John, you want to see my room?" Rich asked.

I nodded, said sure, and he led me back down the hall to the staircase, which creaked loudly as we started to climb. "Barbara's apartment is downstairs," Rich said, over his shoulder. "Girls live on the second floor. The guys are on the third floor. My room's the tower." He pronounced the last sentence proudly.

We rounded the second floor landing and climbed to the third, the oak stairs crying with every step. I reached the top, panting, and followed Rich down a short hall. He opened a door, stepped through it, and waved me in after him. "This is my place," he said, squaring his shoulders. We stood in a six-sided room in the top of the turret which ran up the southeast corner of the house. Three large windows side by side on three of the room's facets looked out into the tops of empty trees. It was a small room, and so packed with furniture and full shelves and countless objects of a hundred different kinds that I felt pressed toward the large windows and the open space beyond them. For a moment I literally felt that I might stumble forward over the bed toward the windows and the long plunge to the yard below.

"Want to sit down?" Rich said. I looked around. He motioned toward the bed which stood near the windows and was covered by a red plaid blanket. I sat there and looked up at Rich standing in the room among his things. He leaned against a darkly stained five-drawer bureau, on top of which stood a pyramid of old Schmidt beer cans, each printed with a different outdoor scene—pine woods, deer, streams, snowy mountains, leaping fish. Above the cans, on the wall, hung a pair of antlers fastened to a wooden plaque. To the right, a small desk was littered with crumpled papers, pens, and markers, its surface lit by an old floor lamp with a red shade trimmed in gold tassels which hung down around its bottom edge. Above the desk, four shelves held curiosities probably gleaned from among the castoffs left at the Earth Day salvage depot. In the welter I could see an Oldsmobile hood ornament in the shape of a jet, a six-inch Eiffel Tower, and a pair of bronzed baby shoes. On the top shelf stood an eight-socket wrought iron candelabra with no candles in it.

On Rich's other side, to my left, there was a closet door and then a wall with only a carved wooden crucifix hanging on it. On the floor under the crucifix, near the foot of the bed, sat an immense turquoise stuffed bear. Rich saw me staring at it and said, "I won that at the fair. I knocked down three bottles with one ball. Do you want a Coke?" I looked up and nodded. Rich went out and I heard the stairs creak as he started down for the kitchen.

I took a deep breath, gathered myself, and went to the bureau. There were only clothes in the drawers. I opened the closet, reached in, and pulled the string to turn on the bulb in the closet's ceiling. When the light flashed on I saw that the inside of the closet door was papered with pictures cut from magazines. There were hunting dogs, race cars, airplanes, and pinups. Mainly pinups. And hung among them at eye level was a small mirror. I looked into the mirror and saw my face. Around it, naked women reclined with their arms raised over their heads and their backs arched. I turned away and looked into the closet.

At the top, on a shelf, stacks of magazines reached almost to the ceiling, dangerously close to the hot lightbulb. Below them hung Rich's shirts and pants. To one side of the clothes, a wooden folding chair leaned against the closet wall. On the floor sat two pairs of shoes and a cardboard box piled with boots, scarves, and gloves. I knelt and went through the box, tumbling and sifting the contents in my hands and listening for the creak of the stairs through the pounding in my ears. When I finished I remembered to breathe. I had not found my glove.

I stood, turned off the light, and closed the closet door. I went to the desk and gazed at the bewildering collection heaped on the shelves above it. One shelf held dozens of old pocket knives, a dented canteen, and a broken compass. Another was piled with intricately carved canes and walking sticks that lay on their sides in a precarious heap. On their whittled handles were the forms of vines and faces and snake heads. The seeming randomness of the clutter made me feel a little dizzy.

I dropped my eyes and idly picked up one of the balls of paper lying on the desktop. I uncrumpled it and smoothed it on the surface of the desk. It was a sheet of cheap typing paper with the outline of a woman drawn in an unsure hand. It looked like it had been traced out of a magazine. I picked up another ball, opened t, and found the same thing. I heard the stairs groaning. Quickly, I looked into the wastebasket under the desk and found it half filled with crumpled sheets. I knelt and hurriedly opened half a dozen, one after another. They were all the same.

The creaking of the stairs stopped and I slid back to my place on the bed. In a moment, Rich came in carrying two Cokes and handed one to me. Then he went to the closet, got out the folding chair, placed it across from me, and sat down. We opened the Cokes and drank them out of the cans. "Well, what do you think?" Rich said.

"This is quite a room," I said. "Where did you get all these things?"

"The depot, mostly," he said. "I fixed this desk myself." He ran a hand over its surface in a circular motion, knocking some of the balled papers onto the floor.

"Looks like you've been using lots of paper," I said. "If you want more, I can give you some. Do you need drawing paper or writing paper?" I asked.

"Thanks, John," he said. "It doesn't matter." He gazed at me tranquilly with his good eye and took a sip of Coke. I waited. There was nothing more forthcoming.

"When you got out the chair I couldn't help noticing the inside of your closet door," I said. "You've made quite a collage there." Rich looked at me blankly. "It's an interesting collection of pictures," I said.

"I just cut out what I like," he said. "But I wish I could draw like you." It was the most solid indication I'd heard that Rich knew what kind of work I did away from Earth Day, and I pressed the opening.

"Well," I said. "I don't get to draw very much these days." I looked him in the eyes. "Did you know I was arrested?" Rich looked away and nodded. "Do you know what I was arrested for?" I asked. He nodded again. He was looking down, staring at the big bear near the foot of the bed. We sat in silence for a few moments. Rich took another drink from his can. Finally I said: "What do you think of that?"

Rich spoke without looking up. "Don't worry, John," he said. "Nothing bad can happen. It wouldn't be fair. I know you didn't do it." I looked at him steadily as he gazed down at the bear. His other eye seemed to search for an object to fix on.

"That's good of you to say, Rich, but I'm not sure I can prove it," I said. "How do you know I didn't do it?" I held my breath.

"I just know," he said. He looked up at me and I searched his face. It stood completely open, guileless and relaxed. "Besides," he said. "It doesn't matter. We're forgiven. We're all brand new, now."

I could make no answer. The things that occurred to me to say—the inevitable "nevertheless," the reminder of my still-impending trial—seemed at that moment unsayable. He was speaking to me from across a gulf, out of an order of experience I didn't understand, and with a simplicity I did not have the heart to complicate.

Rich finished his drink and put the can on his desktop. "We're friends, aren't we, John?" he said.

"Yes, we're friends," I replied.

We sat still for a while. The floor lamp glowed through its red shade. I heard a breeze move through the dark treetops outside the windows behind me.

Rich stood and moved to the door. Then he turned back to me and said, "I smell popcorn. You want to go downstairs?"

It's 11:00 and I'm back home at my kitchen table. The rest of the evening at the Earth Day house was filled with what I can only call "horsing around." We went downstairs and ate popcorn with some of the others and bantered in the kitchen and went out to the driveway and shot baskets under a floodlight with the sweat cold on our skin in the chill air. Though Rich must be in his middle thirties and Kevin somewhere in his twenties, it felt to me like a return to junior high school nights—those edgy, bored weekend nights before dating started, when we felt ourselves teetering between childhood and adulthood, when every trivial thing we did was charged with an energy that was really about something else, something we couldn't yet name but could feel out there all around in the gorgeous dark. Finally, still sweaty, I jogged home through the dark streets. And since then I've been sitting here, writing and thinking—thinking about Rich—and thinking what a bottomless thing it is to try to know another person.

Your friend,

John

10

John Ordway
423 River Street
Delphi, Iowa

April 8, 1991

Dear Wyatt,

Yesterday afternoon was mild and bright. I pulled on a sweater, took my bicycle out of the garage behind the apartment, and went for a ride. I skirted the business district, crossed the river, and went past the sign at the entrance to the park at Redding's Spring. I pedaled on, with the river to my right and the ridge of limestone palisades to my left. When I crossed the intersection at Quarry Hill I glanced up in the direction of Caroline's house, but continued straight ahead. Soon I came to the entrance of another small park with a paved, one-lane road that loops up through woods to the top of a ridge overlooking the river and the town. When the road became steep, I got off and walked. Beside the road, clumps of green had sprung up among last fall's brown leaves and the early wildflowers were blossoming—small, white flowers of two or three different kinds. Even some of the low bushes were beginning to bud out under the high, empty branches of the big trees.

I made the top of the ridge and looked out over the town. The stores, of course, were closed for Sunday, and the downtown streets were empty. The only figures moving were some kids I could just make out in a vacant lot far off to the left, playing ball. Directly below, along the town's edge, the river was a silver band of reflected light.

I looked out for several minutes. The town seemed empty and the sky over it was clear and blue and deep. I felt a familiar, nagging restlessness. And then I knew something. It was like standing in a room and finally turning to look at something that was there. I climbed on my bike and coasted down the hill, the gray trees blurring to my right and left. I rode to the bridge and went back into town to the Shell station and the phone booth on the corner. I went in and called Caroline and when she answered I said hello and she recognized my voice.

I told her that I wanted to see her. I said I was out on my bike and asked if I could ride over to her house. I said I'd be careful, like the time before.

She didn't say anything. For what seemed like a long time there was silence on the line. I looked through the glass booth out to the empty street. A single car approached slowly and stopped at the traffic signal. It waited, though there was no traffic, then the light turned green and the car pulled away.

"John," Caroline said, "you can't come here. You just can't." There was another long pause. The line was perfectly quiet. I waited. Then I heard her take a deep breath. "Maybe we could go for a drive," she said. "Is there someplace where I could pick you up, someplace where you could leave your bike?"

I understood what she meant. I told her she could meet me in the park that I'd just come from. "I'll show you the wildflowers," I said. "Then we can go for a drive."

I went back to the park, rode halfway in, then walked my bike into the underbrush and laid it down behind a big, moss-covered slab of limestone. Then I returned to the road and started to walk.

In a few minutes I heard a car approach and slow down. I turned and Caroline waved from behind the steering wheel. I got in and she drove on into the park. We went slowly with the windows down and the fresh air coming in. "Look at all the little white flowers through here," I said, reaching across and pointing out the window on her side.

"Yes, those are snowdrops," she said. "And those are Dutchman's-breeches. See the way the cleft in the puffy blossoms makes them look like little pairs of pants?" She turned to me and smiled.

We made a slow loop through the park without stopping. When we came out, Caroline turned onto a gravel road that went over a small hill and wound away from town. In a few miles she turned onto blacktop and we cruised past dairy farms on the right and left. "Have you ever been to Guttenburg?" she asked. I shook my head. "It's a small town on the Mississippi south of here. It's pretty. It's about an hour's drive. Would you like to see it?"

I nodded and settled back. The countryside slid past under the clear sky and there were almost no other cars on the road. Caroline reached over, turned on the radio, and found some music.

"I was with Rich last night," I said. She glanced over and then back to the road. "I'm very worried. I feel myself deciding that he must have done it. But I don't think I can know for sure without asking him a direct question. And that seems like a big step."

"Yes," she said. "It's hard to know how he'd react. And if we're wrong . . ."

"I don't think I can do it until I've exhausted every other possibility," I said.

She nodded. "Do you know of others?" she asked.

"Not really," I admitted. "Nothing strong."

It was quiet for a while. Then she said, "We could have talked about this in the office tomorrow, or on the phone. This isn't why you wanted to meet."

"No," I said.

She looked over at me and I looked back. And when she turned again toward the road she took her right hand off the wheel and held it toward me. I took it and our two hands rested together on the seat between us.

In Guttenburg, for the space of an afternoon under the open sky, we forgot everything. We walked together down the town's main street, past the shops on one side and the big river on the other, careless of the possibility that someone would recognize us. We went into a simple restaurant and sat at a table by the window looking out over the Mississippi and ate lunch and drank wine. We went into the tiny, riverfront aquarium and looked at the fish in their tanks. Then we walked the neighborhoods, down streets named after famous Germans—Goethe Street and Mozart Street—lined with plain, wood-framed houses. And then we walked back to the little main street because Caroline wanted to show me a gift shop she knew.

Its owner was an importer and a world traveler who had discovered his most unusual wares along the way. In a large back room there were African masks and a folding ladder for mounting an elephant and there were wind chimes from around the world and carved toys painted in bright colors. And there were camel bells hanging from the ceiling. Caroline told me to strike one. There was a stick for the purpose. I picked up the stick and tapped the largest of the big, oblong bells. A low, clear tone rang through the store. Everyone turned to look, then smiled and turned away. You could feel the tone in your chest as it sounded in your ears. Caroline took the stick from my hand, chose another bell, and struck it lightly. A different tone, equally clear, issued from it. We grinned at each other with pleasure. And so we had to hear them all.

The bells were pitched so their sound would carry through the desert air, Caroline explained, and each was unique so an owner could recognize his camels, even at night, by the sounds of their bells.

"Choose one," I said. "I want to buy it for you."

She turned and struck one of the smaller bells, looked at me, and smiled. It sounded for a long time—light and clear. "This one," she said.

When we returned from Guttenburg it was late. We had lingered in its narrow riverfront park, gazing at the wide river, and on the drive home we stopped to spread a blanket and eat sandwiches that we had bought. The sun went down in a brief, orange blaze, and as we made the last turns on the road to Delphi our headlights swept the dark fields.

We topped Quarry Hill and Caroline turned into her long, wooded driveway. Without speaking, she stopped at the house, got out of the car, and walked to the front door. I followed, feeling my way up the unlit stairs to the open door. Inside, she took my hand and led me through the dark to a stairway that went down. We entered a room lit only by the dim glow of the night sky showing through double glass patio doors at the far end. Caroline stood in front of me, holding both of my hands, but I couldn't see her at all. She leaned forward and placed her ear against my chest. "Your heart is pounding," she said. I put my face in her hair and breathed deeply the clean, animal smell.

The faint glow from the room's far end was like the far-off mouth of a cave. Nothing inside was visible. By touch, we undressed each other, and Caroline drew me to the bed. When we made love it was with a sudden desperation that shocked me until my mind became a blank and something gave way and we fell together and then another floor gave way and we fell again. I clung to her and gasped like a man drowning and she clung to me as if I could save her and then we drowned together and died and kept falling, calmly now, through the deep water.

I woke in the dark room, slick with sweat in Caroline's arms. I got up and made my way toward the dim glow across the room. When I reached the glass doors I pressed my face and then my whole front against the cool pane. I leaned there, breathing deeply and easily, my skin cooling. I heard a stirring behind me. Then the flat of Caroline's hand moved down my back in a long, even stroke. "Cooling off?" she said.

"Yes," I said.

"Does it feel good?" she said.

"Yes," I answered.

She stepped to my side and leaned against the glass next to me. "You're right," she said. "It feels wonderful."

We stood there, side by side, leaning against the cool glass doors. Outside, where the backyard sloped away, I could see over the tops of the near trees to the pinpoints of streetlights below and the sprinkling of stars above them. I leaned my left cheek against the glass and looked toward Caroline. She was a partial silhouette that merged with the darkness behind her.

"It feels good," she said, "but it's strange." I heard her start to laugh softly in a low voice.

"Yes, it's a little strange," I said. I turned to her and we held each other, and then we went back to bed.

I woke up again a little before dawn. I looked past the foot of the bed to the doors and the milky, predawn light. I looked at Caroline and she opened her eyes. "I should go," I said.

We got up and showered together, washing each other in the bright light of the small bathroom. Caroline reached up as far as she could to shampoo my hair, grinning at me as she used the balls of her fingers to work up a lather. I knelt with one knee on a folded washcloth to wash and rinse her legs. Then I took the cloth and washed her belly, stroking softly across the cesarean scar.

We finished and dressed. Then Caroline drove me to the park where the trees and shrubs and rocks were assuming their forms in the first light. She let me out and waited while I found my bike and carried it back to the road. She lowered her window and I came around. She reached her arm out the window and I took her hand and held it. "I won't be coming to your office anymore," I said. She nodded. Then we let go and I coasted away through the chilly air.

I arrived home just as the sun was coming up. I approached from the back, put my bike in the garage behind the house, and quietly made my way around the house and up the steps to the apartment. As I went I could clearly see Officer Paley—I'd learned his name from Ron—sleeping in his car with his chin on his chest. Inside, I made a pot of coffee. I filled a mug, went down the stairs, and crossed the street. I rapped lightly on the window of the squad car and Paley's head bobbed up. He rolled down the window and looked up, focusing his eyes the best he could. "Good morning," I said. "You must be tired." I held out the mug.

"Good morning," he said, still focusing. He looked bewildered, but, with instinctive good manners, accepted the coffee. "Thanks," he said.

"You're welcome," I said and went back upstairs.

Today in the small sitting room of my apartment I made a new painting. I worked on it steadily for six hours, putting into it everything about the night with Caroline. I used only one color, and, when I finished, the canvas was completely black.

Everything is there, but there's nothing to see. It has nothing to do with looking. It is a painting only in the fact that it is made out of paint. There is no reason to show it to anyone. It would only be mistaken for something that has already been done by someone else for other reasons. But, having made this only for myself, I can remember the movements of my hand, the strain of my whole body, and the way I finished with my eyes closed, applying the last strokes, feeling the last emotion which was broad enough to be wild at one edge and calm at the other, and that emotion was gratitude.

John

April 11, 1991
Dear Wyatt,

We found the red pickup. Ron took a day off and at midmorning he and I were driving through the little town of Selden, about 20 miles northwest of Delphi. "There it is," Ron said. "Bingo."

I asked him if he was sure.

"Positive," he said.

It was parked next to a Sinclair station. Ron slowed, pulled in, and stopped at the pumps. He got out, topped off his tank, and we both went into the station to pay for the gas. The attendant at the cash register was a clean-shaven high school kid with sandy hair. "Is that your pickup outside?" Ron asked.

"No, that's Chuck's," the kid said. "He's the mechanic." He gestured over his shoulder toward the garage bay.

"I'd like to ask him something," Ron said.

The kid stepped to the door and shouted, "Hey, Chuck. Somebody wants you." I looked over at Ron but he was staring straight ahead.

A tall man came to the doorway, wiping his hands with a red rag. He was probably in his mid-thirties. His dark hair was combed to one side. He wore a mustache.

I couldn't imagine what Ron was going to say to him. I had the panicked thought that he was going to confront him with an accusation, right there. I turned toward Ron to catch his eye and head him off, but it was too late.

"That's your red pickup parked outside?" Ron said.

"Yeah," the man said.

"Your name is Chuck?" Ron said.

"Chuck Denny," he said. I thought he was starting to look annoyed.

"May I ask you something?" Ron said. I braced myself against the next question.

I felt as though Ron had just lit a match and was preparing to toss it into a pool of gasoline. "Where'd you get those custom wheels?" he said. "I might like to put a set on my truck." He gestured toward his gray Dodge parked at the pumps.

"Sure," Chuck said. "Got them at Daly's Custom Shop in La Crosse. You like them?"

"Yeah," Ron said. "They're great. Thanks a lot." They both nodded and Ron and I walked back to his truck.

I got in, slumped in my seat, and looked over at Ron. "That was good," I said. "But you scared the shit out of me." Ron grinned and stared through the windshield.

We drove straight to Decorah and Ron went to the sheriff's department. I sat outside in the pickup while he gave his information to the sheriff. When he came back out he said, "They'll talk to him right away."

On the drive back to Delphi, Ron said, "It was eerie seeing him again, remembering that afternoon in the rain."

"Do you think he recognized you?" I said.

"No. I had my ball cap on that day and I was drenched. But I remember him clearly now. That was him, all right."

We drove the rest of the way in silence. Ron dropped me at Earth Day and promised to let me know as soon as he heard something. I'll keep you informed.

John

April 12, 1991

Dear Wyatt,

Today the sheriff's office told Ron that Chuck Denny was at a church potluck supper the evening of the break-in at Ellen's. Then he and his wife and another couple watched videos until past midnight. A man with secret habits, perhaps, but he's not the one.

This was a last hope. To have lost it, now—it feels like someone's hit me in the stomach. The beginning of my trial is less than three weeks away. Someone will have to talk to Rich.

John

April 13, 1991

Dear Wyatt,

I don't know whether it was the sound that woke me or whether I'd been lying in bed half awake when I heard it. At first I thought it was inside me—that light, clear tone—but then I could hear the distance in it. It had come from outside.

I sat up and saw the clock: 1:00 A.M. I went to the half-opened window and looked out. Snow was falling—a lot of it—big flakes drifting straight down. An inch of it already covered the ground. When the tone sounded again I recognized it. I dressed quickly, found my jacket, and went outside.

First I crossed the street and rapped on Paley's window. His head bobbed up and he turned to look. When he rolled down the window a crack, I said, "I'm going for a walk in the snow. I'll be gone for about twenty minutes. Can I bring you anything first?"

Eyes wide, struggling to focus, he managed to shake his head. "No," he said. "No, thank you."

I started down the block, rounded the corner, and doubled back down the alley. There she was, a dark form under the eve of the garage. "So it works," she said, striking the bell again lightly, then slipping it into the pocket of her wool coat. I stepped up and put my arms around her.

"What are you doing?" I said. "And what's happening? It snows here in April?"

"Sometimes it does," she said. "Two years ago we got four inches on the 24th." We were smiling at each other like crazy.

"How did you get here? Where's your car?" I asked her.

"I walked," she said.

"That's three miles," I said.

"I woke up and saw the snow. I wanted to be out in it and I started walking. And when I started walking I wanted to come here." She took my hand and we strolled down the alley and out into the dark, snow-hushed neighborhood. The big flakes fell through the cones of light under the streetlamps.

"When did you get so reckless?" I said. "What if someone sees us?"

"When did you get so cautious?" she said, teasing. "I believe I'm just reciprocating for your visits. I'm very polite. Hadn't you noticed?"

"Yes," I said. "Everyone here is. Everyone for miles. The county seat, Decorah, should be called Decorum."

She laughed. "Decorah was an Indian chief. But what's wrong with a little decorum? It helps people get along."

"Right," I said. "And then they can visit you in your office and tell you what's *really* going on."

She laughed again. "That's right," she said. "Would you rather they just knocked each other down in the streets?"

It was my turn to laugh. And then we must have walked for an hour, saying very little. It was not terribly cold, but the snow kept falling. It built up on the sidewalks in front of the darkened houses and we shuffled through it, leaving a double trail. Once Caroline stopped and pulled me to her. Our faces were cold when they touched, but our mouths were warm.

When we looped back to my block we entered by the alley and stopped in the shadow of the garage. "What now?" I said. "You're a long way from home."

"Then you'd better invite me up," she said.

"My house is still being watched," I told her. Caroline didn't look down and she didn't say anything. "Wait here," I said.

I left the alley and rounded the block, coming down the sidewalk in front of my house. Paley's car was still parked across the street. Its windows were entirely covered by snow. I went to the stairs at the side of the house and waved Caroline over. She came out of the shadows and we went up together.

Inside, we went straight to my room and undressed. Her solid, compact body was a charged space in the dark. We made love hungrily, without thought or restraint—without delay or decorum. We were famished and we took our satisfactions, offered freely and taken freely, like air to breathe and water to drink.

We made love and fell asleep. I did not dream and my sleep went by all in a flash.

When I woke up it was light. I looked at Caroline sleeping. I got up carefully, without disturbing her, and went to the window. It had stopped snowing. I looked into the backyard and, with a start, saw our tracks in the snow leading from the alley toward my stairs. I put on a robe and went to the kitchen and looked out the window of the door and saw our double footprints in the snow on the steps. I looked across the street. There was smoke coming out of the tailpipe of Paley's car and the windows were clear. Then his door swung open and I saw him climb out and start across the street.

He walked to the stairs and started to climb them, looking down at the snowy treads. I stood and watched him coming. When he reached the landing and looked up, we saw each other through the glass in the door. I hesitated for a moment, then opened it.

Officer Paley, all alert now, reached out with his right hand. There was something in it. It was an empty coffee mug. "Here," he said. "I kept forgetting to return this. Thanks for the coffee."

I took the mug. Paley turned and went back down the stairs. I watched him cross the street, get into his car, and drive away before I remembered to shut the door against the cold.

I went back to the bedroom. Caroline was lying awake in the bed. I got in next to her. "Who was that?" she said.

"Officer Paley," I said. Her eyes widened. "He came up to return a coffee mug."

She covered her face with the blankets and laughed. I watched the bedding quake. Then she uncovered her face and shook her head. "Poor Frank," she said. "He's getting near retirement and he's been on the night shift for twenty years. He must be getting very tired."

"I wish I could laugh," I said. "I didn't know what was going to happen. I thought he was tracking us."

"I shouldn't laugh," she said. But then she did again. The thought of Frank Paley tracking us through the snow cracked her up. She rolled onto her back, closed her eyes, and laughed, not just with relief and amusement, I thought, but also with deep pleasure—like a bell tolling.

Caroline stayed all day. It was Saturday so we lounged and read and listened to music. Her slacks and socks hung from the shower rod in my bathroom, the snowmelt from our walk drying out of them. She wore one of my sweatshirts and a heavy pair of socks to keep her feet warm. The sweatshirt reached to her knees. At noon I toasted some bread and heated a can of soup for our lunch. In the afternoon we listened to music and talked. I told Caroline about finding the red pickup and about my last meeting with Storley. I said I wanted to learn more about Ellen's ex-boyfriend, Charlie Anderson, the guy in Des Moines. And then, if he was clear, someone would have to talk to Rich. Caroline agreed.

"I think Charlie and Jerry are friends," she said. "You might ask Jerry if he's seen him here in town since Christmas. And Jean might have some impressions of Charlie. I didn't know him."

I nodded. "I'll talk to them," I said. We looked at each other and the seriousness of things bore down on us again. My trial would begin in eighteen days.

A feeling of dread swept over me. To fight it off, I picked up a sketchbook and pencil. I was sitting on the floor of the middle room, leaning against a bookshelf with a pillow behind me. Caroline was sitting on the red couch with a book in her lap. I began to draw her—the curve of the couch back framing her, the heavy socks falling around her ankles—then thought better of it and closed the sketchbook. What if the police searched my apartment again? I told myself. What if they found drawings of Caroline? But maybe that's not why I stopped.

Caroline had seen me put the sketchbook down. She looked at me for a long moment, then set her book aside. She stood and came over to me and held out her hand. I stood and took it. Then she stepped back, away from me, and took off the sweatshirt and socks. The light in the room was bright off the snow. She stood, naked, across the room. She looked me in the eyes and said: "I'm forty-six years old. I have short legs. I've had an emergency cesarean." She paused. And then her voice was softer. "It's me, Caroline," she said.

I crossed the room and put my arms around her. Then we made love, slowly this time, tenderly. In the middle, Caroline rolled on top of me, put her hands on my face, and opened my eyes. She held my eyes with hers for a long time until, at the end, we couldn't keep our eyes open any longer.

Afterward, we rested on the floor in each other's arms. Caroline lay with her head on my chest. Gradually, our breathing quieted. Then she raised herself on her arms and looked at me. "John," she said. "I want you to paint me."

I was surprised. I said the first thing that came into my mind. "I don't think I should," I said. I looked up at her. "I can't," I said.

"But I want you to," she answered. Her dark eyes, beneath their fierce, dark eyebrows, took me in.

I hesitated. "I'm afraid I'll hurt you," I said. "That's what always seems to happen."

"No," she replied. "You won't."

"But the risks . . ." It seemed very dangerous to me, in more ways than I was prepared to say.

Caroline put her finger across my mouth. "Shhhhhhhhh," she said, then kissed me.

At suppertime I went to the store and brought back steak, potatoes, lettuce, and mushrooms. We cooked together and ate hungrily. After dinner it was dark, but Paley hadn't arrived yet. I went down the stairs, then waved Caroline down. We crept to the garage, got into my car, and I drove her home. On the way, she said, "This is exciting. It's my first time."

"Your first time for what?" I said.

"My first time leaving someplace under cover of darkness."

I looked over. There was laughter in her eyes. I grinned at her and shook my head. "You're really crazy, you know that?" I said. "I had no idea you were this crazy." She grinned back at me, happily.

John

April 14, 1991

Dear Wyatt,

I worked with Caroline for the first time, today. She's persuaded me. It is terribly important to her. I still wonder if it's wise. What does it mean to her? Is it some kind of sacrificial gesture, in the interest of getting me back to work? An extension of my therapy? That may be something she tells herself, but this is for her as much as me. I suspect she wants to feel the equal of Jamie, Ellen, and Jean in this regard—to have modeled for me as they did. If there is some sense of buried competition here, it makes me nervous. How will she feel about the paintings? Caroline is wonderfully attractive, but not conventionally "beautiful"—not in the way the other women are. What kind of rendering does she expect?

I did charcoal and pencil work today. I'll have to figure out some way to get my other materials up to her house. I'll probably have to load the car in the middle of the afternoon, drive around, and come over Quarry Hill the back way when there's nobody else on the road. All this subterfuge seems ridiculous sometimes.

Including today: as usual, I had to ride my bike around, hide it, and climb the wooded path up to Caroline's house. The snow was no problem on the bike—the streets had been plowed—but the trail was slippery. I climbed through the wet snow hoping none would fall from a branch onto the rolled paper sticking out the top of my backpack. I arrived at noon as we had arranged. Upstairs Caroline had pushed the living room furniture around and had hung a white backdrop over the bookshelves adjacent to the big glass doors and the windows overlooking the town. She'd brought the round, glass-topped table and patio chairs in from the deck and placed them just inside the doors, in front of the backdrop. The table was set with two places and there were rolls, a coffee pot, and a bowl of fruit. In the middle of the table was a vase of red gladiola. Caroline was barefoot in a light blue robe.

We ate first. She was in high spirits, bright with excitement, speaking lightly. When we finished she sat back, holding her cup near her mouth with both hands. "Well, then, maybe we should get started," she said.

I asked her where she wanted to pose. Part of our agreement, at my insistence, is that she's in charge—she decides when we work, for how long, how she poses. She said she thought she'd pose at the table. She stood to clear the dishes, but I asked her to leave things as they were. I liked it.

Without my easel, I needed a drawing board. I took the leaf from the dining room table and taped sheets of paper to it. Then I pushed my chair to the middle of the living room and sat down with the board propped against the back of the couch.

Caroline had remained at the table, in the sun, sipping her coffee. "Shall I take off my robe now?" she asked.

"Actually, I like the robe," I said.

"You'll tell me if you need me to do anything, won't you?" she said.

"You can do whatever you like," I said. "You look wonderful there. I need to warm up."

I felt the gritty slide of charcoal across paper, that familiar glide and tug. It felt good—the resistance and give. And the sound of the trace across the smooth paper was soothing. I swept out the flattened oval of the tabletop, the straight sides of the vase, the spray of glads.

"How still do I need to be?" Caroline asked. She was sitting back and holding her cup in both hands, as before. "I'm a rank amateur," she said. "You need to teach me." I told her she could move as she wished, that I'd let her know if I wanted her to hold a particular pose. She put down her cup and leaned back in her chair. I stroked in the drapery of her robe and the short curls around her face.

It was a delightful scene—"complacencies of the peignoir"—but the southwest light at noon was harsh, especially with snow on the ground. The snowlight off the deck made for hard light and deep shadows. The shadows on the table and in the creases of Caroline's robe were deep. And there were shadows in her eyes and next to her nose. It was no good for the line drawing I was doing. Starting again, I did a quick study in value, composing by shadow. Then I tore that sheet off and started again, still warming up.

It's always an event when you start with a new model. Doubly so when you already have a different kind of relationship with her. I remember the first time I drew Jamie. We'd been seeing each other for just a few weeks and were in that first flush of pleasure at what was happening between us. I told her I was doing a series of nudes and asked if she wanted to pose for me. Without hesitation, she said, "Sure." She'd posed a fair amount before, at art school and afterward when money was tight. It wasn't a big deal for her. But, since we were already involved, it was charged with that. We went over to her studio space at the Loft one Saturday morning, having spent the previous night together. She wore loose clothes so she wouldn't have lines. I warmed up with several minutes of gesture drawings. Then she took off her dress and sat upright in a chair. I sat in another chair at an easel across the room and drew, but my mind wasn't on my work. I guess she felt the same because in about ten minutes she stood up, walked over, and put her arms around my neck. Somehow we knocked over the easel and wound up making love in the chair. Afterward she said, "Well, that was productive," and we laughed hard, rocking back and forth together. It was several weeks before we tried again.

Caroline, though, was all intent on our work today. It's not surprising that she's self-conscious, never having posed before. She wanted to talk quite a bit, and that was fine. She said that posing in her robe while I was across the room fully dressed was like dreams she'd had in which she's the only one at a party without clothes. She said it's a common dream and asked if I'd ever had it. I said I hadn't. But I told her about a recurring dream I do have from time to time—the one where I wake up in my own bed in the morning, in my familiar room, but paralyzed. I can't move at all. I struggle to turn my head or draw a breath. There's pressure in my head and chest, and the effort to move only makes it build. I strain to lift an arm or a finger, to break the spell. I can't breathe and the pressure builds. Inside myself, I'm frantic now. I think I'm going to explode. Then an arm breaks free and I wake up with a jolt—I'm really awake this time. My head is clanging with my pulse, and I'm panting and sweating. But I'm breathing, now, and I can move. Gradually, I settle down.

I glanced up from my drawing and saw Caroline looking at me with concern. "How awful," she said.

"Yes, it's miserable," I said. "But I haven't had it for a while."

"Good," she said. Then she got up, walked over, and stood behind me. She kneaded my shoulders with her hands. On the drawing board, the charcoal study was heavy and dark. Too much shadow.

"The light is harsh today," I said. We agreed to try again tomorrow.

John

April 15, 1991
Dear Wyatt,

I managed to get my easel, canvases, and paints to Caroline's without incident. She'll keep them in a utility room off the kitchen when we're not working. Today she arranged to meet with all her clients in the morning hours and I worked at Earth Day, as usual. Tomorrow she's got to be at her office all day, which is fine. I'm scheduled to work with the Stortzes on their portrait.

I arrived at Caroline's at 2:00. She'd placed the patio furniture in the living room next to the windows again. By now, though, the snow had melted off the deck, so the light was better. When we started, she sat, as before, in her light blue robe, half-reclining in the chair with her legs stretched out under the table in a straight diagonal. As yesterday, there were gladiola in a vase on the table. I warmed up with some rapid charcoal sketches, then switched to pencil for some closer work.

She asked me if we would do any nude work today. I told her that was up to her, but that, at the table, the robe worked well.

Today, at first, the subject seemed merely conventional to me: a woman at a table. You think of the French, of domestic breakfasts or public cafés. There is food. There's a woman. There's a woman with food. Pleasant enough, and flattering enough to the appetites, but it hardly needs to be done again. As I continued, however, I saw the arrangement more formally. The composition has three elements: the lines of the robe running down from the upper left, the horizontal of the table-top cutting through the middle, and the flowers rising in the upper right. Seeing them together, there's a kind of hydraulic: what flows beneath the table's plane from the left, like groundwater, bursts up through the vase on the right. The cool blue of Caroline's robe geysers back up as the red spray of flowers.

I was just beginning to see this when Caroline spoke. "You want to keep me covered," she said. She spoke quietly. By the tone of her voice I could tell that it wasn't an accusation, but a realization. I looked at her face. Her expression had darkened. A vertical crease had formed between her eyebrows and she was looking down at the floor between us. She was hurt.

I told her about the robe, the way its folds going down were like water. She didn't look up. I knew it sounded like a rationalization to her.

I remember just what she said then. She said: "You don't want to look at me. It's my body. You're dodging it."

"That's not true," I said. But I was defensive, and I said some ridiculous things. I said, "It seems unnatural to paint you naked at a table, as if that's the way you eat your breakfast. And then I said: "Besides, wouldn't you rather have a painting you could hang here in the living room?"

"I don't want a piece of furniture!" she said, her eyes flaring. "We're not doing home decorating here, are we? Was it any more 'natural' when you painted Ellen and Jean lying naked on a platform? I thought this was supposed to be real. I feel like you're humoring me." Her voice was all sharp edges now.

But I'd thought I *had* been doing real work, or I'd just been on the edge of it when she'd spoken up. I was angry now, too. "All right, then, open your robe," I said.

"I will *not*," she replied, staring back at me hard.

"Fine," I said. "That's what I want, anyway. Whether you believe it or not, this composition interests me." I started drawing again, a little fiercely, and kept talking. I told her the movement in the picture was from the upper left to the lower middle to the upper right. It started with her, I said, moving down the length of her body. The drapery lines of the blue robe were like water going down below the ground level of the table. The cylindrical vase was the way back up, but the aperture was small, the force more intense. That's why the flowers are red and spray up hard.

She was listening now. And her face was open, interested. I kept drawing. I wanted to paint this, now. I thought about getting a canvas and starting to lay out the picture, but decided not to break up the session.

Then Caroline untied her belt and opened her robe. It surprised me. It may have been an act of rebellion—giving me what I'd said I didn't want. I'm not sure. But it was just right: working over the top of the robe's lines, I drew in her naked breasts, the curve of her belly, the dark triangle below it. Her womanly shape struck me then like an ancient formula, something to be carved into a bone or stick. What a charm the female shape has! For all its use and all its debasement, it is never to be worn out, never to be wholly debased. How right that it be carved in marble. I think of the Erechtheion, of its caryatids: women holding the temple roof on their heads! Deliberately or not, Caroline had showed me the force that charged the space under the table and fountained up in the flowers.

I kept drawing. But I was thinking, now, of a walk I took one Saturday in the early spring—it must have been about a year ago. Jamie and I had gotten up early. We were going to work soon, but wanted to stretch our legs first. It was one of the first days after the snow had thawed and we could smell the ground. We were cutting through the parking lot of a small block of apartments when we heard, from above, the unmistakable sound of a woman's love cries. We both looked up at the open window of a second-floor apartment. Then we looked at each other and grinned. We kept walking. "That was loud!" Jamie said. And I remember the way I'd felt. Not aroused, exactly, but *cheered*. We'd been working hard that week and were tired. And here was this animal sound of abandonment and pleasure. It bucked me up like a fresh breeze, like the smell of the thawing ground. Life was still happening.

I was drawing intently. I think Caroline could see that. She spoke evenly, now, calmly. "I want you to *see* me, John," she said. "I want you to see *me*."

John

April 16, 1991

Dear Wyatt,

So, Jamie has been subpoenaed. I'm not surprised to hear that she isn't very happy about it. I wish this weren't necessary, but Storley feels strongly that it is. He says the jury needs to see as many women as possible speaking well of me. He says the testimony from Caroline, a health professional, and Jamie, the woman I lived with for years, is very important. I should drop Jamie a note of apology.

I'm at the desk in my bedroom listening to the water drip off the eaves and into the puddles by the foundation in the backyard. The snow from three days ago is disappearing in today's rain. The winter was long, and its only sound was the wind. It seems like an age since I last sat and listened to the rain, the sound of things finally letting loose.

At Earth Day this afternoon Rich helped me with a high chair I found at the salvage depot. He'd already sanded it and today we glued the joints. We worked in one corner of the sorting room. We got glue into the shaky joints and then Rich, with surprising expertise, bound them with a cord so they'll dry securely. Linda, who's working half days now, came over to see what we were doing. She stopped a few feet away and leaned to look, as if wary of entering a forbidden zone. "Who's that for?" she asked.

"It's for Jean Weller," I said.

She nodded, took a last look, and turned away.

Rich and I were squatting by the high chair, picking up the glue and leftover cord. "When does the baby come?" he said.

"Just about any time," I said.

Rich nodded. "Are you the dad?" he said.

I nearly lost my balance. I caught myself, glared at Rich, and said, "Of course not. Jerry, Jean's husband, is the father." I was whispering—hissing actually—glancing over my shoulder to see if any of the others were listening.

"Why isn't *he* fixing the chair?" Rich asked.

I told him I was helping out, as a friend, because Jean and Jerry weren't getting along right now. I said they'd had an argument and were living apart for a while.

Rich shrugged and shook his head. "Too bad," he said. We stood up. "The glue has to dry for two days. Then we can paint it," he told me.

"Thanks, Rich," I said. "I wouldn't know how to do this by myself."

"I know," he said, nodding briskly.

Earlier this evening I had my third session with August Stortz and his family. I understand what he wants, and I'll try my best to give it to him. He wants his family preserved in a moment like the one when they stood in church on Easter morning in their Sunday best. It is the moment in which winter and Good Friday have passed and are as far away as they'll ever be. Soon the bells will ring and the trumpets sound and the five of them will step out onto the churchyard's greening grass.

But for now they stand in a group, scrubbed and poised and dressed for heaven, bright as coins at the mint.

We work in August's living room, with the family arranged in front of the brick fireplace. A farm scene with grazing cattle hangs over the mantel, a photo reproduction of a genre painting, expensively framed. August and his tall, handsome son-in-law stand in coats and ties, groomed to the point of unreality. August's wife and daughter sit in front of them in formal chairs, their dresses pressed and carefully arranged in their laps. Their hair has been styled and immobilized with lacquer. They all smile seriously. Only little Tracy, the four-year-old, moves. It has been suggested that she lean against the arm of her mother's chair, and she does so, crossing and recrossing her legs, sighing and slouching in her green velvet dress. Her long brown curls, subdued by a system of ribbons and bows, gradually free themselves. I've made it clear that she can come and go as she pleases while I work out the painting's general structure, and sometimes she goes to the couch to rest or to the kitchen for a glass of apple juice. "Don't spill on your dress, honey," her mother calls after her. I've told them all that they can move as they like, trying different postures, relaxing when they need to, but they pose with discipline, as if at any moment a treacherous shutter may trip and catch them unawares.

They are the deathless ones, arranged by every art they know to exclude time, change, illness, unhappiness, doubt, and confusion. And my job, behind the easel, standing on the drop cloth which protects the white carpet from the mess of my paints, is to fix forever the heroic illusion. It sounds like I'm judging them. And I'll admit that at the end of a session I'm almost rigid with the tension I've absorbed from the brittle air. But I, of all people, should understand the impulse toward idealization. And I should understand the consolations of an art that conceals.

When the sitting ends, the tableau thaws. August and Tom slip off their jackets and let their shoulders sag. Emma rises and whisks Tracy off to put her into play clothes. Ruth hurries to the kitchen, ties on an apron, and plugs in the coffeepot. There will be pie and ice cream, all of us sitting around the dining room table. I must not leave until I have eaten two pieces. And I am in no hurry to go. The affection around the table is real. The hospitality is heartfelt. They have returned now from the austere plains of art. They roll up their sleeves. Their wrists and elbows reappear, flexing again in the familiar alternations of work and repose. Tracy, in a flannel jumper, sits on her mother's lap and carves her ice cream with a small spoon. Only the women's hair remains immobile, like the helmets of sopranos playfully worn to the party after the performance.

John

April 17, 1991

Dear Wyatt,

It surprises me that Caroline and I quarreled last time. It's something new for us, and not something I do easily. My parents never argued in front of me. I never fought with Jamie when we were together, though sometimes I think she wanted me to. So the memory of the flare-up with Caroline disturbed me all the time we were apart. When I saw her yesterday, though, she seemed perfectly at ease. She had gotten angry, I had responded, then something else had happened and we had gone on. That's the way it was for her, I guess. But it's not that easy for me. In an argument, I always feel like something's breaking—irreparably. I'm afraid of it, but I see that Caroline isn't.

I prepared a canvas and, in pencil, laid out the composition of Caroline at the table with flowers. She seemed unself-conscious as we began. She posed as before, her open robe flowing down on each side of her. She had gotten fresh flowers—the same red glads. I worked quickly, easily, referring sometimes to the sketches from the previous session. After several minutes of silence, Caroline asked if we could talk while I worked. I said, "Sure."

She was leaning back in her chair, relaxed, reflective. "My husband always liked this room," she said. "We planned the whole house around it. When he was sick and couldn't work he would sit here in the sun for hours. Sometimes he would read, but most of the time he was too tired. He always seemed to enjoy the light, though, and the warmth and the view." She was gazing through the windows, looking out over the town. I was drawing in the lines of her legs beneath the tabletop. "He was a very gentle man, a very kind man," she said. "But I wouldn't say that he was a passionate man. Except about ideas. He had a keen sense of justice. And I remember the way he handled his books. Most of the books on these shelves are his. He was perfectly at ease, perfectly knowing with a book. In fact, I usually picture him now standing with a book open in one hand, moving through its pages with the other hand, quickly finding the right passage. He was graceful, then, but in general he was a little awkward, physically." A wondering smile spread over her face, then her expression darkened. "I think he only really paid much attention to his body at the end, when he was very sick. The pain dragged him down into it, made him deal with it. Physical comfort—little pleasures—meant a lot to him then. He enjoyed the sun and his hot tea."

I was working on the bottom half of the canvas, on the legs of the table and chair. There were too many straight lines—I had to change them. I needed curves like wrought iron, curves that could dissipate themselves in the suggestion of circles near her legs. I was still thinking about water. Down at the bottom I needed turbulence and undertow.

After a long pause, Caroline began again. "When you were growing up at home," she said, "was there nudity? I mean, did your parents get out of the shower and walk down the hall naked to the bedroom to get dressed?" I looked up from the canvas. Caroline was looking out the window, thoughtfully.

"No," I said. "I'm not sure I ever saw my parents undressed."

"Mine did," she said. She shifted in her chair and the robe slipped off her near shoulder. "It really meant nothing to them. And I remember playing naked in the garden when I was a little girl. This was in Virginia. We lived a little ways into the country and had a vegetable garden in the backyard."

I was finished laying out the bottom of the canvas. The middle had been pretty well established by the earlier drawings. The top needed a mass, but not a heavy one—perhaps the suggestion of a thin fabric umbrella. Something to contain the painting at the top, but lightly, with held sunlight.

I noticed that Caroline had stopped talking. "I thought you were from St. Louis," I said.

"I grew up in St. Louis after my father died and we moved back to be near my mother's family," she said. "I was eleven."

"I didn't know you'd lost your father so young," I said. "I'm sorry."

"We were in Virginia because my father did work for the Navy," she said. "He was a mathematician and did special equations, something very advanced about displacement and buoyancy, my mother told me. But he taught school, too. The Navy work was irregular after a while."

I walked over and put Caroline's robe back on her shoulder because now I was thinking about that part of the painting. I returned to the easel. The diagonal from shoulder to foot was not long enough. I'd have to lengthen it. The legs could be longer—*should* be longer to get the fluidity I had in mind—but the whole figure would have to be reworked. Starting with the torso again, I wondered: if the woman in the painting were a mythological figure, who would she be? This woman is everywhere in the painting, I thought, even in the flowers, pushing the red flames out of the green stalks.

Caroline had been talking about her father some more. But now she was talking about her mother. "She was worried when I went up to Minneapolis for college. 'You'll freeze to death,' she said. And just before I left she got out her long fur coat—the one Daddy had given her when he got the Navy contract—and gave it to me. I was speechless."

I had a thought and skipped back to the top of the canvas, sketching in the curved line of an umbrella's edge so it repeated the shape of the tabletop. I had realized something. The painting was about levels: the underground below the table, the sky's light caught in the umbrella's fabric, and the world in the space between.

When I'd finished drawing in the edge of the umbrella, I moved back down to the torso. Looking at Caroline's belly—at the thin, purplish line running from navel to pubis—I realized that I had decided, unconsciously, to exclude the scar. It's not part of this composition, I told myself. That's not what this painting is about.

"Excuse me for a moment," Caroline said. She jumped up and ran downstairs. In a few moments she came back with a deep brown fur coat in her arms. "Here it is," she said, smiling brightly. She slipped out of her robe and put the fur coat over her shoulders. I had been absorbed in my drawing, and this break in the pose jolted me. The white of her skin down the coat's open front was bright against the dark fur. I was transfixed. It was lovely—and it was very sexy. I put down my pencil and started to come around from behind the easel. But when I looked up to her face again I saw that she was crying. She didn't make a sound, but wet streaks ran down both of her cheeks. I stopped. "What's wrong?" I said.

"Oh, nothing," she said, as if she were exasperated with herself. "It's just this silly coat."

"It makes you think of your father?" I said.

"No," she said, then: "Well, yes. But it was stored in the study downstairs, and it smells like pipe tobacco. It smells like my husband, Terry." She took a deep breath and forced a smile. But then she pulled up the coat's collar, dropped her face into it, and sobbed.

I went over and put my arms around her. She leaned into me hard and cried.

John

April 18, 1991
Dear Wyatt,

I got home very late from Caroline's last night, and I'm tired today. I wouldn't have come home at all if my apartment weren't being watched. I worked at Earth Day this morning while Caroline met with her clients. And then we were able to start with more drawings this afternoon. Caroline insisted. But I've abandoned the painting of her at the table with flowers. That was a mistake. It wasn't really her. She's asked me to paint her in the fur coat.

The patio table has been returned to the deck, and all the furniture in the living room is in its place. For our work, Caroline stands in front of a black backdrop. When I asked if she didn't want to wear something under the coat, she said, "You paint nudes, John. It should be a kind of nude. Anyway, that's what I want."

Somebody told me that Weston, when he was working on his famous nudes, said that you could photograph a woman's face or you could photograph her sex, but you could never do both at the same time. You have to choose. In this painting I will try to prove him wrong.

John

1 1

John Ordway
423 River Street
Delphi, Iowa

April 19, 1991

Dear Wyatt,

I saw Ron tonight and had a chance to ask Jerry about Charlie Anderson. Ron came by my apartment at dinnertime and asked me to go with him to the Friday night fish fry at Sammy's. It was a clear, cool evening so we walked downtown. The sun had gone down but the sky still glowed at its edges a deep, transparent blue, like blown glass cooling. As we walked, Ron said that Iris had stayed over in Decorah for some kind of office party.

"Oh! And you weren't invited?" I said, teasing him.

"I was invited, all right," he answered, "but I don't care for that kind of thing. Everyone will eat and drink standing up, trying to hold their plates and plastic cups in one hand and eat with the other. When I eat standing up, making conversation with strangers, my stomach stops. I'd wind up with a bellyache and jumpy nerves, nodding my head while one of the guys in the firm explains why Kirby Puckett should be the American League MVP."

"Who's Kirby Puckett?" I asked.

"Never mind," he said. And he seemed to sink into a black humor, having conjured the misery of the party he was skipping.

"But Iris likes these parties?" I said.

"She has to go," he said. "But I don't think she minds them. She wishes I'd go with her." We walked under a streetlight and our shadows grew in front of us, then faded as we left the circle of light.

"You and she have been together for a long time, haven't you?" I said. Ron nodded.

"You don't have to answer this," I said. Ron looked over at me. "But do you two ever talk about getting married?"

"I don't mind," Ron said. "Yeah, we've talked about it."

"Do you think you ever will?" I asked. Ron took a deep breath and exhaled heavily, as if about to put his shoulder to a great rock at the foot of a hill.

"I don't know," he said. "It's complicated." We walked along in the dark between streetlights. "Iris may want to move away from here someday. She talks about the opportunities she'd have in a city—more schooling, a better job, excitement." He sighed again. "I don't know. I came back here after college because I couldn't live in Chicago. I'm not looking for excitement. Excitement makes me nervous." He laughed at himself and I grinned at him in the dark. "I don't know, maybe things are best the way they are. Iris knows me well enough to realize that I'd be a load to take on full-time. Now we can be together as much as we want, but she always has her place in Decorah to get away to for a while. We get into a rhythm. It gives us both a little space." Ron fell silent, but seemed as though he had more to say. I waited. In a dark space between lights Ron continued: "Both of us—Iris and I— have . . . What shall I call it? We've both had affairs since we've been together. And I think that makes us nervous about getting married, too."

I tried to take in the possibility that Ron had had an affair with Ellen. Was Storley's rumor true? But Ellen and Iris were best friends. It couldn't have been Ellen, or else Iris didn't know. The possibilities swirled in my head. We passed under another light and our shadows grew from under our feet, took our true shapes and proportions for a moment, then stretched and faded into the surrounding darkness.

The business district was well lit. The names of beers, written in neon, glowed in the windows of the bars we passed. As we approached Sammy's we could smell the fish fry. Inside, there was a big Friday night crowd. A group was just leaving a booth, so we sat there. Sammy was behind the bar, but Ron caught his eye and waved two fingers in the air. Sammy nodded. In a couple of minutes Roxanne brought out two paper plates heaped with battered and fried northern, cole slaw, and dinner rolls. "Beers for you two?" she asked. We nodded.

As we ate, I noticed Jerry sitting at the bar. I gestured in his direction and asked Ron, "How's he doing lately? I've got to talk to him."

"Jerry?" Ron said. "He's all right, I guess. I haven't seen a lot of him. He seems kind of angry, kind of sullen. You know Jean's got her own apartment now." I nodded.

"I should talk to her, too," I said. "I'm trying to find out what I can about Charlie Anderson. I guess they both knew him pretty well."

"I think so," Ron said.

The food tasted good to me, and I had a second beer. Then I got up and walked over to where Jerry sat at the bar, staring up at the TV screen. The sound was inaudible over the noise in the bar, but a man and woman were walking on a beach. He handed her a bottle of beer. There was a close-up of the bottle and of their hands near their hips as she took it by the neck. Then a wave splashed against a rock, spraying them with spume. They embraced and laughed, tipping their heads back and opening their mouths. There was an open stool next to Jerry and I sat down.

He noticed me, straightened up, and balled his hands in the pockets of his worn jean jacket. He leaned back, as if I were too close for him to see me clearly. The glass in front of him was half empty. "Can I buy you a beer?" I asked.

"No thanks," he said. He waited for me to explain myself.

"You know Charlie Anderson, don't you?" I said.

"I know Charlie," Jerry said.

"Do you mind if I ask when you saw him last?" I said.

Jerry continued to lean back, holding his chin up a little, as if he were regarding me through eyeglasses that had slipped down his nose. "I do mind," he said, and he turned back toward the TV.

I went back to the booth and sat down across from Ron. "He doesn't like me," I said.

"Does that surprise you?" Ron asked. I shrugged. "He probably thinks you attacked Ellen and wonders about the time you spent painting Jean." He paused. "I wasn't sure I should tell you this, John, but I've been asked whether Jean's baby might be yours."

"That's ridiculous!" I said. Suddenly my face was hot and my heart was pounding. "You don't think Jerry believes that?"

"Probably not," he said. "But it would be bad enough for him to feel like other people were talking that way." I slumped back in the booth. "If I were you," he said, "I'd be sure Storley puts Jean on the stand to testify that you behaved yourself."

"Yeah," I said. I felt weak. I asked Ron if he was ready to go.

We walked away from the closely spaced lights of the business district out into the dark and light of the neighborhoods. We walked a few blocks and then Ron turned off to take the direct way back to his house. I continued on, contemplating the dimensions of the suspicions I had aroused. When I passed under a streetlight, my shadow grew in front of me, stretching to a grotesque length, then fading into the darkness all around.

John

April 21, 1991

Dear Wyatt,

Thanks for your letter of the 17th. I'm glad to know Jamie's travel plans. I don't know why she has to come so early, either. The 23rd is eight days before the trial begins. Both Storley and the county prosecutor want to depose her, I'd guess, but I still don't see why they need to schedule it so early in the week. And then she'll have that dead weekend before the trial starts Wednesday. I don't blame her for being upset about it. I'll try to drive over to Decorah and see her. I should thank her in person and apologize for all the trouble.

This evening after work I went to see Jean. Her new apartment is on Lime Bluffs Road, a couple of blocks away from where Jamie and I lived. It's a bright, clean place on the ground floor of a house that's been cut up into apartments. Her entrance is off a small back porch and walks into a big kitchen with nice windows that look into the backyard. The only other rooms are a small bath and two bedrooms, one of which Jean's made into a nursery. She seems happy there and excited for the baby's arrival.

After she'd shown me the apartment, we sat across from each other at the kitchen table under the windows, drank ginger ale, and talked. Jean's long dark hair was tied back. She was as beautiful as ever.

"Did you know that today is my official due date?" she said. "The doctor says first babies are a little late sometimes." She smiled almost continuously as she spoke. "It must be a boy," she said. "He's kicking the daylights out of me."

"Right now?" I said.

"Yeah, you want to feel him?" She drew my hand across the table and placed it on her stomach. In a moment a bulge rolled under my hand. The smooth, rolling motion made me think of the way a dolphin breaks the surface when it breathes.

"I felt that," I said. "That's really something." I took my hand away and sat back.

"I can hardly wait to meet him," Jean said. She poured me some more ginger ale from the green plastic bottle between us. "You want some crackers or something?" she asked.

"No thanks," I said. And then I asked her what she could tell me about Charlie Anderson. I said I'd tried to ask Jerry about him, without success.

"You wonder if maybe he's the one who broke into Ellen's?" Jean said. I nodded. "I wouldn't think so," she said. She paused. "But it's always been hard to tell about Charlie." She paused again. "In high school he was one of the popular kids and a favorite of the teachers, but he didn't want to miss any of the fun, either."

"What do you mean?" I asked.

"Oh, he partied as hard as anybody. And he'd raise hell when a bunch of guys got a little crazy. But he was good at not getting caught." Jean walked to the cupboard, brought back a box of crackers, and sat down. "Once he and Jerry wired a car and took it off Redlen's used car lot. They'd been drinking and Charlie drove the car in a ditch a mile out of town. Charlie stayed with the car while Jerry walked back to town to bring a truck and chains to pull it out. When Jerry got back the sheriff was there, but not Charlie. Jerry never told on Charlie, either." Jean paused. "That was all a long time ago," she said. "We've all grown up a lot since then."

"When was the last time you saw him?" I asked.

"He was here in February," Jean said. "He and Jerry went ice fishing on the Mississippi."

"Does he have a mustache?" I asked.

Jean paused. "He wore one on and off," she said. "Almost everybody around here does. But I don't think he had one the last time I saw him."

We talked a little more about other things. I told her that the last coat of paint on the high chair that Rich and I had repaired was almost dry and that I'd bring it over later in the week. And then I left. I was eager to call Storley. I thought the fact that Anderson had been in town more recently than his parents knew was significant. I went to the drugstore and used the phone. Storley promised to do some more checking. Then I snuck over to Caroline's to tell her what I'd learned from Jean.

I took the usual precautions, but Caroline hadn't known I was coming and that made her nervous. She sat on the couch facing the big windows and fidgeted in a chair across from me. I reported on my attempt to talk to Jerry Friday night and on my growing suspicion of Charlie Anderson. She nodded distractedly as I spoke. "I suppose you and Storley have to explore every possibility," she said. She'd been gazing at the floor, but now she looked me in the eyes. "How long do you think you can put off talking to Rich? John, your trial starts in ten days!" She was almost pleading.

"I've been thinking about that a lot," I said. "I just can't imagine how to do it." I looked at her and shook my head.

"You really shouldn't have to." She spoke quickly and firmly now. "Maybe it's time to talk to Storley about him. Maybe Rich should be questioned officially, so if he does say something important the right people will hear it."

"He'd have to have a lawyer with him, wouldn't he?" I asked. "And maybe somebody like you, somebody sensitive to what it would be like for him." She nodded. I thought about it for a minute, then said: "It sounds awful. If I could just ask him myself, first, and give him a chance to tell me he didn't do it. I'm sure he wouldn't lie to me."

Holding my eyes with hers, Caroline got up, walked over, and sat down straddling my lap. She took the front of my shirt in both of her hands and balled her fists. "Talk to him, John," she said. "Talk to him now." Her eyes were dark and fierce. She'd cut Rich loose. She'd decided for me. "We need to know the truth now. Don't you want to know the truth?"

"I do," I said. "I do." But even as I said the words I knew that, deep down, part of me was afraid to learn what the truth might be.

John

April 23, 1991
Dear Wyatt,

Thanks for your good wishes on the phone last night. And, yes, I'm sure I don't want you to travel out for the trial. There wouldn't be anything for you to do. But I do appreciate the offer. Everything will be fine and I'll call you often.

I saw Jamie today. Her first meeting with Storley is tomorrow. I drove to Decorah late in the afternoon and went to the motel at the edge of town where you told me she'd be staying. I was determined to see her, but I didn't want to simply turn up at her door, so I got her room extension from the desk clerk and called from the lobby phone.

"Hello," said a woman's voice. It didn't sound like Jamie, but I wasn't sure. I wondered if I'd reached the wrong room. "Hello," the woman said again.

"This is John Ordway," I said. "I'm trying to reach Jamie Stevens. Do I have the right room?"

"Oh," said the woman. "Just a minute." And I recognized Andrea's voice.

There was a muffled conversation in the room, then Jamie came on the line. "Hello," she said.

I told her that I was in the lobby, that I wanted to see her—to say thanks for coming back to testify and to apologize for the inconvenience. I told her I only planned to stay for ten minutes, then I was going back to Delphi. Okay, she said, but could I wait a minute? She was just freshening up after traveling all day. She'd flown to Minneapolis and Andrea had picked her up at the airport and driven her down here. They'd just arrived. I told her I could wait.

I sat in the small lobby, staring at the worn, plaid carpeting. I don't remember thinking anything. I was just waiting for what would happen next. When someone appeared, it was Andrea. She was wearing a long, tan raincoat that made her look taller than ever. I stood up.

"Hello, John," she said, curtly. "You can go down to the room now. But first, would you mind coming outside with me for a minute?"

I followed her out the door. She turned and we stood between two parked cars just outside the front door of the motel. A light drizzle was falling.

"You have no idea what you're doing, do you?" she said.

"What do you mean?" I said.

"You're poison and you don't even know it," she said. Her head was cocked and her eyes fixed me hard. I felt like I was looking down the barrel of a loaded gun.

"You almost smothered Jamie, pulling her away from everything she knows in New York. Never mind what's good for her; you can't even imagine that. And then she's supposed to come running when you have that breakdown of yours, or whatever it was." She was biting off her words. "I guess she's supposed to feel guilty. But, anyway, she's got to come to the rescue. You *need* her." She drew out the word "need" as if it made her sick.

"And now one of your models gets roughed up." She shook her head back and forth, then fixed me with her eyes again. "You claim you're innocent—and everybody's supposed to help you get off. But it's pretty clear to me what's going on. You're pissed at Jamie, and you take it out on the woman who's handy."

"Wait a minute," I said. "If you're suggesting . . ."

"You wait a minute," she said, cutting me off. "I'm not suggesting anything. I'm telling you. You're out of control, mister, and I hope they lock you up."

She turned and strode across the parking lot, got into a car, and slammed the door. Then she just sat there, waiting, I suppose, for me to make my visit and leave. I leaned back against the car behind me. I was breathing hard. I felt like I'd been in a fistfight.

The drizzle turned to rain. I went back into the lobby and sat down. I sat there for a couple of minutes wondering if Jamie felt the same way that Andrea did. And then there were only two things to do. I could leave or I could go to the room and see Jamie.

I heaved myself up and started down the hall. When I reached the door I knocked. Almost immediately the door swung open and there she was. I was not prepared. Her sudden presence struck me like another blow. The clear, green eyes, the copper-colored hair, the familiar sweep of the long, poised body. I felt as though I were seeing a ghost, but a ghost fleshed with a preternatural intensity. My face burned. It was as though she had opened the door and slapped me or kissed me hard on the mouth.

She stepped aside to let me in. She left the door open behind us and gestured toward a chair in the corner of the room next to a small, round table. I sat there and she sat on the edge of the bed with the table and another chair between us. She sat with her back straight and her hands folded in her lap. She looked at me and waited. The reality of my impending trial struck me hard. The shock of seeing Jamie again—of realizing that something powerful had brought her back here against her will—drove home once and for all the scope and the public nature of what I'm involved in.

I gathered myself. "I'm sorry that you've had to come back here," I said. "I know it's the last thing you wanted to do, and I'm sorry for the trouble." She sat still and listened. "But it means a lot to me," I said, "and I wanted to come over and thank you in person."

Finally she spoke. "You don't have to thank me for coming," she said. "I didn't have much choice." I looked down and nodded.

"Just the same," I said. "I'm grateful that you're here." There was a long, awkward silence. I'd made my little speech. What was left to say? More moments passed.

"I saw Andrea," I said. "I guess you know what she thinks."

"Yes," Jamie said.

"She's wrong," I said.

"I really don't want to get into it," Jamie said. She shook her head as if a fly had buzzed near her. When she did, her hair swung around, then settled again, as smooth as before. "I'll answer the questions that I'm asked," she said. "I'm pretty sure what they'll be." She looked me in the eyes. "I'll tell the truth: You never hurt me or forced me. And, as far as I know, you were faithful to me while we were together."

"I was," I said.

She nodded. "I know," she said.

We sat quietly in the room for a few more minutes. This morning she'd been in New York. The shape of her earrings and the cut of her clothes brought the city back to me, like a forgotten dream. The strange familiarity of her presence continued to strike me in subtle shocks. It seemed a wonder that she was here. A great distance had been overcome, but more than that, an expanse of time. The four months since I'd seen her last seemed like continents. We had stood in the snowy parking lot of the Lilac View Motel. And then it was as though the months that followed were years of continuous travel. But here we were, in another room with stained carpet and strange, bland pictures on the walls. We sat there, silent, the same two people, but changed. For all her remarkable presence, and for all the memories that came with it, she was withdrawn, contained, and absent to me. And I was elsewhere, too.

I stood up. "I should go," I said.

Jamie stood up and nodded.

I went to the door, turned, and said, "Good-bye."

"Good-bye," she said. And then: "Good luck."

I drove back through the rain as the afternoon darkened into evening, arriving at Delphi just as the streetlights were coming on. Around their globes, I could see that the crooked branches and twigs had broken out with swollen buds and the first, crumpled yellow-green leaves. The space around each light was lacy with them. I reached my apartment and boiled water for tea. And now I've been writing at the kitchen table while the rain continues.

This life we are living is stranger than any story. We make plans, we work ahead, trying to have things turn out right, but from a deep well somewhere events arise. There's more surprise than we can take in as we go along. And then one day we straighten up to look around and everything has been changed. Part of us is already used to it and goes on ahead, but another part steps back and wonders at the strangeness of it all. How did we get here? What is this place? And why does it feel so much like home?

John

April 24, 1991

Dear Wyatt,

I went to Caroline's house today and we worked on the painting of her in the fur coat. I want to finish it before I have to be in court every day, and before . . . Well, I don't know what will come after that. I told Johnson at Earth Day that I needed to prepare with my lawyer, and Caroline has cleared her appointment book for the next few days. The painting is something we can finish, if I work quickly enough, whatever happens next.

I've been brooding about the painting since our last session. It feels to me like no other I've attempted. And as Caroline and I worked today in her sunny living room, the remarkable thing was the talk. Strangely, it wasn't distracting. Caroline told me more about her mother, Sonya, a remarkable woman, apparently, who still lives in St. Louis in the house where Caroline grew up. When the two of them returned to St. Louis, Sonya went to work at a small publishing house that specialized in botanical books. She started as a secretary and in ten years was a senior editor. By then Caroline was at the University of Minnesota, where her father had gone to school. She stayed on there for graduate work, and when she finally left the Twin Cities to come to Delphi she'd been working as a clinical psychologist for eight years.

"After eighteen years in Minneapolis, why did you move?" I asked. "And what made you come *here?*"

Caroline shifted her weight from one leg to the other. She lifted the coat's collar to her face, breathed deeply in it, and let it fall. "My work with families had verged into social work, and some of it wound up in the courts," she said. "That's how I met Terry. Some of his practice was in family law. We were involved in the same custody case once, and after that I called him for advice when I needed it. A year later we worked together again." She paused.

"It was another custody case," she said. "A social worker and I were trying to get a four-year-old boy away from his parents. He was terribly abused. We lost. Eight months later the boy was dead."

Caroline looked past me, her face set in a mask of concentration. "It wasn't the only hard case that year," she said, "but it was the hardest. I was wearing out. I needed a change." She paused again and looked out the windows. "That spring, driving down to see my mother, I stopped for gas in Delphi. All during the rest of the trip I daydreamed about starting over in the little town with the river running under the bluffs, of marrying and having children of my own. I was thirty-six. When I got back to the Cities, I walked into my office and couldn't breathe. I literally could not draw breath into my lungs. Two months later I was in Delphi, living in a rented house on River Street not far from where you live now."

"Wow," I said, stupidly. "So your body told you to leave."

"I guess you could put it that way," she said. "I kept seeing Terry that year," she continued. "Sometimes he came down here, sometimes I visited him in Minneapolis. Finally he agreed to join me here. That was ten years ago."

"And you built this house," I said. She nodded.

I thought about the empty rooms downstairs, the law study for her husband, the nursery for the child, and I saw the pattern of losses that had shaped her life. The men and children had always been taken away. Her father, the abused boy, her own son, her husband. She was an independent professional woman, and her purpose was helping others. But she couldn't save the closest ones. They always disappeared. And now she was letting me get close, another man, and an endangered one, at that.

I knew who I was painting now. I looked at her and wondered at her capacity for risk. She stood in the coat that her father had given her mother, that her mother had given to her, that carried the scent of her husband. And she showed herself to me. She faced me squarely, her arms in the coat's sleeves, her hands in the pockets. The short, dark curls around her face blended with the black background, like the dark fur of the coat. From her face to her feet, down the coat's open front, her pink skin started out, a vulnerable-looking strip of flesh against the dark around it. She looked directly at me then. Her expression was one of calm resolve. Her clavicles were pronounced. Her breasts were wonderfully full and round, doubling her frank gaze at me. Vertically down her belly ran the thin line of the scar. I would not exclude it. The dark hair below it connected with the coat and the dark background. Her legs were solid. Her thighs were dimpled, touchingly. Her beautifully shaped feet were set surely on the floor.

John

April 25, 1991

Dear Wyatt,

Caroline and I have been very foolish. I feel like I've been shaken out of a dream. I don't know what we were thinking, what we were imagining.

I arrived for our session at noon, today, having taken the usual precautions. Caroline let me in and I sat on the couch facing the big windows. She went to the kitchen, brought back two glasses of cranberry juice, and sat beside me. We didn't feel the need to speak. Caroline rested one hand on my leg and leaned her shoulder against me. A great inexplicable calm fell over me.

We sat and sipped our drinks. I was sorry when Caroline broke the spell. "We may as well get to work," she said. "Your things are still in the closet. You can get them out while I undress."

At that moment the crunch of gravel came from outside. Caroline jumped up. "A car's in the driveway!" she said. I stood as she rushed to the front door and looked out its small window. "It's Ellen!" she said.

I stood still, thinking too many things at once to be able to act. Caroline ran to me. "Go downstairs," she said. "Go into the bedroom and shut the door."

"But maybe this is our chance," I said. "Maybe the three of us . . ." A car door slammed.

"Oh, please!" Caroline said, her voice twisting as it rose. "Please don't be stupid! Go downstairs and stay there until I come down for you." She noticed my glass on the low table, picked it up, and pressed it into my hand. "Promise me!" she said.

I did what she wanted. I went downstairs, went into the bedroom, and eased the door closed. I stood still and heard the two women greet each other at the front door. They crossed the room above me and kept speaking. I could hear the voices but not the words.

I stood still and listened hard. Ellen was speaking most of the time, her voice rising and falling, fast and emphatic sometimes, then slower and more deliberate. In between, Caroline spoke briefly or asked a question. As hard as I strained, the words wouldn't come clear.

I pictured Ellen upstairs in the bright room. I imagined Caroline on the couch, leaning forward, listening and nodding. Why was I hiding down here? I should have trusted my instinct, exerted my will, and stayed upstairs. This had been a great stroke of luck. Ellen, unknowingly, had come to *me*. It was the perfect chance to talk to her, to sort things out.

It wasn't too late. I could still go upstairs. Ellen would be startled at first, but Caroline would be there to reassure her. It really was the perfect situation. The three of us could talk. Together, Caroline and I would make Ellen realize that I would never have attacked her. Ellen had to have doubts, already. Seeing me again, she would realize it couldn't have been me. This moment had to be seized.

I stood in Caroline's bedroom, telling myself these things, standing so unnaturally rigid that my legs began to quiver. I pictured myself in the doorway upstairs at the moment when the two women turned and saw me. I imagined Ellen's face— the initial surprise, confusion, and fear. I imagined Caroline's face and saw the shock and betrayal in it. And I remembered the way she had fixed me with her eyes and said: "Promise me!"

I sat on the floor and leaned against the wall. I ran both hands through my hair and took deep breaths. I heard the light, quick movement of Ellen's voice, rising and falling. I heard the lower sound of Caroline's replies. In the evenness of Caroline's voice I heard the tightness—the anxiety and the strain of duplicity. I put my elbows on my knees and my face in my hands. I would not go upstairs. I did not know whether I was being loyal or cowardly.

The voices upstairs continued and I continued to hide. The agony of indecision gave way to a sudden heaviness and fatigue. I slumped to the side, lay on my back on the floor, and stayed that way for a long time. I told myself that I was doing the right thing, that I was protecting Caroline from talk in the town, that I was preserving her credibility as a witness in my trial, and that in staying away from Ellen

I was obeying the terms of my release from jail, but these thoughts came dully through a haze of lassitude. The minutes dragged on and on.

At last—I don't know how long it had been—I heard footsteps cross the floor above me. There were a few more words, then the front door opened and closed. I heard the car start and pull away. Moments later I heard Caroline come down the stairs. She opened the door and looked down at me lying on the floor.

She knelt and then lay down on her side next to me. She put an arm around my chest and pulled herself close. "Oh, that was hard," she said, sighing heavily.

"Yes," I said.

"Thank you, John," she said.

"Okay," I said.

It was quiet for a while.

"We have to stop," she said. "Something terrible will happen."

Then it was quiet again. The light outside was dimming. We lay there for several minutes, recovering the best we could. Finally I asked: "What did Ellen say?"

Caroline, speaking softly and slowly, recounted the conversation. She told me that Ellen had been accepted into the Master of Fine Arts program in painting at the University of Wisconsin at Milwaukee. "She's pleased," Caroline said, "but she's having troubles. Since the attack she's had a hard time leaving her mother's house. She's had a lot of fears—especially since the night the man peered in at her. She doesn't know how she's going to be able to live in Milwaukee." Caroline paused. "She asked me to help her," Caroline said. "I told her I couldn't until your case was concluded. I guess she hadn't known I was going to be a witness in your defense."

I rolled onto my side and faced Caroline. "How did she react?" I said.

"It brought her up short. I gave her the name of someone she can see in Decorah. I tried to reassure her," Caroline said.

"Does she think I attacked her?" I said. We were lying on our sides, our faces close together.

Caroline put her hand on my cheek. "All she knows," Caroline said, "is that what happened to her was real. It was terrible for her. She told me again how the man's hand clamped over her mouth, how the other one moved all over her body while his mustache rasped across her shoulders. She bit him as hard as she could and when he ran she lay in her bed and shivered with her teeth clenched on the leather in her mouth."

Caroline paused. I felt chilled. Caroline said, "She doesn't know what to think. She isn't thinking. She's afraid almost all the time now. It's terrible for her." Caroline stroked my cheek, as if in comforting me she could comfort Ellen.

"She asked me what I thought," Caroline said. "I told her that I knew you. I told her you hadn't done it."

"And what did she say then?" I asked.

Caroline was almost whispering, now, stroking my cheek over and over. "She got a funny look on her face," Caroline said. "And she asked me, 'How can you be so sure? Do you really think you know him that well? Does anyone really know him? He doesn't even know himself.'"

The sun had gone down. We lay on the floor in the dark for a long time. At last I kissed her on the cheek and said, "I have to go."

"Be careful," Caroline said. "Be careful." Her voice, dreamy with exhaustion, came from a long ways away. I got up, slipped out, and made my way home in the dark.

That night I dreamed again. Ellen was in my arms. Her bright hair shone in the dark. I ran my hands down her sides, but I couldn't feel anything. It was as though my hands were asleep. I stood up and looked at them. I stood in the dark, naked, and looked at the thick gloves on my hands. When I squeezed my hands into fists blood oozed from the leather.

Am I crazy, Wyatt?

John

April 28, 1991

Dear Wyatt,

It's Saturday night—the middle of the night—and I've got a lot to tell you. I've been to jail again—and to the hospital—but I'm all right. I'm back home at the apartment now. Listen to this:

I arranged to visit Rich Friday evening. We made plans to shoot baskets over at the house and I was determined to speak to him alone before I went home. We'd finished the high chair and the last coat of paint had dried, so I'd taken it back to the apartment with me. I was going to have supper downtown, drop off the high chair at Jean's, and continue on to the Earth Day house.

It was a beautiful evening, mild and clear. I walked downtown, the trees lining the streets lacy with catkins and young leaves. When I got to Sammy's, Ron was there, as I'd hoped he would be. As usual, there was a big Friday night crowd. I left the high chair under the coat rack in the corner of the bar and joined Ron at his table. As I sat down he looked past me, staring at the high chair. "What are you thinking of, bringing that thing in here?" he said. His eyes were a little wild.

"I didn't think about it," I said.

"Well, Jesus," Ron said. He cut his eyes toward the bar. "Jerry's here and everything." I looked toward the bar and saw Jerry, half turned on his bar stool, staring at me.

"Honestly, I didn't think about it," I said. "Do you really think people . . ."

"Of course they do," Ron said. There was a plaintive note in his voice. "What do you suppose this looks like to them?"

"I still can't believe I'm being *watched* like this," I said. "They don't miss anything, do they?" I was starting to get angry. "And you're telling me I should go around acting guilty and hiding things to prove I haven't done anything wrong?"

Ron looked down into his beer glass and shook his head. He looked disheartened and embarrassed. He seemed uncomfortable with me there, and suddenly I wasn't hungry, so I got up and left. Outside, I put the chair under one arm and walked down the main street, breathing in the cool air and feeling defiant as the sky darkened and the streetlights came on. To hell with them, I thought. The trial's in five days and we'll get this all out into the open.

It was about four blocks to Jean's, and I had to walk past my old studio on Raven Street. Mrs. Tolman's backyard was tidy and bare. The only trace of the tree I'd burned was a neatly raked patch of dirt scattered with grass seed. By the time I reached Jean's place, I'd settled down a little. I was surprised to see Caroline's car parked out front. I hesitated for a moment, wondering whether I should come back another time, then went to the door and knocked.

Jean swung the door open, smiled broadly, and let me in. She leaned forward precariously and kissed me on the cheek. As she did, I saw past her into the kitchen. Caroline sat at the table, leaning forward with her hands around a coffee cup. She smiled, but I thought she looked nervous about me being there.

Jean straightened up and I said, "I can't stay. I'm on my way to shoot baskets with Rich and Kevin. But I wanted to bring you the high chair. Rich helped me with it."

Jean was delighted. She had me put the chair beside the table and she ran her hands over its smooth back and tray. "This is wonderful," she said. "So white and clean. And it fits right in with this kitchen. It's starting to feel like home." Then her eyes looked past me, toward the door.

As I turned to see what she saw, I heard a loud bang that made me duck and jump back. The screen door had flown open at an odd angle, half off its hinges, and a figure rushed by me and struck Jean. She fell hard and landed on the floor with her back against the refrigerator. Caroline fell to her knees beside Jean. "Hey!" I shouted, as if the air had been forced out of me by a blow to the chest.

Jerry wheeled and faced me. "You son of a bitch," he snarled. "Stay away from my wife!" He stepped toward me with his fists balled up and his face red as steak. "Haven't you and that whore Ellen done enough? Why do you have to come around here?" He was shouting now, rocking up on his toes. "I've been watching you!" His voice boomed in the kitchen. "And now you come downtown waving *this* around." He reached and picked up the high chair by its back. He poked it at me once, like a lion tamer, then swung it at me as hard as he could. I raised my arms, but it hit me across the head and shoulders, its legs shearing off and bursting into pieces.

Then I was on my back on the floor. My tongue was thick and the taste of iron was in my mouth. I lifted my head and saw the others across the room. Jerry stood over the two women, still gripping a stick from the broken chair, shaking it in front of them. Jean lay against the refrigerator, both of her arms thrown across her belly. Caroline was on her knees with her arms around Jean's shoulders. Jerry was still shouting, but my ears were ringing. Both women stared up at Jerry as he bent over them, shaking the stick from the broken chair.

It was like a tableau. It was like a painting I had seen somewhere, but I couldn't place it. My mind moved slowly and I felt as though I were looking at them from a long way off, through a window or through a telescope. Then Jerry reached with one hand and grabbed the front of Jean's dress, as if he was going to haul her to her feet. Caroline shouted something, stood up, and tried to push him back. Jerry let go of Jean and pushed Caroline away, sending her sprawling across the floor.

I got up. A wave of dizziness almost knocked me over and I had to hold the counter behind me. Jerry had grabbed the front of Jean's dress again. Caroline was on her hands and knees beside the table, starting to get up. I pushed away from the counter and ran at Jerry as hard as I could. I tackled him from the side, throwing my arms around his neck. We both hit the floor and I hung on. I was behind Jerry and under him, with my arms around his neck, while he twisted and flailed his arms and kicked his legs. He flailed like a madman and I held on so hard I could hear his breath screeching. We kicked over the kitchen chairs and sent them clattering across the floor. Jerry was reaching back, grabbing at my face and hair.

He twisted and rolled and I rolled with him, my arms aching. I was losing my grip. I could feel Jerry slipping in my grasp, and I shouted: "Caroline, call the police."

"I am," she called out. "Hang on."

Jerry had twisted around so that we were front to front on the floor. He was on top of me and I clung to his neck to keep him close so he couldn't hit me. His breath was hot on the side of my face and it stank like beer. Then I felt his hands around my neck, his thumbs crushing the front of my throat. I couldn't breathe and the room was spinning.

I felt a jolt and heard a crack. Jerry rolled off me and struggled to his feet. My throat screeched as I drew a breath. And then I could see Caroline holding a cracked kitchen chair in front of her. Jerry was going toward her, but he stumbled sideways, toward the refrigerator where Jean lay half propped against its door. He tripped over Jean's legs and fell to his knees, then got up again, panting hard. I pulled myself up, gasping for breath, and took a step forward. The three of us made a triangle—Caroline with the chair in front of her, and Jerry and I stooped and gasping. Jean watched from the floor. Then Jerry lunged past us to the doorway and ran out into the dark.

Caroline fell to her knees next to Jean and asked her how she was. I could see now that Jean was sitting in a pool of pinkish water that was spreading across the linoleum. Then I heard a siren and saw lights flashing outside. A moment later two policemen came through the door, looking around warily. One of them came over and put his gloved hand on my arm. The other stood in the doorway. Caroline shouted, "These two have to go to the hospital right away!"

"Are you hurt?" I said to her.

"No," she said. "He just knocked me over."

"What happened here?" said the policeman in the doorway.

"Her water's broken and he was hit over the head with a chair," Caroline said. Her explanation was so short that I wanted to laugh. I pictured a scene out of a slapstick movie. Then the room started to swirl again and I sat down hard on the floor. "*Please* take them to the hospital, now," Caroline said.

The policemen did as Caroline asked. I have a vague recollection of her choreographing our movements. I wound up in the backseat of the squad car, still feeling woozy. I saw Caroline's car pull away with one of the officers driving. I glimpsed Caroline in the backseat cradling Jean's head against her chest. And then the squad car pulled away from the curb and I rode to the hospital.

On the way, the policeman glanced at me in his rearview mirror and said, "How did this happen?"

"Jerry was there," I said. "Jerry Weller. We fought." The officer picked up his microphone and spoke into the radio. I slumped in my seat, let my head tip back, and shut my eyes.

At the hospital emergency room I was taken into a bright, tile-floored room and was put onto a gurney. A nurse pulled curtains to close off a small area around us, put on rubber gloves, and began to wipe my face with gauze pads that came away bloody. Then she gave me water in a paper cup and had me rinse out my mouth and spit into a curved metal bowl. The police officer who had driven me to the hospital stood in the corner of the small space and watched.

When the nurse began to wipe my face again I asked her how Jean was. She said she'd try to find out. Then the doctor came in and examined me and told me I had a concussion. He said he didn't think it was too bad, but he wanted to keep me for a few hours to watch me. The officer told him that I was in police custody, pending an investigation. The doctor nodded. Then they left me alone and I shut my eyes to rest.

When I did, the whole scene at Jean's apartment replayed in my mind—I saw Jerry's red face again as he shouted, blaming me and Ellen for estranging his wife from him—and then, exhausted, I must have slept.

I heard the curtain pull back and I opened my eyes. The doctor came in, looked into my eyes with a light, and asked me how I felt. When he left, Caroline came in. I sat up and then lay back down because my head hurt. She asked me how I was and I told her. And I asked if she had been hurt.

"Not really," she said. "My arm's just a little sore from landing on it."

I asked about Jean.

Caroline broke into a broad smile. "She's fine, just fine," she said. "And so is little Ellen. She was born about half an hour ago. They did a cesarean."

"Ellen!" I said. "That's wonderful." I sat up again and steadied myself, my feet hanging over the side of the gurney.

"She's got dark hair, just like Jean," Caroline said. "She's beautiful." Caroline's eyes filled with tears and she leaned forward and pressed the side of her face against the front of my shirt. "It's such a relief," she said. I put my arms around her and we held each other.

We were quiet for a while. Finally, I said, "What a night."

"Yes," Caroline said. "And there's something else." She stepped back, looked at me, and put her hands on my knees. "Listen to this," she said. "When Jerry was shaking that stick at us, I noticed his hand. There's a terrible scar. His middle finger was all red with it."

"Which hand?" I asked.

"Left," she said, without hesitation.

"Have you told anyone else?" I asked. She shook her head. "We need to call Storley right away," I said.

Caroline went out and found the nurse, who came in and showed me to a nearby phone. I reached Storley at home and told him the story of the evening. He said he'd contact the sheriff. I asked him to call the Delphi police, too, and he said he would. Then the nurse told me I should lie down some more. Caroline squeezed my hand and left to go check on Jean and the baby.

About an hour later, the doctor came back and examined me again. He said I was going to be fine, and as far as he was concerned, I could leave. Then the policeman came in—a stocky man in his late thirties, with a full head of blond hair. He said he needed to ask me some questions, if I felt all right. And so I told him everything that I'd told Storley. He took notes and asked me to wait while he went out to make a call. When he came back he said I'd have to spend the night in jail. As he took me out to his car I looked for Caroline in the waiting room and the adjoining hallways, but she must have been with Jean and little Ellen. And just a few minutes later I was in the one-cell Delphi lockup, lying on my back on a cot with an ice pack on my face.

Moonlight poured in the barred window, making bright stripes on the gray cinderblock wall. I may have slept off and on, but I was too excited to rest well. Every time I closed my eyes the night's events replayed in my mind. At one point I lay for a long time with my eyes open, staring at the moonlit wall. When I finally shut my eyes again I saw Caroline standing in Jean's kitchen the moment after Jerry had fled. She held the cracked kitchen chair in front of her and she looked at me with the eyes of a wild animal. And at that moment, lying in jail with my eyes closed, a phrase came into my mind. It said, "We are married now," and the word "married" sounded to me like it never had before. It did not sound like the name for a social arrangement, something you agree to become. It sounded instead like a geological term, hard and exact, a word for the way two minerals melt down and bond together and cool to make a new mineral.

John

12

John Ordway
423 River Street
Delphi, Iowa

April 28, 1991

Dear Wyatt,

I ended before I was finished last time. It was 3:00 A.M. when I stopped writing—something like that. My head started to hurt again. I'll send that letter and this one together. Anyway: I was asleep in my clothes in jail when Storley arrived to get me out at about 10:00 Saturday morning. That would be yesterday. My sense of time is a little mixed up. I've been sleeping strange hours. Storley was with a policeman who opened my cell door and motioned me out. When I sat up my head clanged. In a few minutes—almost before I realized what was happening—I was standing outdoors in the bright sunlight and Storley was saying, "I'll give you a lift to your apartment." We got into his car and I looked across at him for an explanation. He was rumpled—his white shirt was wrinkled and his tie hung loose around his neck. "I had a long night," he said, "but I've got good news."

"I had a long night, too," I said. "Tell me."

"The sheriff picked up Jerry," he said. "They found him pulled off the highway north of town puking into the ditch and took him in on OWI. The Delphi police had contacted the sheriff's office about the violence at Jean's place, so Jerry was held at the county jail for questioning. After your call, I went down and got a look at his hand. There *is* a scar. He says he caught it in a machine at work, that he has witnesses. But, along with that red mustache of his, it was enough to convince the sheriff to get a warrant and type his blood. It's the same as yours—the same as the blood inside the glove. And when deputies searched around Jerry's cabin they found your other glove in a trash bag stuffed inside an old washing machine out in the woods." Storley pulled to the curb in front of my apartment, beamed at me, and reached across to shake my hand. I shook his hand, thanked him, and slumped back in my seat. This was the possibility that had kept me awake most of the night, but the sudden news left me stunned.

"They're sending the glove to the state lab for more tests," Storley continued, "but it's really all over but the paperwork. I expect the county attorney to file for dismissal Monday morning."

I got out of the car, then leaned down to the window and asked Storley to call Caroline and tell her what had happened. My headache was throbbing and I didn't think I could make it to the drugstore to call her myself. Storley looked at me, suspended in a moment of realization, then nodded and pulled away.

I went upstairs, took some aspirin, and went to bed. When I got up again it was dark—the middle of the night. I fixed myself some soup, ate it, and went out to my landing at the top of the stairs. Everything was changed and everything was the same. The moon, cool and bony, was near its full, and the tips of the twigs around the streetlight's globe flamed yellow-green. I breathed in the cool air. There was no car parked across the street.

This morning—Sunday—I woke up early wanting to go to church and see Rich. Of course, I'd never made it over to the house Friday night, and I'd slept all day Saturday. So I woke up today wanting the simple pleasure of seeing him, of being around him, without questions or suspicions. Also, I hoped Caroline would be there.

I got up and drove to church, arriving just as the organ prelude began. I found Rich, Kevin, Linda, and Patty in the back pew on the left, as usual. They all looked up with questions in their eyes—I'd stood them up Friday, and here I was with a bruised and swollen face—but they quickly slid over to make room for me. I settled in next to Rich and we sat quietly as the organ played. And then someone in the aisle next to me asked, "Is there any more room here?" I looked up and saw Caroline smiling down. We all shifted again, squeezing a little, and she sat down next to me.

So, there we were, all in a row. When we stood for a hymn, Caroline shared her book with me, and I followed the verses with my eyes as she sang softly. Rich sang on my other side, in his familiar, heartfelt drone. During the sermon, Caroline slipped her arm around mine and we sat like the other couples as we listened. Actually, I didn't hear the sermon and I don't remember much of the service. I just sat there between Rich and Caroline, awash with relief and gratitude.

Afterward, we spilled out into the churchyard with the rest of the congregation. As the six of us stood in a loose knot among the others, Rich asked, "What happened to your face?" I told him that I'd been in a fight, that Jerry had hit me and that he was in jail. I said that he was being charged in the attack on Ellen and that the charges against me were being dropped. Kevin and Linda and Patty listened and nodded pleasantly, as if I were telling them about my dinner plans. Rich reached out and shook my hand. "I told you," he said. Then the four of them said good-bye and they filed off toward the curb where Barbara was waiting in the Earth Day van.

I turned back to Caroline, who was speaking with a friend of hers, a woman in a smart yellow dress. Sensing me at her side, Caroline slipped her arm around mine. I saw the woman's eyes glance at the gesture and then quickly back to Caroline's face. We stood side by side as she talked to her friend in the yellow dress. When there was a pause in the conversation, Caroline said, "Have you met John?"

"No, I don't believe I have," the woman said, looking at me for the first time.

"Elizabeth, this is John Ordway," Caroline said, nodding toward me. "John, this is Elizabeth Downey."

The woman smiled formally and I smiled back. "I'm glad to meet you," I said.

"I'm happy to meet you," she said. Then we all said good-bye.

"She's very nice," Caroline said as the woman walked away. "She's on the hospital board. Her husband is a contractor." I nodded. "Are you hungry?" Caroline asked. "Do you want to go to lunch somewhere?" And so I began to enter the wider world of this little town, with Caroline's rehabilitating arm around mine.

After lunch we went to the hospital to visit Jean and I got my first look at little Ellen. We found the two of them in bed, Ellen sleeping at Jean's side. Jean waved us in and each of us bent to kiss her on the cheek. Jean reached up and touched my temple on the right side and said, "Ooh."

"It's all right," I said. "The headache's gone."

Jean sat up in bed, unwrapped Ellen, and pulled the tiny knit cap from her head so we could see the surprisingly long, dark hair. Ellen stirred and reached her fists up and yawned. Her miniature arms barely reached to the top of her head when she stretched. Her ankles were crossed, demurely. "My god! She's so tiny!" I said.

"You've never seen a newborn?" Jean said.

"I guess not," I answered. "Not one this little."

"Or this beautiful," Caroline said.

"Do you want to hold her?" Jean said to Caroline.

Caroline picked up the baby, carefully, and then looked at me. Caroline seemed to glow. I looked at her and had to take a deep, slow breath. My emotions were on a hair trigger. The world had gotten suddenly more intense, or more near. I took another deep breath. "Are you feeling okay?" I asked Jean.

"Yes," she said. "I want to thank you both." She looked from me to Caroline. "I can't believe you hit Jerry with a kitchen chair!" she said to Caroline. "I didn't know you were that strong!"

Caroline's face got a little red, and we were all quiet for a moment, remembering the ugly fight. "Jean, I'm sorry about Jerry," Caroline said.

"Well, don't be," Jean said. "I'm relieved, mostly." She shifted in the bed and tugged at her blankets. "Things were real good for quite a while. We had a lot of fun. But then he got angry and started hurting me." She looked down and smoothed her blankets nervously. "Before I was pregnant my modeling was a 'turn-on' for him, but afterward he didn't like it." She looked at me, then past me to the window. "He couldn't stand to see me pregnant. And he couldn't stand the idea of you painting me that way. He thought it was shameful. And he was sure you and Ellen had been talking against him, telling me to keep the baby. But I never dreamed he could do what he did." She paused.

"In the end I guess he just lost himself," Jean said. "But look at this little wonder." She reached out her arms and Caroline handed Ellen to her. The baby fussed a little, so Jean opened her gown and put little Ellen to her breast. It was lovely.

Caroline put her hand on Jean's shoulder. "We'll let you rest for a while," she said. "I'll see you tomorrow."

I spent the rest of the afternoon at Caroline's house. It was a mild, clear day and we sat on her porch looking out over the town, enjoying the sun. I gazed to the horizon under the open sky. The young leaves showed as a thin, green fog hovering in the neighborhoods. We passed a quiet afternoon and fixed ourselves a supper of chicken and little red potatoes. Afterward, we sat on the couch in the high-ceilinged living room, listening to music and sharing a bottle of wine.

It was dark outside now, and the big windows had become black mirrors. As I sipped my wine, I looked at our reflection and saw the two of us on the couch together in the big room. I still felt a little stunned. I had to remind myself that things had changed, that we didn't have to hide anymore. Now that the prospect of the trial has been lifted away, I hardly know how to think about the days and weeks ahead. Before, there had been a sense of emergency as the trial approached. We lived with a kind of "last days" abandon, as though I might be taken away, like her husband. Now the threat is lifted and the future stretches ahead of us. What do I want? What does Caroline want? And how should we behave in the eyes of the town? Caroline has a life here. If I were to flaunt a certain kind of relationship with her and then leave, what kind of position would she be left in? And how can I say that I'll stay here over the long term, keeping books and sorting cans at Earth Day?

It was about 10:00. I stretched myself and said, "I guess I should be going home." I didn't want to be presumptuous. I watched for her reaction.

She looked down at the square of couch between us. Then she looked up. "I suppose you're right," she said. "I'll drive you home."

We were quiet in the car. When she pulled to the curb in front of my apartment, I turned in my seat to face her. I leaned forward and kissed her, hard, on the mouth, and she kissed me back. Then we straightened and looked at one another.

"See you tomorrow?" I said.

"Okay," she said. "Good."

5/1

Today—Wednesday—would have been the first day of my trial, but instead I went to Earth Day as usual and did the books. Ate lunch with the crew out back in the sun at the picnic table, then worked in the sorting room for a couple of hours. In the sorting room, Linda stood by the conveyor belt picking the 7-Up cans out of the passing jumble and dropping them into a bin next to her. Across the way, Kevin methodically counted cans, taking them one at a time out of a bin and filling the large clear plastic bags with the proper number and tying the bags closed. Sitting on a stool not far from where I worked, Rich wore heavy gloves to protect his hands as he tore the metal rings from the necks of glass bottles. I walked home at two o'clock.

This afternoon the apartment is quiet. I'm sitting at the kitchen table as I write this letter. In the next room the radio plays. It only makes the apartment seem more quiet.

John

May 3, 1991

Dear Wyatt,

Storley was here this afternoon. I had found a white metal table and chairs in the garage, cleaned them up, and put them in the backyard. So we sat in the mild sun in our shirtsleeves while we talked. Here's the story: the charges against me have been dropped, as expected. Confronted with the evidence against him, Jerry's admitted attacking Ellen, though he claims he wasn't going to rape her. He just wanted to shake her up, he says. He thought if she got scared and stopped modeling for me, the studio scene would fall apart. He says he was trying the only way he knew to get his wife back—away from Ellen's influence, and mine. Storley reported these things, which he'd learned through the prosecutor's office, then leaned back in his chair and put his hands behind his head.

"So Jerry's trying to sell himself as the wronged husband," I said. "What about storming into Jean's apartment and knocking her down?"

"That's a problem for him," Storley said. "Trespassing and assault, minimum. He's definitely going to jail, but he's fishing for a plea bargain. My guess is that the most he'll end up serving will be something like two years of actual time, probably less." He shrugged.

We sat for a minute. Then Storley started forward in his chair: "Oh, about the gloves," he said. "Jerry says you left them on a table at Sammy's one night, and that's where he picked them up. My guess is, that's when he got the idea of setting you up. He probably planned to lose one at the apartment during the attack, but not the way it happened."

"You think Jerry's that rational?" I said.

"He had quite a plan," Storley said. "The week of the attack he was on vacation up on Lake Superior and slipped down that evening without seeing anybody. And more than that: his first morning back at work he caught the middle finger of his left hand in a drill press. Everybody there saw it, and I think he did it on purpose to cover the wound from Ellen's bite." There was a note of admiration in Storley's voice that chilled me, but I let it pass. "His emotions got the better of him, though," he continued. "I guess the sight of you parading around with that high chair for his wife really drove him crazy."

"Also, he drank too much," I said. Storley nodded.

We sat for a moment, contemplating the man. Then I asked, "When Jerry gets out of prison, what about Jean?"

"She ought to divorce him," Storley said. "That would make it easier to get a restraining order to keep him away from her and the child." I nodded.

"So, for me, it's really all over," I said.

"Yes," Storley said. "Just tell me where you want your paintings sent. They're no longer needed as evidence."

Strangely, I hadn't thought about the paintings. There wouldn't be room to keep them in the apartment. "I'll have to find storage space," I said. "I'll call you."

We stood up and shook hands. Storley rolled his sleeves down and put on his jacket. "Oh, I almost forgot," he said. He drew a brown envelope out of his jacket pocket and handed it to me, then he walked to his car and left. The envelope contained a voucher for my bail money. I took it to the bank and had them make out a money order payable to you, which I've enclosed here. Wyatt, thank you. Thanks for everything.

John

May 11, 1991

Dear Wyatt,

I got your letter of the 8th. Yes, I could crate up the paintings and ship them out to you, but somehow I don't feel ready to do that. Caroline says she has plenty of room, so, for now, I'll have the sheriff deliver them to her place. In fact, she's eager to see them. For all the times we've talked about my painting, she hasn't seen any of it. That seems strange, when I think of it.

For the past two weeks Caroline and I have been—what shall I call it? The word that comes to mind is "dating," but that doesn't sound right. We see each other several times a week, but we're being careful with each other, almost formal. She's stopped by my apartment after work a few times, and we went to a movie earlier this week. We've cooked dinner together at her house twice. But we're both be-having with a lot of restraint. It seems absurd, but maybe there's a kind of sense in our behavior. It's as though we've backed up to fill in a stage we missed earlier. Maybe we're just learning how to be together in public. And that brings with it a lot of questions. For instance: can I imagine a future here?

I'll have to break off. Caroline's at the door. Ron and Iris have invited us over for supper. Until later,

John

May 13, 1991

Dear Wyatt,

I've enclosed the photo of the Stortz portrait that you asked for. I think they're pleased with the painting. They've hung it over the fireplace in their living room, replacing the cows at pasture. Your idea is an interesting one. I can only promise to think about it. You're right—doing portraits would be at least as interesting as keeping the Earth Day accounts and sorting cans. And, yes, the fact that you've al-ready been able to arrange one commission—if I decide to come back—does seem promising. I'll think about it.

You're determined to get me out of here, aren't you? You've got it all figured out: a week in your client's apartment in Rome before I come back to New York to paint portraits and whatever else. A week's vacation in Rome is quite an inducement. It's very tempting. But to leave so soon? Two weeks from now seems very sudden. I realize there's no flexibility in the arrangement—the dates of your client's trip to

New York are all set, then he's going right back to his place in Rome, etc. But are you sure you and Alice don't want to take him up on his offer rather than passing this plum on to me? Surely you could get away if you set your mind to it.

You say I have no future in Delphi. I know you're right. But the idea of leaving raises some hard questions. I'm thinking of Caroline. I don't know how I'd put it to her.

John

May 16, 1991
Dear Wyatt,

Caroline took me to a dinner in the church basement yesterday evening. It was "potluck" and she made her Waldorf-Astoria red cake in the afternoon. I stood in the kitchen, leaning against the counter and sipping iced tea as I watched her mix the ingredients. Her hands moved lightly, deftly, as she sifted flour, poured oil, cracked eggs. Soon the three round pans were in the oven and she was mixing the white frosting. "A red cake," I said. "I don't think I've ever seen one before."

"The red is food coloring," she said. "I suppose it isn't something you'd want to eat every week, but people seem to like it. The main flavoring is the cocoa. It's gotten so I'm expected to bring it every time—Caroline's red cake, they call it. There's never a slice left to bring home afterward." She looked back over her shoulder and smiled at me. I stepped up and put my arms around her from behind. She put one finger in the frosting, held it up for me to taste, leaned back into me, and closed her eyes. The afternoon stretched out before us, spacious and calm.

At 5:30 we went to the church. I drove and Caroline held her covered cake pan in her lap. It was a bright, mild evening. In a yard that we passed, the bottom half of a forsythia bush was in bloom and the top was bare. Only the part that had been protected from the hardest cold by the snow held a sprinkling of yellow blossoms. At the church, we went downstairs to where the Wednesday night Lenten suppers had been and Caroline found a place for her cake. The food was arranged on long tables at one end of the room and the rest of the big area was filled by round tables, each with six chairs around it. Already people were lining up, filling their plates, and finding places in small groups to eat and visit.

This is a food culture. People express their bonds by feeding each other, by eating together. Upstairs they kneel at the railing for little wafers and tiny sips of wine. Later, they gather in the basement—in the fellowship room—for the real thing:

barbecue beef sandwiches, noodle casseroles, and green beans in a sauce of mushroom soup with little onion rings on top. And then the homemade pies and cakes. And the coffee. Always coffee—brewed weak so they can drink it all day. The food is heavy and satisfying. Afterward you sit back, slowed and ballasted. You can almost feel the layers going on against the long winters.

The "fellowship room"! When Caroline and I had gotten our food and sat at one of the round tables, nobody joined us! We ate and looked around as the others clustered in cozy little groups. The sound of amiable chatter rose in the big room. I watched Caroline as she glanced up at the people going by to find their places. She would brighten with recognition when she saw a friend, then glance away when they glided past. At one point, the woman Caroline had introduced me to after church came toward us—the woman in the smart, yellow dress. Now she had on a tailored blue dress with a lacy white collar. She and Caroline made brief eye contact. The woman threw a tight, social smile into the air somewhere over our heads, then swerved like a fish in a tank and made her way to join another group across the room. Caroline dropped her eyes and pushed the food around on her plate.

I was becoming uncomfortable and wanted to leave, so I tried to move things along. "I'd like to have a piece of that cake now," I said. "Will you have one with me?" Caroline looked up, forced a smile, and stood with me. We got our desserts, returned to our table, and ate in silence.

Finally, when we were nearly finished, August and Ruth Stortz came up. "Okay if we join you?" August said.

I nodded, gratefully. "Please," I said. "It's good to see you."

It felt as though a spotlight had been lifted off of us when they sat down and filled in two of the spaces at the big table. "We just came for a little cake and coffee," Ruth Stortz said. "I wouldn't miss Caroline's cake."

August took a bite. "It's delicious, as always," he said. Caroline smiled at him.

We finished our cake and sipped our coffee. The talk was light and easy. Gradually, the people at the other tables began to finish and depart. And then August and Ruth said good-bye and left, too. "You two take care," August said. And I saw Ruth give Caroline's hand a squeeze.

When they were gone Caroline turned to me and said, "Well, I guess I can get my cake dish, now. And then we can go."

I walked with her to the long table at the front of the room, stopped, and looked. There were only four pieces missing from Caroline's cake. We both saw it at the same time. I looked at Caroline's face. Then there was an almost unbearable moment, as I watched the realization soak in. Her face dimmed. It was like seeing the current to a light swiftly turned down. The room literally seemed to darken. She was being shunned.

Caroline pulled her eyes from the cake—the white frosting swirled by the easy turns of her wrist, the dark red inside showing like a gash—and went back to the kitchen to retrieve her dish cover. She returned, covered the cake, and picked it up. We walked outside without speaking.

We were silent as we drove back to Caroline's house. I stopped in the driveway next to the front door, put the car into park, and turned to her. Before I could speak Caroline said: "Please come in, John. I want you to."

When I turned off the car and got out, she led me directly downstairs to her bedroom. It was early evening and the light was just beginning to soften beyond the sliding glass doors at the end of the room. The deepening blue sky stretched like a dome over the little town. I could see the steeple of the church pointing up. Caroline strode to the doors and jerked the curtains closed. Then she found me in the dark and kissed me hard. She kissed me defiantly, as though there were others in the room and she wanted to wound them. Then she drew me to the bed. We made love with most of our clothes on, urgently, almost ferociously. Hurt and anger impelled us through a trajectory that was thick and red at the beginning, then thin and silvery way up at the top where we could barely breathe, gasping in the high air. And then, at last, we fell back into the darkness of the bed and our bunched and rumpled clothes.

We lay side by side in the dark bed for a long time. I felt spent and calmed, but soaked with something, saturated with it. It wasn't anger, now, but a sense of ruin. I opened my eyes but it was like staring in a cave. I could feel Caroline next to me, her deep and even breathing, and I could smell her clean hair, but I couldn't see anything. The world was gone. I had thought I was a maker, but I felt like a destroyer. A chain of thoughts began to run in my head and I couldn't stop them. First I had lost Jamie, driven her into a loneliness that finally made her leave. And then Ellen. My work with her, and with Jean, had made them targets—they'd both been attacked. *"Women with their heads shadowed or cropped, and their torsos arched for the male gaze sweeping over them. So much surveillance and plunder. We've had quite enough."* The words of the review came back to me and my stomach turned over. And now Caroline. In the dark I saw the parishioners swerve away from us like a shoal of fish.

We lay in bed, the curtain drawn against the town below. Caroline shifted, her chin nestling against my shoulder. "Are you sleeping?" I whispered.

"Mmm. No," she said.

"Caroline, I should go," I said.

"Oh, do you have to?" she said.

"I mean, I should leave," I said. "I should leave Delphi."

Caroline lay still and quiet in the dark. The silence stretched out and lasted. As it did, a pressure built in my chest, hard and round. And then a sob escaped me. And then Caroline sobbed. And we cried and held each other until our faces and arms and chests were slick between us. "I knew this was coming," Caroline sobbed. "I just didn't know it would be so soon."

"I'm sorry," I cried. "I'm sorry."

"I know," Caroline said. "I know."

"I can't stand to see you hurt," I said.

"It's all right," Caroline said. "It'll be all right."

"I'm sorry," I said.

"I know you can't live here," she said.

"I couldn't stand to see you hurt," I said. "When I'm gone . . . things will be all right."

"We'll be all right," she said. "It'll all be all right," she said, bitterly.

5/17

Expect my paintings to arrive in about a week. I'll drive over to Decorah to get them tomorrow. Today I'm getting the crating materials together. I'll pack them at Caroline's. There's space there to do the work and she said she wanted to help. I love her, Wyatt. I should leave as soon as possible.

Tell your client I'll be happy to stay in his apartment for a week while he's away. Rome a week from now, and then New York. That means I'll need a place to stay in New York in just two weeks. I'll call Judd and see if he can help me find something. I was able to save the check from the last painting you sold, and that will cover airfare and some of my expenses for the week in Rome. Then I'll just deal with things as they come. Sell any of the old paintings you can, even if you have to lower the prices (take the reduction out of my share, of course). I need to get together as much money as I can. But don't sell any of the new things I'm sending. And don't show them. Thank you, Wyatt.

John

May 20, 1991
Dear Wyatt,

I picked up the paintings yesterday. They'd been stored under sheets in a locked side room in the courthouse and appear to be in good condition. It was a shock to see them after all this time. One of the big blue nudes of Ellen shook me. Looking at it there in the courthouse, with a deputy standing next to me, I could only see it through the county prosecutor's eyes. Ellen's own eyes stared back at me out of the canvas. She sits, upright and stiff, with her hands folded in her lap, the blue tones of her skin as chilly as midwinter. A woman on ice, I thought. A cold needle moved in my chest.

I carried my sketchbooks and the portfolio of drawings out to my car. Then the deputy and I maneuvered the paintings one by one down a big staircase, out to the parking lot, and placed them in the back of a sheriff's van. The deputy was courteous and formal. He handled the paintings carefully. He seemed to be taking pains not to look at them.

He drove the van to Delphi, following me. I sat in my car, behind the windshield, with the gray ribbon of two-lane highway twisting and straightening in front of me. Caroline was waiting. I thought as I drove: Well, now she'll see. She'll see this contagion I carry. It must show in the paintings. Really, it will be a good thing. She'll understand why I have to leave and why I can't ask her to come with me— if she even thinks about that. But how could she? How could she think seriously of leaving the town where she's lived for the past ten years, the town she chose as a haven when her life in Minneapolis became intolerable? (If she left Minneapolis for small-town life in Delphi, why would she consider going to New York?) She has her work, the people she helps, and her friends. She has her wonderful house poised on the hill, the house that she and her husband designed and built. I've damaged her in the eyes of the town, that's certain. But when I'm gone she'll heal back into her life, and the town will heal around her. Against the solidity of all that—against the whole history and logic of her life—leaving with me would be like riding off into the sky on a soap bubble.

Behind the wheel, looking out at the fields and sky and the highway lines ticking past, I felt like an empty space hurtling through the landscape, an absence bordered by the windshield's sheet of glass.

I pulled into Caroline's driveway and stopped. The deputy parked the van behind me and helped carry the paintings inside. As Caroline watched, we leaned them in a stack against the bookshelves in the bright living room. I thanked the deputy and he left. As soon he was gone Caroline asked me to show her the paintings, so I placed them around the room, leaning them against the walls, the bookcase, and the backs of the furniture. Carrying the large canvases in front of me, I felt like a man behind an X-ray panel, his bones and organs exposed for examination. Caroline sat next to the big windows and I felt her watch me as I worked. I spread out the canvases, one by one, and the nakedness in the pictures became my nakedness. When I had finished, I retreated to the three wide steps leading from the living room to the dining area and sat down. My heart knocked hard in my chest.

The big pictures—several of them 48" x 72" or bigger—were propped all around. The spacious room was crowded with them. Caroline stood and moved among them, looking intently. "This isn't ideal," I said, nervously. "You should be able to look at them from farther away." Caroline nodded without speaking and without lifting her eyes from the painting she was looking at. It was one of the draped figures of Jean. She lay with her eyes closed, her dark hair fanned out around her head, and the black fabric draped in folds around the curves of her torso and belly. Her face and hands—the only light areas on the big canvas—loomed forward against all that darkness. Caroline looked for a long time, then stepped to the next canvas.

There was the small nude of Jamie in the mauve room looking out a window—the one you shipped back to me after I asked you not to sell it. There were the two big nudes of Ellen done in the blue midwinter light, with orange highlights from the glow of the space heater's coils. There were two later nudes of Ellen and three of Jean at various stages of her pregnancy. And finally there were the three draped figures done during the war, two of Jean and one—the most recent—of Ellen.

As Caroline walked among them I sat on the steps and busied myself by looking through the sketchbooks. As I did, I could remember each of the sessions with Jean and Ellen, from those first days almost a year ago when they were strangers to me down to the last sessions in February just before the attack. The two of them have become dear to me. They're my friends. I turned slowly through the studio drawings and through the sketches I had done in August's slaughterhouse. That they were both in the same sketchbook seemed brutal but true. When I looked at the small painting I had done of Ellen wrapped in the black fabric, it filled me with grief. She's lost to me now, I thought.

Caroline stood across the room, contemplating a large painting of Jean lying on her side with her body curled around her belly late in the pregnancy. Caroline turned and saw me watching her. She came over and stood in front of me. "These paintings . . ." She spoke quietly and paused. I didn't know how to interpret the expression on her face. It made me think of a lake composing itself after a rock's thrown into it. She spoke again, softly. "The paintings are very intimate," she said. She paused again. "But they're not about being excited. They're about being calm." She was searching for her words. She looked over her shoulder back at the roomful of paintings, then back to me. "They're about being vulnerable," she said, "but safe, after all."

"Safe?" I said.

"When I look at them," she said, "it's almost as though they're all the same woman. She's in danger, somehow. Like that one." She pointed at the big nude of Jean late in her pregnancy. "The way she curls around her stomach," Caroline said. "Everything revolves around it. It's something big that's going to happen to her. It's all-important, and threatening." I nodded. I could see what she meant. "But even with the danger, there's something very reassuring about the paintings—about *all* of them." She continued, searching for the right words. "I don't know what it is. Something about the way they're painted. They're so careful. When I look at them I can almost feel each brush stroke, so light and careful."

She reached and pulled my head to her chest. I could hear her heart beating. I was facing the picture called *Acteon* that leaned against the stairs next to us. In its top half, in the background, a billboard advertisement features a bathing Aphrodite. Ellen is the model. In the foreground a man walks past a parked car while two Dobermans strain out its window, snapping at him. Their teeth are sharp and white, and the man looks like he's about to fly apart.

"Safe," I said. "You think the women in the paintings look safe."

Caroline took a step back and turned toward one of the draped figures. In it Ellen is held in a moment of sleep. The sheer black fabric swirls in folds across her torso. One arm is visible, extending out of the sack on one side, its hand open and the wrist turned up. Ellen's eyes are closed and her face is relaxed. Her skin glows in the late afternoon light like the tip of a lit candle.

"Yes," Caroline said. "Like I said before. Safe, after all."

She sat down next to me on the stairs, then. She said: "I'd like you to finish your painting of me. The one in my mother's coat. Do you think we can finish it before you go?"

"Yes," I told her. "I want to. Let's start tomorrow," I said.

John

May 24, 1991

Dear Wyatt,

We worked hard this week and the painting is finished. It means as much to me as anything I've done. Of course, it will stay with Caroline. It's hers. I'll photograph it and send you a slide. I want you to see it. In its subject—and in the feeling of the picture—it reminds me a little of *Hélène Fourment in a Fur Coat*, though I'm not claiming I've accomplished what Rubens did. Do you remember? I'm looking at the Rubens again, now, in one of my books. It seems more like a snapshot than an arranged pose: she reaches to catch the coat that slips from her shoulders, holding it together around her hips with her other hand. Though she's almost entirely unclothed, I can't call the painting a nude. She's not a poised ideal. She's too much herself to be that. Her slight awkwardness, the creases under her arm, the fat dimpling her legs, make her appear excruciatingly naked. But she looks out from the painting—alert and serene—at the unmisgiving painter, her husband.

Caroline and I worked in her living room with a black backdrop falling behind her and extending out across the floor where she stood. All around us were the other paintings. We haven't put them away. We worked hard for three days—three good days of working and talking. We felt very close to one another. Only one thing was difficult. As I painted with the pictures of Jamie and Ellen and Jean all around, it was as though Caroline was becoming one of them—one more lost woman saved into paint.

I'm ticketed to fly out of Minneapolis Sunday. Ron has said he will drive me up. I'll see you and Alice that night. Then my flight to Rome leaves at 8:30 A.M. It will be good to see you both.

John

May 25, 1991
Dear Wyatt,

Ron and Iris threw a bon voyage party for me at Caroline's last night. I was completely surprised. Caroline got me out of the way by driving me to Guttenberg. She said she wanted to buy me a bell. So we drove down and walked through the small town next to the wide river and went through the motions of having a lovely day together. But underneath us ran an undertow of sadness. I was reminded too much of that day in April—our first day together. And Caroline was too—I could see it in the tightness of her mouth. We both strained to be cheerful. In the past days, we'd somehow agreed, without saying anything, to approach our separation with a stoic cheerfulness. But late in the afternoon when we got into her car to drive home, Caroline turned to me and said, "I thought this would be a good idea. I guess it wasn't." We had decided not to buy a bell, after all. We hadn't even gone into the shop.

We were quiet on the drive home. I was too sad to speak. And Caroline, I'm sure, wasn't in the mood for the party she had helped to arrange. But, according to plan, she drove us to her house and asked me in for a drink. When I stepped through the door all the lights went on and a crowd shouted, "Surprise!"

The living room looked like a ballroom strung with crepe paper streamers that rose from the walls to the apex of the high ceiling. The deck off the living room was rigged with Chinese lanterns and its railing was hung with life preservers. Iris had come up with the idea of decorating Caroline's house like a ship, though I'll be traveling on a plane. Below the deck, in the backyard, Ron's fishing boat sat in the grass with oars in its oarlocks. Three cardboard shark's fins erupted from the grass, encircling the boat. I had to laugh when he showed me.

Some of Caroline's friends from work were there, and Jean and baby Ellen, and Rich, Patty, Linda, and Kevin. Also Johnson, the Earth Day director, and his wife. And the whole Stortz family was there.

Food and punch were spread out on the dining room table, in the area above the living room. Out of some romantic notion of ocean liners, Iris had searched out big band records to play, and she moved through the house encouraging everyone to dance. This was a party with a script, apparently, and Iris was the recreational director. Soon a handful of guests were moving across the floor in stately pairs. So there was music and dancing and the buzz of conversation. It seemed that everyone knew each other, at least slightly.

As the party progressed, I stood next to the punch bowl and spoke to my friends as they came up to me. A couple of hours passed in easy conversation, and I was touched by the warmth I felt. It made me certain that Caroline would be happy among these people. I looked out over the party. Caroline was dancing with Ron. Iris was dancing with someone I didn't know. And then I saw Johnson go to the door to let in a late-arriving guest. It was Ellen. From across the room, Jean spotted her and went right over. They greeted each other with a hug and then Ellen took the baby in her arms and the three of them went to a far corner of the room and sat down. I watched them talking, Ellen holding baby Ellen in her lap.

I had seen Rich dancing with Patty, then he disappeared for a while. When I saw him again several minutes later, he was emerging from the stairway that leads to the lower floor. He saw me in the dining room, next to the food, and made his way over. "I went to the bathroom," he said. I nodded and waited. "I got lost," he said. "I saw your paintings." They were stored in Terry's old study downstairs, stacked against the walls.

"Oh," I said. "What did you think?" He picked up a cracker, smeared it with cheese, and put it into his mouth.

"I like them," he said, chewing. He paused and looked out across the living room. His wandering eye seemed to scan the ceiling. "Is that the blond girl in the paintings?" he said. He was looking at Ellen, who was standing near the windows now, talking with Johnson. She wore a pink knit sweater buttoned to the throat with round, pearl-like buttons. It matched the top of Johnson's head, which was a little sunburned.

"Yes," I said. "Her name is Ellen." Rich nodded without looking at me and started across the room.

My first impulse was to go after him, but I stopped myself. I watched him squeeze between the clusters of people who stood talking around the edge of the room. Then he stepped up behind Ellen, who was still speaking with Johnson, and tapped her on the shoulder. She turned and I could see that Rich was saying something to her. Her eyes widened and she turned to glance at Johnson, who stared at Rich with a startled look. Ellen turned back to Rich, hesitated, then nodded helplessly. At her reply, Rich raised both of his arms. He held his left hand open in the air, palm up, and reached around with his right arm to place that hand on Ellen's back. Ellen placed her right hand in Rich's left and they began to sway back and forth together, stiffly.

An old Glenn Miller tune was playing. Rich executed a halting two-step, glancing down at his feet from time to time. Ellen followed the best she could. She's fairly tall and Rich isn't, so when he wasn't checking his feet Rich gazed somberly forward at Ellen's chest. Johnson still stood by the windows, incapacitated by anxiety.

As the song continued, Rich warmed to the dance. His face was still fixed in intense concentration, but his steps became broader. He swooped one way, paused, and swooped back. Ellen swayed with him from side to side, balancing for a moment on one leg, then swinging the other way, like a slow metronome. She looked over the top of Rich's head, her mouth pursed and her eyes wide. I started across the room.

As I neared them, the music stopped. Rich stepped back from Ellen, said thank you, and made a little bow. I stepped forward, and when Rich saw me he broke into a wide grin and strutted away. Johnson thawed, took a deep breath, and headed for the punch bowl.

I turned to Ellen. "His name is Rich," I said. "I work with him at Earth Day. He's all right." She nodded. "You and Johnson looked scared to death," I said. "What did he say to you?"

"He just asked me to dance," Ellen said. "Really, he was nice. He said, 'I would be very happy if you would dance with me.'" She smiled, self-consciously.

The next song began, another slow one, with clarinets on the melody. "Well, then," I said. "I'd be very happy if you would dance with me." A look of fear flashed through her eyes, but then she nodded.

We moved to the middle of the floor and began to dance slowly with the three or four other couples there. "I haven't had a chance to congratulate you," I said. "I'm very happy about art school."

"Thank you," Ellen said. She held herself stiffly as we danced. And why not? It was strange, after all that had happened, to be at a party together, dancing. She had thought I'd broken into her apartment, that I'd tried to rape her. She'd imagined that about me, and somehow, after all the time we'd spent working together, it had been plausible to her. After months of suspicion, how could she just erase all that? My chest ached at the thought.

"How are you, Ellen?" I said.

She drew back and looked at me, then stepped forward again and sighed. "I'm okay," she said. "I've found a place in Milwaukee, and school starts in September. I've been talking with Caroline and she's been a lot of help."

"Yes, she's wonderful," I said.

Ellen nodded. "I've felt better since Jerry was arrested. It all makes more sense, now." She paused. "When I thought it might be you . . ." She glanced up at me quickly, nervously. "Or when I thought it could be just anybody . . . That scared me a lot. It just seemed crazy. It made me feel like anything could happen."

We were both quiet for a while. I suppose we were both thinking that anything can happen.

The music continued, and as we danced it occurred to me that, for all the intimacy of our work together, this was perhaps the first time I had touched Ellen. I couldn't remember even an incidental brush as she'd handed me a cup of tea or as I'd passed her a section of the newspaper during a break. And as she'd modeled for me, the easel had separated us like a proscenium arch.

All that looking and all that distance. Her back felt tense under my hand.

The song ended and we both stepped back. There was an awkward moment, and then Jean was there. "Will you dance with me now, John?" she said. "If you don't mind, Ellen?"

Ellen turned to Jean and took the baby, hugged the child eagerly, and smiled at Jean. "No, of course not," she said.

The next song started and Jean eased smoothly into my arms. We danced to two songs, chatting the whole time. Jean wanted to know all about the trip, where I would stay and what I would see. Then Caroline came over, and she and I danced for a long time. She rested her head against my chest as we made slow circles among the others.

At about midnight Iris called out, "Everyone get your glasses, we're opening the champagne!" The corks popped loudly, and Ron and Iris made their way around the room, filling glasses.

Then Ron stepped up into the dining room and offered a toast: "Here's to my good friend, John. Have a fine trip. And good luck back in New York. We'll miss you." There was a murmur of assent and everyone raised their glasses.

Iris put her arm around Ron and called out: "The ship departs in fifteen minutes. Last dance! Everyone on the dance floor!" Then she circulated around the room, herding and coaxing. In a few minutes everyone was on the floor: August and Ruth Stortz, their son and daughter, Ron and Iris, Caroline and I. Johnson and his wife glided by, and Johnson nodded at me and said good luck. I saw Rich across the room, dancing with Patty again, but craning his neck to look around. Ellen held the baby while Jean danced with a blond man who worked with Caroline at County Services. Then Jean took the baby and Ellen danced with the blond man.

The glass doors were open and some of the couples had moved onto the deck, where they continued to dance. Caroline and I followed them out. Linda and Kevin were there, swaying together under a red lantern. Caroline waved at them and Linda waved back and smiled.

Caroline looked up at me as we danced. "Nice party," she said.

"Yes," I said. "And if Iris lived near a seaport, I think she'd have a real future at this." Caroline laughed softly and moved closer. The cool air outside smelled sweet.

There must have been some kind of signal then, because all the guests drifted out of the house and down to the backyard, below the deck. From there, they blew plastic horns and threw streamers and shouted good-bye. Caroline and I shouted back and waved, as if from the railing of a departing ship. Then everyone turned and moved toward their cars, leaving us under the lanterns, waving after them.

When I woke up later, in the middle of the night, and thought about the party, I thought of couples dancing. I saw men and women circling each other. The old steps of the old dances. Caroline turned in her sleep, shifting in my arms, and I smelled the clean scent of her hair.

Then I thought of Ellen. Yes, I had touched her once. I remembered now. I had adjusted the drapery around her shoulders and down her torso during that last afternoon session. I remembered the slight electricity of trespass I had felt. Ellen had been at ease, though. She'd even fallen asleep. I had worked quickly, virtually finishing the small painting in an afternoon.

And then I remembered another touch: that time in the snowy park when she hit me hard on the chest and I echoed like an empty drum.

My chest ached again. I pictured the damage in Ellen's eyes as she'd danced, frightened, with Rich. Lying in the dark, I felt a sharp pain in my chest, like a needle turning. But I didn't mistake it for guilt. I knew it was grief.

Caroline turned again and sighed deeply. "Are you awake?" I whispered.

"Yes," she whispered back. She was facing away from me, and my arms were around her.

"You know," I said, "when everyone was in the yard and we were standing on the deck together with those streamers coming down all around, it was like we were leaving together."

"Mmm, that would be nice," Caroline said sleepily. "I've always wanted to see Rome."

"Do you mean it?" I said. "How would people treat you? What would they say when you came back?"

Caroline turned toward me in the dark. She put her arms around me and pressed her forehead against my cheek. When she spoke I could feel her breath against my throat. "Who says I have to come back?"

I drew away and tried to see her face, but the room was too dark. "You mean you'd go away with me?" I said. "You'd leave everything you have here?"

"What do I have here, John?" Caroline said.

"I mean, your work and your friends, this house," I said. "I thought you came here to get away from what had happened to you in Minneapolis."

"Oh, John," she said. "This is where I came to start a family. Didn't you know that?" We were lying together in her bedroom, next to her dead husband's law study and the empty nursery. "I came here to start a life that didn't happen," she said.

"I couldn't give you that kind of life," I said. "I just . . ." Caroline reached up and put her hand over my mouth. Her fingers were soft against my lips.

"Shh," she said. "It's too late for all that." Her hand moved from my mouth to my cheek.

It was my turn to say something. She wanted to leave Delphi. She wanted to come away with me. If I asked her to, she'd sell this house, leave her practice, and ride off on a soap bubble that could burst under her at any moment. Hadn't something in me broken before? And hadn't the women either fallen or vanished? Fear for both of us welled up in me like rising water.

"God, I've scared the daylights out of you!" Caroline said. "Your heart is going like crazy."

I took a breath and then another breath. I lay on my back, floating in the dark. "Will you come with me, Caroline?" I said. "Will you leave with me and not come back here?"

Caroline's voice came out of the dark beside me. "Yes," she said. "Yes, I will."

John

6-1-91

Wyatt—You'll have to settle for postcards now, but I'll write as small as possible. Our last day in Rome today. It was hot, so we did fountains and ice cream. Paid homage to Fellini and Anita Ekberg at the Trevi, then laughed at the Fountain of the Naiads in the Piazza della Repubblica. Four bronze nymphs lounge naked in the spray (a scandal at the 1901 unveiling, according to our guidebook). The vulgar creatures, each reclining on a different beast, are supposed to symbolize oceans, lakes, rivers, and "subterranean waters." But they are sexual cartoons. Dinner was fabulous—melon, bruschetta, gnocchi, Parma ham with sage. And your client's apartment is wonderful. Tonight in the shower Caroline struck a pose. "Which naiad are you?" I asked. "The nymph of modern plumbing," she laughed. Cheers! John.

Paris

6-4-91

We splurged on dinner tonight: boeuf bourguignon at a small restaurant near where we're staying. Our room here is small and simple—up six flights of stairs, too. But it has a little balcony with a wonderful view. Last night we sipped wine and gazed out at the lights. What a sense of freedom we have! Some afternoons we are happy just to walk the streets, look at the shops, and rest when we find a park. Bought sausage and flowers from a woman in a tiny shop today, who kissed Caroline on both cheeks and beamed at me. All best. John.

Paris

6-7-91

Caroline and I are happy to tell you that we were married here yesterday by a civil magistrate. He was very solemn and official throughout, then when we'd finished, he shook our hands, smiled warmly, and gave Caroline a carnation out of a small bouquet on his desk. We celebrated with crêpes in the street, feeding each other like two sparrows on a wire. Then had a fine dinner that night—in Montmartre. We leave for Vienna tomorrow for two days in the museums. As arranged, will check at American Express there for any messages. Cheers. John.

Vienna

6-11-91

A remarkable day at the Kunsthistorisches Museum. I had wanted to show Caroline Rubens's *Hélène Fourment*—and that was wonderful, of course—but hadn't realized there was a virtual series of women in fur coats here: paintings by Giorgione, Titian, Rubens, and a beautiful late pastel by Manet. What is it about this subject?—the *faces*, the *eyes*, are wonderful in each. What tender pictures they are! It was a huge day: *Susannah and the Elders*, Vermeer's *Artist in His Studio*, the Rembrandt self-portraits. We tumbled out of the museum and into the nearest park to lie in the grass and recover. Caroline complained, "The women are lovely, but why are all the naked men either dead or dying? To be fair," she joked, "we should go to Greece for the kouroi." Who knows, maybe we will. John.

John Ordway
Wild Pension
Lange Gasse 10
Vienna

June 15, 1991
Dear Wyatt,

A brief letter this time. Received in good order the money you wired here. Many thanks. I'm glad your client was still interested in that small painting of Jamie by the window. If you keep this up, we may never come back, you know. But we *have* talked about what comes next. Caroline, of course, has an agent working to sell her house. And she's contacted someone in St. Louis to look for something there. She wants to be near her mother, who is approaching eighty now. I've told her I'm game to try St. Louis.

About the paintings: Remember that I've asked you only to store them. I don't want them shown or sold. If I've begun to accomplish anything, there's no one with eyes to see it. It's just the wrong moment. And I suppose the people who would buy the paintings—who are buying my old ones!—are confirmed reprobates. I'd probably despise them if I met them. I'm tired of the whole thing! Let's just watch the world turn for a while and hope it gets somewhere new.

John

Crete

6-20-91

In the mountains, here, the air smells like sage. I believe I could live on bread and wine and olives. (Roasted potatoes out of a stone oven on the Lasithi Plateau were wonderful, too.) After we saw the Minoan frescoes in Athens—those beautiful men and women in their light, colorful clothes—we had to come here to visit the palace sites. C. got up early this morning, and when I saw her standing on our balcony, I wanted to paint. There's much to learn about the nude. But not for a while. It's worn me out. We napped together on a blanket in an olive grove this afternoon. When I woke, it was fine to lie next to Caroline and look up through the leaves, watching the blue change above us. I think I could spend a year or two just painting the sky. John.

About the Author

Robert Schultz's books include two collections of poetry, *Vein Along the Fault* and *Winter in Eden,* and a novel, *The Madhouse Nudes.* He has received a National Endowment for the Arts Literature Award in Fiction, Cornell University's Corson Bishop Poetry Prize, and, from *The Virginia Quarterly Review,* the Emily Clark Balch Prize for Poetry. A native Iowan, Schultz grew up in Humboldt and Iowa City. He attended Luther College and pursued his graduate studies at Cornell University. In 1985 he returned to Luther, where he taught writing, literature, and film for 19 years. He is currently the John P. Fishwick Professor of English at Roanoke College in Salem, Virginia.

Acknowledgments

Thanks are due to many people who helped me complete this book. Attentive readings at various stages by Paula Deitz, Gail Hochman, Suzanne Jones, Lise Kildegaard , Martin Mohr, Mary Hull Mohr, Frederick Morgan, Lisa Russ-Spaar, Becky Saletan, Sally Schultz, John Whelan, and David Wyatt were invaluable. Special technical information of various kinds was provided by Marion Beatty, Susan Frye, Lincoln Perry, Bobbie Morton, and Jenny Thompson. The pottery described in this book is based on the work of Dale Raddatz.

I would also like to acknowledge, with gratitude, fellowships from Luther College and the Virginia Foundation for the Humanities and Public Policy, which provided time, space, materials, and encouragement.